I will be working quite close together, after all."

Ah, God. So it was to be this particular male, was it? She swallowed hard as anxiety and dread and a strange electric excitement settled under her skin. Would she have preferred it to be one of the more open, cheerful fellows? Certainly. Hell, she would have even preferred Mr. Parsons and his dark brooding. Anything was better than Mr. Ethan Sinclaire and the dangerous distrust in his eyes.

But perhaps this was for the best. After all, wasn't there something to be said for keeping your friends close but your enemies closer? And there really was no getting closer than what she planned for this man. Her cheeks burned hot just thinking about it. But now was not the time for nerves. She would counteract his distrust with seduction and undermine his suspicion with kisses. And in doing so she would clear the way for their success.

Though as she slipped her hand in his, and his strong fingers engulfed her own, she felt quite literally as if she were sealing a bargain with the devil himself.

Praise for Christina Britton and Her Novels

"This alluring, emotionally charged Regency proves hard to put down." —*Publishers Weekly* on *The Duke's All That*

"A charming and thoughtful regency romance."
—*Kirkus* on *What's a Duke Got to Do With It*

"For readers who like to feel all the emotions of a story."
—*Library Journal* on *Some Dukes Have All the Luck*

"Endearing, complex characters."
—*Publishers Weekly* on *Some Dukes Have All the Luck*

"Sigh-worthy fare."
—*BookPage* on *Some Dukes Have All the Luck*

"This is a knockout." —*Publishers Weekly* on *A Duke Worth Fighting For*, starred review

"First-rate Regency fun!"
—Grace Burrowes, *New York Times* bestselling author

"Moving and heartfelt."
—*Kirkus Reviews* on *Someday My Duke Will Come*

"Swoonworthy romance."
—*Publishers Weekly* on *Someday My Duke Will Come*

"Christina Britton proves she has mastered the craft of engaging Regency romance."
—*Shelf Awareness* on *Someday My Duke Will Come*

"Readers will be hooked." —*Publishers Weekly* on *A Good Duke Is Hard to Find*, starred review

"This was my first book by Christina Britton. It won't be my last."
—*TheRomanceDish.com* on *A Good Duke Is Hard to Find*

To Heist
and
to Hold

Also by Christina Britton

A Good Duke Is Hard to Find
Someday My Duke Will Come
A Duke Worth Fighting For
The Duke's Christmas Miracle (novella)
Some Dukes Have All the Luck
What's a Duke Got to Do With It
The Duke's All That

To Heist and to Hold

Christina Britton

FOREVER

New York London

This book is a work of fiction. Names, characters, places, and incidents are the product of the author's imagination or are used fictitiously. Any resemblance to actual events, locales, or persons, living or dead, is coincidental.

Copyright © 2025 by Christina Silverio

Cover design by Daniela Medina
Cover art by Judy York
Cover copyright © 2025 by Hachette Book Group, Inc.

Hachette Book Group supports the right to free expression and the value of copyright. The purpose of copyright is to encourage writers and artists to produce the creative works that enrich our culture.

The scanning, uploading, and distribution of this book without permission is a theft of the author's intellectual property. If you would like permission to use material from the book (other than for review purposes), please contact permissions@hbgusa.com. Thank you for your support of the author's rights.

Forever
Hachette Book Group
1290 Avenue of the Americas, New York, NY 10104
read-forever.com
@readforeverpub

First Mass Market Edition: September 2025

Forever is an imprint of Grand Central Publishing. The Forever name and logo are registered trademarks of Hachette Book Group, Inc.

The publisher is not responsible for websites (or their content) that are not owned by the publisher.

The Hachette Speakers Bureau provides a wide range of authors for speaking events. To find out more, go to hachettespeakersbureau.com or email HachetteSpeakers@hbgusa.com.

Forever books may be purchased in bulk for business, educational, or promotional use. For information, please contact your local bookseller or the Hachette Book Group Special Markets Department at special.markets@hbgusa.com.

ISBNs: 9781538769119 (mass market); 9781538769126 (ebook)

Printed in the United States of America

BVG-M

10 9 8 7 6 5 4 3 2 1

For Eric

Acknowledgments

A huge thank-you to my fabulous agent Kim Lionetti. Your guidance and support helped me not only in the creation of my Wimpole Street Widows Society, but in building the career of my dreams. I'll be forever grateful.

To my wonderful editor Madeleine Colavita, and to Grace Fischetti, Dana Cuadrado, and everyone at Forever. I'm so thankful to be part of the Forever family.

A very special thank-you to Christopher Sugg with CIBSE Heritage Group for his help with nineteenth-century gas lighting (any inaccuracies are mine alone to fit the story).

Thank you to Jayci, Hannah, and Julie for always being there for me and cheering me on.

Thank you to my incredible readers. I adore each and every one of you so very much.

Thank you to my husband and children for never wavering in your support of my work…even though I STILL haven't put a sword with a secret compartment in the hilt in my books. I love you so much.

And, lastly, thank you to BTS and their song "Dionysus" for inspiring the name for Ethan's club.

Author's Note

CONTENT WARNING: *To Heist and to Hold* contains content that may distress some readers. For content warnings, please visit my website:

http://christinabritton.com/bookshelf/content-warnings/

Also, any mention of medicinal plants in this book should not be taken as medical advice.

Affectionately Yours,
Christina Britton

To Heist *and* to Hold

1

Late spring 1821

Mrs. Heloise Marlow tensed, her half boots making a whisper of sound on the flagstone floor as she widened her stance. Locating the hulking figure in the shadows from the corner of her eye, she surreptitiously brought her hand up to the collar of her pelisse, sensitive fingers locating the narrow hilt there, gripping it tight along its carefully etched grooves. With a flick of her wrist she silently freed it from its disguised sheath, the thin three-inch blade glinting in the dim light before, with one swift lunge, she spun and drove her hand forward, embedding the steel between her opponent's ribs.

Or what would have been ribs if the figure had been alive.

"Nicely done, Heloise," Sylvia Lutton, Lady Vastkern, murmured, moving closer to the straw dummy. She bent forward, peering at the hole in the waistcoat left by the lapel blade before accepting the small dagger from Heloise and inspecting the edges. "This newest batch is wickedly sharp. And the finger grips are a genius addition. Did you find the handling improved?"

Heloise flushed with pleasure. "I did," she replied, stripping off the pelisse the blade had been hidden in and laying it aside. "Euphemia's leather sheaths in the collar have improved as well. Though I do wonder," she continued with a small frown, the momentary pleasure gone as she accepted the blade back from Sylvia and ran her thumb over the narrow channels she had gouged into the grip, "if I couldn't make the hilt a bit lighter."

Sylvia chuckled as she took up the pelisse and inspected Euphemia's meticulous stitches attaching the thin leather sheath to the underside of the collar. "No matter how much I may tell you how utterly brilliant your work is, you will never be satisfied. You need to stop overthinking things, my dear."

Heloise worried at her lip with her teeth. "But if anything were to happen to one of the Widows while out on assignment, and it was caused by some flaw in my work—"

Sylvia laid a staying hand on Heloise's arm, her expression gentling. "You cannot take every bit of responsibility onto your shoulders," she soothed before grinning. "No matter how very strong those shoulders may be. What you have accomplished is above and beyond what anyone else could have done; now put your trust in the Widows—and in yourself."

Heloise nodded and smiled, though it was a hollow thing. What worth did she have to these women if she did not excel at her craft? What reason did they have to keep her around if she did not exceed their expectations?

But Sylvia was waiting for something more, wasn't she? "You're right," she said with as much conviction as she could muster. Which must have been enough to be convincing. Sylvia gave her an arch smile.

"Of course I'm right," she replied. "I'm always right. A fact which my darling Laney would be more than willing to agree with," she continued in a louder voice as Mrs. Laney Finch entered the smithy.

"I will agree with whatever you wish me to agree with, my love," Laney said with ready cheerfulness, wrapping an arm about Sylvia and planting a kiss on her upturned lips.

"Well, that is a promise I will certainly not pass up," Sylvia murmured, turning in Laney's embrace, with a look in her eyes that Heloise had become all too familiar with in the two years since coming to stay with the women at their Wimpole Street house.

Smiling, Heloise reached for the pelisse still in Sylvia's hand, gently tugging it from her grip. For their part, the two women seemed not to notice her, their attention fixed quite firmly on one another. Heloise slipped out, silently closing the door behind her. Though she could not work on her blades just then, her time would not be wasted. There was Euphemia to confer with regarding the efficiency of her newest creation now that she had properly tested the hidden sheaths. And she could always use the time to practice her sword skills or go over her notes regarding her designs for the newest batch of weapons she was crafting. No, not a moment would be spent in leisure. She had to earn her keep, after all.

The sharp click of her boots echoed as she made her way through the house, the quiet halls proof that the other Widows were busy at their respective positions in the household. Though just what those positions were would surprise anyone outside of their small, tight-knit group. The Wimpole Street Widows Society, as they were known, seemed innocuous enough, a group of women with the shared experience of having lost their husbands, collected under one roof to support one another in their widowhoods. And they had vigorously tended that misconception, like a gardener cultivating a particularly unassuming plant, when beneath the surface the roots were far reaching and powerful.

She amused herself imagining what the good people of London would say were they to learn the true purpose of the Widows—or what went on under the roof of the Wimpole Street town house. She chuckled. She rather thought that the sale of smelling salts would expand considerably were it revealed that not only were the fine arts of pugilism and swordplay practiced daily, but those of disguise, lock-picking, and poisoning as well. She herself had taken no small amount of time and effort to come to terms with it when Sylvia had first asked her to join the Widows. Even now, she found it hard to believe that there was such a society—or that she herself had somehow been lucky enough to be invited into its inner sanctum. A luck she would never take for granted.

Just as she was turning into the front hall, Mrs. Strachan, their housekeeper, approached. Rather, she stormed across the shining inlaid wooden floor toward Heloise, like a stout marauder intent on causing mayhem.

"Mrs. Marlow," she barked in her gravelly Scottish brogue, her face pinched in its perpetual frown, "how many times do I have to tell you that I am far too busy to play hostess to a barrage of guests at all hours of the day and night? I cannae take time out of my schedule to deal with the comings and goings of every blasted Sassenach who chooses to cross our bleeding doorstep."

Heloise forced a smile. God knew what had set the woman off this time, but she was not so much of a glutton for punishment that she would say or do anything that might make matters worse. Self-preservation, she had learned, was key to dealing with the brusque housekeeper.

"Hello, Strachan," she said, all sweet complacency. "You are looking lovely today. Are you doing something new with your hair?"

Strachan narrowed her eyes. "If you think I'll be turned to a puddle by your compliments, you have got another think coming, gel. Now go see to your own visitor in the drawing room. I've got things to do." With that she sniffed sharply and spun about, the staccato sound of her sturdy heels sharp and determined, like a drummer going into battle.

Letting out a breath of relief that she had managed to escape the woman with a minimal ear blistering, Heloise gave up any intention of seeking out Euphemia and headed for the stairs and the drawing room. Though Strachan fairly terrified her on a good day, she could not deny the woman was frighteningly good at her job, not only keeping the house in order but also assisting the Widows in their work. Heloise could put up with a bit of mild terror for their continued success.

She entered the pleasantly chaotic room, a perfect blend of the Widows' personalities with its mismatched furniture and peculiar blend of patterns, and immediately spied a familiar head of pale-blond hair pulled back in a severe bun topping a slight and subdued form. In an instant her worries disappeared, delight taking their place.

"Julia!"

Miss Julia Marlow, sister to Heloise's late husband, turned, a smile on her face. But there was a brittle quality to it that sent alarm bells pealing through Heloise's brain.

"Heloise," she said, stepping forward, hands outstretched. "I'm sorry for coming unannounced. I know it is not our normal day to meet."

Heloise laid the pelisse aside on a nearby chair and took the girl's hands in her own, noticing with concern that Julia's fingers were not only trembling ever so slightly but also ice cold through her gloves. Whatever had brought the girl here today, her visit was not a mere social call. Frowning, she rang for tea and led Julia to a settee before the hearth.

"I always have time for you, you know that," she said, sinking down beside her. "But something is wrong. What is it?"

Julia huffed a small laugh, but the sound was more hopeless than amused. "Did I give away so much already?" she asked. But her composure did not last long, her delicate features crumbling. And then, with a shaky sigh, she dissolved into sobs.

Alarmed, Heloise gathered Julia in her arms. "Dear God, what's happened?" she exclaimed. But it was all too obvious that she would not soon get an answer; the girl had become incoherent in whatever grief had hold of her. Her body shook, her breath coming in ragged gasps as she cried into Heloise's shoulder. For Heloise's part, she could only act as a kind of port in the storm while Julia clung to her and questions flooded her head: Was Julia ill? Had she lost her position? Was she in trouble? She felt at sea, unsure how to deal with the emotions pouring out of the girl.

Gregory would know what to do. The thought came unbidden, all the harsher for how unexpected it was. At the remembrance of her late husband, a deep guilt took hold of Heloise. She had made a vow to Gregory just before his unexpected death that she would watch over Julia. The two had been very close, and his passing had left a gaping hole in the girl's life—one that Heloise fully blamed herself for. If she had only taken care of things herself, if she had not asked for help, Julia would now have a brother to protect her.

Closing her eyes, she laid her cheek on the crown of the sobbing girl's head, even as she fought against the burn of tears that lodged in her throat. Julia was so fragile and sensitive. She and Gregory had had only each other for so long, and he had been incredibly protective of her, his anxiety over her future nearly consuming him. It had been the main reason he had married Heloise, to give the girl a kind of mother figure as she grew. And Heloise had filled that space as well as she had been able to. Even so, the bond between the two siblings had been strong, and she had often felt an outsider. His concern for his sister's well-being had been his one coherent thought as he'd lain feverish and confused on his deathbed, begging Heloise to protect her, his eyes glazed, skin pale and clammy, hand like a claw about her own in that one last burst of desperate energy…

She broke free of the memory with a gasp. What else could she have done but agree to his request—as incapable as she had felt of fulfilling it? She would have promised so much more to give him a bit of peace.

Despite her fears that she would muck the whole thing up, she had done her best to keep that vow. She'd made sure Julia had everything she needed, nursing her when she was sick, surprising her with the small trinkets and treats she thought Gregory might have chosen, cheering for her when she secured a position as companion to an influential countess.

But it had not been enough. Julia's tears seemed proof that she had failed at the one thing Gregory had asked of her.

"Julia, please let me know what's wrong," she tried again, desperation coloring the words.

Blessedly, the sound of her voice seemed to finally calm Julia. Gulping in several large breaths, sniffling loudly, she pulled away from Heloise. Tears glistened in her lashes and streaked down her pale cheeks, and she retrieved a handkerchief from her reticule and pressed it to her running nose. "I hardly know where to begin," she managed around the material.

"There is no better place than the beginning," Heloise said firmly, patting her arm.

Yet even with the encouragement—and despite that she had obviously visited with the express purpose of revealing her troubles to Heloise—Julia seemed at a complete loss. Blessedly, the tea came then, a maid bringing the tray in and depositing it before them. Heloise busied herself with preparing their cups and doling out generous plates of delicacies, giving Julia the time and space to gather her thoughts—and hiding that she was devoured by worry for the girl. Finally, when she had served them both and was left with nothing further to do except clasp her hands in her lap to keep herself from tearing her hair out from anxiety, Julia spoke up.

"I don't know where else to turn, Heloise. If you say you cannot help me, I don't know what to do."

Which was far too ominous a sentence. Swallowing hard, Heloise placed a steadying hand on Julia's arm. Though truthfully it was as much for herself as it was for Julia.

"What happened?" she asked.

Closing her eyes as if beyond weary, Julia whispered, "Dionysus."

Heloise stilled. "Dionysus? The *gaming hell*?" Surely she'd misheard.

Julia nodded mournfully. And Heloise suddenly felt sick to her stomach. Blowing out a sharp breath, she leaned back in her seat. Dionysus was known as a place of immorality, synonymous with decadence and excess. There was not a highborn family that had not been affected, for better or worse, by chances taken at Dionysus's tables.

But how had Julia, as innocent and naive as she was—not to mention that she was most certainly not from a well-to-do family—become entangled in such a place?

No matter how Julia had become involved, Heloise needed to focus so she could help in whatever way she could. Sitting forward, taking up her cup and swallowing a deep draught, letting the bracing heat of the tea work its way into her stomach, she turned back to Julia. "Tell me everything," she demanded. "And I mean everything."

2

At the end of an hour, after wading through a good many stops and starts and tearful words that she could barely comprehend, Heloise finally managed to extract the whole story from her distraught sister-in-law. A story that made her equal parts terrified and furious, mingling with a guilt that deepened with each agonized word.

But now was not the time to allow those emotions to take control, not if she was to save Julia from the loss she'd incurred at Dionysus's tables. She saw the other woman out, promising to help in every way she possibly could, before retreating to her bedroom.

But as she moved to the window to stare down into the back garden, fear sat dark and heavy on her shoulders. How could she possibly save Julia? After all, Dionysus was a massive beast, far reaching and frightening and powerful, while she was just...Heloise.

She didn't know how long she stood staring out the window. But she was no closer to a solution when a sudden knock sounded on her door, scattering her troubled thoughts like clay marbles in a children's game. She would find an answer somehow, she vowed. No matter how hopeless it seemed.

Smoothing her hands over her skirts, she called out, "Come in."

The maid, Kristen, peeked her head in. "Lady Vastkern sent me to remind you of the weekly meeting in the drawing room, Mrs. Marlow."

Damn, she had forgotten about that. "Thank you, Kristen," she said before taking a steadying breath and following the maid out.

The Widows were already gathered about a low tea table in a lively discussion when she entered. They greeted her with smiles as she took her place in the circle.

"Was that Miss Marlow I saw leaving a short while ago?" Euphemia asked, placing a neat stitch in the bit of fabric she was working on. A former theatrical costumer and therefore a master with a needle and thread—as well as a whole host of disguise techniques—she had the power to transform in a moment into anyone she chose. A veritable chameleon when it came to clothing and makeup and mannerisms, she was an invaluable tool in the Widows' arsenal of talent.

"It was," Heloise replied. Before she could open her mouth to continue, however, Mrs. Iris Rumford spoke up.

"You do not seem happy to have seen her." She frowned slightly, unconsciously scratching at her scalp under her mass of upswept blond curls, dislodging a leaf from the mess. Their resident botanist, who had a peculiar talent for lock-picking and safecracking, she was indispensable to them. She also had the tendency to think in a very linear, logical fashion that, while useful for her profession, left her confused by the minutiae of social interactions and rules.

"It's nothing," Heloise replied hurriedly. This was her

family's mess; she didn't wish to drag the others into it. "But what were you discussing when I arrived?"

"Miss Amanda Sheffield, it seems, has settled quite nicely into the cottage left to her by her grandmother," Laney said, referring to their latest case, in which they had assisted a young woman who had been robbed of her inheritance by her vile uncle. She peered at Heloise closely. "But why do I have the feeling we have a new mystery to solve right under our noses?"

Heloise, who had been in the process of biting into a biscuit, promptly choked. Truly, it was maddening—as well as awe inspiring—just how quickly the Widows picked up on even the slightest tell.

"Do you know, my love," Sylvia murmured to Laney, even as her eyes narrowed on a watery-eyed Heloise accepting a cup of tea from Euphemia, "I do think you're right. Heloise, dear, what happened with your sister-in-law to trouble you? And don't think to deny it. You know we can spot a lie a thousand feet away."

Heloise lowered her cup. "There really is no hiding anything from you, is there?"

"You know there is not," Sylvia said cheerfully before indicating with a wave of her hand that Heloise should answer the question.

Heloise sighed. "Julia has got herself in a bit of trouble is all. But it's not anything I cannot handle."

Sylvia, however, was not to be fooled so easily. She pursed her lips, stirring her tea with a soft tinkle of silver on porcelain. "Why don't you let us decide that for ourselves, my dear?"

But Heloise shook her head. "I've no wish to involve any of you. It's my family's problem."

"Which means it is very much our problem," Sylvia

said, her voice gentling. "You are our family, too. Anything that affects you affects all of us."

It was not the first time one of the Widows had told her this. No doubt it would not be the last. All the women in this house were uncommonly close, after all, and did indeed act more like family than anything.

But Heloise could not allow herself to be so complacent. If there was anything that growing up in her uncle's unwilling care had taught her, it was to know her place and to stay in that place.

Sylvia must have sensed her continued reluctance. Her expression shifted, turning almost sly as she considered Heloise.

"You know," she murmured, "we're at loose ends just now, and have been since Miss Sheffield's problem was taken care of. You would be doing us a favor if you gave us something to do."

The rest of them nodded enthusiastically, their voices echoing Sylvia's, working in concert with the fear corroding Heloise's insides, crumbling her determination. What harm could it do to tell them?

"If you're certain." They all enthusiastically gave voice to that certainty, and Heloise took a breath, trying to ignore the relief that blossomed in her chest.

"Julia has come with rather unfortunate news." She bit her lip, trying to control the anxiety and rage the past hour had dredged up in her. "And it all centers around Dionysus."

Laney frowned, sitting forward. "The gaming hell? What does Miss Marlow have to do with such a place?"

"Much more than I would ever like to admit," Heloise muttered. And then, because she could not have remained still if she tried, she rose and began to pace, her boots making quick work of the floral carpet beneath her feet.

"My sister-in-law has certain…skills. Skills that my late husband possessed as well, an innate ability to remember seemingly mundane things…including what cards are played in games of chance."

There was a heavy silence. When she chanced a glance up, all the Widows were staring at her with expressions of shock mingled generously with reluctant humor and admiration.

"Do you mean to say," Laney asked slowly, "that Miss Marlow attempted to count cards?"

Heloise nodded miserably. Which caused Sylvia to let loose a bark of laughter. "I didn't know the girl had it in her."

Euphemia, however, frowned. "Wait, she attempted this at Dionysus? But *how*? And *why*?"

"I have a good idea both of those questions can be answered fairly easily," Sylvia murmured. "This has to do with her employer, Lady Ayersley, does it not?"

Heloise stared at her. "How did you know?"

Sylvia gave her a pained smile. "The countess was infamous for her fervor for gambling some years back. Her husband, of course, forbade it after she nearly lost him the bulk of his fortune, and she has been quiet for quite a long time. But seeing as Miss Marlow has been pulled into Dionysus's jaws, it's a safe assumption that Lady Ayersley was somehow involved."

"Yes," Heloise managed. "When her employer learned of her ability, she forced Julia to attend Dionysus's quarterly masquerade with her and play on her behalf."

"An impressive plan," Sylvia mused. "Not only would it enhance her chances of winning, but it would allow her to keep her promise to her husband that she herself would not gamble."

"And Julia was found cheating, was she?" Laney shook her head somberly. "The partners at Dionysus would not have taken it lightly. They are known to be a ruthless lot."

"Actually, no," Heloise replied with no little wonder. "She succeeded in hiding it from everyone."

Iris frowned again. "If so, why you were upset when she left?"

"No doubt because Miss Marlow went to a gaming hell in the first place," Euphemia explained.

"But that's not it at all," Heloise replied, her anxiety returning tenfold when she recalled Julia's face pale with fear. "I am upset because, before she quite knew what was happening, she lost quite heavily. So much that Lady Ayersley put up her ruby jewelry so Julia might continue playing. Jewelry that was quickly lost to Dionysus. Jewelry," she continued, unable to keep her voice from shaking, "that Lord Ayersley gave his wife upon their engagement, and that he has since decreed she must wear to their anniversary ball in a month's time. And if Julia does not somehow produce the rubies by then, Lady Ayersley has threatened to accuse her of stealing them."

The Widows fell into a stunned silence. "Which would mean," Euphemia managed, eyes wide, "she will either be hanged or transported."

"Yes," Heloise said through a throat tight with fear.

"How horrible," Iris whispered.

Sylvia, however, quickly rallied, waving a hand in the air. "It seems an easy enough fix. If she put the jewels up as collateral, we simply need to go to Dionysus and produce the funds to secure the necklace."

Heloise shook her head. "Julia has already tried that. They claim they have no record of the necklace."

That seemed to give the viscountess pause. She raised

one silver brow. "No record of it? How strange. I hear Dionysus is quite meticulous and aboveboard in everything."

"Perhaps they are not as 'meticulous and aboveboard' as they would like everyone to believe," Heloise said darkly, the anger from before sizzling hot under her skin.

Laney sat forward, no doubt sensing there was much more than anger behind the words. "What do you mean, Heloise?"

"Julia is certain she witnessed the dealer at her table manipulating the deck, and that is the reason she lost so heavily."

A silence fell over the room once more, this time electric with shock.

"Dionysus, cheating?" Laney breathed, finally breaking the spell Heloise's revelation had cast. "I have never heard anything of the sort said about that hell. Their reputation is a source of pride to them."

And Laney would know. Once an acclaimed pugilist, she was the Widows' doorway into London's underground gaming empires. Judging by the disbelief stamped on her face, she was having trouble wrapping her head around such a piece of news. Truly, Heloise didn't blame her. It was an astonishing piece of information, after all. While the lower-class "copper hells" were known for their shady dealings, the upper-class "golden hells" thrived on their reputations for fair play. And Dionysus, by all accounts, was the most trustworthy of the bunch.

Sighing, feeling more alone than ever—which truly was saying something, considering how adrift she typically felt—she opened her mouth to excuse herself.

Sylvia, however, was once again quicker than she.

"Well then," she declared, sitting forward, "let us begin to plan what needs to be done to recover those jewels."

Heloise stared at her. "What are you talking about?"

Laney smiled widely, an excited gleam entering her eyes. "Oh yes," she said to Sylvia, clasping her hand, "let's begin. I can see this will be quite the job."

"Job?" Heloise gaped at them. "What job? There is no job."

"Of course there is," Iris said, taking up the notebook and pencil she always kept with her, opening to a blank page, and looking about in expectation.

"And an exciting one, as well," Euphemia said with a grin, putting her stitching aside, a fresh enthusiasm lighting her face.

Heloise shook her head, frowning at the lot of them. "I cannot allow you to get involved in such a mess."

"You're not *allowing* us to do anything," Sylvia declared. "This is what we do, after all, protecting the innocent, righting wrongs. We go into this quite willingly, I assure you." When Heloise made to protest once more, the viscountess held up a staying hand. "We shall all be part of this, and so you may as well accept it. You cannot take on Dionysus alone. And besides, it is the least I can do." She gave Heloise a pained smile. "I'm afraid my guilt will allow me to do no less."

"Your guilt?" Heloise asked with no little disbelief.

"Certainly. If I had given you proper warning of Lady Ayersley's past propensity for gambling, you might have discouraged Miss Marlow from accepting a position with her, and she might not now be in this mess. And so you must allow me to make reparations."

Which was as far-fetched a reason as Heloise had ever heard. Yet she found she could no longer fight their help. The truth of the matter was, she was frightened nearly witless at the danger to Julia. She would do anything to help her. Anything. Even if that meant adding to the massive debt she owed these women for taking her in when she had been beyond hope.

Blinking back tears, she nodded. "Very well," she replied. "Where shall we begin?"

3

As part owner of a gaming hell, one of those houses of vice that the general population decried as the embodiment of evil, one would think that Mr. Ethan Sinclaire wouldn't give a damn what was being said about him. After all, he was a peddler of sin, someone who went against what every decent member of society deemed proper, and he did it with a smile on his face.

And yet here he was.

Laying his quill down on the blotter, he leaned forward, resting his forearms on the desk and threading his fingers together, spearing the man seated before him with an intense stare, the better to observe every flicker of a reaction, every nuance of meaning. "Tell me again," he said. "And tell me slowly."

Russell Keely, onetime pickpocket, now working solely—and in certain cases secretly—for Ethan, rubbed his knuckles on the leather arms of his chair. "There are whispers, sir, about your tables. Nothing concrete, mind you," he hastened to add, no doubt due to some darkness that had fallen over Ethan's face—given how Ethan was feeling, he wouldn't be surprised if he appeared like the devil incarnate. "Just speculation that there may be something...unsavory afoot."

"Unsavory." Ethan tested the word on his tongue, rolling it around in his mouth. He pulled his lips back from his teeth as the bitterness of it overwhelmed him. *Unsavory* could be nothing at all in his line of business, of course. Or it could be a death knell for everything he had worked for and built up. Especially after what had happened three years before.

Gavin.

But he would not think of the time when the person who should have been the one he could trust most in this world had betrayed them so brazenly, when everything had nearly been lost because of his brother's greed. No, he would focus on the here and now, and he would make certain there was no repeat.

Although he might very well be too late for that, if what Keely was telling him was true.

Leaning heavily back in his seat, he pinched the bridge of his nose and sighed. "Perhaps it's someone who wishes to bring us down," he muttered, more to himself than to Keely.

"I'm not certain that's it, sir," Keely replied, picking at his dirty nails. "If that were the case, the rumblings would be loud. But they're quiet, only found if someone knows where to look."

Meaning whichever patron it originated from was not keen on making it public, due to fear of either scandal or retaliation. But with the rumblings already starting, it was only a matter of time before they transformed into actual rumors that would tear through London like wildfire.

"Damn and blast it all to ever-loving hell," Ethan growled. He speared Keely with a sharp gaze. "Is there anything else? Any details about this *unsavory* reputation?"

"Aye. Something about unreliable tables. It seems someone has begun to have suspicions that the house is cheating, but they don't have enough evidence to blab it about." He smirked. "And your own formidable reputation is such that they don't dare come right out and say it without proof."

"Thank God for small favors, I suppose," Ethan muttered to himself.

Keely, apparently done with what he had come for, rose. "Will there be anything else, sir?"

"Not presently," Ethan replied. Pulling a wad of bills from his desk, he thrust them at the young man, whose eyes widened at the bounty. "But keep your ear to the ground. Squash any further whispers and come to me with any additional intelligence, and there will be more where that came from."

"Yes, sir," Keely said with a toothy grin before, with a tug on his forelock, he fairly bolted from the room. No doubt to spend a good portion of it immediately on women and drink. The scamp truly did live in the moment.

Ethan pressed his lips tight. That was not something he himself could afford to do. No, every ounce of his energy was focused on one thing and one thing only: seeing that the reputation of his club was flawless. There could be no chinks in the armor, no vulnerabilities. The walls he'd put up about him had to remain completely impenetrable.

Once more his brother's face swam up before his mind's eye, dark eyes laughing. They, along with their youngest brother, Isaac, and their two closest friends, had dragged themselves from the gutters to become the youngest gaming hell owners in London, their rise painful and daunting but the burn of their success bright, like that of a shooting star across the heavens. Ethan had believed nothing could touch them.

Until his brother, not satisfied with what they had accomplished, had become greedy and wanted more, and had cheated to get it. And in the process had become that shooting star, burning out into nothing more than ash and dust.

He closed his hand into a fist, reining in his swelling anger lest he swipe the whole damn desk clear and send everything crashing to the floor. Damn and blast Gavin for all he had done. Blessedly, word had never gotten out, Gavin's tragic death smothering any rumors that might have come to light. But though Dionysus's reputation had remained spotless, though it drew powerful patrons who lauded his club as one of the premier establishments in London, he never felt he could completely wash away the invisible yet indelible stain of what his brother had done—or the sense of betrayal. It stayed embedded in his skin, like the scars that crisscrossed his back. He rolled one shoulder, wincing as the puckered skin pulled tight. And like those scars, the pain would forever be part and parcel of him.

"That is the most hellishly frightening expression you've got there, Brother."

Ethan glanced up at the sound of his younger brother's voice. Isaac looked as carefree and devilish as ever, with that lopsided smile that never failed to charm even the most irascible patron—not to mention a good number of the women of London. He sauntered into the office, closely followed by their two partners, the combined mass of the three men enough to make the spacious office feel decidedly close.

"And that is saying something," Hardwick Teagan continued, cocking a thumb at the man at his side, "considering how frightful Parsons here is."

"You're a bloody nuisance, did you know that?" Parsons grumbled, his voice like crushed gravel, before pushing past Teagan and lowering himself into the chair Keely had vacated minutes before. Known only by his surname—Ethan had never learned the man's given name, though he had known him since boyhood, and he very much doubted anyone but the man's mother and whatever God he chose to believe in knew it—Parsons was as far from his namesake as one could be. Large and rough, with frightful scars that cut across his pale face and long nearly white hair he kept pulled back in a perpetual queue, he appeared more demon than man of the cloth.

Teagan chuckled as he followed Parsons into the room. He was the opposite of Parsons in every way: graceful where Parsons was rough, lean where he was large, friendly where he was reserved. Like now as he leaned a hip against Ethan's desk, teeth flashing a grin in his dark face. "I only grate on you because you're such a surly beast. Ethan and Isaac, on the other hand, adore me."

"*Adore* is a strong word for what we feel for you," Ethan muttered. "More like *tolerate*."

Teagan, however, wasn't in the least offended. As usual. The man was blasted hard to insult.

"I will take being tolerated, and happily," he quipped. "But while Isaac is a forgiving fellow and cannot stay angry to save himself, we all know you're an untrusting bastard, and you tolerating someone is as good as you saying you esteem them greatly. And so I am honored." He sketched a shallow bow, his lips kicking up in a smirk.

Isaac chuckled, dropping into the seat beside Parsons. But he had no sooner crossed his long legs and settled himself in the deep leather armchair than he turned a sober eye on Ethan. "But what was Keely doing here?"

Ethan's momentary good—or at least neutral—mood vanished. Though they knew Keely worked for him, they all believed he hired Keely for menial jobs, running letters and fetching purchases and the other hundred small tasks Ethan required done on any given day. He had made certain that no one, not even his brother—perhaps especially his brother—guessed at the true nature of his business dealings with Keely, who ferreted out information for him regarding Dionysus. He would not be caught unaware and defenseless again.

It was all to protect Dionysus. And as Dionysus was the living, breathing beast that had been their salvation, the creature that continued to save them even now, it was to all their benefit. Had he been doing it in secret for the past three years since Gavin betrayed them? Yes. Was Isaac, Teagan, or Parsons at all responsible for what Gavin had done? No. They had been duped just as heinously as Ethan had.

But despite that, he could not confide in them. It was his fault, after all, that he had let down his guard and been oblivious to what Gavin was doing. And if his own brother, someone he had trusted so completely, could have done something so heinous, couldn't anyone? Against his will his gaze tripped over the three men, the past like a spill of ink on the present and the future, staining his vision. No, he would not make the same mistake again, would keep the door shut tight on the lure of Midas, so that no hint of temptation ever led another of them astray again. Even if that meant deceiving his last surviving brother.

He was certain that what he was doing was right. So why did he feel so damned guilty keeping it from them?

Maybe it was Keely's revelation that the calm waters they were sailing in had something dark and dangerous lurking beneath the surface. Who was responsible for it this time around? Who had turned their back on Dionysus and all it stood for? And could it be any of the men before him?

But Isaac's question still hung heavy in the air. And his brother was not the only one waiting for an answer. All three men's faces revealed a suspicious alertness that grew more pronounced the longer he remained silent. Making certain his features didn't betray even a modicum of his internal disquiet, Ethan replied, "I've decided to refuse Lady Weyland's advances. I sent the boy off with my reply."

There was a pause, no longer than a breath, that exposed the fact that the men didn't fully trust that he was telling them the truth.

Well, the feeling was mutual.

"Poor Lady Weyland." Teagan arched one brow. "I can't deny I'm surprised. She's quite the beauty and known for her...generosity in the bedroom. I thought for certain you would agree to her proposal."

"I find I grow tired of such affairs." Which was the truth. While at first he'd enjoyed the attentions of the highborn women who pursued him, he'd quickly realized he was no more than a novelty for them, a means of flirting with the taboo.

He made a great show of retrieving his pocket watch and checking the time. "But what brings you all here at such an hour? I know it's not just to see my handsome face."

"Handsome," Isaac snorted, raising a dark eyebrow, the carefree look back in place. Though there was still a lingering something left in his eyes, like the dirt left at the bottom of a tub after it was drained.

Parsons, however, was not about to disparage anyone's looks. He was sensitive enough about his own, though he would pretend otherwise.

"We need to plan another event," he said. He shifted in the leather seat, which creaked under his weight. Parsons was always shifting in discomfort in some way, appearing as if he would rather be anywhere but where he was, even when in the comfort of his own home.

"We've got the masquerade in just over a fortnight, haven't we?" Ethan said, frowning as he reached for his calendar. They had been hosting their quarterly masquerades for years. They were among Dionysus's largest draws, providing a way for people of all genders and from all walks of life to join in the festivities and indulgences in complete anonymity.

"Actually," Teagan said, plucking a heavy glass paperweight from Ethan's desk and turning it over in his hands, "we're thinking perhaps something in addition to the masquerade." When Ethan gave him a quizzical look, he hooked a thumb in Parsons's direction. "It was his idea. He's been spending time with Beecher from Brimstone, you know."

Which caused Ethan's one raised brow to rise even higher up his forehead. Augustus Beecher was part owner of Brimstone, the only other gaming hell in London to hold a candle to Dionysus. Well, he supposed Beecher was the sole owner, since his previous partner, the Duke of Buckley, had sold him his portion and sailed off in domestic bliss with his new bride. It was no secret that Beecher was looking for a new partner, someone to rule Brimstone alongside him. That Parsons had been spending time with the man had alarm bells pealing in Ethan's brain. Could it be a coincidence that Parsons had befriended the owner of their rival hell just as whispers had begun about Dionysus having crooked tables?

Add to that Parsons glaring at Teagan before giving Ethan a defiant glower, and it did not look good. Not at all.

"What has Beecher said to make you think we need something new here at Dionysus?" he asked the man.

"Brimstone will be hosting a boxing match soon. Perhaps you've heard of it?"

"I have," Ethan replied, steepling his fingers, filing away the fact that Parsons had not answered his question but had instead merely repeated a truth that half of London already knew. "And we have held boxing matches in the past, lest you forget."

"I'm not a simpleton," Parsons snapped, brows lowering dangerously over stormy eyes. "But we have not hosted one in some time. And with Brimstone inching ahead of us in popularity, we need to counter their moves. If our patrons leave us for them, their money goes with them."

He leaned forward and tossed a missive on the desk. Ethan unfolded it, and a small card fell out and into his lap. But he hardly gave it a glance before his attention was snagged by the bold writing in his hands and one very familiar name.

"Mrs. Finch?" he asked, glancing at the other men before returning his attention to the letter. "Mrs. Laney Finch, the famed pugilist? She wishes to fight at Dionysus?"

"So it seems," Isaac joined in. "It appears to be a gift from the heavens, doesn't it? Most of London would clamor to see Mrs. Finch come out of retirement to box again."

"Indeed," Ethan mused. Yet another coincidence. And if there was anything Ethan did not trust, it was coincidences. As the other men discussed the possibility of such an event taking place at Dionysus, Ethan studied the small card that had fallen into his lap. Was it all connected, the whispers of cheating and Parsons falling in with Beecher and the sudden—and suspiciously well-timed—gift of Mrs. Laney Finch wishing to box at Dionysus? Could this all possibly be a ploy on Parsons's part to join Brimstone as a partner, and was he hell-bent on destroying Dionysus from the inside out before that happened?

A sourness settled in Ethan's stomach. As Teagan recounted how he had seen Mrs. Finch box when he was a lad and how this could be just the thing to elevate Dionysus above even Brimstone, Ethan glanced at Parsons and fought to keep himself from rubbing at the ache in his chest. Despite the walls he had built about himself when Gavin had betrayed them, he had too much history with these men—and, indeed, shared blood—to completely shut them out of his trust. The very idea that one of them was capable of intentionally hurting him and all they had worked for was much more painful than he would ever willingly admit. Especially after what he had been through in the past. He had known better. And still he had been duped.

Well, no more.

"As we are all in agreement that this would be the best thing for Dionysus," he said when Teagan finally shut up, "I'll call Mrs. Finch and her manager here to talk over the details."

"Splendid," Teagan exclaimed, rising and going to the sideboard to pour glasses of whisky to toast with. As Ethan tapped his glass with the others' and downed his drink, he thought that there was no better way to protect Dionysus than to keep his enemies close. His gaze drifted to the small calling card he had left on his desk. And he would start by meeting with Mrs. Finch's manager, Mrs. Heloise Marlow.

4

Heloise stared up at the quietly elegant building that housed Dionysus, its soaring columns and intricately carved friezes and white granite shining in the sunlight in the middle of St James's Street, and tried with all her might to dredge up the confidence she knew she would need for the upcoming meeting with the gaming hell's owners. But all she felt was a vague kind of nausea.

No, that wasn't true. There was nothing vague about it. It was quite solid and horrible and causing a faint sheen of sweat to take up residence on her upper lip. But she would deal with the nausea, and gladly, if it meant she could save Julia.

"Are you certain about this, Heloise?" Laney asked. Heloise knew the other woman wasn't asking if she was certain about infiltrating Dionysus, nor about playing the part of Laney's manager, which they had all agreed was the best way for Heloise to gain access to the club regularly. No, she was referring to an additional part of their scheme, something Heloise had decided upon on her own. For she had quickly come to the realization that her playing at a boxing manager could get them only so far, into public spaces that any vendor or worker might access.

Seducing one of the owners, however, could open the more private, secret areas of the club that would otherwise be closed to them—with the added benefit of gaining the trust of those men in charge. She had tried with all her might to come up with alternatives to such a plan. Yet with each hour that passed she had seen with increasing clarity that there was no other way, not if they were to succeed in this. Dionysus, after all, would be very much like a fortress. And she would have to use every weapon at her disposal to infiltrate it.

That did not make her any easier over her decision, however.

She scowled at Laney now, more to hide her own disquiet than anything else. "You don't think I'm capable of seducing someone?" Not that she would blame Laney if she didn't. Even in her youth Heloise had never been exactly sought after. She had not the softness and gentle curves that so many men preferred, instead sporting a leanness and muscled tone that her work at the anvil had built.

And even if one could overlook her form, her face was another matter entirely. She was not what anyone would call a beauty. No man would be inspired to ardor and devotion by looking at her, her features too strong, too stubborn. And so she had possessed no dreams of undying love when she'd accepted Gregory's suit, one born solely out of necessity. Their relationship had eventually transformed into friendship, but regardless, their union had not been built on any great passion. She had no experience in seducing a man, much less one who no doubt had all manner of women throwing themselves at him.

Panic clawed at her chest, making it hard to breathe. What had she been thinking, announcing that she would seduce one of Dionysus's owners? She didn't know the first thing about seduction, or what men liked, or how to be feminine and desirable.

In the next moment, however, common sense prevailed. Or at least it tried its hardest to be heard over the uncertainty screaming away in her brain. How hard could it be to seduce someone? Sex and desire were natural, instinctual parts of being human. And while she wasn't the most stunning woman in the world—not even close—she was not exactly disgusting to look at. She could do this. She hoped.

"Of course I think you're capable of seducing someone," Laney soothed with a fortifying smile. Her auburn eyebrows did not get the message of comfort that the rest of her was trying to impart, drawing together in blatant concern.

"Certainly I can," Heloise reiterated almost defiantly, though whether for Laney's benefit or her own she didn't have a clue. "And with men who give themselves up so willingly to desire, it should be a walk in the park."

"Oh, I have no doubt of it," Laney declared bracingly.

"Not to mention," Heloise continued, her words coming faster, as if the sheer speed of them would help drive home the questionable idea that she was capable of doing this, "that we have researched the owners extensively, and I am confident that, whichever man I'm to work most closely with during the preparations for the match, I will be able to seduce him with little trouble."

"Little trouble at all," Laney said. And, by some miracle, Heloise found she was actually beginning to believe the lies they were telling themselves.

But whatever confidence she was able to drum up fizzled to nothing when they knocked at the massive front doors and those doors immediately swung wide to reveal a solidly built man dressed in an elegant set of clothes that would have done any Bond Street dandy proud. One look at his rough features, however, and Heloise had the disturbing impression he had cracked more than his fair share of heads together.

Before they could say a word, the man spoke. "Mrs. Finch and Mrs. Marlow?" At their nods he bowed. "I'm Copper, the floor manager. The partners are expecting you. If you'll follow me?" Then, stepping back, he motioned with one meaty hand for them to enter.

Laney, ever fearless, smiled wide and stepped inside with alacrity. Heloise, however, was not so eager to be swallowed by the den of iniquity. And swallowed she was as Mr. Copper closed the door behind them, shutting them off from all outside sound and light. But this was not a heavy, cramped space, as she'd expected. This front hall would rival that of any mansion in Mayfair, with a soaring ceiling, a wide, sweeping double staircase, and silk-covered walls.

But that was where the similarity ended. There was nothing of the cold, sterile homes that the aristocracy used to show off their wealth. No, this place appeared to be built on passion, the colors too rich, the materials too opulent, every line and curve seeming to have been formed by an artist bent on seduction. As someone who had never allowed herself to explore that side of herself in all her two and thirty years, Heloise found that it fairly bombarded her senses, making her want to gasp for breath. It felt as if Dionysus were a living, breathing monster and she had just willingly entered its gaping maw. Before she could calm her overactive imagination and tell herself that she was being a silly ninny, Mr. Copper started off across the shining marble floor of the entrance hall, between the twin staircases, to another heavy door beyond. He flung it wide, ushering them through. To Heloise's shock, the disconcertingly sensual hall was positively tame compared to this new room, which could only be described as the great, cavernous belly of the beast itself.

Their steps echoed on the highly polished dark wood of the floor as they crossed the space, bouncing off the empty tables, traveling to the vaulted ceilings. A quick glance up and Heloise firmly expected to see the outline of a rib cage. Instead she saw, just barely discernible by the dim lamplight, a bacchanalian scene of mythological revelry. And the painted ceiling was not the only bit of excess to be found. With opulent chandeliers that dripped like heavy constellations from the arched ceiling, walls that appeared papered in a rich red damask, furnishings of deep mahogany, and heavy velvet drapes hiding God knew what, this place was nothing short of extravagant.

They headed to one of the velvet curtains now, and the floor manager pulled it aside to reveal a sturdy, intricately carved door. Even before he opened it, however, Heloise became aware of a deep rumble on the other side, like thunder, a sound that made the hairs stand up on the back of her neck. But it was no such tame natural phenomenon waiting for them on the other side. No, what was waiting was infinitely more treacherous, a collection of mismatched males who stood as they entered, each looking more dangerous than the last.

Goodness, but the owners of Dionysus were striking. She'd done her research, of course, but even so she was not prepared for the combined allure of them. They were not handsome in the same way, and one not handsome at all. Yet each had his own special something that drew the eye, a magnetism that left Heloise tongue-tied. How on God's green earth could she hope to capture the attention of even one of them?

"Thank you, Copper," the leanest of the four said, sending

a flirtatious smile their way as Mr. Copper retreated. "And welcome, ladies. Please, make yourselves comfortable. We have tea coming momentarily."

"Tea?" Laney said with a cheeky grin as she took a seat. "I did not know gaming hells had such innocuous drinks available."

The man chuckled. "We have everything your heart could possibly desire. That is what we cater to, after all, the soul's most secret desires." He raised a black eyebrow suggestively, his eyes heavy lidded in appreciation as he gazed at her. "If you prefer, we can certainly supply something a bit more to your taste."

"Oh, I have heard of you," Laney said archly. "You must be Mr. Teagan."

"I see my reputation precedes me," he drawled, sinking into the seat beside Laney, clasping her hand in his. "But what an honor, that *the* Mrs. Laney Finch knows who I am. I followed your career when I was a lad, and was lucky enough to witness you fight. It is an honor to have you in our establishment."

"Why, Mr. Teagan, you make me feel positively ancient," Laney rejoined. "But please allow me to present my manager, Mrs. Heloise Marlow. It was her idea that I come out of retirement."

"And what a brilliant idea it was," Mr. Teagan effused, turning his attention to Heloise.

For Heloise's part, she was so overwhelmed with wondering if this could be the man she would be working closely with, she was caught completely unawares when he turned his eyes her way. "Ah, er, thank you," she managed. Her cheeks burned hot, something that seemed to please Mr. Teagan if the satisfied look in his eyes was any indication. No doubt he believed her being flustered was caused by his allure, an attitude that could only help her if he was indeed the man she would attempt to seduce.

But she would not succeed if she acted like a ninny every time one of these men so much as looked at her. No doubt she would soon learn which of them she needed to focus her attentions on; in the meantime, she would prepare herself as best she could. While all the partners had similar backgrounds, having risen from the poorest parts of London to unimaginable heights of power and wealth, their personalities could not be more different. Smoothing her skirts, she hastily went over the information Sylvia had supplied just that morning while Mr. Teagan turned his attentions back to Laney. That man had already proved that he was a consummate flirt. But as she studied his expertly tailored clothing and the unconcerned curve of his lean body as he sprawled in his seat, she recalled he also possessed a genius mind that had made him a partner not only in one of the most successful gaming hells in London, but also in other ventures, lesser known but equally successful. Such an active mind could lead one to do troubling things if it was kept less than completely stimulated.

On the other side of that coin, there was Mr. Parsons. She dipped her head as Mr. Teagan finally halted his flattery and introduced that partner, a hulking man seated just off to the side of the group as if he could not be bothered to be a part of it. Unease settled under her skin as she studied him. No matter that his features were craggy and unforgiving, bisected by a pale, tight scar that went from one side of his forehead across the bridge of his nose and puckered across the opposite cheek; that part of him truly did not bother her a bit. Rather, it was the air of warning about him, a heaviness, as if anyone who tried to get close to him would be swallowed whole and never be able to escape. He had been an enigma even to their informants, a person who held all cards close to his chest and revealed not a single tell. She swallowed hard, sending up a little prayer that she did not have to attempt to seduce that particular man.

It was with relief that she followed Mr. Teagan's direction and settled her gaze on Mr. Isaac Sinclaire, youngest of the three Sinclaire brothers. Or, at least, there had been three before the middle brother's untimely death several years prior. Mr. Isaac Sinclaire seemed to be as popular with the ladies as Mr. Teagan. But where Mr. Teagan had the air of someone who was constantly busy, constantly seeking, constantly needing something, Mr. Isaac Sinclaire had a much calmer feel to him. He looked at Heloise and Laney in turn with a small, open smile on his face. Heloise chewed on the inside of her cheek. He was young for a man in his position, the very same age she herself was, and with his milder disposition and quiet good looks, he seemed the preferable of the three thus far for a seduction. But he was also the least powerful. No, the most powerful position at Dionysus was held by one man and one man alone.

Which naturally led her to the fourth prospect, Mr. Isaac Sinclaire's eldest brother, Mr. Ethan Sinclaire. A man who was known for his fierceness yet also for his honesty, whom people feared yet were strangely loyal to. A peculiar combination indeed. She turned to greet him as Mr. Teagan made the introduction—only to have her breath ripped from her lungs as her eyes met his. She had given him a cursory glance when she'd entered the room, of course. But she had not looked him fully in the face, and what she saw had her equally confused and transfixed. His features were careworn, rough, as if the hardships he had experienced had etched themselves into every line and sharp angle. With his heavy brows, crooked nose, and sharp cheekbones, there was nothing soft about him at all. Except for his lips, which were strangely full, an incongruous lusciousness, like that of a vibrant flower in a rocky landscape. But it was not his lips that so thoroughly captured her attention. At least, not completely. No, the thing that hooked into her and would not let go were his eyes. She felt as if those strange, piercing, nearly black orbs of his could see straight to her soul. Which, of course, must be what accounted for the peculiar tension that suddenly electrified her body, from the top of her head to the tips of her toes and every single inch in between.

"Mrs. Finch, Mrs. Marlow," he said with a slight dip of his head. His voice was rich and unbelievably deep, like browned butter and sugar and molasses all mixed together in a delicious concoction of temptation. "Thank you for coming to meet with us. We were intrigued and honored to receive your letter."

Heloise blinked. He sounded the farthest thing from honored that there could be. In fact, he sounded very much as if he distrusted them. She shivered slightly as his cold gaze drifted over her, as if taking stock of her. Ah, yes, he did not trust them at all. Which meant either distrust was part and parcel of his personality, or he had seen through their ruse. The former they could work with, of course. But if it was the latter, they could be in trouble indeed.

Blessedly, the tea came just then, giving Heloise the space to gauge Laney's reaction as Mr. Teagan went to work preparing the beverage. Had her friend sensed Mr. Sinclaire's tone as well? From the slight tightening at the corners of her eyes, she rather thought Laney had. Her smile was that much brighter, her teeth flashing as she dipped her head in acknowledgement of Mr. Sinclaire's comment.

"That is kind of you to say," she said. "I have missed the

sport so much and have ached to get back in the ring. When Heloise and I were discussing where best to do so, we could think of no finer establishment than Dionysus. As I'm sure you're all aware, your club is one of the best in all of London." She laughed lightly. "If not the very best."

Mr. Sinclaire's lips quirked at one corner, but there was no humor in the action. "Indeed."

Mr. Teagan chuckled. "And Sinclaire here is humble as well. Please, pay him no heed. He's a surly beast at the best of times. Now, Mrs. Marlow," he continued with a smile Heloise's way, "how do you take your tea?"

The next minutes passed pleasantly as Mr. Teagan saw to their tea and Mr. Isaac Sinclaire passed out delicacies in the form of small cakes and biscuits. It was quite the most bizarre experience of Heloise's life; it would have been a tea worthy of the finest London drawing room had they not been in a gaming hell talking of women's boxing. And if there had not been such a strange collection of males present. Indeed, so aware was Heloise of Mr. Sinclaire at her side glowering over the proceedings, she could hardly force herself to take a sip of her drink. But she would not allow the man to cow her. Purposely recalling Julia and the devastation on her face as she recounted what had happened here in this very hell, she straightened and attempted to remember her part in this strange dance—and how important the outcome was.

"We do hope you will consider working with us, gentlemen," she said, determined to play her part to the hilt. "Mrs. Finch is quite eager for it to happen and would be horribly disappointed should we fail to entice you to host her comeback match."

"Oh, there is no enticing needed," Mr. Teagan said with a wide grin. "It has already been decided."

"Teagan here is such an admirer of yours," Mr. Isaac Sinclaire joined in, chuckling, "that it was not a matter of *if*, but *when* we could host your match."

"Oh, splendid!" Laney cried. "I cannot thank you enough."

"It is we who should be thanking you," Mr. Teagan effused. "Even more so should you be ready in a fortnight, in time for our quarterly masquerade. It is Dionysus's biggest draw, and having your comeback that evening would be the very thing to transform this particular event from *incredible* to *spectacular*."

"You do have a way with words, Mr. Teagan," Laney replied.

A fortnight. Heloise's mind whirled with all that needed to be done. Granted, they had hoped for a short time, the Ayersleys' anniversary ball taking place in just under a month. But could they manage this? She placed her barely touched tea down and sat forward, catching Laney's eye. "It is quite close; our preparations for the event will have to be rushed. Do you think we are up for something of this magnitude in so truncated a time?" Her friend, she knew, would understand all she left unsaid. She meant they would have to infiltrate Dionysus much quicker than anticipated in their search for Lady Ayersley's jewels.

Not to mention Heloise's need to seduce one of the partners to secure their success.

But Laney did not hesitate. She knew better than Heloise what the Widows were capable of.

"I have every faith that we're up to the job," she said with a steady confidence that did much to allay Heloise's uncertainties.

Or it would have been enough to allay them had Mr. Sinclaire not then turned to face her fully and held out his hand to her.

"To seal our bargain," he murmured when she looked in alarm at him. "You and I will be working quite close together, after all."

Ah, God. So it was to be this particular male, was it? She swallowed hard as anxiety and dread and a strange electric excitement settled under her skin. Would she have preferred it to be one of the more open, cheerful fellows? Certainly. Hell, she would have even preferred Mr. Parsons and his dark brooding. Anything was better than Mr. Ethan Sinclaire and the dangerous distrust in his eyes.

But perhaps this was for the best. After all, wasn't there something to be said for keeping your friends close but your enemies closer? And there really was no getting closer than what she planned for this man. Her cheeks burned hot just thinking about it. But now was not the time for nerves. She would counteract his distrust with seduction and undermine his suspicion with kisses. And in doing so she would clear the way for their success.

Though as she slipped her hand in his, and his strong fingers engulfed her own, she felt as if she were sealing a bargain with the devil himself.

5

"And here is the space we'll utilize for the match."

Ethan stepped aside as the other partners guided Mrs. Finch into the large room, Mrs. Heloise Marlow trailing in the rear. It was a good space, large enough for a boxing ring and rows of seating, with a vaulted ceiling and generous lighting and a balcony that ran the entire circumference of the room to provide an unimpeded view of the fight. Ethan, however, didn't so much as glance about. Yes, he was as familiar with the room as he was with the back of his hand. But that was not the reason for his inattentiveness to his surroundings. That was solely due to Mrs. Marlow.

He watched her closely as she moved around the perimeter of the room, separate from the others in their busily chattering group, trying and failing to understand what it was about this woman that set him on edge. He had not trusted her from the moment she'd set foot inside Dionysus, that was certain. No, it had started before that, with the letter from Mrs. Marlow and the coincidences surrounding its timing. It had all been suspiciously fortuitous.

But his reaction to her was so much more than simple distrust. He frowned, his eyes roving over her as she sidestepped a chair. There was something powerful and yet graceful about her that had captivated him from the start. It was as if each movement, even while doing something as innocuous as taking a sip of her tea, was carefully calculated, as if she did not do anything without thought.

That same trait was in her eyes as well, those peculiar pale blue eyes that were strikingly offset by her sable hair. There was a watchfulness in them that had set his hackles up, as if she was planning and plotting something. A watchfulness as well as an uncertainty, a peculiar emotion indeed considering how very capable and sure of herself she appeared. Like right now, as she refrained from joining the others in the group, who were just then climbing the stairs to the top level, instead returning to Ethan with determined steps and a small smile on her face. She seemed confident in herself and her position as manager to one of the world's most famous women pugilists.

But he, who had made his living in games of chance, who had learned to read tells in others to survive, saw what she no doubt had no wish for him to see. Such as the tightening at the corners of her eyes, the way her fingers nervously brushed a nonexistent lock of hair from her cheek, how she could not seem to look directly at him. And when she did manage to look at him, her cheeks immediately darkened. He was not so vain that he believed it had anything at all to do with his looks. He knew he was a rough, homely bastard, that women pursued him only for his power and wealth, as well as the novelty of fucking someone who had crawled from the literal gutter. Yet this woman was blushing as if she were a debutante and he were her beau.

Something was definitely suspicious about Mrs. Marlow.

"I do believe this space will do nicely," she said with a nod, taking another glance about the room—though he had the distinct feeling that she did it more to avoid his gaze than to take in her surroundings.

He studied her profile, his gaze tracing along the delicate slope of her forehead, down her straight nose, over her plump coral-pink lips, around her surprisingly strong jawline. It was as he studied the long arch of her neck that he realized with a start he had ceased looking for proof of her nerves—of which there was an abundance—and was now merely appreciating the alluring contrast of power and fragility her features exuded. Giving himself a sharp mental shake—this was no time to be distracted by a pretty face—he cleared his throat and took a step away from her, more to steady himself than anything.

"We will be building a raised platform for the ring," he explained, sweeping a hand out to indicate its positioning, making certain he didn't so much as brush up against Mrs. Marlow, who was still much too close to him for his comfort. "There will also be benches along all four sides, and seating along the balcony above. As you can see, no seat will have a disadvantage, each providing an exemplary view."

"It sounds wonderful, exactly the kind of venue we were hoping for, and that we were certain we could find in Dionysus. Though," she continued, turning a small frown his way, "are you certain it will be ready by the required date? Between the building of the ring and seating, as well as advertising the event, it seems a fortnight will not be enough time for all that needs to be done."

He should be able to answer without hesitation. As the lead on this particular project, he had already gone over the schedule with meticulous care and was certain that everything would go off without a hitch.

But when her pale eyes met his, he lost the power of

speech. How was it that there was a shade of blue in all the world like her eyes? And why in God's name did it feel as though he were tumbling headfirst into a fathomless pool?

Blessedly, he was able to quickly gain control of himself and his errant and wholly unwelcome musings. Angry as he was at himself for his wandering thoughts—he was never anything but in control, yet here he was spouting mental nonsense about Mrs. Marlow's eyes, of all things—his response to her was much more curt than he had intended.

"Of course everything shall be ready by the required date," he snapped. "We are not novices, Mrs. Marlow."

The young widow blinked and took a step back. He didn't blame her; he was acting like a petulant child. A large and dangerous petulant child, if the alarm in her expression was anything to go by. Silently cursing himself, he took a steadying breath and tried again.

"We will have the room readied in time," he continued in a calmer tone. "You've no need to worry on that score."

Her cheeks once more brilliant pink, she nodded jerkily. "Very good. That is, I'm relieved." In the next moment she set her chin—that peculiarly stubborn-looking chin—and said in a much firmer voice, "I, of course, will be beside you every step of the way. The schedule shall be quite tight; I shall need to make certain nothing occurs to derail our plans for Mrs. Finch's return to the ring. We have much riding on this."

Why the hell did the idea of her shadowing him give him such a thrill? Anticipation burned in his chest at the thought of her beside him, spending her time with him, sharing her thoughts with him. He scowled, feeling like an inexperienced green boy.

But while he would love to refuse her suggestion, he could not deny that the arrangement would be of benefit to him. Having Mrs. Marlow close at hand so he might watch her every move was an ideal situation.

"Of course," he finally answered. "I would expect no less."

She nodded, apparently satisfied. "I'm glad that is settled, then. And, of course, we shall expect you to work with the Pugilistic Club to keep everything aboveboard. Mrs. Finch treasures her reputation of fair play and will not have any doubt put on the outcome of this match." She paused. "It is something I'm sure you can understand. From what I hear, you are a stickler for fair play and honesty yourself."

He stilled, narrowing his eyes on the young widow. Was that a note of challenge in her tone? And why? Surely she could not know about the whispers swirling in the miasma that was London. Even his partners did not know about them.

No matter what had prompted it, however, it only solidified his certainty that his suspicions regarding Mrs. Marlow were correct. The woman was up to something.

"I understand very well," he replied. "I'm glad we're on the same page. I can assure you, madam, I will do everything in my power to see that nothing unscrupulous occurs under my roof."

It had been a threat, plain and simple. Only a person acting dishonestly would have heard it. And Mrs. Marlow understood it, if the way her eyes widened for a split second in alarm was any indication.

In the next moment her expression transformed, like a mask falling into place, a too-bright smile fairly splitting her face. "I'm happy to hear it," she said in a cheerful chirp. "But I should fetch Laney. She had best begin her training in earnest if she's to be ready in a fortnight." With that she dipped her head in farewell and turned toward the stairs.

In her haste, however, she stumbled, one foot tripping over the other. Her pale eyes widened in alarm, her arms flailing as she toppled over. He reached out blindly, his arms coming about her as she careened toward the hardwood floor. His scars pulled uncomfortably, but he hardly registered it as he dragged her body against his. And there they stayed, frozen, staring at one another in mutual disbelief. A disbelief that quickly transformed to something hot and altogether consuming as he became aware of the utterly alluring combination of soft curves and firm muscles beneath his suddenly sensitive fingers.

He had not been wrong; she was unusually strong. It was in her arms as she clung to him, in her fingers as they gripped his shoulders tight. In the balcony above the others spoke, oblivious to the peculiar scene unfolding beneath their feet, their cheerful voices and laughter echoing about the room. But he hardly heard it over the sound of Mrs. Marlow's ragged breath in his ear, a perfect accompaniment to his own. The air he dragged into his lungs brought with it the scent of violets, surprisingly delicate given how capable and strong she appeared. He swallowed hard, his fingers unconsciously clenching in the dark blue of her gown even as he felt as if he were the one tipping head over arse, falling once more into the clear pools of her eyes.

It was her voice, faint and breathless, that finally broke the spell. "I-I think I can manage now."

Ah, God, had he just been standing there holding her? He hastily straightened, righting her. She cleared her throat, patting her hair, back to looking at anything but his face. That faint flush on her cheeks was back as well, like the stain of crushed summer strawberries on her skin.

He frowned. And apparently his inner poet was back as well. Truly, what the devil was wrong with him? He felt a stranger to himself where she was concerned. It must be his suspicions of her. He didn't trust her, and it was affecting him in a very visceral way. Yes, that *had* to be the reason.

Something he would think on later, once he managed to get himself under control.

"But you were about to fetch Mrs. Finch," he said. "I shall take myself off, then."

Before she could respond, he hurried from the room. All the while telling himself he was *not* fleeing her presence. Certainly not.

6

It had been a successful meeting. Heloise was certain of it. They had gained access to Dionysus through the planned match, Laney had begun to work her magic on the club's partners with her undeniable charm, and they were all one step closer to their goal of locating Lady Ayersley's jewels and saving Julia. She should be feeling confident, hopeful about the outcome, ready to start the hard work to see to their plan's success.

Why, then, did she want nothing more than to stay safe in her bed the following morning and never emerge?

She sighed as she rose and began her preparations for the day—much earlier than she was used to, as most of the work for the boxing match would be done just after Dionysus closed at dawn. But no matter that she had gone over her blunders with Mr. Ethan Sinclaire a hundred times in her head, no matter that she could still feel his arms about her when she had been so foolish as to trip over her own feet, she would not let those things petrify her and keep her from moving forward. Besides, this was her plan, her scheme. She would go through hell itself to see it succeed. She set her back teeth tight together as she thought of Mr.

Sinclaire and his hard, suspicious eyes. Even if that meant sleeping with the devil himself.

Unfortunately, being determined to sleep with said devil was quite different from actually doing so, a stark fact that Heloise finally admitted to herself a half hour later as she discarded yet another gown on her bed. It seemed everything she owned was too staid, too plain, chosen for comfort and ease of movement and not for the vague possibility of having to seduce a worldly gaming hell owner who was much too ruggedly handsome for his own good.

Stupid, naive past Heloise.

But it was not just her lack of appropriate gowns, was it? No, the truth of the matter was, she had no idea how to go about seducing anyone, much less someone as alluring, magnetic, and most of all experienced as Mr. Sinclaire. A fact that had her body fairly thrumming with anxiety, as well as some foreign emotion that was much like…what? Excitement? Eagerness? No, surely not. She was planning to seduce him because it would further their chances for success, after all, not because she desired him. No matter how attractive the man was with his broad shoulders and piercing dark eyes and too-full lips…

She hastily halted those thoughts in their tracks, the very idea that she could become lost in his appearance causing her anger toward herself and her own ineptitude to grow. So much that when a knock sounded at her bedroom door just as she yanked the last gown from the armoire, she called out, "Come in," with far more aggravation than was warranted.

It was Iris who entered. "Strachan ordered me to tell you the carriage is ready," she said, pushing a stray blond curl from her cheek. She stopped then and blinked myopically as she took in Heloise's state of undress and the pile of gowns strewn haphazardly across the unmade bed. "But you are not ready to leave."

"No, I'm not," Heloise groaned, tossing the last gown into the mound of cottons and calicos and muslins, sinking down into a nearby chair and dropping her head into her hands. "I suppose I could always just go in what I'm wearing now," she muttered through her fingers. "Seduction would be much easier, I'm thinking, in nothing but my chemise."

There was a beat of silence, then the sound of Iris's light steps as she came closer. "It's the seduction aspect you're worried about, then?" the other woman queried, sinking into the chair beside Heloise.

In a calmer frame of mind, Heloise would have been able to recall that Iris was not one who understood sarcasm. Agitated as she was, however, she found herself blurting with far more bite than the question warranted, "What else could I possibly be worried about?"

"Well, there is infiltrating a gaming hell," Iris replied without a bit of guile, "as well as feigning to be a pugilist's manager, attempting to locate valuable jewelry, the danger to your sister-in-law's very life—"

"Yes, thank you," Heloise choked out, holding up a hand to stop Iris from adding to the veritable mountain of anxieties she was buried under. "There's plenty to worry over. But in this moment, my most pressing concern is seducing Mr. Sinclaire."

Saying it out loud unfortunately led to an increase in her agitation—if that was at all possible. But Iris was looking at her with her brows drawn in that way that proclaimed louder than words that she did not comprehend what was going through a person's head. Heloise sighed. "I have never had cause to seduce anyone before," she explained lamely.

"If you're so anxious about it and not certain how to go about it, why did you volunteer?"

Which was a completely valid question. And one she had asked herself hourly since she had declared her plans. Truly, what had she been thinking, to volunteer for such a task, and at absolutely no one's suggestion?

What answer could she give, then, but the truth? "Because we require intimate access to the club that cannot be had with me posing as a mere pugilist's manager, and by seducing him I will give us our greatest probability of succeeding."

"Ahh." Iris's gaze tripped about the room, indicating she was deep in thought. And then she said the thing Heloise least expected. "Why don't I assist you?"

"You?" Heloise blurted with more than the necessary shock. Truly, anyone else would have been affronted at the amount of disbelief coloring her words.

Not Iris, however. She nodded firmly. "Certainly. I am nothing if not an observer of human habits." Here she paused, her expression slipping into a look of vague frustration before she shook her head and continued. "I have studied the courting rituals of young women and men in society, and I do believe that, though I have not had cause to utilize them myself, I can give a good overview of what must be done to attract the attentions of a man."

Which made perfect sense to Heloise in that moment, sitting as she was in nothing but her underthings, the time to seduce Mr. Sinclaire looming closer, while she had not a clue how to do so.

She turned toward Iris. "I would very much appreciate hearing your theories."

A soft flush of pleasure colored Iris's typically pale cheeks before she cleared her throat and clasped her hands in her lap. "I will endeavor to assist you in any way I can. Now, first and foremost, we must ascertain the male mind."

Heloise certainly hadn't expected that. She blinked. "The male mind?"

"Yes." Digging into the pocket in her skirt, she extracted her ever-present notepad and pencil, quickly flipping past sketches of plants and pages of small, close writing until she came to a blank sheet. With nimble fingers she quickly made a rough sketch of a human form—with much more detail than Heloise had expected.

"Oh," she said faintly, face suddenly hot as Iris made a particular portion of the male anatomy even clearer.

Iris, blessedly, was completely oblivious to her discomfort.

"Now," she said, all business, "we of course know that the human male tends to be driven by a healthy sexual desire. These portions of his anatomy are especially sensitive to such urges."

Here, to Heloise's further mortification, Iris began circling areas of the figure. Circle after circle appeared, with Heloise unable to take her eyes from the sketch. That area? And that, as well? She swallowed hard. Goodness.

"But while direct contact with these areas may garner the response you seek, it is prone to be short-lived. I assume you require the affair to continue at least until the jewelry is recovered, do you not?" Here she turned wide, curious eyes Heloise's way.

"Er, yes," she choked out.

With a nod, Iris turned back to the sketch. "Therefore, we must eschew these areas for the time being and focus on this particular portion of the anatomy." Here she made a large circle around the entire head.

"I'm...not sure I understand," Heloise said.

"His mind," Iris replied, tapping the tip of her pencil against the head, leaving several dots of graphite there, giving the appearance of beady eyes watching her. Which made the whole situation even more unsettling. "You shall need to feed his ego. That is the one thing I observed during my short time in society that seemed to work to the best effect, the constant stroking of male egos. They appear to quite enjoy that, and it seemed the young women who were most successful at it found their mates the quickest." She turned to gaze at Heloise with a smile. "Appeal to this base nature. Many men like to be made to feel superior. Flirt with him, feign helplessness, play to his ideal that he is of the stronger sex—though you and I know much better—and I am certain you shall find success."

As Iris took her leave to convey to Strachan that the carriage should wait a while longer, Heloise bit her lip and returned to the pile of gowns. Flirt? Play to his ego? She'd never had cause to practice those things—she had gone from her uncle's house to her husband's house without so much as smiling coquettishly, her skills with sabre and foil seemingly much more important than anything else.

But was she to bat her eyelashes and simper and *giggle*, for God's sake? Her hands stilled on a forest-green gown as she blanched. Quickly recovering herself, she worked at pulling the gown over her head. She would do all that and more if it meant the difference between failure and success. Even if it killed her pride. Which, she thought wryly as she considered her reflection in the looking glass and tugged her bodice down as far as it would go, it just might.

7

The carpenters, as scheduled, were at Dionysus early the next morning, ready to begin building the boxing ring and seating for Mrs. Laney Finch's upcoming match. As luck would have it, however, so was Mrs. Marlow.

Ethan stumbled to a halt just inside the event hall, eyeing the woman as she conversed with the head carpenter and feeling not a small dose of exasperation—as well as a disturbing amount of anticipation. Why anticipation, he didn't have a clue. God knew she was already a thorn in his side, and he had not known her a full twenty-four hours.

They should, of course, be perfectly aligned in what they wanted from all this. They both were working to make certain the boxing match was successful, for Mrs. Finch's and Dionysus's benefit. They should be in complete accord.

Yet that was not what he sensed from her at all. Mayhap because he suspected she was somehow involved in the looming devastation to the club's reputation, it felt as if she was more his opponent than anything. And if he was correct that she was up to something shady, he knew in his bones she would be a challenge. And he had not had a good challenge in a long while.

Again that anticipation, though sharper now. He narrowed his eyes, watching her as she inspected the planks of wood that ran the length of the room, her body moving with an easy grace as she maneuvered around the material. Strange, that. He had thought her graceful the day before as well. Why, then, had she tripped over apparently thin air and landed in his arms?

He recalled with a certain impressive clarity the exact feel of her pressed up against him. Mrs. Marlow was not some soft society matron, that was certain. Which he supposed was obvious, given she was working with Mrs. Finch. Yet he couldn't help but think that managing a famed pugilist was only the tip of the proverbial iceberg when it came to Mrs. Marlow.

She glanced up then and spied him. And would someone tell him why his stomach twisted in the most disconcerting way when she smiled at him?

"Mr. Sinclaire," she called out over the general din of craftspeople filling the space. With a long-legged stride she made her way to him. "Good morning. I trust you slept well and are ready for the day's work?"

He scowled. Truly, it was the only expression he could think to use considering how disoriented he felt as his skin shivered more with awareness and his heartbeat pounded louder in his ears the closer the woman came. "I have not yet slept," he responded, perhaps more curtly than was called for. "Lest you forget, Dionysus is open through the night. My hours are not typical."

"Oh! Of course, how silly of me." She blinked. Several times, in rapid succession. If he didn't know better, he would think she was fluttering her eyelashes at him. And then she did something wholly unexpected—or, rather, another thing wholly unexpected, although he was beginning to think that going against predictable behavior was a normal phenomenon with Mrs. Marlow—and took his arm, pressing herself up against him. He reared back, startled, but she merely held on tighter, blinking rapidly in that myopic way, lips curled up in what he could only describe as a disturbing attempt at a smile.

"But you must be exhausted. How hard you must work. Do you live on the premises? Or if not, mayhap you wish to return to your lodgings. Do allow me to accompany you there, and we may talk on the way."

He would later realize that it had taken him much too long to react to whatever the hell Mrs. Marlow thought she was doing. But in the thick of it all, with the woman attached to his arm like a limpet and gazing up at him with an expression that was at once determined and uncertain and frighteningly focused, he could not comprehend how he should react. And when the shock began to fade, he was dealt another jarring realization: that of just how wonderful her body felt pressed up against his side, most especially his arm, which was currently cradled in the valley of her breasts. He swallowed hard, painfully aware of just how pert and firm and yet incredibly soft they were as they hugged his bicep. Which led his attention farther down, to his forearm, where the faint curve of her belly was. Which drew his attention even lower, to the part of her that was pressed up against the back of his hand...

The staccato clatter of a plank of wood hitting the floor echoed through the room then, blessedly jarring him back to his senses. Pulling his arm forcefully from her grip, he took several healthy steps back from her. "Ah, er, there's no need for that," he said, stumbling over the words much more than he liked. Which, naturally, led him to scowl again. Truly, this woman had the most frustrating effect on him. And he did not like it, not one bit.

"Like I said," he continued, "my hours are not typical. I am ready to continue working. Which I must do if we are to complete the necessary preparation for the match. Now if you will excuse me."

With that he quickly located the lead carpenter and headed his way. It was not until he had received the plans for the build from the man and was looking them over that he noticed he was not alone in his perusal. Over his left arm was Mrs. Marlow again.

Sighing heavily, he closed his eyes in a bid for patience before glancing her way. "Can I help you with something, madam?"

She smiled brightly. "Not at all. Please, pay no attention to me."

Again he sighed. Though this time it came out a bit more aggressively than before, a sharp exhalation of breath, stirring the plans in his hands. "There is no need for you to remain," he managed through teeth he was quickly threatening to grind to dust for all he was pressing them together so tightly. "I have things well in hand."

She nodded enthusiastically. "Of course you do," she replied in a breathy voice, her hand finding his arm again, fingers lingering on his sleeve. "I can tell you are quite adept at what you do. It is admirable, Mr. Sinclaire. Admirable indeed."

What the absolute devil? Though he had not known her more than a day, he did not believe such fawning behavior was typical of her. Before he could make sense of it all—or pick his jaw up from his chest, where it had dropped—she continued.

"But I do believe I informed you yesterday during the tour of your facilities that I would be sticking close to you for the fortnight leading up to Mrs. Finch's match. It is imperative that it be a success. Which I'm certain it will be," she hurried to say, her wide smile widening even further, something he had not thought possible considering how her cheeks had seemed to be nearly split in two. "If someone as capable as you is in charge, it can only be successful. But it is my job to make certain everything that can be done is done. You understand, don't you, Mr. Sinclaire?"

Once more she fluttered those long lashes of hers, so rapidly it was a wonder they did not create a whirlwind to blow him away. He narrowed his eyes, the back of his neck tingling, much like a dog sensing an approaching storm, no doubt. Something was brewing, coming closer, looming over him and Dionysus and everything he had worked so hard to build, ready to rain down on them all. And this woman could very well be part of it.

Oh, she might not be the center of the storm. He had no doubt at all that someone who worked for Dionysus was there at the eye of the hurricane. But the only way to ascertain how big a part Mrs. Marlow might play in it was to keep her as close to himself as possible. He pressed his lips tight. Despite his wish to do otherwise. A wish he would insist was real, no matter how much his heart thrummed whenever she was near.

Blessedly, it seemed she was doing her damnedest to make certain they were in close proximity. Well, far be it from him to disappoint her.

"I am in complete agreement, Mrs. Marlow," he murmured, dipping his head in her direction.

That seemed to stall her. She blinked, her smile faltering. "You—you are?"

"Absolutely. But there is much to do. And there is no better time than the present. Shall we?"

Without waiting for her answer, he spun about, ignoring the flare of excitement in his gut as she scurried after him.

* * *

A short time later, however, he was ready to curse his former self for being so bloody clever.

Mrs. Marlow leaned forward in her seat across the carriage from him, the better to peer out the window as they pulled away from Dionysus. The slight movement sent a waft of sweet violets his way, and he gritted his teeth tight against the sudden clenching of each and every muscle in his body. It had perhaps not been the best idea to bring her along with him on today's errand; the carriage, while spacious and easily able to accommodate all four partners, was somehow much too cramped just then. He hooked a finger under his cravat, trying to ease the sudden tightness in his chest. Though she was slender, hardly taking up any physical room, the air fairly vibrated with her presence. Or perhaps the sensation was confined to his body; it felt as if someone had taken a tuning fork and stuck it in the top of his head.

Mayhap things would be less tense if they were to talk. This charged silence was wreaking havoc on him in ways he could not have ever believed possible.

"I did not expect us to venture from Dionysus today," she said now.

No, he had been wrong. Her voice, with that faint huskiness, was so much worse than silence, acting like a physical touch. He cleared his throat against the sudden heat that sizzled along his skin to parts of him he would rather not think about just then. "It is imperative that we secure Mrs. Holburn as Mrs. Finch's opponent," he replied as evenly as he was able. Which, to his frustration, was not very.

"And we could not simply write her?" She turned from the view at the window to peer at him with that overbright smile of hers that nonetheless did nothing to hide some peculiar frustration beneath the surface. "This seems a waste of your time when a messenger could get the job done just as well."

Why did she appear discontented? Seeing as Mrs. Finch's opponent was quite possibly the most important aspect of the match, Mrs. Marlow should be eager to be involved in this portion of the process. Truly, the woman was growing to be more of an enigma with each interaction.

"There is no time for a back-and-forth with Mrs. Holburn and her manager," he replied. "We need to confirm her participation today if we are to have the advertisements and flyers prepared in time."

"Ah." She flushed, giving one last look out the window in Dionysus's direction with an almost wistful expression before turning to face him once more, that same blank-eyed brightness from earlier back in place. "Of course you're right. I should never have doubted you. You are a professional, after all, and have things well in hand. It's an honor to work with someone with your experience and care."

What the devil? The compliments poured from her tongue like wine. Yet though they sounded sincere enough, they tasted more like vinegar to him.

Not knowing how to respond, he leveled an emotionless stare at her. His utter lack of response to her compliments seemed to confound her. Her smile trembled, a small muscle twitching at the corner of her eye. But where most others would have settled back in silence, she proved as stubborn as her strong jaw indicated.

"Might I sit beside you?" she asked, those eyelashes fluttering once more. "While I appreciate you giving me the forward-facing seat"—here she paused, her expression saying she thought him a consummate gentleman, something no one had ever accused him of in his life—"I do like to see where I've been, rather than where I'm going." Then, without waiting for a response, she half rose from her seat, twisting her body, and slid herself onto the seat beside him.

Ethan could do little more than freeze, every part of him going rigid at the feel of her pressed so close to him. And yes, that body part went rigid as well. He swallowed hard. Damnation, one would think he had been without a woman for years the way he was reacting to something so innocuous as Mrs. Marlow's warmth beside him. Which was not lessened a moment later when her fingers curled around his arm.

"There now, isn't this nice?" she said brightly.

No, not a damn bit. Or, rather, it was too nice. So nice, in fact, that it took every ounce of willpower for him not to lean in and drag the sweet scent of her into his lungs, every bit of strength not to turn toward her and bury his face in her neck and taste her skin. Instead, he ripped his arm from her grasp and lurched across the carriage, falling in an incongruous heap on the opposite bench. Which was still warm from her bottom, something he was trying very hard not to think about.

"As you aren't going to make use of it," he muttered when she stared wide-eyed at him, "I may as well. Please," he continued, louder now and with a raised hand, as she leaned forward, appearing as if she would follow him to this seat as well, "enjoy yourself there. I would not wish to take away the enjoyment of that view from you."

He thought she would sit back and lapse into blessed silence for the remainder of their journey. It appeared that way at first, her body easing, the overly exuberant expression falling from her face. He very nearly breathed a sigh of relief.

Nearly.

Until that stubborn jut of her chin manifested once again, a strange, determined gleam sparking in her eyes. Why, he thought a bit wildly as she gripped the cushion beneath her and leaned forward to move across to him once more, did she want so badly to attach herself to his side? It was not as if they were separated by some great distance in this godforsaken carriage. Before her bottom could so much as rise from her seat—ah, God, why did he have to think of her bottom again?—he blurted, "So tell me, how long have you known Mrs. Finch?"

Which, blessedly, was enough to stop her forward momentum. Once more she dropped back, her eyes blinking myopically at him. "Mrs. Finch?"

"Yes," he said, perhaps a touch too eagerly, desperate to keep her distracted. "Mrs. Finch. When did you first become acquainted with her?"

"Oh." More blinking. "Er, two years?"

It was his turn to blink. "Are…you asking me?"

"No." She flushed, that summer strawberry stain blooming across her cheeks again. "Two years. I've known her for two years."

That out of the way, she nodded and looked pointedly at the seat beside him, her intentions clear. Which, of course, prompted not only his shifting to the middle of the seat but his next hasty question as well.

"And who did you manage before then?"

He really didn't give a good damn whom she'd managed before, the question merely an attempt to distract her. But her answer, as utterly peculiar as it was, snagged his attention completely.

"No one."

"No one?" A surprising thing. If one had been hired to manage one of the most famed women pugilists in England, one should have had some experience. Especially for something so important as a much-lauded comeback.

"Were you involved in pugilism before?"

"No," she replied without hesitation, her attention still on his seat, which he was doing his damnedest to fill completely. "I'd never even been to a boxing match before meeting her."

"You never attended a boxing match? Ever?"

His disbelieving question finally seemed to distract her from her goal of joining him on his bench. She stilled, pale blue eyes widening as they flew to his. Why did she suddenly look like a rabbit caught in a snare? "N-no?"

He raised one brow. "Are you asking me again?"

Again that delicious flush, though this time it crept down her throat to the modest neckline of her gown. "No. I'm not asking you. I'm telling you, no, I never attended a match before meeting her."

"And you've only known Mrs. Finch two years?"

Here her chin, that delightfully, maddeningly stubborn chin, rose a fraction, as if in defiance. "Yes. Why is that surprising?"

His instincts were on high alert, like those of a hunting dog catching the scent of prey. Leaning forward, he rested his elbows on his knees. It was her turn to pull back now, alarm flaring in her eyes.

"It's just surprising, is all," he murmured, watching her closely. "Why would someone of Mrs. Finch's caliber hire someone with no knowledge of the sport to manage her career?" He paused, narrowing his eyes slightly. "Don't you agree?"

There was a beat of silence, the only sounds the jangle of the tack and the clatter of the cobbles beneath the wheels and the horses' hooves. And in that short time, a myriad of emotions flitted across her face, from haughtiness to determination to fear. Oh yes, fear was there in spades, though it was quickly stifled.

"Well, of course I've been involved in sport," she replied, waving a hand in the air as if the very idea of her not having some sort of experience were laughable. "My husband was Gregory Marlow of Marlow Fencing Salon. Perhaps you've heard of it?"

Oh yes, he'd heard of it. It had been a popular place up until the owner's death some two and a half years before. And then...nothing. It had seemed to vanish off the face of the earth. He frowned. So this woman was his widow, was she?

"And you were involved in the running of the salon?"

"I was." That chin came up a fraction more. "Not only the running of the salon, but I also instructed classes and forged our own weapons."

That last gave him pause. "Forged your own weapons?"

"Yes." She smoothed her skirts. "I assisted in my uncle's blacksmith forge before my marriage. I brought those skills to my husband's home."

A blacksmith. The woman was a blacksmith. Which would account for the incredible strength he had felt beneath his palms when she'd tripped and fallen in his arms just the day before. This new bit of her history should have given him a better idea of who the woman was. Yet she was even more of an enigma than before. And in the space of a moment, she had suddenly gone from intriguing and maddening to being the most fascinating woman he had ever met in his life.

Something that did not help with his unwelcome reactions to her, he thought as the carriage, finally at their destination, came to a stop. He stole a glance at her as she gathered her things, intensely aware of the rapid pounding of his heart. He unconsciously rubbed a hand over his chest. No, it did not help him one bit.

8

Well, that could have gone better.

Heloise blew out a sharp breath, tilting her head to one side and rubbing at the ache in her neck. Then, grabbing the tongs and pulling the metal from the furnace, she positioned it over the anvil and brought her hammer down on the glowing piece, sending a shower of bright sparks flying. The heat of the furnace pulsed through her muscles and sent sweat trailing between her breasts, the reverberation from the contact of metal against metal traveling up her arm and making her bones shudder. And yet, though she had been aimlessly pounding at the bit of iron since her return to the Wimpole Street house an hour past, though her work typically cleared her mind of its troubles and relieved her tension, it seemed only to be adding to it, making her mind race and the strain in her neck and back become almost unbearable.

She scowled down at the scrap of metal she was currently abusing, taking great pleasure in imagining that Mr. Sinclaire was in its place before she deliberately brought the hammer down on it again. The whole morning had been fraught with frustration. It had been bad enough that the man had kept her clear of Dionysus for most of their time together. She'd had little opportunity to become familiar with the place, and every moment counted. But even when she had put aside her aggravation and done her best to seduce him during their outing, he had done everything in his power to physically keep away from her. An impressive thing, really, considering their proximity inside the carriage. Worse, he had managed to confuse and fluster her to the point that she had made several blunders, mainly in disclosing information about herself that she would have preferred he not know.

But she would not, *could* not, think about her stumble now or she would go mad. Instead, she would focus on one very important question about the whole morning: how had Iris's suggestions for seducing him gone so horribly awry?

Truly, she didn't know what she had done wrong. She had followed Iris's instructions to the letter. She had simpered and fawned and done her best to build up the man's ego, though each mindless compliment had tasted as bitter as Iris's tinctures in her mouth. Truly, she felt as if she had betrayed her very soul in attempting to portray herself as a helpless female in awe of the big strong male. She paused in her work, swallowing down the bile that rose in her throat at the lengths she had gone to. There had to be a better way.

Yet she still didn't have a clue how to succeed. In fact, she felt even more in the dark about it than before.

But these ruminations were getting her nowhere. And she did not have the time for trial and error to figure out how to get herself in his bed. She had to seduce the man, and fast. But that would never happen if he continued the little dance of avoidance he had perfected as the morning wore on. She frowned. Though, strangely enough, he had also made certain to keep her near him, hadn't he? A nearness that had at times distracted her from why she was there.

Not that she had ever forgotten her purpose. No, she had always been fully aware of what needed to be done. But that did not mean she did not appreciate how muscled his arm had been under her fingers, or how delicious the spiced smell of him had been, or how when he'd looked at her with those nearly black eyes of his she had felt as if she were about to topple over into a fathomless abyss that she was strangely eager for...

She shook her head to dispel the disturbingly tantalizing thoughts. The inescapable truth was that she had not managed to take a single step forward where he was concerned. In fact, with Mr. Sinclaire's constant movement, constant momentum, constant working, she had quite possibly taken two gigantic steps back instead. Gritting her teeth, feeling the full weight of her responsibility on her aching shoulders, Heloise raised the hammer, bringing it down on the metal with as much force as she could manage. The clang of it rang through her skull, bouncing about, mingling with the aggravated words that spilled from her lips.

"That frustrating"—*clang*—"utterly maddening"—*clang*—"bastard." *Clang.*

"Shall I assume you're talking about the enigmatic Mr. Sinclaire?"

Heloise, in the process of administering a particularly brutal thwack with the hammer, started at the unexpected sound of Sylvia's voice. The ball tip of the tool veered off course, bouncing off the iron in a wild manner. Scowling down at the hammer as if it had done it on purpose and were somehow in league with Mr. Sinclaire, she felt the tension in her boil over, and she cried out, "The man never stops!"

"Well, that sounds promising, darling," Sylvia drawled, sinking onto one of the stools in Heloise's forge, carefully rearranging her skirts as she did so. "That could only be a boon in a potential lover."

The woman's words succeeded where Heloise's work had not. Oh, they didn't banish her frustrations. No, there was not much in heaven or on earth that could accomplish that just now. But Sylvia, however unknowingly, had reminded Heloise that there were other people involved in this job that she had brought to their door and was in essence responsible for. She had to do well. And that started with hiding her uncertainties regarding her abilities. If the other Widows guessed that she had no confidence in herself, they would lose their confidence in her. And that she could not bear.

Fortunately, Sylvia saw none of her internal conflict. Unfortunately, however, she was still quite focused on Mr. Sinclaire. She leaned forward, her eyes sharp as she considered Heloise. "Do tell me, though, what Mr. Sinclaire did to frustrate you."

Heloise forced a laugh. "What hasn't he done?" She moved about the forge, hanging up her leather apron, putting things to rights, more to avoid Sylvia's too-knowing gaze than anything else. "But he is a man in a position of power; it is no wonder that dealing with him would be somewhat difficult."

There was a beat of silence, and then Sylvia spoke, her voice softer than before. "You know, you don't have to seduce him, Heloise. I'm certain we can find another way to access the private areas of the club."

A suggestion that did not sound at all confident on Sylvia's lips. Putting the last of her things away, Heloise turned to face the woman. "We have racked our brains, Sylvia," she replied firmly. "There is no other way. Dionysus is as protected as any castle would be during a siege, everyone involved in the place like foot soldiers closing ranks against an enemy. Even Euphemia's disguises would not get past the public rooms there." And it was too true. Heloise had taken in every small detail she could while sprinting about after Mr. Sinclaire that morning, and every employee in attendance had looked at her with a healthy dose of distrust. It would not be easy getting past them.

Which, of course, was where Mr. Sinclaire had to be used. While they treated her like the outsider she was, watching every movement she made with narrowed eyes and crossed arms, they had looked at Mr. Sinclaire as if he were their savior, come down from on high to grace them with his presence. She could not recall witnessing such unwavering loyalty to anyone in her entire two and thirty years. Which, unfortunately, only solidified her certainty that she had been right in planning to seduce him. Damn it.

But she did not want to think about taking the enigmatic Mr. Sinclaire to her bed just then. Shaking her head to clear it of a particularly vivid image of the man's strong, scarred hands on her body—goodness—she forcibly turned her attention back to Sylvia and, more importantly, the business at hand.

"I'm sorry for not coming to you straightaway when I returned from Dionysus to give you a summary of my time there."

"Oh, pish," the woman said, waving a hand in the air. "You know very well you don't need to report every little detail to me. I trust you."

Which shouldn't have affected Heloise as it did. Clearing her throat of the sudden tightness there, she took up a clean cloth and wiped her face, praying the action also hid the emotions flooding her. No doubt the woman had only said it to be kind. Heloise could not afford to be complacent in her position here. Being complacent would mean being the weak link in the chain. And that she would not do.

"If you have time," she said, with perhaps more firmness than was warranted, "I'd like to go over it with you now."

To which Sylvia said…nothing. For a moment the woman merely gazed at her with an expression that appeared almost sad, as if she had seen beneath her bravado to the frightened woman beneath. Heloise tensed, ready to…what? Fight? Flee? Whatever it took to continue concealing her doubt in herself.

Blessedly, Sylvia soon reverted to her typical mischievous expression, the laugh lines bracketing her mouth and radiating from the corners of her eyes back in place as she stood and shook out her skirts.

"You know I always have time for you. Shall we walk while we talk? I have been seated at my desk all morning writing correspondence, and I could use the exercise."

So saying, she linked arms with Heloise and guided her from the forge and out into the brilliance of the back garden. And Heloise did not know whether to be relieved or sad that her subterfuge had worked so well.

* * *

By the time Heloise's meeting with Sylvia had concluded, Heloise wanted nothing more than to retire to her bedroom and take a nice long nap. While recounting the details of her morning had helped her to put her thoughts in order and conclude where best to place Euphemia in their scheme—she always took such a vital role in their proceedings, in the very thick of things with her intricate disguises—it had not done a thing to ease her mind over the much-needed seduction of Mr. Sinclaire. Could she have asked Sylvia for tips on how to insert herself into the man's bed? Certainly. But had she? Of course not. It was one thing to talk privately with one of the other Widows. But Sylvia, as their leader and, most importantly, the one who had taken the biggest gamble in bringing Heloise into their group, was another matter entirely. And so Heloise was just as much in the dark about that aspect of their plan as she'd been when they'd started. Her lips twisted wryly as she trudged up the stairs to her private chamber. No, she rather thought she was worse off now, considering how abysmally things had gone that morning.

Finally her room was in view, the familiar mahogany door beckoning her within. She nearly slumped with relief, her body eager to relax. Just then, however, she passed by Euphemia's open door. The other woman was bent industriously over a bit of something in her lap, and Heloise recalled belatedly that there was one more important job she had to accomplish before finding the comfort of her bed.

Heaving a sigh that was more than a bit mournful, she turned and rapped softly on the doorframe.

Euphemia started slightly, looking up from the plain brown pelisse she was working on.

"Oh!" she exclaimed, smiling widely at Heloise. "Are you back from Dionysus, then?"

"I've been back for some time, actually."

Euphemia blinked, looking to the clock on the mantel. "Goodness, is it that late already? I quite lost track of the afternoon." She laughed lightly, putting aside the pelisse, rising and stretching her arms above her head as she headed for the pair of seats before the hearth. "But come in and tell me all about it. How did it go?"

"Fine, fine," Heloise replied, sinking into the chair beside Euphemia, trying for a breezy tone and confident smile. She must have failed spectacularly, however, if the concerned look the other woman gave her was any indication.

"Are...are you certain it was fine?"

Heloise sighed. "Perhaps *fine* is not the word for it. However," she continued with determination, "it will be fine. I'm certain of it. Especially as I believe I have found the perfect way for you to infiltrate the club."

Which, blessedly, seemed to distract the other woman from her worries over Heloise. Euphemia's gaze sharpened as she sat up straighter. "Splendid. Tell me all about it."

Heloise smiled, a true one this time. "How do you feel about carpentry?"

Over the next hour the two women went over every aspect of how they could insert Euphemia into the score of craftspeople working day and night on the venue for the boxing match. A secret set of eyes and ears in the very heart of the proceedings was imperative to obtaining pertinent information—such as which valve controlled the main gas line and where easily accessible exits were—in case Heloise should fail at securing the jewels before the night of the masquerade and they were forced to put their plans in place to infiltrate the club en masse in a last desperate attempt. Finally done with this all-important piece of the puzzle, Heloise made to rise, her bed already singing a lullaby from the next room. After her lack of sleep the night before and her stressful morning, she wanted nothing more than to fall into a dreamless slumber—preferably one that did not remind her of her horrendous failures with Mr. Ethan Sinclaire.

Euphemia's sudden words, however, had her entire body tensing once more, all thoughts of sleep vanishing in a moment.

"And how is the planned seduction of Mr. Sinclaire going?"

"Fine," Heloise squeaked, fingers clenching the carved wooden arms of her seat. "Everything is fine."

Which was quite possibly the least convincing response she could have made. Especially with Euphemia, who was incredibly—and frighteningly—insightful when it came to others' emotions, more so than all the other Widows combined. Heloise ducked her head, attempting to hide her grimace as she waited for the barrage of questions that surely must be about to pour from the other woman's lips.

But, to her shock, not a single question emerged. Instead, Euphemia rose and stood before Heloise, holding her hand out and smiling broadly. Heloise stared at the proffered hand, with its small scars and dry skin and calluses, with a vague kind of confusion.

"That is wonderful to hear," Euphemia said. "But now that we've got that out of the way, come, I've a mind to get some exercise."

With that she grasped Heloise's hand in hers and pulled her to her feet, dragging her unceremoniously from the room. Heloise, for her part, could only spare a quick, longing glance back at her bedroom door before they turned the corner. By the time they reached the stairs, her confusion had worn off. And when Euphemia glanced back at her as they made the front hall, brown eyes dancing, a giggle bubbling from her lips, Heloise found an answering lightness filling her chest. Where only moments ago she had been about to cry from exhaustion, now she found a new energy running through her. When they ducked into the music room—despite its name, there were no instruments of any kind here, the place having been cleared for practice in swordplay and self-defense and pugilism—and Euphemia rushed to the wall where a collection of fencing foils hung, she smiled for what felt like the first time that day.

"You wish to practice fencing?"

"And why not?" Euphemia grinned, taking down a foil, balancing its weight on her hand. "Especially when I have the best fencing master in all of London at my beck and call."

"Poppycock," Heloise muttered, face heating. Yet the very thought of taking up a sword and stretching her muscles had the remainder of her exhaustion evaporating in an instant. Excitement finally thrumming in her veins, she rushed to the armoire in the corner, throwing the doors wide, taking out the necessary equipment. Soon they were both dressed in their wire masks and high-necked canvas jackets and loose breeches, and they took their positions on the bare floor. In no time they were lunging, parrying, the metallic clang and scrape of the foils mingling with the sounds of their sharp exhalations and their feet moving over the floor, broken occasionally by Heloise making gentle corrections to Euphemia's form.

"Watch the alignment of your arm," she murmured as the other woman lunged forward. "Good, good. Now try to hit the mark. Well done."

She could just make out Euphemia's grin through the wire mesh mask. "I'm improving, I think."

"More than improving. I would say you are a star pupil." And she meant it. Euphemia, and indeed all the Widows, had shown incredible proficiency at the basics not only of fencing, but of all manner of swordplay.

Euphemia lunged forward, hitting just shy of the small heart on Heloise's padded leather plastron with the cotton-covered ball tip of the blade. "Now, that is something I never heard in all my years of schooling." She let loose a breathless laugh, an almost wicked sound. "I was always better at other, more intimate things that did not require book learning."

Heloise choked on a sound between a laugh and a gasp. "Euphemia!"

The other woman shrugged before—taking advantage of Heloise's distraction—she quickly knocked her foil aside and lunged forward, hitting the mark on her chest once again. "I am a physical creature. For instance," she continued archly, "I was able to nab my husband with one kiss, and on our second meeting to boot. Granted, entering into that union was not the best decision I've ever made." Here she paused, shoulders drooping momentarily. Then, seeming to rouse herself, she made a particularly forceful lunge. "But even so, I cannot deny I have always been proficient in such things."

Which succeeded in capturing Heloise's attention. She straightened, lowering her foil and removing her mask. Euphemia followed suit, brushing a damp lock of light brown hair from her cheek as she looked at Heloise in some expectation.

"Yes?"

Heloise cleared her throat, stepping closer. "You are proficient, you say?"

"Yes," Euphemia replied evenly, not so much as breaking a smile. Yet her expression shifted completely to one almost of satisfaction. Why satisfaction, Heloise didn't have a clue. Nor did she particularly care in that moment. All she knew was that this was too good a chance to pass up.

"I don't suppose you would care to elaborate on that?"

Finally the woman smiled, bringing to mind the cat that got the cream. "Absolutely."

9

The following day Mrs. Marlow was once more at Dionysus bright and early. And as Ethan, upon entering the boxing venue, spied that now-familiar head of shining sable hair next to Mr. Ferris, the lead carpenter, he couldn't help but scowl. Not because he was displeased to see her, but rather because he was *pleased* that she was there and had been looking forward to seeing her since they'd parted the day before. Damn it all to ever-loving hell.

Even more frustrating was the fact that he was eager to spend the day with her. Not to keep an eye on her because he did not trust her, but just to have her near. This was all for the sake of protecting his business, he reminded himself severely, trying to leash his rogue thoughts. It was certainly *not* for pleasurable reasons.

Which, unfortunately, was like a spark to dry tinder when it came to his imagination. Against his will he began to dream up all manner of pleasurable reasons to keep her by his side. Mostly ones that did not include anyone else about. Or clothing.

Shaking his head to clear it of a much-too-tempting image of Mrs. Heloise Marlow without a stitch on amid the rumpled sheets of his bed, he growled low and spun about, intending to stalk back to the sanctity of his office. Lusting after the woman would not help one bit in his keeping his head where she was concerned, something that was imperative if he was to successfully guard his club against whatever she was up to. Unfortunately, his exit was not fast enough. Before he had taken two steps, a slender yet surprisingly firm hand was on his arm, holding him in place.

"Mr. Sinclaire, how wonderful to see you again this morning."

Closing his eyes to control his body's completely treasonous reaction to the woman's now-familiar voice—one that was sweet and lilting, yet with the faintest huskiness—Ethan steeled himself and turned back to face Mrs. Marlow.

"Good morning, madam."

She smiled up at him. But it was not the too-bright simpering of the day before, with fluttering eyelashes and coy glances. No, today her eyelids were heavy, her lips turned up in what he could only call a knowing curve. That, combined with the way her fingertips seemed to linger on his coat sleeve, and his body burst into flames.

Her smile widened, as if she knew her effect on him. "I look forward to working closely with you again this morning. Shall we get started?"

Get started? Get started with what? As she spoke she pressed closer to him, her breasts brushing up against his arm—with a much more purposeful air than the day before—and his mind simply stopped working altogether.

Blessedly, just at that moment, Teagan sauntered up. Still dressed in his evening wear from the night before, he looked his typical devilishly handsome self. Which should not have perturbed Ethan as it did, especially when Mrs. Marlow turned her heavy-lidded gaze his way.

"Mrs. Marlow," the other man said with a grin, sketching

a slight bow. "How lovely to see you here this fine morning. You have such a wonderful dedication to your job."

She laughed lightly. "I firmly believe that anything worth doing should be done right."

Ethan felt those words straight to his...toes. Not that there had been anything sexual about what she had said. Yet they affected him just as viscerally as if she had whispered them in his ear and then licked him for good measure. He cleared his throat and shifted from foot to foot, more to break contact with her than anything else. Good God, if he kept up like this, he would embarrass himself in front of everyone present.

"Well said, madam," Teagan replied. "And may I say, your lovely face is a welcome diversion amidst the crush of unattractive male visages I'm forced to look upon. Present company included," he continued in a drawl, his sly eyes sliding to Ethan. "But forgive me for interrupting, Sinclaire. Mr. Kendal has arrived early with the playbill and advertisement mock-ups. I've shown him to your office; he's waiting for you there. And as you have not yet eaten this morning, I'll have the kitchen staff send something up to you after he leaves."

Ethan scowled. "I'm not hungry."

To which Teagan rolled his eyes. "Did you know, Mrs. Marlow," he said to the woman in a loud aside, "that Sinclaire here is quite the most stubborn man alive? He will gladly starve himself if it means thwarting my care of him. Which is why I shall call on you to help make certain he eats everything I send up for him. But have you breakfasted yourself? I shall send something up for you as well. We have quite the fabulous spread; you will not want to miss out."

The damn bastard, always interfering. But whereas

his interference was typically harmless fun, now it most assuredly was not. Not that Teagan knew just how troublesome this bit of strong-arming was. Or did he? Ethan narrowed his eyes. Could the man possibly know how much Mrs. Marlow affected him, that the very idea of being in such close, private quarters with her was akin to torture? As usual, however, the man gave not the smallest tell as he continued to gaze at Mrs. Marlow with that maddeningly mild yet altogether too-flirtatious smile on his face.

Just as Ethan was about to denounce the idea, however—while he needed to keep her in his sight, he did not have to be alone with her to do it, thank you very much—the woman spoke up.

"That sounds lovely, thank you." Bidding goodbye to Teagan as that man—the utter arse—dipped his head in a small bow and sauntered away, whistling all the while, she turned to Ethan, reaching for his arm, sliding her fingers into the crook of his elbow. Ethan jolted at the contact, more surprising for the fact that she seemed to caress his bicep, her fingers wrapping about the muscle as if taking stock of his strength. It took everything in him not to purposely flex.

She smiled in expectation up at him. "Please, Mr. Sinclaire, lead the way."

What could he do but comply? Gritting his teeth, he led her back down the hallway and away from the boxing venue. Behind them, the steady pounding of nails being driven home, the sawing of wood, and the busy, deep chatter of the workmen's voices droned on. It all grew fainter when, just before they reached the main casino floor, he guided her through a nondescript door to his right and up the narrow staircase to the floor above.

Not a word was spoken between them. Yet with her hand

still curled almost possessively around his arm, he could not fail to feel her reaction when the first-floor hallway was revealed to her. She started, her fingers clenching on his sleeve, and for the first time that day he smiled slightly. Most people did not expect such a drastic change when entering the long row of offices. Whereas the public spaces were decadent and dark, with rich colors, heavy fabrics and wood, and low lighting that made you feel as if you had stumbled into some kind of prequel to hell, the floor above—save for the hall containing the owners' suite— was the opposite. Light-colored fabrics dominated, with large windows and landscape paintings showing a bucolic paradise. This space, he knew, would not be out of place in even the finest English estate.

He did not know what had prompted his interior design choice here when they had first taken over the place. Perhaps it had been a need to escape the grimness that his life was, to garner some semblance of calm and peace and beauty. From birth he had been cloaked in a heavy gloom, nearly suffocated in the churning miasma of misfortune that his life had brought, something he fought against even to this day. He hunched his shoulders almost self-consciously, feeling the familiar pull of the tight, scarred skin on his back. A constant reminder that, though he might try to leave his cruel past behind, he would always be tethered to it, like a dog on a chain.

This small slice of beauty shining from ugliness normally succeeded in easing the band about his chest. Now, however, with the baffling, maddening, tempting woman at his side, he found it hard to focus on much else but her. Especially as they drew increasingly close to his office and, beyond that, his private apartments, the place he called his own. Just the thought of her so near where he ate and bathed and slept was enough to cause every muscle in his body to seize up. If Mr. Kendal had not been awaiting them, he would have dragged her far away from here.

But the man was, and so they kept going, right through the open door of his office. Kendal stood when they entered, doffing his cap and sketching a bow.

"Kendal," Ethan intoned, striding forward, taking the man's proffered hand, "Thank you for coming with the material on such short notice. This is Mrs. Marlow; she is Mrs. Laney Finch's business manager and is working closely with me on the event."

"Pleased to make your acquaintance, Mrs. Marlow," the man said, sketching a short bow. "All of London is abuzz over Mrs. Finch's upcoming match. It is an honor to be working on the advertisement for it."

She smiled in a way that set Ethan's heart thumping in a strange rhythm. It was quite the most genuine expression he had seen from her thus far, lifting her cheeks and causing fine lines to radiate from the corners of her eyes. It made her, quite honestly, even more beautiful than usual.

"How kind of you to say," she replied, taking the man's hand in a warm shake. "But I do hope this last-minute work has not made your life difficult."

"On the contrary, madam," Kendal said with a warm expression, his other large hand enclosing hers, "it has been a joy to work on, an absolute joy."

Which should not have affected Ethan in the slightest. They were merely expressing respect for each other, after all. Yet watching the two fawn over one another had Ethan seeing red. Or, rather, green, though why that particular color had popped into his head he didn't have a clue. Before he knew what he was doing, he pushed between the two.

"Now that we have gotten that out of the way," he said

loudly, guiding them to the semi-circle of seats before the hearth, "let us see what you have come up with, Kendal. The sooner we finalize the design, the sooner we may begin promotions in earnest. We do not want to give Mrs. Finch a subpar welcome."

Kendal flushed as he hurriedly reached for the rolled papers he had brought with him. "Of course, of course. My apologies. Let us get to it, then."

The next minutes were spent going over the man's work, discussing the changes that needed to be made, conferring about a timeline. But though Ethan tried his hardest to focus solely on the work at hand, time and time again he found his eyes drawn to Mrs. Marlow. That small divot between her brows as she focused should not be so attractive. The line of her neck as she bent her head to look closely at Kendal's artwork should not be so alluring. And he should most definitely *not* wish to press his lips to the small hollow behind her ear.

He had never in his life had such trouble focusing on work as he had in that torturous quarter hour, and so it was almost with relief that, upon the completion of their meeting, he saw Kendal out of his office. Then he turned back to the room and spied Mrs. Marlow gazing at him, and he recalled that the worst was, in fact, yet to come.

* * *

She should not feel this nervous about being alone with Mr. Sinclaire.

Well, perhaps she should be at least a bit nervous. After all, she was planning on taking this man, one powerful in both body and status, to her bed. And she finally had him alone.

Yet as he turned back to her and gazed at her with those

piercing dark eyes shadowed by his heavy brow, a brow that was knotted in consternation more times than not when he looked at her, she knew this was more than nervousness roiling in her gut. There was something else underlying it, a vibrating energy deep in her bones that she could not begin to understand. Why did this man affect her as he did? He was the means to an end, nothing more. And now that she finally had him not only alone, but in the more private area of the club, she was not going to turn tail and run. No, she was going to see this through, come hell or high water.

Remembering everything Euphemia had told her about how to gain a man's attention—though thus far that advice had not seemed to affect Mr. Sinclaire at all—she made a concerted effort to relax her body into languid lines, dropping her shoulders from where they had inched up near her ears, letting her hands fall elegantly over the arms of her chair, easing her features into a look of heavy-lidded interest.

"Mr. Kendal is a master at his craft," she murmured, in that husky tone Euphemia had tutored her to use. "His work is nothing short of wonderful. I do believe it will prove the much-needed draw for Mrs. Finch's match." She smiled. "Not that holding it here at Dionysus isn't a draw in and of itself."

"Yes, Kendal is worth his weight in gold," Mr. Sinclaire said. But he did not move from his spot at the open door.

Heloise's smile faltered. Was he avoiding being near her? Did he find her repulsive? The thought polluted her mind with uncertainty and not a small amount of self-pity. She had spent more than three decades looking at her reflection in the glass and already knew she was not what most men—if any—wanted.

But no, she reminded herself, it did not matter how plain

she was. What mattered was the confidence that she could successfully seduce this man. As Euphemia had said, confidence could do much to garner the interest of another. No matter how utterly false—not to mention foreign and uncomfortable—that confidence felt.

"Are you waiting for something?" she asked in a tone that was much calmer than she felt. Thank goodness her voice, at least, would not betray her nerves.

"Waiting? Ah, yes." He cleared his throat. "The food should be here momentarily."

As if he had magicked the meal into being, a maid appeared behind him just then with a tray.

"Mr. Sinclaire, sir," the girl piped, "Mr. Teagan said to bring up food."

He flinched, cheeks darkening, before he turned and took the tray from the girl. "Thank you, Mary," he murmured.

The girl smiled brightly, with a quick bobbing curtsy and a curious sideways glance for Heloise, before she hurried back down the hall.

"What perfect timing," he said as he returned to the semicircle of seats. Heloise blinked. Was that a hint of sarcasm in his voice? But no, his expression remained neutral as he deposited the tray on the low table.

"This looks delicious," she said as Mr. Sinclaire removed the silver lids from the dishes. And indeed it did look delicious. The plates were piled high with myriad breads and fluffy yellow eggs and thick slices of pink ham that had her mouth watering. And that was not the only sustenance they had been provided. Dionysus's kitchens, it seemed, had thought of everything. There were steaming cups of dark coffee, a small pitcher of chocolate, pots of butter and jam, fresh fruit. The morning fare at the Wimpole Street house was satisfying, but it was also plain, the menu created by Strachan and reflecting the woman's no-nonsense way of living, something she had brought with her from her beloved Highlands. Indeed, throughout Heloise's life she had eaten similarly, the focus on sustenance rather than decadence, survival instead of excess. Until her arrival at Wimpole Street, she'd never had a choice but to live in such a way.

This, however, was on a whole other level. The savory and sweet smells wrapped about her like a warm hug as he placed one of the plates before her. At which, to her utter mortification, her stomach gave a loud rumble of appreciation.

He paused, hand outstretched with a cup of coffee for her, eyes flying to meet hers. Face hot, she dipped her head in thanks, taking the cup from him. She should perhaps have focused as she did so and turned their inevitable brush of fingers into something seductive. Instead, however, her mind had been filled with embarrassment over her body's unwelcome auditory reaction to the food, and so when their fingers did touch, there was no deliberate caress meant to entice. She jumped, and he jumped, and the coffee, in the ensuing chaos, did as well, sloshing over the side of the cup—right onto Mr. Sinclaire's hand.

The man sucked in a sharp breath. Heloise, her mortification mingled now with concern, hurriedly took the cup and placed it down, lurching forward to take his hand in hers, dabbing gently at it with a napkin.

"Oh dear," she fretted, looking over his reddening skin. "Oh goodness. Mr. Sinclaire, are you quite all right? Does it hurt very much?"

The man said not a word, which in and of itself should not have been strange. He seemed to not be particularly verbose, after all. Yet as she tended to his hand, the silence stretched on, becoming heavier with each passing moment. And when his fingers, those long, scarred fingers, suddenly curled around her own as if of their own volition, enveloping her in heat that did not have anything to do with the hot liquid that had recently bathed his skin, she froze and looked up—into sharp, dark eyes that seemed to pierce her very soul.

How long the moment stretched she would never know. All she did know was that the combination of his gaze on hers and the clasp of his fingers seemed to stop time itself. It was long moments before she became aware of anything but him, and only because he finally blinked, breaking the spell, and pulled back from her. But why did that last drag of his hand against hers make her want to cry?

He cleared his throat. "No harm done," he said in a deep rasp before, eyes dropping away from hers, he took up his fork and dug into his food, shoveling it into his mouth as if he could not eat fast enough. It was as loud as words: He wished to eat quickly and get back to work.

But Heloise, finally back to her senses now that the charged moment had passed, was not going to give up this chance so easily.

"It appears I do not have to make good on my promise to Mr. Teagan after all."

Food halfway to his mouth, he glanced sharply up at her, eyes hard. The bit of egg impaled by his fork quivered in the air. "Promise?" he demanded. "What promise?"

She blinked. That was most assuredly not the reaction she had expected. More than a little baffled, she nevertheless tried for a smile. "That I should make certain you eat. It seems to me you are making good progress yourself without any assistance from me."

He looked at his fork and then at his plate blankly, as

if he had not even realized he had been eating. "Ah," he finally said. "Yes, I suppose not."

"It is kind of Mr. Teagan to wish to make certain you eat."

He shrugged. "It is of benefit to him, and so he does what he must."

That took her aback. "Of benefit to him?"

Again a shrug, his mouth tightening at the corners as if in pain. With his fork he began pushing about the remainder of his food. "It would not do anyone any good if I were to keel over from malnutrition, would it?"

The comment was rough, self-deprecating. As if the man could not imagine that anyone could worry about him for himself alone, as if he fully believed that people could care for him only due to what he could do for them and how he benefited them.

It should not affect her as much as it did. Even so, pity for this man settled in her heart.

Though her stomach was still quite ready and willing to partake of the fare before her, she moved to the chair closest to him, placing her hand on his sleeve. "I'm certain Mr. Teagan, and indeed everyone at Dionysus, thinks much more of you than you believe." She smiled. "Their loyalty is commendable."

He looked at her hand, his expression unreadable. When he finally did raise his gaze to hers, she sucked in a sharp breath at the pain in his eyes. In the next instant, however, it was gone, like a mirage, leaving only cool disdain in its place. As he continued to stare at her with something akin to defiance, she searched his face with increasing frustration for a hint of the emotion she had unintentionally seen, even as she asked herself why she wished to uncover it again.

"Do you always have such an optimistic view of others, Mrs. Marlow?"

She gave a startled laugh, pulling back from the faint censure in his voice. "I hardly think anyone would call me optimistic. But I don't think my observation of how the people around you view you is based solely on optimism. I'm merely stating fact."

He lifted one heavy, dark brow. "And you have managed to observe that after only two days?"

She shrugged. "Oftentimes it does not take even that long for one to get the scope of a situation. I daresay it did not take me above five minutes in your case."

That, finally, seemed to pique his interest. He placed his fork down on his plate and turned more fully toward her, the sardonic line of his brow turning to one of curiosity.

"You must be a good judge of character, then."

There was something almost soft and amused in the statement, as if he were teasing her. It took her aback, that tone; it was one she had never expected from him. Nor had she expected that his features would subtly rearrange themselves, transforming them into something even more compelling than the aloof handsomeness she had grown accustomed to.

Instead of becoming flustered, however, she felt herself relax, her stomach releasing the tension she had not even known it was holding, her posture easing. "I would not say that," she hedged with a small smile. "But I can usually quickly understand a situation."

His gaze roved over her face, as if he were trying to read something there. "Then tell me, Mrs. Marlow," he murmured, "what is the situation you believe you have read here at Dionysus? Do you believe it is all rainbows and goodwill?"

She rolled her eyes. "You tease me, sir."

"No, I am truly curious. Tell me, what is it you see?"

She pursed her lips, considering him. Yes, he was teasing her. But there was a genuine desire to know beneath the light question. "Very well," she finally said, leaning back and crossing her arms. "You are a hard man, who demands the best from those around him. Yet you have not only a partner who is concerned for your well-being and makes certain you eat—"

"Which as we discussed is not due to any love for me," he interrupted.

She held up a hand. "So you say. But if you would allow me to continue?"

He crossed his arms over his wide chest, brows drawing low again. But there was no aggravation in the action, especially when his full lips—so incredibly full—tightened at the corners in an obvious attempt to keep from smiling. An expression that made him much too attractive for her peace of mind.

"Please do, madam," he said.

Purposely ignoring how the rough baritone of his voice ran along her skin like a physical touch, Heloise dipped her head. "As I was saying, not only was Mr. Teagan concerned that you eat, but the maid who brought the food tray was quite at ease with you. There was no lowered head, no scurrying away, no fearful look in her eyes." She gave him a triumphant look. "You can tell much about a person by how their employees act around them."

"Is that so?"

She nodded emphatically. "It is."

"So let me understand this," he said, the slight quirk to his lips deepening, softening his features even more. "Because of the actions of one maid, you have come to the conclusion that everyone at Dionysus is loyal and cares a great deal about me? You must be a novelist. Your imagination knows no bounds."

"You may laugh if you like," she replied archly. "But it is plain as day to me."

"Oh, I have no desire to laugh. In fact," he continued, leaning toward her, "I find it fascinating. You have a unique way of seeing the world, Mrs. Marlow."

Why was it, she thought a bit wildly as his face came closer to hers, so close that she could see the warm brown in the dark depths, that her heart was beating so much faster? It felt as if it would be only too happy to burst out of her chest. Taking a steadying breath, she replied, "I have had a unique life, I suppose."

"I do believe I would like to know more about that 'unique life' of yours," he murmured. "It must have been interesting indeed."

It was only when Heloise felt the peculiar sensation of falling headfirst into his intense gaze, wanting to tell him everything he wanted to know and more, that she finally realized the danger she was in. What the devil was she doing? She was supposed to be seducing him, getting into his head and his bed. She was most assuredly *not* supposed to make him wonder who she was and why she was here— or actually want to reveal it all to him. That way lay only danger, for her and the rest of the Widows, not to mention Julia's increasingly dire future.

"Oh, it is a boring story, to be sure," she said, taking on that husky tone again. Leaning closer, so close she could feel his breath, still sweet from the bit of pastry he had eaten, caress her face, she let her hand run up his sleeve. "Not like your own. How fascinating it must be. But we have some time; won't you tell me about it now?"

Surely such a ploy would work. Euphemia had been quite adamant that men reveled in talking about themselves above all else. That, combined with her rather blatant flirting, and Mr. Sinclaire should be a puddle at her feet.

To her bafflement, however, it seemed to have the very opposite effect. At once his features closed up, the new openness gone in a blink. He physically drew away from her as well, his body angling so far from hers she would not have been surprised if he fell out of his chair.

"Your food grows cold, madam," he said, frost settling over his voice, turning the words into unforgiving sleet that stung as they hit her. "Shall we finish our meal and get back to work?"

With that he turned to his own nearly finished plate, and though they still sat next to one another, Heloise felt as if the whole of the ocean had suddenly flooded the space between them. Frowning, she returned to her seat and tucked into her food. But though moments before she had been fairly salivating with hunger, now it took every morsel of effort to take even a bite, the still-warm eggs and tender ham like sawdust in her mouth. Since her husband's death, she had tried so very hard to make amends for her part in his passing and to honor his last wish by protecting Julia. Yet time and time again she had failed. And if she could not recover those jewels—which, if she could not get Mr. Sinclaire to let down his guard, seemed more than a possibility—she would fail yet again. Her fingers tightened painfully around her fork. And that she could not do, not with Julia's life on the line.

10

Failure, however, seemed imminent as, not ten minutes later, Heloise was practically booted out of Mr. Sinclaire's office. *What a blasted mess.*

Face flaming, she fought the overwhelming urge to duck her head and hurry back to the ground floor. Instead, she forced herself to slow her pace, eyes furtively scanning every nook and cranny of the bright and surprisingly welcoming hall. She could not pass up this opportunity to take stock of this portion of the private area of the club. Goodness knew when she would get an opportunity like this again—if ever.

But even as she made a mental list of all she saw, from the number of doors to the placement of the windows to the light sources, she could not put from her mind the look of disdain on Mr. Sinclaire's face when, after the disaster of a meal was over, the man had summarily dismissed her. No, not just dismissed; he had appeared as if he would gladly pack her bags and send her off to hell.

Her feet faltered and then stopped on the runner as she dropped her face into her hands, letting out a muffled groan. And things had been going so well, too. Or, at least, she had thought they had been going well. During that short interlude when she had let her mask drop, in a misguided attempt to comfort him, he had seemed to respond to her. For the first time since meeting him, she felt she had seen through the rough, unwelcoming veneer to the man beneath. And she had begun to respond to him as well. She blanched as she recalled the effect he'd begun to have on her, her skin tingling and her heart about to gallop out of her chest. But no, she would not think of that. She needed to focus on the change that had come over him when she had returned to using the skills Euphemia had taught her to assist in seducing the man.

She dropped her hands, turning to frown at a bucolic painting of brilliant green pastures bookended by towering trees on the wall beside her. His attitude toward her had most definitely changed the moment she had begun to use those feminine wiles again. But could that possibly mean that he preferred her when she was being herself, and not the femme fatale she had thought she needed to be?

She snorted a laugh. Of course the man would not prefer her natural personality. That was preposterous. Shaking her head, she made it the rest of the way down the hall, slipping through the door that led to the staircase and the lower floor—only to freeze before her foot had descended even one tread. Just as she closed the door, submerging herself back in the rich, opulent extravagance that marked the rest of the gaming club, the light from the hall caught ever so briefly on a bit of metal on the far wall of the landing.

There were burnished gilt sconces here, of course, gas lamps turned low, as well as all manner of richly appointed frippery and opulence. Yet there was something about that small flash of metal that snagged her attention. It appeared like nothing so much as the handle to a door.

Frowning, she paused and bent down. Yes, it did indeed appear to be a handle, right in the middle of the wood paneling. A quick perusal of the wall, her fingers running lightly over the polished wood, revealed the definite delineation of what appeared to be a door.

Blinking, she straightened. A hidden door. Which could mean only one thing: This area of the club was not a place most people were typically invited.

Heart pounding, Heloise cast a glance down the dark stairs to make certain there was no one about before, taking a steadying breath, she reached for the handle and gave it a careful turn.

It made not a sound save for the slightest click of the latch releasing, the hinges no doubt carefully oiled. The door swung inward, revealing yet another hall, this one darker and more richly appointed than anywhere in the club she had seen thus far. It was adorned with a plush runner as red as blood, velvet-topped benches, and all manner of gilt-framed paintings depicting Greek gods in various states of undress and merriment. Legs shaking beneath her, feeling as if she were walking into Hades itself, she stepped into the hall, letting it swallow her up, carefully closing the door behind her.

For a long moment she stood frozen, hardly daring to breathe, listening. But even the work of the carpenters one floor down was a mere echo here. Unnerved by the quiet, she peered down the hall, making out not only more doors but also a dark opening on the far right wall, perhaps a continuation of the corridor. She swallowed hard, wondering just how vast this place might be, wishing that she had a ball of thread to lead her out to safety, like Theseus in King Minos's labyrinth. Unconsciously reaching for the collar of her pelisse, she found a bit of strength when her fingers came into contact with the blade hidden there. Then, jaw set and senses on high alert, she moved down the hall.

With utmost care she tried the handles of the two doors

closest to her. Each, however, was locked tight, refusing to give even a bit. She exhaled in frustration, biting back a curse. If only Iris were with her. Her talent for picking locks was unmatched; she would be able to access the rooms without a problem. But though Heloise had learned a thing or two about lock-picking, and in a pinch could use the specially made pins in her hair to gain entry to just about any room, her skills were nowhere near on par with Iris's. Such a thing would take time, and that she did not have; while there was no one about now, she did not know how long that might remain true. She had to hurry if she was to take stock of this place. Giving the doors a furious glare, she continued on, pausing at the turn in the hall, peeking around the corner before slipping around it.

She had not taken two steps, however, before she heard deep male voices rumbling in conversation. And they were coming from the stairwell behind her.

Breath stalling in her chest, Heloise pressed her back against the wall, head tilted and ears straining. Mayhap it was yet another vendor here to meet with Mr. Sinclaire. But her small half-hearted prayer was dashed as the voices suddenly grew clearer, louder, and she realized that wonderfully silent door that had assisted her just moments ago had been opened and the men were, in fact, coming her way.

She hastily clamped a hand to her lips to hold her squeak of alarm at bay. Looking wildly about, she made for the first door she could see, one heavier and more ornate than the others. *Please*, she begged silently as her hand gripped the handle, *please let this door be unlocked.* She fully expected her plea to be ignored. Hadn't every other door she'd tried been locked? To her complete and utter surprise, however, the handle turned easily in her hand. Without a second thought she slipped through...

...And was dealt a shock—or, rather, another shock—as

she entered a large, opulent room with a wall made entirely of glass. Glass that looked over the casino floor.

But she did not have time to fully take stock of this jarring fact before, to her horror, the men's voices came closer, stopping right outside the door. Acting on instinct alone, Heloise leaped forward, toward the first item that could be used to hide her. Which happened to be a very large, very plush, very sensual-looking sofa. She had no sooner rearranged her skirts behind the thing than the door swung open and two sets of heavy footsteps entered.

"I don't give a good damn what Teagan wants," a gruff voice—one Heloise recognized as belonging to Mr. Parsons—said. "The private women's games should be opened to a larger pool of patrons. Do we really want only noblewomen in the upper echelons of society to be able to partake of Dionysus without the benefit of the masquerades? The rest of us agree; why does he have to be the one stubborn arse?"

Heloise frowned. Private women's games? She had been under the assumption that women were allowed into Dionysus only during the quarterly masquerades. She set her teeth tight. Those same masquerades that Julia had been forced to attend.

But Mr. Parsons was referring to something quite different, something separate from those nights of bacchanalian pleasure when the sexes mingled under a cloak of anonymity.

"You know Teagan," a second man grumbled. From his peculiar raspy voice, she immediately recognized him as Mr. Copper, the floor manager who had admitted them that first day. A nearby chair creaked as he sank down into it. "Though he grew up in the gutters alongside the likes of us, he wants to distance himself from it. And that means mingling with the nobility as much as he can."

Parsons grunted. Heloise, peering under the sofa, watched as his large black boots crossed the room to the wall of glass. Even though she could not see above his knees, she could sense the tension in him as he stared down into the casino. "The damn fool. As if the nobility is good to us for anything but parting them from their fortunes at our tables."

Mr. Copper gave a rough laugh. "Something you're extremely talented at."

"This ugly face is good for something. But I don't give a damn what Teagan says. Gather the requests for admittance to the private games and bring them to me later today."

"Aye." The man rose, heaving a sigh as he did so. "But Teagan ain't going to like it."

"I don't give a damn what Teagan likes," Parsons growled. "It's three against one; I refuse to allow him to hold us all hostage to his whims a moment longer. You're the manager; make it happen."

Chuckling darkly, Mr. Copper moved for the door, letting himself out into the hall, closing it with perhaps more force than necessary. Leaving her alone with Mr. Parsons.

Which was entirely too unnerving. The quiet of the place was unforgiving, betraying the slightest sound. She focused on controlling her breathing lest it expose her presence. Even so, it sounded ragged and overloud to her ears, bouncing off the sofa on one side and the wall on the other in a horrible, unending echo. Minutes—or perhaps hours; she had no clue how much time passed, tense as she was—ticked by, she certain that at any moment Mr. Parsons would realize he was not alone.

Yet the man continued to stand eerily still at the large window, gazing down at who knew what. Just when she thought her rapidly cramping legs would give out, the man slammed his fist into his palm, the sickening sound of flesh hitting flesh mingling with the low, rough curse that exploded from his lips, causing her to jump and nearly topple over.

"Fucking bastard," he snarled. Then, without another word, he stormed from the room, slamming the door behind him.

Heloise dug her fingers into the rug beneath her as she listened to the sounds of his retreat, forcing her disordered thoughts into place as best she could. There were two very important things she had to do. One, she had to escape from this place before she was found out; there was no way her luck could hold if someone else were to enter this room. And as it appeared for all intents and purposes to be the owners' suite, a place where they could watch over their domain like angry gods from on high, that seemed very likely.

And two, she thought with determination, rising from her place behind the sofa, ignoring the screaming muscles in her thighs as she made her hasty way from the room, she had to secure a place for Sylvia at Dionysus's private women's games. For if there was anyone who had the clout to gain admittance, it would be the viscountess.

* * *

Damn it all to hell, what the devil was she still doing here?

Ethan, who had hidden away in his office for much longer than he was willing to admit to avoid Mrs. Marlow and her baffling array of fluctuating personalities, had finally dragged himself back down to the casino floor to confer with Isaac about a minor detail of the upcoming masquerade when, out of the corner of his eye, he spied her. Not that she should have garnered his attention. She was, as usual, dressed in staid clothes, with not a single bow or bit of lace or lowered bodice in sight.

And yet...

He scowled. And yet she nevertheless drew his eye like nothing else ever had. And, blast it, she was headed his way.

Without even the morsel of a thought behind the action, he quickly ducked behind a nearby velvet curtain, heart pounding heavily in his chest. Isaac, who had been standing next to him, was silent for a charged moment before he said in a voice much louder than it had any right to be, "Ethan, what in hell are you doing?"

"Shut your blasted mouth," he hissed desperately, "and pretend you didn't see me."

"Pretend I didn't...?" Isaac muttered, the words trailing off—which Ethan was soon to learn was due to Mrs. Marlow's arrival on the scene.

"Mr. Sinclaire," she said, and Ethan, behind his curtain, dug his fists into his thighs to try to curb the electric jolt that ran through his body at the sound of her voice. "How nice to see you again."

Isaac did not respond, and Ethan held his breath, hoping that the damned fool wouldn't say something to give him away. Blessedly, his brother was not stupid and quickly rallied to become his typical cheerful self.

"The feeling is mutual," he replied, the smile evident in his voice. "And how is Mrs. Finch? Looking forward to the event, I hope."

"She is at that. I have never seen her so focused on her craft. It's quite thrilling."

"Splendid. I cannot wait to see her fight. Teagan has filled my head with how inspiring the sight is, and I'm eager to witness it for myself."

"Laney will be happy to hear it. But I had best take myself off. Good day then."

Ethan listened with bated breath as her footsteps began

to recede. Just as he was about to exhale and slip from his hiding spot, however, she spoke again.

"Forgive me, but I've heard something altogether interesting about your club and was hoping you could help me."

"Of course," Isaac replied. "Anything at all."

She cleared her throat delicately, the rustle of her skirts reaching Ethan as she seemed to move closer. "I have heard," she went on, voice lowered in an intimate way that affected Ethan in places he would rather not think about, "that you hold private games for females?"

"We do indeed," Isaac replied, amusement lacing his voice as he lowered his tone to match Mrs. Marlow's. "Are you thinking you would like to join?"

"I would, as would Mrs. Finch, I daresay. But it is more for Mrs. Finch's partner, Lady Vastkern. She is quite keen on games of chance, you see. I don't suppose you could secure her a spot at one of your tables. The viscountess would be most appreciative."

It was an innocuous enough request. They received dozens of them a day from women wishing to join in those private games, all hoping to get a taste of what their husbands and sons and fathers could indulge in freely anytime they wished.

Why, then, did the hair at the nape of his neck stand on end, telling him that there was something decidedly suspicious about Mrs. Marlow's inquiry?

"Oh, certainly," Isaac responded. "Anything for Mrs. Finch and her partner. Anything at all. When were you all thinking of joining in?"

"Tonight, if at all possible."

Tonight? He frowned. There was something too eager in the request. Not for the first time, he wondered what the hell Mrs. Marlow was up to.

But Isaac was apparently free from Ethan's suspicions as

he proceeded to explain just what the women had to do to gain access that evening. When they were done and Mrs. Marlow finally took her leave, Ethan was not so quick in attempting to leave his hiding spot, and not only because he feared the woman might turn around once again. Could she simply wish to secure a coveted spot for this Lady Vastkern? Certainly. But as he had distrusted her motives from the very beginning, his suspicions could not help but be roused now. He growled in frustration. What he wouldn't give to get in Mrs. Marlow's head and see just what she was up to.

Which, unfortunately, led to wondering what it would be like to get into other parts of her. Which, in turn, made him desperately happy for the cover of the drapery.

Of course, that was when Isaac yanked back the heavy velvet and stood staring at him with no little confusion.

"Why the hell did you wish to hide from Mrs. Marlow?" he demanded.

Before Ethan could come up with a plausible response—truly, he was drawing a complete blank for a reason that would satisfy his brother without revealing his suspicions regarding the woman and Dionysus in general—Teagan sauntered up.

"You're hiding from Mrs. Marlow?" He snorted. "I've never known you to shy away from a seduction before."

Which was not anything he had expected. He frowned at his partner, certain he must have heard him wrong. "Seduction? What the devil are you talking about?"

To which Teagan rolled his eyes so violently Ethan was surprised they didn't roll out of his head. "Don't play stupid, man. It's obvious to everyone that the woman is trying to get you in her bed."

Ethan could only stare. Teagan was known for his sarcasm; the man could write a book on the fine art of underhanded ridicule. Yet this time there was nothing but the ring of truth to his words. And suddenly everything regarding Mrs. Marlow—or, at least, everything regarding her baffling actions toward him the last few days—clicked into place. She was trying to seduce him.

Holy hell.

A soft breath escaped him. He had been so focused on his suspicions, as well as on controlling his body's unwelcome reactions, that he had not seen her attentions for what they were. Now, however, thinking back on every touch, every glance, he saw it with a clarity that struck him like a brick to the head. She truly had been trying to seduce him in her own awkward, strange way.

Teagan, watching him the whole while, laughed outright. "And I thought you were smart."

"Wait," Isaac said, holding up a hand, his eyes wide in surprise. "Mrs. Marlow wishes to sleep with Ethan?"

"Hard to understand, I know," Teagan drawled, giving Ethan an amused sideways glance. "Of course, the question is: What is Sinclaire here going to do about it?"

A very good question, Ethan thought as the two men sauntered off, laughing at his expense. He looked to the large double doors of the casino, now firmly closed after Mrs. Marlow's departure. And one that did not take a great deal of thought to come up with an answer to. While she might simply wish to have him in her bed, she could also be looking for an opportunity to harm the club. He narrowed his eyes as he considered how allowing Mrs. Marlow to seduce him could provide him with the opportunity to keep a close eye on her and thwart whatever scheme she might have in mind—determinedly ignoring the flare of hot excitement that trailed over his skin at the thought of the intimate details that affair would entail. He smiled slowly. If the young widow wished to take him to her bed, who was he to refuse her?

11

Despite its being nearly summer, the night was brisk as Heloise, along with Laney and Sylvia, made their way down the narrow alley that backed Dionysus. Behind them the streets were busy with bodies desperately trying to hang on to the last bit of the London Season before they had to return to the quiet boredom of their ancestral homes. All was gaudy, the street lit up with bright flames to stave off the night, the people almost manic.

The alley in front of them, however, was silent, light shining at intervals in a muted gold, flames flickering behind amber stained-glass lamp covers, the only people the two hulking guards that flanked a single door.

Apprehension vibrated along Heloise's nerves, growing more intense the closer they got to those overlarge men and the door that stood, looking innocuous, beneath that flickering golden light.

Sylvia and Laney, however, did not share her disquiet. No, it seemed they felt the very opposite, their excitement palpable as they strode along, arm in arm, at Heloise's side.

"Goodness," Sylvia said, voice electric with her eagerness as she hugged Laney's arm tighter against her, eyes glittering bright in the gilded light, "this is all quite thrilling, isn't it?"

"It is indeed," Laney joined in. She grinned at Sylvia. "It gets the blood pumping."

Sylvia laughed, the sound like tinkling bells in the still, close air of the alley. "Heloise, I have said it once and I shall say it again: This plan was positively brilliant."

Heloise, momentarily distracted from her spate of nerves, felt the warmth of that compliment down to her toes. But she would not allow herself to soak in the pleasure of it. No, now was not the time for complacency. Eyeing the guards, who were nearly within earshot, she said in a low voice, "You will be fine investigating the dealers at the tables while I attempt to make further headway into Dionysus's inner sanctum?" Which, of course, meant trying—once again—to get close to Mr. Sinclaire, something all the more imperative after her near discovery while trying to search the private hallway that morning. She felt the full weight of all her failures with that man. If she didn't succeed tonight, she didn't know that she would ever be able to. It was one thing to fail at seducing the man during the day when stark, cold business was at the forefront of their time together. It would be quite another to fail when Dionysus was at its most atmospheric, when the whole mood of the place was focused on excess and sensuality.

Dear God, if she failed tonight, she might as well enter a nunnery for all the good she could do in this particular department.

"Oh, of course," Sylvia said, waving a hand in the air, the massive rings on her fingers—worn more for attention than style—winking in the low light. "Besides my ability to squeeze information from even the most taciturn person,

I also happen to have quite the talent for play, as my dear Laney can attest to."

"Sylvia truly is a fine card player," Laney agreed, giving Sylvia a heavy-lidded look. "And money is not the only thing she has won at the tables."

Again Sylvia laughed, though there was a certain huskiness to it now that told of a very interesting story indeed.

They reached the guards then. Heloise stepped up before them, gripping her hands tight in her skirts to stave off their shaking. She had a part to play, and she'd best play it for all she was worth.

"Mr. Isaac Sinclaire invited us to this evening's game," she said with a certain haughtiness she did not feel. "This is Lady Vastkern and Mrs. Laney Finch, and I am Mrs. Heloise Marlow."

There was not a flicker of emotion on the men's faces, yet they reacted immediately, opening the door and stepping aside, motioning them to enter. With only the barest pause, Heloise stepped forward into the dim hallway, Sylvia and Laney following.

The moment the door closed behind them, Heloise stopped. She didn't mean to. She meant to stride forward with confidence, as if she knew exactly what she was about. But now that she was here, she couldn't seem to help herself. Which was silly, really. She had, of course, been inside the hell before. She had become used to its strange, sultry atmosphere, and this visit should be no different.

Yet it *was* completely different. It felt as if with the coming of night Dionysus had awoken, as if it were a living, breathing thing that had sucked her in and would not soon let her go.

Laney placed a gentle hand on her shoulder. "Heloise, are you quite all right?"

"What? Oh! Yes, I'm fine, perfectly fine," Heloise replied, perhaps more brightly and loudly than warranted. Straightening, she turned a wide smile to the two women. "My apologies. Shall we?"

Without waiting for an answer, she started off again, following the faint sounds of low, feminine laughter and clinking glasses. And then they were at the end of the hall and stepping through an open door into a large room filled with the most fashionably dressed women Heloise had ever seen.

"Goodness," she managed. She had never witnessed such riches and extravagance in her life. Each woman was draped in the most luxurious fabrics, the most glittering jewelry. It was as if some unseen hand had reached into every London ballroom and plucked out only the most stylish ladies present. As if she were in a soaring aviary of the most elegant birds in existence.

Just then Mr. Isaac Sinclaire approached them. "Mrs. Marlow, you have come," he said in his cheerful way, that wide smile that seemed part and parcel of his features lifting his cheeks. "Mrs. Finch as well. How wonderful to see you again. And this must be Lady Vastkern." He bowed over her proffered hand, starting only slightly when the large jewels adorning her fingers caught the light, winking in his face. "It's a pleasure to make your acquaintance, my lady. Welcome to Dionysus."

"The pleasure is all mine, I assure you," Sylvia replied. "It is an honor to have nabbed one of the coveted invitations to your private games. I have heard they are difficult to come by."

Mr. Isaac Sinclaire chuckled. "Anything for someone so important to Mrs. Finch and Mrs. Marlow." His gaze once more flickered to the rings on Sylvia's fingers. Heloise, watching him carefully, narrowed her eyes, thinking of

Lady Ayersley's jewels and how the person who had fleeced Julia must have been eyeing them from the moment they'd entered the place.

"But please," he continued, gaze once more firmly on Sylvia's face, "come this way. I have the perfect table for you."

He turned, leading the way across the room. Heloise, frowning, made to follow—until a very large, very warm hand on her arm stopped her. Letting loose a small gasp, she spun about, only to come face-to-face with Mr. Ethan Sinclaire.

The breath lodged tight in her chest. The man was wickedly handsome in the daytime, in a rough and incredibly masculine sort of way that always had her feeling slightly off-center. But now, in the evening, dressed from head to toe in stark black—even his cravat—he looked like Hades rising from the underworld. She swallowed hard. And from the way his eyes glittered beneath the heavy shadow of his brow, she had the fanciful notion that she was Persephone about to be spirited away.

"Mrs. Marlow," he said, his voice a low, intimate rumble that tripped over her skin like sensual fingers. "I did not expect to see you here this evening."

She might have been able to settle her thoughts had it not been for his large hand still on her arm, his fingers gentling to almost a caress. She cleared her throat, intensely aware of how hard her heart was pounding. She had intended to locate him tonight but had fully expected it to be no easy feat. Dionysus was large, after all, and as owner he no doubt had much to do and many places to be.

Yet here he was, in front of her, seeking her out. She could not have planned for such a fortuitous outcome. Which, naturally, made her immensely wary.

Something she could not show. She smiled, allowing his light grip on her arm, though she didn't have a clue what to do with it, as he had always made it a point to keep from touching her before. "Your brother was kind enough to secure places for Mrs. Finch and her partner Lady Vastkern at your tables," she explained.

"And you?"

She blinked at the loaded huskiness of his voice, which was settling low, so very low, in her belly in the most disconcerting way. "I'm sorry?"

His full lips quirked up on one side, making him look at once boyishly charming and dangerously attractive. "Will you be joining them at the tables?"

"Oh!" She flushed, more for the fact that her body continued to respond in the most baffling way to his tone than any embarrassment that she had not understood him. "I do believe there is a place for me should I wish to. And as those places are quite hard to come by, I would be a fool not to." Then, in a voice that shook ever so slightly for all she dared to try it, "Unless there is someplace better I should be spending my time."

To her utter shock, his half smile transformed into a full smile, something she had never witnessed from him, his gaze turning heavy-lidded as he looked her up and down. She felt that gaze like a physical touch over every inch of her body.

"I do believe," he murmured, his voice dark and rich and delicious to her suddenly oversensitive senses, "that there may be someplace much more interesting for you to spend your time here tonight."

Before she knew what he was about, his hand traveled down her arm to her hand. And then his fingers—his warm, calloused fingers—were gripping hers, and he turned and walked from the room, pulling her with him.

While she had become familiar with the layout of much of the ground floor of the club in the past days, tonight it felt like a completely different place. He silently guided her down the hallway, the twists and turns making her feel disoriented, dizzy. Just when they reached a portion she recognized, the scents and sounds and dim, sultry lighting had her senses veering off again. But, to her shock, she did not feel the apprehension she had expected to. No, there was only a buzzing anticipation deep in her gut, radiating from that place where their bare palms met.

Suddenly they came to the end of the hall and Mr. Sinclaire paused, pushing open the door before him. Noise and gilded light flooded into the dark hallway, and she caught a quick glimpse of brilliant gaslights casting a glow upon highly polished wood tables, each surrounded by elegantly dressed men with glasses in hand and wide smiles on their faces. But there was nothing joyous about the atmosphere; rather it was almost threatening, jarring, a shock to her senses, and she unconsciously shrank back from it. She had not realized just how comforting the dark and quiet—as well as Mr. Sinclaire's presence—had been.

He spoke to someone on the other side of the door then.

"Please let anyone who asks after me know that I will be indisposed for some time."

"Aye, Mr. Sinclaire," the unseen man replied.

Before the man was done speaking, Mr. Sinclaire shut the door and, closing his fingers more tightly about hers, opened the door at his side and pulled her through.

Ah, yes, now she knew where they were, the dark stairs that led to the offices above. Just as he had that morning, he led the way to that long, quiet hallway to his own office at the end of it, closing the door behind them when they were inside.

Every nerve in Heloise's body came alive at the soft click of the latch. Lamps were already burning here, but though she had spent time there just that morning, their low light made the place feel strange, foreign.

"I thought," he said, his voice quiet as he stood still against the closed door, dark eyes glittering in the shadows, "that it might be good for us to get to know one another better outside of work."

How was it that a voice could be the very embodiment of touch, that you could feel it trail over your skin and through your bones at the same time? *Keep your senses sharp*, a small voice admonished in her head. *You must keep the upper hand.* But that voice was hard to focus on, fuzzy as her mind was becoming as she stared into those mesmerizing nearly black eyes overshadowed by their heavy brows.

Nevertheless, she would succeed here. Everything depended on it, Julia's livelihood and very life included. Though, she realized as she looked at him, noting the way his gaze lingered on her as it hadn't in the past days of her attempting to seduce him, it looked very much as if she might succeed tonight.

Dear God.

Knees shaking, she reached out blindly for the nearest object, which happened to be one of the overstuffed leather chairs they had eaten their breakfast in that morning. "Goodness," she managed faintly when he straightened away from the door, apparently alarmed at her sudden lurching, "it's quite warm in here, isn't it? Perhaps a drink might help."

Yes, that was it, alcohol. Alcohol would not only make certain he was receptive but help ease her nerves as well. Her mouth watered as she glanced around the room, searching for a sideboard or something similar, anticipating strong spirits to help calm her. Surely the man had some liquor here.

But when he finally moved, it was not to pour generous draughts of brandy out of sparkling cut glass decanters. No, he came up behind her, out of her line of sight, his steps as he drew closer reverberating up from the floor and through her body. "I'll help you off with your wrap first, shall I?" he murmured. And then his hands were on her shoulders, and he was slowly pulling the wrap away.

She froze. Though she was fully dressed beneath the shawl, she felt as if she were being bared. She could blame it on the gown itself, of course. Sylvia had insisted Heloise borrow one of her more daring evening dresses, as nothing Heloise owned could possibly do for a night at the famed club. Heloise had accepted it with reluctance, only the assurance that this was best for her goal for the evening and, by extension, for their job as a whole prodding her to take it. She had thought surely Sylvia must be exaggerating. There was no way a gown could invoke the reaction she needed.

It was only now, however, as the deep red silk was revealed, with its nearly bare shoulders and plunging décolletage, and she heard Mr. Sinclaire's sharply indrawn breath behind her, that she realized just how brilliant Sylvia had been. And then Mr. Sinclaire's warm—no, hot, they were definitely hot—hands were on her again, this time curling around her upper arms, and all thought fled from her head.

"Mrs. Marlow," he rasped, his voice hoarse, his breath stirring the loose curls that trailed along the nape of her neck, "I don't suppose I could call you Heloise tonight?"

Before she could think to respond to that—not that she was capable of thinking just then—his lips were suddenly pressed against the arch where her neck met her shoulder.

It was the lightest of touches, his full lips barely brushing her skin. Yet it sent a jolt of something molten through her. A tremor ran through her, her body tensing in shock, the very breath stalling in her lungs. He must have felt her reaction, for he stilled. His uneven breath bathed the sensitive skin of her neck, his fingers tightening infinitesimally on her arms. And then he released her, stepping back, and for some strange reason Heloise, somewhere in the midst of the utter riot her mind had become, had the overwhelming urge to cry out at the loss of him.

"My apologies," he said in a rough rasp of sound. "I must have misunderstood your intentions these past days. I'll return you to your party."

Which finally succeeded in snapping her back to the plan at hand. Dear God, she finally had a chance to get close to Mr. Sinclaire and she was freezing up like some inexperienced girl who had never been with a man. Not that her intimate interactions with Gregory had been anything spectacular. Indeed, they had been bland at best, painful and embarrassing at worst. But still, she had been with a man. She knew the ins and outs of doing the deed. And Mr. Sinclaire's actions these past minutes were proof that he was open to something between them. All she had to do was grab the bull by the horns, so to speak, and act.

Which she did. Sucking in a sharp breath to steady herself—for, as clichéd as it sounded, she truly had forgotten to breathe in the last moments and her vision had begun to go spotty from lack of air—she spun about and, taking Mr. Sinclaire's face in her hands, she closed her eyes tight and pressed her lips to his.

12

Ethan hadn't meant to kiss Heloise's neck. What he had meant to do when he had decided to guide her through his club and bring her here to the quiet, intimate privacy of his office was give her a chance to seduce him properly. *If* Teagan hadn't been playing him for a complete fool, that was. Which Ethan wouldn't put past him; truly, the man had the most perverse sense of humor.

But then he had removed her wrap and seen her in that dress—that *dress*, dear God—and had been thoroughly entranced by the mesmerizing curve of her neck. Before he knew what he was about, he had bent his head and pressed his lips to the deliciously smooth skin where her neck met her shoulder. Even with that light touch, even though his lips barely came into contact with her, it was like a drug to his senses. Her own sweet scent of violets filled him up, the warmth under his lips a heady aphrodisiac, making his mouth water. He'd ached to pull her back against him so the strong curves of her body melted into him, to open his mouth on her neck, to drag his tongue over her skin. To *taste* her.

Her reaction, however, had not been what he would have hoped for. Even in his passion-dazed frame of mind, he could feel her flinch, then become utterly still, the shock that permeated every inch of her a tangible thing. Perhaps Teagan truly had been playing him for a fool, he'd thought in the one portion of his brain still coherent. Mayhap the arsehole had been angling for Ethan to make an utter idiot of himself. Doubts began to flood him: Why the hell would she want an ugly bastard like him? How could he hope to attract the attentions of someone as beautiful as she? Never mind that the whole reason he was consenting to her seduction was that he didn't trust her intentions, and acquiescing to her plans, all while carefully controlling what card in the deck was to be played next, was the best way to protect what was dear to him. No, in that moment all he could think about was her, and him, and what it would feel like to strip her bare and feel her against him.

And so he had apologized, and pulled back. And everything was turned on its head again a moment later when she spun, grasped his face in her hands, and planted her mouth on his.

It was his turn to freeze now, and not only at the complete unexpectedness of her kiss. No, the majority of his shock was due to the nature of her kiss. This was no practiced seduction, each movement orchestrated to drug his senses with desire. Truthfully, if he didn't know she was a widow, he would have thought her an inexperienced innocent for the sheer artlessness in her actions. Her lips were pressed tight against his in a prim, ungiving line, her eyes squeezed even tighter as he stared down in disbelief at her. Her hands shook against his cheeks, her body separated from his by several inches of charged air. Truly, it was the most baffling kiss he'd ever experienced in his life.

And yet...

And yet, when she pulled back and looked up at him

with a strange swirl of triumph and uncertainty in her eyes, eyes that said she could not quite believe her own daring, molten heat permeated every inch of his body. How the bloody hell was she, with one strange, innocent kiss, undoing every tightly controlled intention within him?

She stepped back, her hands falling from his face, as if she had done what she'd come to do and was finished with him. But Ethan was not done with her, not by far. With a shaky exhalation he snaked an arm around her waist, pulling her up against him. She gave a small squeak of surprise as their bodies collided, one he quickly swallowed as he claimed her lips with his own.

Ah, God, she tasted sweeter than he could have ever imagined. Like every beautiful thing he had ever dreamed of in his youth while huddled under a threadbare blanket with an empty stomach and emptier heart. She was sunshine at the seaside, and ice cream in the summer, and dew on a field of flowers. She was light and laughter and hope. She shuddered under his onslaught, her hands coming up to grip his shoulders, her fingers curling in the material of his jacket, anchoring her in place. And then he felt it, the faintest pressure of her lips pressing back against his, the slightest arching of her body into his, the tentative acceptance of his kiss sending a peculiar joy rippling through him.

With a moan of pure need he cradled her cheek in his palm, tilted his head, deepened the kiss. She gasped, the soft sound like the headiest aphrodisiac, and he took the opportunity to plunge his tongue into her mouth. Her tongue retreated for a beat before meeting his, tentative at first, then becoming bolder, tangling with his as surely as he wanted their bodies to tangle.

If he'd thought she tasted sweet before, now it was so much sweeter. He felt in that moment he would never get his fill. He devoured her, his kisses becoming wilder, less polished, more raw. She followed, mouth opening hungrily under his as if she had never experienced anything like this in her life and now wanted to make up for it. Her hands inched up into his hair, fingers gripping handfuls, this proof that she was as affected as he going straight to his groin. Needing her even closer, he pressed his hand to the small of her back, forming it to the arch of her spine. The curve of her backside tickled his fingertips, a tantalizing temptation, and he gave in to it, trailing his hand lower until her bottom filled his palm. He pressed her closer, against his erection, savoring the way her soft belly gave to him.

She gasped, her head falling back, revealing the long, strong column of her throat. Trailing his mouth down the length of it, he nipped at her skin, reveling in the small sounds escaping from her lips with each gentle bite, with each slow drag of his tongue. He ached to kiss lower, to pull the edge of her bodice aside, to fill his palm and his mouth with her breasts. More than that, his body throbbed with the need to wrap her legs about his hips, to plunge himself into her and find blessed release in her body.

But he'd be damned if he would take her for the first time—for he had no doubt in his mind this would be the first of many times—standing up, rutting like some damn animal. With a low growl, desperate to get her to his bed where he could undress her properly and finally see the glory that was her body, he tore his mouth free and, with one fluid motion, hefted her into his arms, in the next breath striding across the room to the far door and his bedroom beyond.

* * *

Heloise was quite used to being the strongest person in any room—her profession assured that—so it was an utterly foreign feeling to be lifted as if she weighed no more than a feather. Foreign and, if she was being totally honest, delicious. Mr. Sinclaire—no, *Ethan*, for she could no longer think of him in such proper terms, not after the way he'd kissed her—hefted her against his chest, his arms cradling her to him. So transfixed was she by the sensation, she did not immediately understand that he was taking her across the room, through a door, into a…bedroom?

Mind muddled, she could do little but stare wide-eyed around her as he kicked the door closed behind them and continued on his very focused path. She had just enough time to take in the luxurious fabrics and rich woods, all illuminated by the low glow of the hearth, before she was lowered again. Not to her feet, though. No, he laid her down, in a strangely gentle manner considering how rough and large he was, to the bed.

But she had no time to wonder at the unbearably soft counterpane that surrounded her like a cloud before he quickly shrugged out of his coat and stretched out beside her. And then there was no time to think at all as his mouth found hers again.

Dear God, the man kissed like he was parched and she was the sweetest wine. Though he was half on top of her, though the weight of him was making the heat between her legs build to an almost unbearable degree, she felt as if she might float away any moment, fly off through the heavens and never come down again. She grasped tight to his shoulders to keep herself anchored as he devoured her mouth with his own. How was it lips and tongue could work such wicked magic? Gregory's kisses had been perfunctory, quick, his lovemaking a mirror of that. There had never been any passion. He had focused on his needs and his needs alone. It had been a deed to be done and nothing more.

Ethan's kisses, however, were most definitely not solely for him, his mouth seeming to do its best to draw a response from her. And his hands…good God, his hands. They roved her body as if he were a sculptor and she were his muse. His palm was large and hot as it trailed up her rib cage, his fingers wickedly clever as they skimmed the side of her breast. They hooked in the low neckline of her gown, dragging it down with aching slowness, grazing over her breast and exposing it to the night air. She cried out softly into his mouth as he reached her nipple, one finger trailing across the sensitive tip, and he swallowed the sound eagerly as if it were his reason for living. He tore his mouth from hers then, and she nearly whimpered from the loss of it. But what she did not expect, what she could never have expected, was for his lips to close around the peak of her breast.

The hot ache in the juncture of her thighs flared even hotter as he swirled his tongue about her nipple and drew it farther into his mouth. She pressed her legs tight together, as if it could somehow relieve the tension there. But the ache only grew stronger, making her whimper, making her squirm. As if he sensed what she needed, his hand trailed down her body to the hem of her gown, grasping a fistful of her skirts, pulling them up. And then his hand gently nudged her thighs apart, sliding between them to that place that was quickly becoming the center of everything.

"Oh," she breathed as his palm pressed against her. "Oh, Ethan."

He started, and stilled, and she feared that she had made a fatal error in using his name. But then he groaned in reply, the sound traveling through her breast and down her body, making the sensation between her legs that much more acute.

"Say it again," he rasped, his full lips brushing against her aching nipple, his hot breath coming hard and fast.

Before she could ask what he meant, his fingers found the center of her. She cried out, hips bucking up as pure, raw sensation tore through her body.

"Say it," he repeated, his voice hoarse. "Say my name."

"Ethan," she managed, fingers tangling in his hair as she urged him back to her breast. "Ethan."

"Ah, God," he moaned, the sound almost helpless, a second before he closed his mouth once more about her nipple. His fingers, still between her thighs, quickened their movements, rubbing against her. She threw her head back, hair rasping against the coverlet, even as every muscle in her body was drawn taut as a bowstring. What, she wondered dazedly, would happen to her if he released the string, if he let the arrow fly?

She quickly found out as, leaving her breast and moving down her body, he settled between her legs. His hot breath washed over her as he nudged her thighs farther apart. And then he was claiming that most private part of her with his mouth.

Her breath left her on a long exhalation, her spine arching off the bed, her hands finding and holding on to his head. She would wonder later why she hadn't been shocked to her core, why she hadn't pushed him away and scrambled up from the bed. She had never had anything like that done to her, had never dreamed it *could* be done. And yet...

And yet in that moment, with his mouth and tongue loving such an incredibly intimate place on her body, she could only think how very right it felt. It was as if she had been made for this loving, as if her body had unknowingly yearned for it for years, and now that she was here spread before him it was the most natural thing in the world.

Hooking her thighs over his wide shoulders, he ran his hands over her hips to her belly, the large warmth of them splaying over her quivering stomach to hold her in place. All the while his mouth kissed and nipped and sucked, his tongue dipping within her folds, finding the very epicenter of her pleasure. She gasped as he licked there, fingers tightening on his hair as she pressed up into the open warmth of his mouth. A low growl escaped him, the vibration doing wonderful, wicked things to her, making the pleasure peak until she didn't think she could soar any higher.

Just then, however, his clever fingers found her cleft, and she discovered she could soar much higher, indeed.

His fingers slipped inside her, first one, then two, stretching her, filling her. And all the while his mouth continued working its magic. Helpless whimpers escaped from her throat as the pressure in her body built. Her hips began to work in tandem with him, reaching for something she could not begin to understand. Just when she thought her body could not take a bit more of the almost unbearable pressure, he pulled her into his mouth, sucking deep, and she shattered into a million glittering pieces.

Before she could even begin to put herself together again he was over her, mouth on her breast, on her neck, on her cheek, frantic kisses that made the ache between her legs return. "Can I, Heloise?" he panted in her ear, the rough desperation sending shivers of renewed need through her body. "Can I love you?"

Can I love you? She shuddered at the hot hunger in that question. Not that she had any delusion that he was truly in love with her. Hell, they barely tolerated each other. This was purely physical.

But good God, that question went straight to her soul. "Yes," she breathed. "God, yes."

He groaned, a sound that came from deep in his chest, even as he crushed her mouth under his. He tasted of her, a heady flavor on her tongue, and her eyes rolled back in her head, remembering where that mouth had been just moments before. And then his thigh was between hers, urging her to widen them. She did so eagerly, hands gripping tight to his shoulders as his lean hips slid into the juncture there. The fine material of his breeches rasped against the tender skin of her inner thighs and the swollen flesh at her center, sending a shudder of need through her, making her whimper. One of his hands worked between their bodies, undoing his falls, freeing himself. In the next moment the hot, blunt tip of him pressed against her. Then, after one last pause, he exhaled a hiss of pleasure and carefully pushed into her.

Heloise cried out as he stretched her, her head falling back, fingernails digging into the fine silk of his waistcoat. To her surprise, he paused, pulling back, gazing down at her with a face drawn tight with worry.

"Am I hurting you?" he panted.

She stared up at him, stunned that he would take the time to question her on that. And looking into his eyes she suddenly knew, without a doubt, he would stop here and now if she so much as asked.

Her heart gave an unsteady lurch, and there was the peculiar sting of tears behind her eyes. Confused by her reaction, she hastily shook her head. "No," she managed, a mere breath of a sound. "You're not hurting me." And then, because she could not stop herself if she tried, "Please don't stop."

His eyes turned molten, the heat from the low fire seeming to have transferred into their depths. Cradling her face in his hands, he lowered his mouth to hers. Though this time there was something else to his kiss, an aching need that hadn't been present before. He pushed forward again, filling her. He was so unbelievably hard, and as he began to move, a slow retreat and advance that left her breathless with want, she found this was very different from when he had kissed between her legs. That had been intense, overwhelming. This, however, was so much more. His large body pressed her down into the soft mattress, the weight of it delicious, the sensation of his hips spreading her wide driving her wild. Though they were fully clothed—for the most part—she could feel the rapid, heavy beat of his heart against her breasts, proof that he was as affected as she. And his mouth...God, his mouth never stopped moving, devouring her lips, her jaw, her neck.

But what affected her most was the sounds coming from his lips. Soft gasps and ragged breaths and low, rough moans that seemed to be dredged up from the very depths of his soul. They grew wilder as his movements became almost frantic. And then he reached back, hooking a hand under her knee, and hitched her leg up, spreading her body wider and tilting her hips to receive him more fully. He hit something inside her then, a secret spot that made her explode around him and had her keening her release.

"Heloise," he groaned into her neck, before, pulling himself from her body, he took himself in hand, finishing himself into the coverlet as he threw his head back and shouted his own completion into the night.

The thought that he would surely roll from her and bid her leave managed to worm its way into her hazy mind as he collapsed atop her and his harsh breathing filled her ear. After all, wasn't that what it had been like with Gregory? He'd never liked to linger with her once the deed was done. And she hadn't minded in the least. She had preferred to be alone after.

Surprisingly, the thought of Ethan doing the same made

her oddly mournful. When he finally did rise from the bed, however, it wasn't to kick her from the room. To her shock—or, at least, as much shock as she was capable of with her body and mind in a state of such utter depletion— he bent and took her in his arms, lifting her against his chest. With deft movements he threw back the coverlet and lowered her with infinite care to the sheets. As she watched, stunned, he gently removed her shoes, followed by his own boots, before climbing fully dressed into the bed with her. And not only to lie beside her. No, he gathered her up in his arms, pulling her to his side. Then, hand cradling her head and lips at her temple, he gave a soft sigh, his large body relaxing.

Why, she thought as she listened to his steady heartbeat under her ear, did she suddenly feel like crying? Eyes burning, a sudden languid exhaustion pulling at her, she found her body melting into his, and within moments quickly fell into blessed unconsciousness as sleep claimed her.

13

That sweet peace, however, disappeared the moment she opened her eyes to the near pitch dark of the room, mind no longer dazed from passion, and recalled all that had occurred between her and Ethan. Something that was made all the more vivid when she realized she was still wrapped around him like a squirrel climbing a tree.

She froze, hand splayed over his very wide, very firm chest as mortification filled her. No, perhaps not mortification; she certainly wasn't ashamed of what they had done. She had planned on taking him to her bed—or his bed, as in this particular case. And anyway, physical intimacy between two consenting adults was natural. No, she was not ashamed.

But something uncomfortable was condensing in a horrid amalgamation in the pit of her stomach. Made worse as, quite against her will, she once more recalled the things he had done to her—and how she had responded to them. She pressed her face into the silk of his waistcoat, as if the blood that had rushed to her cheeks had somehow created a blinding beacon in the darkness and she could hide it in his shoulder. She had not thought the things that had happened between them were possible. Oh, she had fully understood the pleasures many experienced from the act. After having lived with Sylvia and Laney, she could not be ignorant of that. They were quite demonstrative.

Her imagination, however, must be severely lacking. She had never in her life expected such a sensation. Even thinking of it now had heat blooming anew between her legs. A feeling that she ached to relieve. But in that moment, the last thing she wanted was to wake Ethan. God, she could not face him just then. Ironic, really, considering how closely their fully clothed bodies were pressed together.

But she was being an absolute ninny. She had come here for the express purpose of seducing Ethan, the culmination of several days of effort. She paused. Not that she had done much seducing tonight. Except for her fumbling kiss, he had been the one to instigate things between them this evening, hadn't he? Strange, seeing as he had tried his damnedest to keep her at arm's length until now. Why had he done such a severe about-face with her?

But she was being unduly suspicious. Things had worked out, hadn't they? Who truly cared how they had gotten here, as long as she had succeeded in what she had set out to do? Now she just had to make certain this affair continued. It was not about getting him into her bed; it was about keeping him there and getting him to, if not trust her, at least let down his guard so she might gain much-needed access to the more private areas of Dionysus and find those blasted jewels. Which she would accomplish only by sticking close to his side. No matter how desperately she wanted to slip from this bed and escape this room so she might not have to face him.

An urge that was growing harder to fight with each tick of the clock. Below them the sounds of merriment could be heard, the club still a hive of activity. What time was it? How long had she been asleep? Had Sylvia and Laney left for home? All the while, as her mind spun like a top, she was very much aware of the large male halfway beneath her, his strong arm hooked about her back, his even breathing in her ear, the very firm muscles beneath her fingers—the way her leg had somehow insinuated itself between his own.

Mayhap it truly would be better to slip from his arms and the room and this club altogether, she reasoned a bit wildly as her lungs seized. Who knew how long he would sleep, after all? Yes, she should definitely find a way to leave…preferably one that did not include waking Ethan. And so on and so on her thoughts spiraled away from her completely sound logic of a moment before.

Until a large, warm hand covered her own and stopped her panicked thoughts in their tracks.

"Are you going to go back to sleep?" a husky voice mumbled, rumbling under her ear. "Or would you like to pick up where we left off?"

"Oh!" she squeaked, intensely aware of his arm tightening about her back, bringing her even closer to his body. He rubbed his cheek against the crown of her hair, a strangely affectionate action that had her heart going from panicked thumping to lurching in…longing? She attempted to swallow the emotion down, but it only grew stronger as his thumb caressed the back of her hand where it lay against his chest.

"I'm sorry I woke you," she finally managed.

"I'm not," he murmured, a second before he rolled her onto her back and came up on one elbow to lean over her. The firelight had died down to faint orange embers, the only light in the room the indirect silver moonlight coming in through the windows. Yet it was enough to glint in the unending depths of his eyes and highlight the rugged plains of his face. To reveal a hunger she had not expected to see, most especially not for her, who had never inspired such a look from anyone in her life.

"It is ironic," he said, the words a deep rumble that fairly vibrated her bones, his fingers going to the bodice of her gown, gently running along the edge in a way that made her breath catch, "that I brought you purposely to this bed to strip you naked, and yet here we are fully dressed."

"Goodness," she whispered, unable to help herself. Then, screwing up her courage, she said in a voice that shook much more than it ought to, "Mayhap we might see that through next time we are together."

He stilled. His gaze, which had dropped to trace the path his fingers were taking along her neckline, rose to meet hers, and to her shock the heat that had been present there seemed to have increased tenfold. "Will there be a next time, then?"

She swallowed hard. "Y-yes?"

His lips quirked, his eyes crinkling at the corners in a way she had never seen in him before. The sudden shift in expression made him appear younger, carefree. "You do have a strange habit of asking questions when you should be answering them. Could it be you're flustered?"

"Why would I be flustered?" But the question had the opposite of the effect she had hoped for, her breathlessness giving proof of it rather than refuting it.

Though she could not regret it as his smile deepened, his teeth flashing in the moonlight. Goodness, and she had not thought he could get more attractive. Her gaze zeroed in on that smile, and those full lips, and she recalled with impressive clarity all the wicked things he had done with them not long ago. With incredible will she gripped tight to the sheets beneath her lest she reach for him and drag him down for a kiss.

Ethan was not so reticent. He lowered his head, capturing her lips with his, making her toes curl and her body fairly melt beneath his. It was over quickly—much too quickly, but she would rather chew nails than admit that—and he rolled from the bed to stand, holding out a hand for her. She stared at that hand several moments longer than necessary, her brain not understanding right away what she was to do with it. Finally, however, she reached out, gripping his fingers tight, allowing him to assist her to her feet.

"I shall hold you to that promise," he murmured, thumb tracing her knuckles. Then, releasing her hand, he moved off deeper into the shadows of the room. She thought he would surely open the door and kick her out. But no, he quickly returned to her with her slippers in hand, bending down before her and gently guiding her feet, one by one, into them.

Why, she wondered as she stared down at his bent head, did she once again feel like crying? Her throat burned with tears as his large hands worked with infinite care to make certain her slippers were secure before he stood again.

"Give me a moment and I'll bring you back to your party," he said.

But the tears that had begun in her throat were somehow quickly moving up to her eyes. Why? Because the man had shown a bit of kindness toward her? *Yes*, a small voice whispered in the back of her mind. Which was too pathetic for her to countenance.

But no matter that she knew better, that did not lessen her sudden need to cry. Worried she would make an utter fool of herself in front of this man, she quickly backed away from him. "There's no need," she said, moving toward the door. "I can find my own way back. I'm certain you're busy." She turned and reached for the handle, throwing the door wide. Golden light from his office flooded the silvery dimness of his bedroom, blinding her, chasing away the last bit of intimacy between them.

Or so she thought. She made the fatal mistake of looking back. He stood in the middle of his bedroom staring after her, looking deliciously mussed with clothing creased and cravat hanging limp and hair sticking up in odd places. But it was the strangely soft, almost vulnerable look in his eyes that had her very nearly closing the door again and rushing back to him.

She shook herself. No, she had to leave, for her own sanity if nothing else. The man was quickly making her lose sight of why she was here in the first place.

She forced a smile. "I shall see you tomorrow," she said before, giving him one last long look, she closed the door.

* * *

Ethan stared through the darkness at that closed door for much longer than he would ever willingly admit. He had thought that by allowing Heloise to seduce him, he might gain the upper hand in their strange dance and understand a bit more of what she was angling for. Yet his mind was even more muddled than before.

He nearly snorted. Allowing her to seduce him? He had damn well nearly jumped her the moment he'd had her alone. Just the sight of her in that damn dress had nearly sent him over the edge. And when she had kissed him... he ran a hand over his face. How was it possible that one simple, unpracticed kiss could affect him so deeply? Even thinking of it now, the small, surprised gasps from her lips, her fumbling hands, kisses that had not had a bit of guile in them, and his cock twitched to life. He would not have been the least surprised if he learned she was an innocent.

Or at least an innocent before tonight. His vision went hazy and his mouth watered just remembering how she had tasted.

He forced himself back to the present. Yanking at his limp cravat and tossing it aside, he padded to the bedside lamp and lit it before striding to the small cabinet in the corner and reaching for the cut glass bottle of brandy he kept there. His hand shook as he poured himself a healthy glassful of the stuff, the staccato clinking like a scolding to ears that had recently heard only the glorious sounds coming from Heloise's lips. Scowling down at his traitorous appendages, he slammed the decanter down and grabbed the glass, sloshing a bit of the expensive liquor over the edge as he did so, before going to the large window looking over St James's. But even as he glared down at the busyness beneath him, even as his eyes took in the carriages still pulling up to the front of Dionysus and milling bodies still hungry for vice traversing the street, he hardly saw it for the image of Heloise resplendent amidst his sheets.

Letting loose a rough curse, he took a deep swallow of his drink, reveling in the burn of it as it traveled down to his stomach. No matter how he had lost himself in her this evening, he refused to lose sight again of why he had allowed this affair to begin with. He would be more in control of himself when he saw her the next day. He swore it.

14

But it seemed that vow held no more water than a colander the moment he saw her again shortly after dawn.

His eyes fairly devoured her as she stood on the other side of the boxing venue, taking in the graceful flare of her hips beneath the modest leaf-green gown, tracing the curve of her breasts, caressing the long line of her neck. She was back to her typical garb, gowns no doubt created for comfort and ease of use. And yet…

And yet she was even more alluring than last night, when she had been draped in scarlet silk, shoulders nearly bare and every curve teased by the luxurious fabric. He had the mad thought to go to her, take her hand in his, and drag her off to the nearest empty room so he might bury himself in her supple body.

Which was probably why, he realized blearily a moment later as he tugged at his suddenly much-too-tight cravat, he had not immediately noticed her talking in a very close, intimate manner to a handsome young man dressed in workman's garb.

He blinked as some strange bitter taste filled his mouth. What the hell was wrong with him? Of course she was talking to the workers. She was here to help oversee the preparations for the boxing match, after all. She had been working hard with all the craftspeople to make certain everything was built to the proper specifications.

Why, then, did he have the urge to stride across the room and take that fresh-faced, much-too-handsome-for-his-own-good worker by the scruff and plant a fist in his face? He could not possibly be…jealous?

He reared back, stunned. Jealous? What the devil? He laughed, an almost unhinged sound, earning him more than one startled glance from the men about him. There was no way in hell or on earth that he was jealous. He was incapable of feeling jealousy, just as he was incapable of feeling most strong emotions. He kept that part of himself in check, a hand he would never willingly show. Proof that his heart had been petrified over the years to the point that those emotions no longer even existed in him. If they ever had in the first place.

Just then, however, Heloise leaned in closer to the worker, seemingly to impart something in confidence, and another surge of bitterness flooded him. Without thinking, he took a step in their direction, his hands fisting at his sides. To do what, he didn't have a clue. All he knew was the deep, driving desire to separate the two with all haste. Blessedly, Mr. Ferris stepped into his path, stopping him from doing God knew what.

"Good morning, Mr. Sinclaire," he said, all jovial good will. Tucking a pencil behind his ear, he motioned to the floor, where the raised platform for the boxing match was quickly taking shape. "We're ahead of schedule, and if things continue at this pace, we will be done with time to spare."

"Good, good," Ethan muttered, only half listening to the

man, his gaze still firmly stuck to Heloise across the room. "But who is that youth with Mrs. Marlow? I don't believe I've seen him before."

Mr. Ferris followed his gaze. "Who, young Herbert there? He's Mrs. Marlow's cousin. She asked that he be hired on for the duration of the project." The man shrugged. "He's a bright lad, and though he's inexperienced, I saw no harm in it."

Heloise's cousin? And just like that the tension drained from his body. Which was all the more concerning, as it proved that his bitterness had indeed been jealousy. Or, at least, it should be concerning. Instead, all he felt was a light kind of relief. Dear God, he thought as Mr. Ferris touched a finger to his forelock and excused himself, what was wrong with him? And why didn't it concern him more? It was all too obvious that Heloise had somehow, someway managed to worm into his affections.

And then even that small concern dissipated a moment later as the woman herself, having bidden farewell to her cousin, spied him and smiled.

His insides melted. *No, this isn't right*, some small voice whispered inside his brain. But then she made her way through the workers and equipment to him, and even that voice disappeared as quickly as it had come.

"Good morning," she murmured when she reached him. She stood several feet from him, yet he could feel the heat of her across the space.

"Good morning," he replied. "I trust you slept well."

Her gaze turned heavy-lidded. Was it just him, or did she look at his lips? His mouth went dry.

"I probably should have." Her eyes dropped to the floor, her fingers nervously playing with the folds of her gown.

"You did not?"

She laughed lightly. "Not a bit, I'm afraid."

Why did that shy comment make his heart lurch? Mayhap it was the blush that rose to her cheeks, proof that her trouble sleeping had to do with one very particular reason. Which in turn made *him* think about that particular reason.

He swallowed hard. "Perhaps it would be better for you to return home, so you might rest properly."

It was a half-hearted suggestion at best. One she blessedly refused.

"I'd much rather stay here," she answered softly. Her gaze rose to his again. "If you've no objection."

Heat flooded him at the husky tone in her voice, and he just stopped himself from groaning. Instead he took her hand and, not caring that they were surrounded by workmen, pulled her from the room.

He should have had the control to take her up to his office. But control, in that moment, was one thing he sorely lacked. Another thing he should have been concerned about. After all, hadn't his life been built on tightly leashed control? Just then, however, all he could think about was having her in his arms. And so when he found an empty room, he pulled her through the open door, slamming it behind them before, pinning her to the wall, he crushed her mouth under his.

* * *

Whatever Heloise had been expecting from Ethan when she'd arrived at Dionysus that morning, it had certainly not been this.

Not that she was complaining. She had not been lying, after all, when she had told him that she had not slept well, nor had she been fooling him about the reason why. During the long hours between her departure from the club last night and her arrival some half hour ago, not a second had gone by that she had not thought of being held in his arms.

Blessedly she had not been forced to recount the events of the evening to any of the other Widows, busy as they had all been with their myriad parts to play. Did she have to eventually let the others in on her success with Ethan? Yes. But for some strange reason, she wanted to hold it close to her for the time being.

That was something she would not look at too closely. Especially now, as he opened his mouth over hers as if he were starving and she were the one food in all the world he craved. She welcomed his kiss with a greediness that surprised her, winding her arms about his neck, gripping tight to his hair. Her body arched against his, remembering the bliss it had experienced at his hands and craving more of it. How was it she had not been satisfied with that? How could it possibly make her want even more with him? But want more she did, her skin fairly sizzling with heat, that place between her legs aching until she could hardly stand it. When he reached down and hitched her skirts up, grasping her thighs and hooking them about his lean hips, she whimpered into his mouth with need.

"Heloise," he rasped as he kissed along her jaw to the sensitive spot just beneath her ear. "Can I take you?"

Why did her heart lurch at the desperate request? It had done the same the night before, when he had asked her permission. It made her feel cherished, respected.

But it was making it damned difficult for her to keep things in perspective. Not that she had managed to keep things in perspective thus far. No, she had lost all common sense the moment he'd dragged her here and kissed her.

But any chance of gaining control of her wildly spinning emotions was lost as he pressed his hardness against her. She gasped, wrapping her legs more fully about him. "Please, Ethan," she managed.

The words had barely escaped her lips before his hand was between them. And then he was freeing himself and guiding himself into her, and the wonderful fullness of his member was filling her.

"Heloise," he hissed against her neck, his breath hot on her skin as he seated himself to the hilt. He stilled, panting heavily, fingers tight on her bare thighs, making Heloise all the more aware of the throbbing of his cock inside her and the deliciously vulnerable feel of being pressed between his massive body and the ungiving wall behind her.

Finally he began to move, a steady rocking. Soft gasps fell from her lips, joined by low, desperate, almost feral sounds from his own, making her wilder, the ache at the center of her more acute. She clung to his shoulders as his movements quickened, her entire universe centering on that place where their bodies joined. And then his hand worked between them again.

"Come for me, sweetheart," he rasped in her ear, his fingers rubbing against her. And she did, breaking apart in his arms, his mouth quickly finding hers and swallowing her cries of completion.

The moment the last wave of pleasure finished, he pulled out of her, gently lowering her feet to the floor. Then he tore a handkerchief from his waistcoat and, his hand on the wall beside her and his forehead pressed to her shoulder, he finished himself off with a low, rumbling groan.

Her legs shook, and she had the rogue thought that she would have fallen over on the spot had his body not been curled around her. They stood that way for a time, their heartbeats gradually slowing, their breaths evening. Somewhere on the other side of the wall, a plank of wood clattered to the ground, and someone cursed.

She should have felt embarrassed—they were barely

feet away from the workmen—but instead a giddy laugh escaped her.

Ethan stilled at the sound. Before she could think what that stillness meant, however, he joined her, rough chuckles tumbling from his lips like rocks down a cliff face. He started briefly, as if unused to the sound, before continuing. Which surprised her into continuing, their laughter mingling.

It was surprisingly intimate, even more intimate than what they had done just minutes before. Warmth seeped into her cheeks as, laughter finally dying down, she chanced a glance up at him. His features were softened, eyes crinkling at the corners in a wholly attractive way, full lips stretched in an easy smile. Her heart gave a quick, heavy thrum in her chest. Unconsciously she pressed a hand over the unruly organ, as if she could somehow tame it. But it continued its thumping, as if waking after a deep, dreamless sleep and wanting her to know it was there.

His gaze caressed her upturned face like he was seeing her for the first time. "I never intended for *this*"—he indicated the small space between their bodies—"to happen when you arrived this morning." A frown furrowed his brow as he looked to the floor. "It was not well done of me. I have never in my life lost control like that."

He appeared bewildered, as if he could not understand how such a thing could have occurred. She blinked. Was he saying he had been so overwhelmed by her he had not been thinking straight? Surely not. As she knew full well, she was not one to stir such emotions in anyone.

And yet…

And yet when he turned his gaze back to hers, the heat there told a very different story. She swallowed hard against a suddenly parched throat. "I'm sorry," she whispered.

He stared at her before letting loose a huffing laugh. "You're sorry? What the devil for? It's my problem, not yours."

Her cheeks, those damn traitorous cheeks, burned hot under his disbelieving stare. "I was not exactly holding myself back, though, was I?" She gave a nervous laugh of her own. "I'm not normally so brazen. I've never done this before. That is, I've done *this*"—she motioned to the space between them as he had done, which was apparently a safe way of indicating they'd had sex without actually saying the words aloud—"but only ever infrequently, and certainly with much less passion…"

She clamped a hand over her mouth and stared up at him wide-eyed in horror. She hadn't meant to reveal that particular truth.

He stared down at her, equally wide-eyed, though in his case it was caused by shock if the rest of his expression was to go by. Mortified beyond bearing, she fumbled along the wall behind her, desperately searching for the door handle.

"But I should get going. I have to check on my fri…er, cousin, to make certain he is settling in well, and then I have an appointment…somewhere." She finally located the handle. Nearly sobbing in relief, she turned it, intending to pull it open and dive through.

His hand on the door above her head, however, stopped her in her tracks.

"I will see you tonight?"

She gaped up at him. "What?"

He appeared confused, as if he could not understand what he was doing. But then his face settled into determined lines, and he asked again, his voice firmer than before, "Will I see you tonight?" He tentatively tucked a stray lock of hair behind her ear, his lips quirking in one corner in a wholly endearing manner. "I would very much like to see you again. Separate from business dealings, that is."

"Goodness," she whispered, the last bit of her self-disgust melting away in the face of this softness. Truly, who knew the man had it in him?

But she had revealed enough of her own inexperience to him; she did not need to appear as an even more pathetic figure in his eyes.

"Yes. That is," she continued, fighting the urge to press her hands to her burning cheeks, "I would like that as well."

Why did his shoulders lower and his face ease as if he were relieved? And why on God's green earth did that small reaction make her insides melt like strawberry ices on a hot summer day?

"Well then," she said, trying to gain some kind of control over not only the situation, but her own unruly emotions as well, "I should be going." With that she looked pointedly up at his hand, still on the door, holding her captive.

"Oh," he said, removing his hand and stepping back.

She hurriedly pulled the door open, peering out to make certain no one was about before slipping through. All the while, as she practically fled Dionysus, she was achingly aware of the rapid pounding of her heart, each thump of that traitorous organ counting the seconds until she could see Ethan again.

15

"Where are you running off to, Brother?"

Ethan, who should have been trying to sleep but had instead been heading out for a good pounding ride in Hyde Park, froze with the key in the lock. He glanced to the side and let loose a low curse.

One door down from Ethan's, Isaac had his dark head stuck out into the hall like a weasel peeking out of its burrow. Knowing his plans for a solitary ride were well and truly over, Ethan turned to face him. His brother sauntered over, hands in pockets as if he didn't have a care in the world. But there was something tight at the corners of his eyes, something almost…suspicious? Why did his expression set the hairs at the nape of Ethan's neck to standing?

"I think that should be obvious," he drawled, indicating his riding attire.

Isaac huffed a laugh, rolling his eyes. "And you think I'm going to accept your departure from your usual schedule without commenting? You, who have not deviated from that schedule once since we've begun Dionysus?"

If only his brother knew how much he had begun to deviate from that schedule since Heloise had come into his life.

Damn it all to hell, but the woman affected him in ways he never could have imagined. And he seemed to have no defense against her. Thus the need for that pounding ride.

But Isaac was waiting for him to say something, and he'd be damned if he'd tell him the truth. "I couldn't sleep is all," he finally grumbled.

"Splendid," his brother replied with a wide smile.

Ethan blinked. "Splendid?"

"Absolutely. I have no desire to go home and sleep, either. Wait just a moment and I'll join you." Then, before Ethan could think to stop him, Isaac disappeared back into his office.

Damn and blast. The last thing he needed was his brother's typical chatter when all he wanted to do was mindlessly ride until he was too exhausted to sit in the saddle. He considered running off before Isaac returned. But he knew that was a futile dream. Isaac would not be opposed to chasing him down.

Ethan sighed heavily, leaned against the wall, and tried not to think about why he needed the ride in the first place. At least with Isaac joining, he told himself bracingly, though not very convincingly, he would not be able to think of Heloise much.

* * *

That pathetic hope was quickly pummeled and left for dead. Just as he and Isaac exited the mews, guiding their mounts down St James's, his brother started up on the one subject Ethan had hoped to avoid.

"You disappeared with Mrs. Marlow last night for some time."

Ethan, who had been busy guiding his horse around a shining black lacquer carriage, started, his hands tightening ever so slightly on the reins. Or perhaps more than slightly; Typhon, typically calm even in the face of the worst London's streets had to offer, shied to the side. By the time Ethan regained control, not only of Typhon but of himself as well, Isaac's attention had been well and truly piqued. He considered Ethan with pursed lips and a raised brow as they turned onto Piccadilly.

"Sensitive subject, Brother?"

"Not at all," Ethan replied evasively. "It just surprised me, is all."

Isaac cast him a hooded sideways glance before, face relaxing into its typical natural ease, he tipped his hat at a lady in a passing open carriage, giving her a sly wink. "It's natural to ask about it, I think," he continued to Ethan. "After you hid from her yesterday, followed by your shock at Teagan's revelation that she wishes to seduce you, of course I'm going to ask about last night."

"Of course," Ethan replied sardonically.

His brother laughed. "If you were in my shoes, you would do the same."

True. But he'd be damned if he'd admit as much.

"If we are to assure Mrs. Finch's match goes off without a hitch," he said instead, keeping his voice as even and bored as he was able to make it, "I will be working with her manager day and night to see it is done, no matter the place or time."

There was a beat of silence as they worked their horses around a particularly snarled bit of traffic. Which was a sight less stressful than dealing with his brother's too-astute comments. While he had gone into this affair with a clear goal in mind, it was quickly being usurped by a plethora of emotions that he wished to avoid looking too closely at—an impossibility with this sudden probing.

But if Ethan thought Isaac was through with the subject, he was dead wrong.

"I am not so stupid," Isaac drawled once they were on their way again, "that I did not notice the way you looked at her when you pulled her from the gaming room last night. Nor am I so nobbed in the head as to have missed your expression when you disappeared with her this morning." He raised a dark brow, eyes twinkling as he considered Ethan. "Mrs. Marlow is a beautiful woman, and I would not blame you at all for taking her to your bed. Though," he continued, ignoring the furious glare Ethan sent his way, "the very fact that you did, indeed, take her to your bed at the club speaks volumes that this is no normal affair."

Which was something Ethan had done his best not to think about. But damned if the whelp wasn't right. He had never, in all the time they'd operated the club, taken a single woman to his rooms. Any affair he'd entered into had been conducted at the woman's residence or an obliging hotel. He had never brought a woman into his inner sanctuary, the one place he felt safest.

Why, then, had he brought Heloise there? He could have just as easily made love to her in his office. While he had never used that space for such a thing, either, it was not as precious to him as his private apartments.

Yet when he'd had her in his arms, he had not thought of protecting himself or keeping her out. No, he had wanted to claim her in the most complete manner possible. And, though it was difficult to admit, he had also wanted to be claimed *by* her, to share something with her he had never shared with another.

But why? That one question had haunted him since he'd parted from her, worrying away at his hard-earned peace. And as he could not answer the query any better than when it had first sprung up in his mind like a particularly unwelcome weed in a carefully cultivated garden, he replied the only way he could think to: with a raw threat.

"Lest you wish to find your pretty face bruised and bloodied," he growled, "I will not hear Mrs. Marlow spoken about in such a way."

Which may not have been the right response to throw his brother off the scent, if his sudden wide smile was any indication.

"Oh, you really do like her."

"Isaac." The one word was like thunder rumbling, his chest vibrating with it.

But his brother had never been particularly quick when it came to heeding warnings. Or rather, he understood the threats given but didn't seem to care a bit for his own safety.

They entered the park at Hyde Park Corner and slowed their horses down, pulling them off to the side of the path. "I don't judge you a bit for it," Isaac quipped, grinning, taking a moment to look out over the sea of people in the park, each of them there to see and be seen. "In fact, if I was the one lucky enough to be working so closely with her, I probably would have done the same—"

Ethan reached across the space between their mounts and lay a hard hand on his brother's sleeve, stopping his idiotic words in their tracks. "Don't ever say anything disrespectful against her again," he gritted when Isaac looked at him in shock. "Do. You. Understand?"

There was a beat of silence. And then, voice more sober than Ethan had heard it in a long while, "I apologize. I was so glad to see you loosening the tight reins you keep on yourself, I went too far." Then a pained smile. "I just want to see you happy for once. I love you, Brother."

Those words, said with such affection, knocked the

breath from Ethan's lungs. He knew Isaac loved him, of course. And Isaac knew he returned that love. They were blood, after all, and had been through all manner of hell together. But they were not demonstrative people, and never actually said the words out loud.

Which gave him pause. Had he ever in his life told his brother he loved him? Never in words, perhaps. But in actions he had let his brother know he cared deeply for him. Hadn't he? He frowned, thinking back, digging through their interactions over the years. Which brought him back much further than he had expected, to the *before* time.

His hand fell numb to his side, Gavin's smiling face swimming in his memories. But even as anger and guilt and pain washed over him, nearly as potent as they had been three years earlier for all he had kept them bottled up and fermenting, he could not help remembering how much easier the three of them had been with one another. Before Gavin's betrayal and death and before their world turned upside down.

He looked fully at Isaac, forcing himself to take in the hint of grief in his brother's eyes. Was that worry beneath the surface? Worry for him? A strange tightness closed his throat.

"I *am* happy," he managed gruffly, looking out over the milling riders and open carriages. "I have everything I need, after all. What more could I possibly want?"

Isaac was silent beside him for a long moment, the lack of sound from him louder than the laughter and conversation and jangle of tackle about them. Finally he huffed a soft chuckle.

"You keep telling yourself that, you pigheaded bastard," he mumbled. Before Ethan could think of a reply, Isaac clapped him jovially on the back. "But I've spotted several of our patrons eyeing us. And as I'm damned tired of dealing with these cocky nobles, let's find a quieter bit of dirt to stretch these beasts' legs, shall we?" Giving Ethan a roguish wink, he kicked his horse on.

Ethan, unsettled and not knowing why, watched him leave. Then, shrugging off the uneasy feeling, he urged his own horse after him.

* * *

No matter how much effort Heloise put into avoiding everyone at the Wimpole Street house, she would not be able to succeed forever. Something she tried to remind herself of as she made her way to Sylvia's suite for their scheduled afternoon tea. Could she have claimed a headache and sat it out? Certainly. Was she going to? She had been tempted. Oh, she had been tempted. But in the end she knew it was best to get it over with. So she raised her head high and threw open the door to Sylvia's rooms, ready for the barrage of questions regarding her planned seduction of Ethan. After the trip to Dionysus the evening before, the others *had* to know something had occurred.

What she did not expect, however, was the absolute disinterest she was faced with.

"I am telling you, Euphemia," Sylvia was saying, pointing a bit of shortbread at her, seeming not to notice as Heloise approached and took a seat nearby, "your skills are improving beyond even my imaginings. When you walked in here this afternoon, I swore some strange man had infiltrated the house. I very nearly called Strachan to deal with you."

Euphemia, still in the craftsman's garb she had used to gain access to Dionysus earlier that morning, laughed delightedly and removed her wig of closely cropped dark hair. "No thank you," she said with a grin, pulling the pins from her pale brown locks. "I'm terrified enough of Strachan; if she were to come at me in full fury I would expire on the spot. Oh, hello, Heloise. My disguise was quite a success, if I do say so myself. Mr. Ferris never batted an eye. Introducing me as your cousin was positively brilliant."

"I do wish I could find a way to help," Iris fretted, fiddling with the spoon in her teacup, nearly sloshing the beverage over the rim in her agitation. "I feel so useless sitting at home."

"My dear Iris," Sylvia drawled, giving her an arch look even as she laid a gentle hand over the other woman's to still her anxious fidgeting, "you are delusional if you think you are not useful."

"Sylvia is right," Laney chimed in as she passed Heloise her cup of tea—plain, without a bit of sweetness, just as she liked it. "Your usefulness is not determined by how often you get into the thick of things. Supporting us from the barracks, as it were, can be even more meaningful."

But Iris was not to be soothed so easily. Placing her cup down with a clatter, she worried at the skin of her wrist with her thumbnail. "If only I was a better actress, I could assist you all within Dionysus as well." Her small pixie-like face screwed up in frustration. "I must have improved somewhat since I started out. Surely if you give me something to do within Dionysus, I can manage to succeed."

"No," Sylvia said, a touch too quickly, an alarmed look in her eyes before she schooled her features into a mild smile. "That is, we need you here. You'll have to be fresh for the night of the masquerade should we be forced to infiltrate the gaming hell en masse, and as you are quite the most talented of us when it comes to picking locks, your help will be invaluable then. Also, I've sent out word through my connections to see if any more of Dionysus's victims can be located. I shall need someone close to home should word come through."

"Oh, splendid," Iris exclaimed, sitting forward, knee precariously bumping her teacup in her relief. "Whatever I can do to help."

Sylvia gave her a small smile. "With you ready in the wings, Laney's plans to practice in the new ring once it is built, my own invitation to play in their private gaming room, Euphemia in place to locate the valve to the gas lamps, and Heloise well and truly ingrained in Dionysus and with Mr. Ethan Sinclaire, our success is practically assured."

Heloise tensed. There it was, confirmation that they knew she had succeeded in seducing Ethan. But once more she was proven wrong in her belief that they would leap to discuss it. The conversation quickly turned.

"Now that we have got that out of the way," Sylvia continued with satisfaction, "I would very much like to begin planning a trip for when this whole affair is done. It will be good to get out of London for a bit as the dust settles. What say you all to a visit to the Isle of Synne? I've a mind to clear my head with a dose of sea air and sunshine, and it's far enough removed from London that we may safely relax there without fear of becoming entangled in the aftermath."

And just like that, the entire atmosphere transformed, everyone joining in with her plans for the proposed trip. Everyone, that was, except for Heloise. Now that her worry had settled some that they would bring up the more intimate aspect of her dealings with Ethan, a new feeling had burrowed under her skin, causing the muscles in her shoulders to twitch. Frowning, she sipped at her tea, trying to make sense of it. It had all the flavor of guilt. But why guilt? She thought back over the past minutes, trying to understand. It was when she recalled Sylvia mentioning the aftermath of their efforts that she realized just what it was that had her uncomfortable and itchy: If she failed to locate the jewels and they infiltrated Dionysus in a last-ditch attempt to save Julia, it could destroy the place's reputation. That fact, of course, had certainly never bothered her before.

Why, then, did it now feel wrong?

She stared down into her cup and the dregs submerged beneath the amber surface. Wrong? There was nothing wrong with what they planned. The club was responsible for the hell that Julia was going through. If not for their crooked tables, her dear sister-in-law would not now be facing possible transportation or death. Yes, it was Julia's employer's actions that had put Julia in this position. That woman had been the one to offer up the jewels as collateral, after all, and was now threatening Julia if said jewels were not recovered—something she had to know Julia had no control over.

But if not for the fact that the gaming had been rigged in the first place, her sister-in-law would not now be living in daily fear.

Yet even as she tried to reawaken the same outrage she'd had when she'd first learned of the hell Julia was being subjected to, she found it was a weak thing. Why? Nothing she had seen or heard thus far during her time at Dionysus had given her reason to regret doing whatever was necessary to recover the jewels.

Well, that is not exactly true, is it? The small, quiet question floated about in her mind, almost like a scolding. Hadn't Ethan shown her incredible tenderness and care? But more than that—for she could not go solely off of their time spent in intimate congress, for God's sake—others showed him an extraordinary amount of respect and ease. He was a man people trusted.

While it was well known in society that he was feared for his power, that he could make a man wet himself with one well-timed glower, his effect on those weaker than he seemed to suggest something else entirely. From the kitchen maid, Mary, to Mr. Ferris heading the boxing ring build to Mr. Kendal in charge of the playbills and advertisements, she had seen him treat them with nothing but respect. Something that showed in their comfortable way of interacting with him, in the relaxed lines of their faces when they spoke to him, and in the way they went about their work without fear. If he was at the root of the cheating, she had not seen a hint of it.

The next moment she downed the remainder of her tea in one long swallow, using the burn of the hot liquid to shock herself back to her senses. What, did she expect the man to advertise that he was a swindler? One could be kind to those working for one and at the same time steal from others. Didn't even the worst criminals have people they had fooled into thinking they could not possibly be guilty?

No matter how she tried to tell herself that Ethan was the great big villain that she had gone into this believing him to be, she could not reconcile that image with that of the man who had held her so tenderly after she had fallen apart in his arms.

"You are strangely quiet this afternoon," Sylvia said in her ear.

"What? Oh!" Heloise's face burned as she turned a wide, false smile Sylvia's way. "My apologies. I'm afraid I was woolgathering."

"No apologies needed, my dear," the other woman replied gently.

That gentleness gave Heloise pause. While Sylvia was kind to them all, while she cared for them all, gentleness was not part and parcel of her personality.

Euphemia leaned forward and handed her a plate full of pastries and fruit.

"Woolgathering is all well and good, but you must eat," she said with sternness colored liberally with affection. "I don't believe you ate a bite this morning before our departure, and I know you did not eat after your return." She grinned. "I asked."

Laney gave her a look of mock horror. "You braved asking Strachan?"

"What, do you think I would willingly don that particular hair shirt?" Euphemia's laughter was like bells, a strange thing indeed coming from her lips, seeing as she still wore the makeup that had changed her from a sweet, unobtrusive woman to the quietly handsome Herbert.

"No," she continued, "I asked Helena in the kitchens." She took up a strawberry and plopped it into her mouth, giving them all a look that said, *And I shall do the same for all of you if you don't eat your fill.*

The next half hour passed pleasantly, with no more mention of Dionysus or anything relating to their plans for that place. Which should have eased Heloise's mind. Yet she could not help noticing that, on occasion, the other women sent curious, concerned glances her way. *Perhaps it's nothing*, she told herself firmly as Iris, in the process of reaching for a small sandwich, looked at her out of the corner of her eye. *Mayhap I'm imagining things*, she thought as Euphemia's laugh faltered ever so slightly when she looked her way.

But she could not ignore the strange way Laney pressed her hand, nor the tighter-than-normal hug Euphemia gave her when they bade each other farewell. They knew, they all knew, and were worried about her, a realization that should have given her some relief that she did not have to tell them but instead filled her with dismay that they could not even stomach bringing the subject up to her. None of them had wanted her to seduce Ethan, after all. But she had seen no other way.

"Oh, but I need to get out of this disguise," Euphemia said, tugging at the limp cravat at her throat. "I feel positively filthy."

"Shall I help you?" Iris asked, hurrying toward her, nearly upending the whole of the tea table in the process in her eagerness.

"Absolutely," Euphemia replied with a smile. Waving their goodbyes, the two women left, Laney quickly following. Leaving Sylvia and Heloise quite alone.

And then Sylvia, patting Heloise's arm, made to leave as well. And Heloise found she couldn't take it a moment longer.

"Is no one going to ask me how things are going with Mr. Sinclaire?"

She tried her best to raise her head high and feign unconcern. But her voice wobbled horribly until it faded off entirely, a complete and utter betrayal. Sylvia heard it, if the way she pressed her lips together in compassion was any indication.

"Anyone can see you succeeded," she said gently. "Just as anyone can see that you don't wish to discuss it."

She came to stand before Heloise and took her hand. Now that they had gotten it out in the open, Heloise could see the stark worry in the other woman's eyes. Warmth filled her chest, tears burning her eyes. She could not recall the last time anyone had worried about her.

Oh, she was certain that at one time, when she had been small, her mother had worried for her, loved her. But then she had died, and her father had been too busy surviving to think of his only daughter. When he had died several years later and she had gone to live with her uncle and his wife, they had let her know in no uncertain terms that she was under their protection only due to familial duty. So she had kept her head down and worked hard to justify her place in their home. When she had left their house and married Gregory, his only concerns had been for his sister and his business, in that order. His wife, he had been fond of saying, was like a well-made broadsword, useful and strong and not needing much maintenance. She had been proud of it then. It had meant she had succeeded in earning her place in his life.

Now, however, with Sylvia looking at her as if she truly mattered, with the memory of the concern in the other Widows' eyes still fresh in her mind, she saw it for the empty success it had been.

"I will, of course, be here for you should you wish to talk things over," Sylvia said before Heloise could begin to understand this new ache coursing through her chest. "As will any of us. You know we are here for you."

Feeling suddenly raw and vulnerable in the face of such kindness, Heloise cleared the tears from her throat and pulled her hand from the other woman's grasp. "Thank you, Sylvia."

"Of course," she murmured with a small smile. The worry adding to the lines of her face, however, did not ease. If anything, those lines deepened, bracketing her mouth, hugging her eyes. "But know that, should Mr. Sinclaire mistreat you in any way, you need only say the word and we shall converge on Dionysus with all the fury of…well, the Furies."

Laughing softly, she winked and made her way from the room, leaving Heloise to thoughts that were much too tender for her to know what to do with.

16

"Mr. Sinclaire, sir?"

Ethan, having managed to snatch only a couple of hours of fitful sleep after his return from the ride in Hyde Park, started at the sound of Russell Keely's voice. He glanced up to find the young man standing in the doorway of his office, looking as if he had been there for some time trying to gain his attention. Damn it all to ever-loving hell, he really had to start being more aware of his surroundings. This being distracted at all hours of the day and night was not conducive to keeping his head, something that was imperative when Dionysus's future was on the line. Not to mention his own sanity where Heloise was concerned.

But the man wouldn't be here now, mere minutes before they opened for the night, if it wasn't important. And considering the particular tasks Ethan had set him on—as well the grave look in his eyes—Ethan suddenly found he was not the least bit tired.

"Come in," he said, motioning the young man to the seat before his desk. Keely, cap in hand, closed the door tightly behind him before doing as he was bade.

"Shall I assume," Ethan continued as the other man

settled into his chair, trying to ignore the tension threading through his shoulders, "that you have something imperative to impart?" And which of the tasks he had given Keely was he here to report on?

"Aye." Keely twisted his cap in his hands, fairly strangling it. "But do you want the boring information first, or the not-so-boring information?"

Ethan blinked. Well, he certainly hadn't expected that. "Er, the not-so-boring information, I suppose?"

Keely pressed his lips tight and nodded. "Righto, then." He took a deep breath, as if steadying himself for an unpleasant task. Which only made Ethan more anxious, something he had not thought possible.

"The grumblings are getting louder about Dionysus's trustworthiness," the other man stated, almost apologetically. "Most are quick to defend the club. And I've done my best to silence what I can. But that hasn't stopped the few outliers."

Ethan cursed softly, leaning back in his chair and running a hand over his face. Like a drop of ink in a bucket of crystal-clear water, a few outliers were all it took to pollute everything. He'd seen it ruin a good many men, destroying their livelihoods, like woodworm in the support beams of a house.

"It's all well and good to say there is gossip about our tables," he said now, not bothering to hide his frustration. "But what exactly are they saying? Where is this information originating from? I cannot fight it if it's so damn vague."

Keely shrugged. "So far they look to be servants to upper-crust employers. Which most likely means it's their employers that are talking behind closed doors, and the servants are getting wind of it."

Ethan went cold. Damn it all to ever-loving hell, if the blasted ton got wind of this, Dionysus was done for. He despised the aristocracy with everything in him, which was why he had no qualms about taking their money from them. If the spoiled fops wished to throw away their inheritance at Dionysus's tables, who was he to complain?

But if those same aristocrats began to distrust Dionysus, they would take their business elsewhere. And Dionysus would cease to exist.

"I've done my best to find out more from them," Keely continued. "But they become close-lipped when I pry." He pursed his lips, studying his grimy fingernails. "Mayhap if I had the blunt to cross their palms, I might get somewhere…" He let the sentence trail off, shooting Ethan a meaningful sideways glance.

"You know I'll give you whatever funds you require," Ethan replied, reaching into his desk drawer, pulling out a small pouch and tossing it at Keely. The other man caught it, testing the weight of it in his palm, giving a satisfied nod as it jingled merrily.

"There's a bit of something for me as well here, I take it?" he queried.

Ethan raised a brow. "Naturally," he drawled.

"That'll do then, I'm thinking," the other man said with a grin.

"Just be quick about it." Ethan frowned down at the broadsheet currently laid out on his desk, the illustration of Mrs. Laney Finch and her opponent, Mrs. Holburn, in full pugilistic poses staring up at him. "I want to get this straightened out before the masquerade and boxing match." God knew the damage this insidious gossip could cause if it remained unchecked.

He eyed Keely, who was still focused raptly on the bag

of coins in his hand. "And now for the boring bit of news?" he prompted.

"Aye, that." The other man cleared his throat, tucking the coin bag in an inside pocket of his coat with deft fingers. "You had me looking into Mrs. Heloise Marlow."

And the tension was back. It was natural for him to wish to learn all he could about Heloise; even if he hadn't been suspicious as hell of her, she was an unknown gaining access to his club, working in close concert with him. He would do the same with anyone coming into Dionysus's purview, and had, often.

Why, then, did he feel so damn guilty?

"Truthfully," Keely said, blissfully unaware of the mental torture Ethan was putting himself through, "I guess it's not exactly boring information. The lady has led a hell of a life." He chuckled.

Ethan narrowed his eyes. "Explain."

Keely held up a hand, ticking off items on his fingers. "Orphaned at a young age; sent to live with her uncle, who she learned blacksmithing from; married the famed fencer Marlow at eighteen and worked in his fencing salon alongside him." He chuckled, a hint of admiration in it. "It's not an ordinary life for a female, is it?"

No, it wasn't. Which was why Ethan had expected some manner of deviation from what little she had told him.

And yet everything thus far matched up exactly. He should not feel such relief. Yet here he was.

"Then Marlow died some two and a half years ago," Keely continued. "His widow tried to keep the salon afloat but couldn't. That's when she joined the Wimpole Street Widows Society."

Ethan blinked. "The what?"

"Wimpole Street Widows Society, a fanciful name

really for what seems nothing more than a harmless group of widows living together. The Viscountess Vastkern began it some years ago. She brings in all manner of women who have nowhere to go after their husbands give up the ghost." He jerked his head in the direction of the broadsheet on Ethan's desk. "Mrs. Laney Finch is part of it, too, as well as several other odd females. There's not a typical one in the bunch." Again that laugh. "Which I suppose is why they all band together, like a flock of hens." He paused, tilting his head. "Do hens flock?"

Ignoring the question, Ethan sat forward, resting his elbows on the desktop, steepling his hands in thought. It would certainly explain why Heloise was so close not only to Mrs. Finch but to Lady Vastkern as well. And why she had been given the job of Mrs. Finch's manager when she had absolutely no experience in the sport.

That relief that had settled in his shoulders sank deeper, melting into his bones at this proof that his suspicions of her had thus far proven completely unfounded. *Don't let your guard down*, he warned himself severely. But it was a weak warning, barely heard over the rushing in his ears.

Which was why he forced himself to say, "Look into the Wimpole Street Widows Society."

Keely, who had been lovingly patting the bag of money in his coat pocket, looked up sharply. The man was not stupid, though he might like to pretend otherwise, and understood far more than he let on. A talent that was invaluable to Ethan, especially in moments such as these.

"Aye," he said, short and succinct, before he rose and made his way from the office. Ethan remained at his desk, listening to the sounds of his footsteps receding down the hall. Soon those footsteps were overtaken by the noise from below, the evening's patrons already arriving for their night of revelry and sin. Which meant Heloise would soon be here.

His heart gave a strange, eager lurch in his chest. He should not be looking forward to her arrival as much as he was. But no amount of stern thoughts could have stopped him from hurrying from his desk into his bedroom, to the large window that looked down onto St James's and the general chaos of a night just begun. He should be concerned as hell at his actions. He was not some inexperienced green boy. And yet that was just how he was acting, thinking with certain parts of his anatomy that should *not* be doing his thinking for him.

Though Keely's report on Heloise had been innocuous enough, Ethan knew he should not be letting down his guard. He should instead be exercising even more caution than before. Something wasn't entirely right; he had felt it from the very beginning. And though his suspicions had quieted some—hell, they'd quieted more than *some*, and would have disappeared altogether if he had not learned about the peculiar Wimpole Street Widows Society—he still wasn't totally convinced that she was innocent of all subterfuge.

It should not be so hard, however, to hold on to that doubt. He ran a hand over his face. Mayhap entering into this affair had been a bad idea. He could not afford to lose control of himself like this. Perhaps he should end it. He had believed that, by playing into her hand in allowing her to seduce him, he could force her to let down her guard and reveal what she had planned for Dionysus. Now that he was flirting with the possibility that Heloise was no threat to him and his, however, he should break things off with her, this time to protect his sanity.

Yet when he thought of her, eyes heavy lidded and lips

swollen from his kisses, ending their affair was the very last thing he wanted to do.

He placed his palms flat on the cold glass of the window, looking down at the long line of carriages below but not seeing them. What, was he so emotionally and physically weak that her kisses sent his mind completely packing? Was he so overwhelmed by the idea of holding her in his arms again that he could not think straight? Truly, one would think he was falling in love with her.

He snorted. That right there was the exact reason he should not end this affair, if only to prove to himself that he was most definitely *not* falling in love with her. Yes, he thought as he straightened away from the window, he would continue this affair and squash any idiotic idea that he was becoming smitten with her. He had never run from anything before in his life. He was most certainly not going to start now.

Though, he admitted ruefully to himself, recalling his reaction to her just that morning, perhaps it would be best if he pulled back some. Letting his desire have free rein over him was not necessarily conducive to clear thinking. Tonight he needed to keep his cock in his pants for as long as possible while in her presence.

A faint knock sounded, and he turned to find Heloise standing in the doorway to his suite. If the way his body reacted to her small smile was any indication, it might not be long at all.

17

From the look in Ethan's eyes when she walked through the door to his suite, Heloise had been certain that he was going to kiss her. The heat in his gaze fairly scorched her, and she felt an answering flame spark to life deep in her belly.

But no matter how much she might wish for him to take her in his arms—and she did wish it, much more than was at all healthy for her peace of mind—she had come here determined to implement the next part of her plan: leveraging herself into areas of the club where she would not otherwise be permitted, to locate the jewelry for Julia.

But he did not move to kiss her. Instead he planted his feet wide as if preparing for a blow and asked with a strange awkwardness, "Did you come with Mrs. Finch and Lady Vastkern?"

She blinked at his strangled tone. "Er, yes," she replied, shifting from foot to foot, finding it strangely difficult to keep from rushing to him—truly, what the devil was wrong with her? "They're in the private gaming room. They're so thrilled to have been invited, they may make it their second home." She laughed, but it came out more like the wheeze from the bellows in her forge, so tight was her chest.

He nodded distractedly and motioned to the office behind her. "Shall we have a drink?"

God yes. The answer fairly screamed through her mind, loud and desperate. While she had planned to keep herself from his bed as long as possible, it was growing increasingly difficult as she looked at him.

"That would be lovely," she replied instead, with what she thought was impressive poise considering the very loud voice in her head urging her to just kiss him already. Silencing that voice as best she could, she retreated to his office, finding a seat as he moved to the sideboard. For a long moment silence reigned, broken only by the faint sounds of the patrons arriving below and the soft tinkle of glass as he poured their drinks. Which only increased the tension threading through Heloise, so much so that, when he returned to her side and handed her the glass, she snatched it from him, the amber liquid nearly sloshing over the rim. Bringing it to her lips with hands that shook ever so faintly, she downed the lot in one long gulp. The burn of it traveled down her throat, through her chest, hitting her nearly empty stomach. There. That should distract her from the fantasy of dragging Ethan back to his bedroom and having her way with him.

But when she lowered the glass, she discovered he was still standing in front of her, hand outstretched, surprise lifting his brows. And she found that just one glass wouldn't do in erasing her desire for this man.

"Do you…wish for another?" he asked, apparently reading her mind.

Her face heated. "Yes, please. Actually," she continued as he reached for her empty glass, holding it tight to her chest like a bit of crystal armor, "why don't you bring the whole decanter? I'm feeling particularly parched this evening."

His brow quirked up with a combination of curiosity and amusement, but he did as she bade. When he returned and poured her a second glass, she managed to gain enough control over herself to sip from it with a modicum of poise. Thank God.

"How is your cousin adapting to working with Mr. Ferris?" he asked as he deposited the decanter on a low table nearby and sat in the chair beside her. She choked on the liquor, wholly unprepared for mention of Euphemia—or *Cousin Herbert*, as Ethan would know her—the brandy doing much worse than burning as she fought to dislodge it from her windpipe. Ethan reached across the small space between them, pounding on her back to assist. That, however, only managed to add to her distress. Truly, could she be more awkward?

Finally, blessedly, her chest cleared enough for her to wave him off. "I'm fine," she croaked. With clumsy fingers she wiped at her streaming eyes. "But you were asking about my cousin." The words came out strangled, and she cleared the last of the brandy from her throat. "He's adjusting well, thank you. Quite excited to learn all he can from Mr. Ferris. It was kind of him to take Herbert on."

Ethan, who was still looking at Heloise with a healthy dose of concern, nevertheless settled back into his seat. "Ferris is a good man," he said, taking a sip of his own drink. He regarded her over the rim, a shuttered look dropping over his eyes. "But if you have family close by, I'm surprised you agreed to live with Lady Vastkern."

Heloise froze. The comment was harmless enough, but an underlying current indicated there was something more to the words than met the eye. Then she realized: She had never told him she lived with Sylvia.

It was a warning, plain and simple: He was telling her

that he had looked into her background. She was, of course, not unduly worried that he would uncover anything damning about the Wimpole Street Widows Society. Sylvia was a master at making certain their tracks were covered, that they appeared for all intents and purposes an odd group of widowed women banding together for support and camaraderie.

Yet that didn't ease the tension that pulled her every nerve tight as she considered Ethan. She had almost forgotten how dangerous the man was. But she would not forget it again. Just as she would not lose sight of why she was here in the first place.

He was watching her closely to see what her reaction to his revelation would be. But, after two years under Sylvia's tutelage, she was no longer a novice.

"If you are looking to shock me with knowledge I never gave you," she said, "you will have a long wait."

His eyes narrowed, his lips kicking up in one corner. "Is that so?"

She nodded. "It would be strange, after all, for someone in your position to remain ignorant of those surrounding him. It makes perfect sense that you would wish to protect Dionysus."

He tilted his head, taking her in from the top of her head to the tips of the slippers peeking out from under the hem of her borrowed sapphire silk gown. "I admit," he finally said, "I did not expect such a calm answer."

She gave a light laugh. "Did you expect me to fall into histrionics over something so mundane? It is no secret that I live in Lady Vastkern's home." She paused for effect. "Anything you wish to know you may ask, and I shall answer you truthfully. I have nothing to hide."

It was an outright lie, of course. And if the sardonic lift

of one of his eyebrows was any indication, he didn't believe her. But he settled back in his chair, pursing his lips. "Anything, eh?"

"Yes." Her eye caught the glint of the crystal brandy decanter, and a wholly inspired idea struck her, one that would not only hopefully quiet any suspicions he might still have about her, but would also provide her with the means to get access to the hidden parts of Dionysus. She grinned, reaching forward and grabbing the bottle, holding it up for his perusal. "But that kind of thing goes both ways, doesn't it? Why not make a game out of it? We may ask one another anything we wish. If the other person refuses, they must pay a penalty. Namely, in the form of a drink." She leaned forward, wagging the decanter back and forth so the amber liquid sloshed about. "You are a man who thrives on chance. What say you, Mr. Sinclaire?"

He grinned. She could tell he hadn't wanted to. He seemed to be fighting it with everything in him. But in the end that wonderful smile won out, transforming his face in an instant. "Very well," he replied. He downed his drink and took the bottle from her. "To see we're on even footing," he explained as he took both their glasses, making certain each had a fingerful of brandy before passing hers back.

"I'll go first, shall I?" he asked. When she nodded, he shifted in his chair, leaning toward her. "How did you come to know Lady Vastkern to such a degree that she would invite you to live in her home?"

She was prepared for this type of thing. It had been part of her training when she had first joined the Widows, how to deal with questions that might arise when in the field. The general rule was to remain as close to the truth as possible. A relief, really, as she was not the most talented when forced to think on her toes.

Even so, it took her some seconds to gather her thoughts. Settling more comfortably in her chair, she adjusted her skirts, smoothing them over her legs. Which, apparently, had the added benefit of serving as a distraction for Ethan, if the way his suddenly hot gaze followed her hands was any indication. A smile tugged at her lips at the very thought that she could affect him in such a way.

But he had asked her a question. "How did I come to know her?" She gave a small sigh, remembering the despair, the darkness. And then Sylvia, there like an angel descended from the heavens.

"My husband had been dead some months," she said softly, lost in the memory, "and I was failing horribly at keeping his fencing salon afloat. People were more than happy to learn from me when a man had been in charge of the place. But once I was the sole proprietor, they would not think of crossing the threshold." She huffed a small, humorless laugh. "Sylvia had heard about it through the normal channels of information, the gossips no doubt finding delight in the downfall of a woman they saw as reaching much too far above herself. She came to the salon just as I was about to give up, introduced herself to me, and offered me a place to stay in nearly the same breath."

She expected him to voice disbelief that she would attempt to continue the business after her husband passed—a typical response—or offer false murmurs of commiseration that held no more water than a sieve—even more typical than the first.

But he did neither, remaining silent as the seconds ticked on. She glanced up, curious, only to see an expression on his face she had never seen before, a softness she had never expected. The breath caught in her throat, not so much at the shock of seeing it, but because it made her want to crawl into his embrace and never leave.

Flustered, she looked away. "But I did not answer your question, did I?" she continued. "You were asking why Sylvia invited me into her home. The viscountess is rather eccentric and likes to surround herself with things that are strange and unusual. As I am rather strange and unusual myself, I was the perfect fit for her little menagerie." She gave a light laugh.

"So she has her own peculiar reasons for inviting you to live with her," he said softly. "But why did you accept?"

The question gave her pause. Not because he'd asked it; it had been completely natural to do so, she supposed.

But the truth of the matter was, she had never really asked *herself* why she had agreed to Sylvia's offer. Yes, her life had been falling down about her ears, her future in a shambles. And yes, Sylvia had offered her a comfortable home where she could pursue her passions to her heart's content. It made perfect sense through such a narrow lens.

But to live in the Wimpole Street house, she had been required to join the Widows in their work, an enterprise that had shocked her to her core when Sylvia had told her of it. And one that she had quickly learned could be dangerous, that took cunning and skill and all manner of talents that she was even now lacking. A thought that had her feeling much too raw and vulnerable.

"Who would not wish to live with a viscountess?" she replied lightly, noncommittally, before fixing him with a stern glare. "Ah, but that is a second question, isn't it?" She wagged a finger at him. "Enough of that. It's my turn now."

He narrowed his eyes, looking as if he would argue with her. But in the end he dipped his head in acknowledgement and indicated with a sweep of his hand that she could proceed.

Hiding a smile, she pursed her lips and pretended to consider it. Not that she had much to consider. This little game was hers, after all.

"How did you meet your partners?" she asked now.

He smiled some. Just with the corner of his mouth, barely enough for it to be considered a smile. But there was something like ghosts in his eyes. The expression took her aback, for it was as if a deep, dull pain lurked beneath the surface, a presence that might rise up and swallow him whole if given a chance.

A dull throbbing started in her chest, and she fought the urge to rub at it. What was this emotion? Concern? Pity? Neither would be conducive to her plans. Shaking off the feeling as best she could, she tried for a light tone as she said, "Remember, if you choose not to answer, you must pay the penalty."

She was rewarded with the slightest deepening of the lines radiating from the corners of his eyes, the scattering of those ghosts in his gaze. "Oh, I'll answer," he replied. "Like you, I've nothing to hide. And the story is well known, anyway. You may have heard I grew up in…difficult circumstances." He waited for her to nod, which she did. Who hadn't heard that he had come from the seedier part of London and risen from the literal gutter? It was part of what drew the nobility to Dionysus, that prospect of flirting with the taboo.

"We ran in the same crowd, Teagan and Parsons and I," he continued, his gaze taking on a faraway, haunted look, as if he were witnessing those days once more. "And my brothers, of course. In fact, nearly everyone who works for me is connected in some way to those days." He paused. "I hoped that connection would ingrain a sense of loyalty in those who work here."

The words fell off, heavy and somber. She had seen that loyalty for herself, had even commented on it. But the dark air coming off him revealed something completely different was going on. Was there disloyalty within Dionysus? She recalled then Julia's tear-streaked face, her insistence that the club's tables had been crooked. Add to that how much the club obviously meant to Ethan, and doubts began to creep in, like tendrils of smoke beneath a closed door, warning of danger on the other side. Was his pain connected to all that, then? Had he heard rumors as well that something unsavory was afoot at his club? Was he not, in fact, part of the corruption within Dionysus, but a victim of it?

Another moment and she shook herself back to her senses. Ethan was not a victim. Commiserating with him, pitying him, would only lead to failure. There was too much at stake, her promise to her late husband and Julia's safety and her position in the Widows included.

That, however, did not stop the small roots of doubt that had crept into her heart.

But she had been silent too long. She shifted in her seat, shooting him a covert glance. He, however, did not seem to notice her distraction, his morose gaze fixed quite firmly on the still-full glass in his hands. She should not feel compassion for this man. She should continue to direct their little game down the path that would give her the outcome she desired.

But nothing could have stopped her from trying to smooth the strange sadness from his brow.

Scooting forward in her chair, she reached out and laid a hand on his arm. He started, looking at it bemusedly.

"Tell me how you met them," she said softly. "What was your friendship like? And this still counts as my one question," she continued louder when he looked up at her. "For you truly haven't answered me."

A spark of amusement lit his gaze. "Is that so? Well then, to save myself from a penalty, I'd better answer, hadn't I?"

She moved to settle back in her chair, strangely pleased at herself for having put a smile, however small, on his lips. When her hand would have fallen from his sleeve, he grabbed it, holding it in place. His large, scarred fingers traced hers, sending shivers of need pulsing through her, and it took every bit of her willpower to focus on his words and not on how his touch affected her.

"I don't recall the exact date," he continued, voice low and almost as hypnotic as his touch. "I was five. My ma had just given birth to Gavin, and she couldn't deal with a rambunctious child underfoot. So I was sent out to find my own adventures. And I did, in the form of two equally dirty, equally wild hellions. We were inseparable after that." He chuckled softly, then quickly sobered, fingers rubbing absently at a scar on the back of her hand. "They were at my side when Ma had Isaac the following year, and when my pa left shortly after that. They helped me gain access to the seedier gaming hells so I might try and use my talents at cards to support my family. And they were there to nurse me back to health when I nearly died."

That, finally, broke the spell of his fingers on her skin. She sat up straighter. "You almost died? What happened?"

He grinned and wagged his finger in her face, a blatant imitation of what she had done to him. "Now, now. I have answered your question. You wouldn't wish to be unfair by not allowing me *my* turn, would you?"

Oh, he was maddening. Shooting him a scowl—her curiosity was quite thoroughly piqued—she pulled her hand from his and flopped ungraciously back in her chair. "Very well," she grumbled. "What do you wish to ask me?"

He chuckled, then sobered, gaze intense on her. "How did you meet your husband?"

She blinked. "Gregory? You wish to know about Gregory?"

"Unless you wish to take your penalty," he murmured, indicating with a jut of his chin the still-full glass in her hand.

"Oh, no," she declared. "Those two drinks have already gone to my head, and I don't fancy another. Besides, I vowed you could ask me anything."

She cleared her throat, shifting in her seat, her mind already traveling back in time, to places she would be more than happy to forget. "To tell you about Gregory, though, I suppose I shall have to first explain what led me to his doorstep. You probably know from the information you gleaned about my past"—here she paused and gave him a pointed look, to which he dipped his head in acknowledgement without the slightest hint of sheepishness—"that I was an orphan, that I was sent to my uncle's house when I was young, that I learned blacksmithing from him. But they had more than their fair share of mouths to feed, and I was not welcome. My aunt, particularly, was eager to see me gone, and was quite fond of letting me know in no uncertain terms that the sooner I came of age and left her house, the happier she would be. My cousins followed her lead, of course, in making me feel as unwelcome as possible. And so I soon became as eager for the day of my departure as they were."

It was meant as a kind of dark humor, this way of explaining why she had left her uncle's home the moment she'd been able to. Yet Ethan did not seem to see it that way. He looked at her with something like sadness shadowing the depths of his eyes. "And you had no one else?" he asked. "No siblings? No grandparents? Not even a friend?"

"Not a one," she replied.

"It sounds to be a horribly lonely existence for a child."

She blinked, for she had never thought of it that way. She

had been surrounded by family, after all, her uncle and aunt and cousins.

Yet she truly had been lonely, hadn't she? "I suppose I was," she replied quietly, suddenly aware of a deep ache in her chest that seemed to have been there for far longer than she had realized.

"But I did my best to be useful to them," she continued, flustered by the foreign emotions bombarding her, her explanation of the situation more a reminder to herself than for him. "Affection cannot be expected, after all. I had to earn my place with them."

But her words did not alleviate his peculiarly mournful mood as she'd intended. If anything, they seemed to deepen it. "No one should have to earn their place in anyone's life, most especially a child."

Shouldn't they? But his quiet words were dredging up emotions she would rather not confront just then. Needing to regain control of the conversation, as well as her rapidly thawing heart, she continued. "When my uncle grew sick and was nearing the end of his life, I knew it was only a matter of time before I was thrown out onto the streets. By this time my fascination with weaponry had taken over everything else. I was haunting Gregory's fencing studio, watching his classes from the street. I finally screwed up the courage to introduce myself, to offer up a partnership of sorts: I would supply him his weaponry and mend his blades and do anything else he needed around his salon if he would offer me a place to stay. He counteroffered: We could marry, a marriage of convenience of sorts, and form a true business partnership." She shrugged. "And that, as they say, was that."

"You make it sound so simple," he murmured.

"I suppose it was. It all fell into place, after all."

"Fell into place?" Disbelief colored his words. He took

up her hand, his fingers warm around her own, giving her a comfort she hadn't expected to receive. "I think you underestimate the strength of character it took to forge ahead when it seemed the world was against you."

Which was so unexpectedly kind, she was unable to speak for several long moments. Flustered, yet unable to bring herself to remove her hand from his, she continued.

"Anyway, though it was not a love match, we grew to become good friends. The time I spent married to him and working alongside him in his salon was a blessing." Then, to remind herself why she was here in the first place, she said a bit louder, a bit more forcefully, "And I gained true family in the form of Gregory's sister. I would do anything for Julia."

Which naturally guided her to her next question. She *wanted* to ask him how he had nearly died. She *wanted* to ask him about the brother he had lost.

But this was not about what she wanted, was it?

"And now it is my turn once more," she declared. Then, taking a deep breath, she asked, "Will you bring me someplace within Dionysus I haven't been before?"

His eyebrows shot up, his surprise at the request evident. "That question is hardly within the rules of the game."

"I said we may ask the other anything we may wish, and if the other refuses, they must pay a penalty. I did not specify that the thing we ask must have a verbal answer."

A bark of laughter escaped his lips. "You're a sly minx, aren't you?" he murmured with more than a hint of admiration. He stood and held out a hand to her. "Come along, then."

Heart pounding in her ears, she took his hand and rose, and together they made their way from his office.

18

As it happened, the place Ethan brought her was somewhere she had already been. He, of course, wouldn't know that, seeing as she had been hidden behind the velvet sofa for the majority of her previous visit.

Yet she couldn't bring herself to dredge up even the slightest bit of disappointment. She told herself the warm glow of pleasure she felt as he guided her into the owners' suite with a gentle hand to the small of her back was from triumph. After all, her plan to infiltrate the inner workings of the club via becoming his lover was working splendidly.

But she knew, deep down, that wasn't what had her chest filling with emotion. No, it had nothing to do with her schemes, and everything to do with the fact that he was letting her in. Something she felt instinctively he did not do easily.

A pang of guilt wormed its way in then: Wasn't she going to betray him in the end? Wasn't this all heading toward complete destruction?

She flinched, an unconscious reaction to the battle being waged in her, so violent it caught his attention. He stilled at her side.

"Is something wrong?"

Ah, God. At this rate all her efforts would be for naught, her damn conscience threatening everything. *Pull yourself together, Heloise.* Forcing her lips up in a smile, she gazed about her as if seeing it for the first time. Which, as far as he knew, she was.

"I'm just shocked, is all," she replied. "I never imagined a place like this existed. You can see the whole of the casino floor from here."

And she could. Walking to the large, tinted window, she took in the scene before her. While she had seen something of this view on her previous visit, it had been nothing like this. Then, the gaming floor had been quiet, the tables empty, the chandeliers dark. Now, however, the whole scene was lit up with the brilliance of the sun, the floor crowded with people, each table surrounded by men who laughed and shouted and talked in a cacophony of sound. It was an undulating mass of fine black wool and jewel-colored silk, like the constant churning of waves against the shore. Placing her hands flat on the glass, heart pounding with a strange excitement, she peered down.

"Goodness," she breathed. "It's…it's…"

"Chaotic, I know," he murmured, coming up beside her, humor coloring his words.

She looked at him then, saw the pride in his eyes as he took in his kingdom. "Actually," she said with utmost honesty, surprised at how true the words were, "I was going to say it's beautiful."

He blinked, looking at her. "Beautiful?"

"Certainly." She indicated the whole of the scene with a sweep of her hand. "The excitement, the drama, the richness and the splendor." She paused, surprised at how much she meant it. Then, because she couldn't help herself, she said, "It's a work of art."

He considered her for a long minute, the muted gold light of the chandeliers that soared over the gaming floor catching in the angles of his face, casting dancing shadows across his features, making it difficult to distinguish whether her words pleased or offended him. She soon had her answer as, giving a low groan, he hooked a hand behind the nape of her neck and pulled her against him, claiming her lips with his own. The muted taste of brandy washed over her tongue, making her mouth water. The next minute, however, she gasped, pulling back sharply.

"Someone might see," she managed, sending a meaningful look at the glass wall and the mass of men below in all their evening finery. A familiar burly figure caught her attention, Mr. Copper, the floor manager, deep in conversation with someone. Just then he glanced up, toward the window, toward *her*. Did he see them? Surprised, she involuntarily took a step back.

When she looked toward Ethan, however, her worry melted away like ice on sunbaked pavement. There was no mistaking his expression for anything but what it was: a hot, intense desire. For her. She shivered, though her body felt consumed by flames, and gripped her hands tight together to keep from reaching out for him.

"We keep the lights low in this room," he explained, "to prevent those below from seeing in. That, along with the bright lights of the casino floor and this tinted glass, is enough to keep it quite private in here."

She cast a glance about the room, but there were no gas lamps here. No, there was only a low fire in the hearth, hardly giving off a glow, casting most of the suite in shadow. It gave the space a surprisingly intimate feeling despite the crush of humanity on the other side of the window. Her heart pounded in her chest in a strange anticipation.

"But," he continued, his voice gone husky, "to add a bit of safety…"

He went to one side of the window, grasping the gossamer drapes there, pulling them across the expanse of the wall so that only the most brilliant of the chandelier lights reached them. Then, taking her hand in his, he pulled her with him farther into the shadows before, snaking an arm about her waist, he drew her flush against his body. "No one can see in," he murmured. "Anything can happen in this room, and no one will be the wiser." He smiled again, and she felt it down to her toes. "I even had the wherewithal to lock and bolt the door."

She *should* say something witty or clever to distract him. She *should* push him away and ask all the questions she needed to about this private area of the club, a place she had hoped, in her seduction of him, that she would be invited into.

She, however, did neither of those things. Instead she reached up, grabbed his face in her hands, and dragged him down for a kiss.

It was all the encouragement he needed. Groaning into her mouth, he stumbled his way to a couch tucked in the darkest corner, then dropped down onto it, pulling her astride him. Then his hand was between them, opening the fall of his trousers, and he was guiding himself inside her.

"Bloody hell," he ground out through tightly clenched teeth as his fingers moved to her hips, bringing her down fully on him.

It was a sentiment Heloise herself would have willingly echoed, had she not been completely devoid of a voice. They stayed that way for a time, breaths ragged. Her inner muscles pulsed around his shaft, and he jumped inside her in response.

"Our game is still not done," he suddenly said, breath hot on her neck.

Still focused quite thoroughly on the feel of him inside her, she did not immediately understand what he said. When she finally did comprehend it, she pulled back and gaped at him. "You still wish to play that game? Are you mad?"

He laughed, the sound strained. "Most likely. I have never in my life done something like this. But it's my turn, is it not?"

"Yes." She gasped as he shifted beneath her, angling himself even deeper within her. "W-what do you want to ask of me?"

With the small portion of her mind still capable of coherent thought, she half expected him to request something intimate in nature. But instead he asked, "How many have there been for you after your husband?"

"Just you," she breathed. "There has only been you."

"Oh God, Heloise," he groaned a moment before, hand hooking around the nape of her neck, he dragged her down for a kiss. And it was not just any kiss, but one of desperation, of need. It branded her, that kiss, as surely as a hot poker pulled from her forge would.

Nearly mindless now, her fingers began working desperately at his clothes, tugging and pushing them from his body. His fingers were busy, too, moving with impressive dexterity down the long column of buttons at her back. Soon the only articles of clothing left on her body were her silk stockings.

She should feel wicked, naked in his arms as she was, with half the men of the ton on the opposite side of the thin pane of glass. Instead, as he pulled her tight against him and the hard, hot expanse of his chest pressed against her sensitive breasts and quivering stomach, she found she could only think how deliciously right this was.

"You feel like heaven," he breathed.

She smiled and kissed his shoulder, a thrill going through her when he groaned and buried his face in her neck. Snaking her arms about his back, she pressed her fingers into the broad expanse. But the skin beneath her fingertips wasn't smooth. In fact, it was rough, a veritable map of ridges. She frowned, momentarily distracted from the feel of him filling her...

Until he pressed an openmouthed kiss to her collarbone. His hands were tight on her hips as he began to move her on him, and she had no more time to think.

"Ride me, sweetheart," he pleaded hoarsely.

She did as he begged, holding tight to him, her hips moving seemingly of their own volition, the friction at the very heart of her building. His low moans and harsh breaths and large hands on her body played in concert with the sensation, and she quickly came apart, splintering into a million pieces. She had no sooner descended back to earth than Ethan lifted her from his member, quickly spending himself in a handkerchief before pulling her back into his arms, holding her more tenderly than she had ever been held in her life.

Some time later—it could have been minutes or centuries for all Heloise knew—she shifted in Ethan's arms, achingly aware of their hearts slowing in concert with one another's, as well as her body's utter unwillingness to move. And so, snuggling closer, smiling as his arms tightened ever so slightly about her, she began a slow, languorous stroking of his sweat-slicked back—only to feel those peculiar ridges against her fingertips again.

She frowned, tracing them, trying to deduce what they

could be. Which was perhaps too obvious; he suddenly stilled beneath her. His hands, which had been doing their own slow exploration, stilled as well, splaying across her back. Face heating, she was about to blurt out an apology when he spoke.

"It's your turn, you know," he murmured, his lips brushing against her neck in the most maddening fashion.

She blinked. "What?"

"Your turn. For our game." He took her shoulders in his hands then, gently pushing her back far enough that he could look her in the eye. "You can ask me something. If you wish." His lips quirked then, his eyes sparkling ruefully in the low light. "If you're not fainthearted, that is."

"You can be assured," she declared automatically, "I am not the least bit fainthearted."

He lifted one eyebrow. Yet she saw the glimmer of something vulnerable beneath it all. He was giving her permission to ask him something that must be quite sensitive, offering to open himself up to her. Her heart swelled.

Even so, she found it difficult to outright ask why his skin was so marred. He must have seen her hesitation; after a pause, he sighed softly and set her on the couch beside him before turning slightly so she might witness what she had only felt.

How she managed to keep from gasping in shock, she would never know. She had seen her fair number of wounds and scars, of course. Working in her uncle's smithy for so many years, she had been witness to countless burns and cuts, not to mention the broken bones her uncle had set and the gashes he had stitched, a blacksmith's job not stopping at mere metalworking.

But this was completely different. Even in the dim light she could see the angry crisscrossing of puckered skin, a veritable lattice of cruelty. With shaking fingers she reached out, traced one particularly deep gouge. He didn't so much as flinch; rather he was preternaturally still, allowing her to explore, to take it in.

"It must hurt still," she murmured thickly.

He shrugged. "Some. The skin is tight and needs frequent stretching."

She swallowed hard. "What happened?"

He turned back to her then, his lips hitching up in one corner, though there was a shadow of pain in the expression. "It's not an uncommon story," he said, voice rumbling in the dim room. He pulled her against him, giving a small sigh as she settled against his side. "I was winning at the tables of a seedy hell, and handsomely, too. I'm uncommonly good at cards, you see. It was how I supported my family after my father abandoned us, the one bit of talent I could use to keep us from starving."

He huffed a small, humorless laugh, and Heloise tightened her arm about his waist. "The owners didn't like it one bit," he continued. "They claimed they didn't have the blunt to pay me and gave me a gold watch worth far more than my winnings. I, fool that I was, accepted it, thinking only of what it could provide to make my mother's life easier. But the owners of the hell cried theft. I was arrested and whipped as punishment."

"They more than whipped you," she said through a tight throat, the image of those scars burned into her brain.

Again he laughed, though there was something bitter in it now. "It seems the man in charge of my punishment liked his job a bit too well. I nearly died as a result."

"And Mr. Teagan and Mr. Parsons were there for you," she said quietly.

"Yes. And after as well, when my mother died from the

strain of it all. She was already unwell from the stress of my father leaving her; my own misstep pushed her over the edge and finally killed her."

"Oh, Ethan," she whispered into his chest, tears burning her eyes at the echo of self-hatred in his voice. "It wasn't your fault."

But besides the faintest tightening of his fingers on her arm, he gave no sign of hearing her. "Teagan and Parsons helped me feed and clothe my brothers and keep a roof over their heads until I was healed enough to work myself." He paused. "They have been by my side for every moment of my life since I first met them until now. I would be a fool to forget that."

She frowned. Why did he seem to be explaining the whole thing to himself as much as he was explaining it to her? As if he was trying to remind himself of something in the telling of it?

But as they lay there wrapped in each other's arms, the cacophony of the club a distant buzzing in her ears, she couldn't help wondering how a man who had been so horribly wronged in the past could lower himself to cheat his own patrons. It made no sense, no sense at all. Was he as much of a victim in this as Julia was? It was a thought that both made her weak with relief and consumed her with a bitter guilt because, no matter the truth, she had to see this infiltration of his club through no matter the cost. Even if that cost could break her heart.

19

"Iris," Heloise called out the following day as she burst into the small greenhouse at the back of the Wimpole Street house. "Are you here?"

A curly blond head popped up over a particularly bushy shrub, one that Heloise would never be able to identify but that Iris no doubt knew every detail about from the tips of its shining deep green leaves to the ends of its twining roots. She blinked myopically, brushing a strand of hair from her cheek, leaving a smudge behind. "Heloise? What is it?"

Heloise stepped around a collection of heavy pots and made her way down the brick path, even as she recalled with vivid clarity the image of Ethan's heavily scarred back from the night before. Though now she had the added memory of the way he'd moved just that morning while dealing with the sundry things needed for the boxing match and the masquerade, how he'd occasionally stretched his arms or given a barely perceptible wince when the skin on his back was pulled. With Iris's knowledge of medicinal plants, she might be able to help alleviate some of the discomfort he felt from his scars. And, she belatedly reminded herself, something of that sort was certain to get him to further trust her.

"Do you have anything that would alleviate pain or tightness from old scars?" she asked now as she reached the other woman.

"Old scars?" Iris's frown quickly cleared, understanding making her eyes go wide and her mouth form a perfect oval. "Is this for Mr. Sinclaire, then?" she asked, excitement infusing her voice. "I can finally help?"

An affectionate smile curved Heloise's lips, her chest warming at the enthusiasm lighting her friend's moss green eyes. "Yes, you can finally help."

"Wonderful!" Iris exclaimed, clapping her hands together, sending a puff of dirt into the air. Then, before Heloise could so much as blink, she darted off, racing for the washbasin at the side of the greenhouse. In a matter of minutes she'd hung up her tools, removed her apron, and washed her hands. And then she was hurrying from the greenhouse without even a glance back, leaving Heloise to stare after her. Bemused, Heloise followed. By the time she reached Iris's rooms, she had already taken down a good quantity of notebooks from her overflowing shelves and was flipping through them with a speed that made Heloise dizzy.

"Just give me a moment," she murmured, eyes scanning the close, cramped text before her, fingers hurriedly turning over page after page.

Not knowing if Iris's idea of a moment constituted minutes or hours, Heloise moved to one of the many bookcases that lined the wall. A hodgepodge of items crowded the shelves, weighty tomes and sketchbooks and framed color prints of plants in various stages of development all interspersed with small jars of seeds, displays of pressed flowers, magnifying glasses and shears and tweezers. It was as Heloise was inspecting a peculiar large green metal cylinder with a strap that had been propped in the corner that Iris gave a loud exclamation of delight.

"I've found it!" She looked up at Heloise, her excitement palpable.

"Have you truly?" Heloise asked, coming closer.

Iris grinned. "Yes! And it will only take a little over a week to complete."

Heloise, who had begun to grow as excited as Iris, deflated in an instant. "A little over a week?"

Iris nodded happily, returning her attention to the open notebook before her. "If I can locate the necessary materials quickly, then yes."

"But that will be much too late. The boxing match is in just over a week, after all. And I will need it well before that."

The smile fell from Iris's face. "But the extraction. The process to extrude the oils takes time."

Time that they did not have. Heloise had felt as if a ticking clock were looming over her ever since she'd begun this charade with Ethan. Now, however, there was something more to it. Yes, she had worried when she'd begun this whole thing that she would not be able to accomplish all she needed to. After all, Lord and Lady Ayersley's anniversary ball was coming fast, the need for that blasted jewelry like an ever-tightening noose about Julia's neck. She rubbed at her own neck, thinking that such an analogy was much too close to what could actually happen to Julia if that jewelry wasn't recovered in time.

Now, however, in addition to that, the end to her affair with Ethan was coming fast, causing a dull throb of pain in her chest. Which was ridiculous. She didn't love him, after all. She had not begun this affair out of any affection for him. This newfound intimacy with him was the means to an end, and nothing more.

Even so, that ache grew, making it hard to breathe.

"Oh, this is awful," Iris sighed. "And I was so excited I could finally help."

They stood there for a time, each mired in her own troubled thoughts. But Iris, bless her, was not one to admit defeat so easily. In the next moment her eyes flew open again, her pale brows drawing together in the middle with a surprising amount of determination.

"I may not have the time to extract the oils myself," she declared. "But give me a day, two at the most, and you shall have what you need."

* * *

Ethan didn't know what to expect several days later when, instead of going over the nearly completed boxing venue with him upon her morning arrival at the club, Heloise informed him in no uncertain terms that they needed to visit his rooms immediately. Or, rather, he hoped for a particular outcome, one including the use of his bed for the next several hours. And no clothing.

As luck would have it, there *was* a no-clothing portion of her plan. Unfortunately, he soon learned that he was the only one participating in it.

"Get in," she ordered, pointing to the steaming copper tub set up before the hearth.

Hot anticipation filled him as he imagined her, bared and lovely, skin glistening with water, limbs entwined with his. "As long as you join me," he murmured, reaching for her.

But to his confusion and consternation, she danced out of his way. "Oh, no you don't," she declared, wagging a finger at him, a mischievous smile on her face. "I have put entirely too much effort into this for it to be pushed aside so swiftly."

What the devil was she talking about? It was then he finally took stock of his surroundings. Much to his surprise, the hot bath was not the only thing she had prepared. Not only was there a carefully folded stack of clean towels and a basket holding several small glass vials by the hearth, but the curtains were drawn tight against the morning sun, plunging the room into shadows. His nostrils flared then as he caught a whiff of something new in the air, a sweet floral scent permeating the place.

He looked at her then, at her beaming smile and the sparkle of excitement lighting her eyes. She had done this for him? Something previously petrified in his chest, the one bit she had failed to reach in his week of knowing her and the days he'd been taking her to his bed, began to soften.

"What's all this?" he asked through a throat strangely thick with emotion.

"It has concerned me," she said, reaching for him, pushing his jacket and waistcoat from his shoulders, "that you still deal with pain in your scars all these years later. And so," she continued, deft fingers loosening his cravat, "I had the incredible astuteness to ask my very dear friend—who is a lauded botanist, mind you—to concoct something especially for you, something that will soothe and heal your scars and give you some relief."

He stared at her, devoid of speech. No one in his life had ever done something like this for him. Ever. Not even his mother, God rest her soul, who'd had too many troubles and too much to worry over to ever coddle him and his brothers. Oh, he'd known she loved them. But she had never been a demonstrative woman, even before her husband had left her alone with three young children and broken her spirit. The way she had expressed her love had been by making certain her children were clothed and fed, and there it had ended. And he would never think badly of her for it.

This, however, was entirely new, a caring he had not ever thought to receive in his life.

Heloise, who must have sensed a shift in him, stilled in her removal of his clothing, her gaze finding his. She scanned his face intently, as if seeing something there for the first time.

"Ethan?" His name came out quiet, almost a whisper, asking so much in that one word.

Looking for answers he was nowhere near ready to give.

Stepping back from her touch, he took over where she had left off. But weren't his fingers shaking as he sat and removed his boots? A fact that troubled him much more than he liked. So much, in fact, that he reverted to gruffness with her, a kind of shield. Though he knew deep down there was no shielding his softened heart. No, she had already infiltrated that traitorous organ, touching him in ways he had never thought another could.

"What is that smell?" he demanded, as much to distract her as anything, her with her curious eyes that saw too much. He sniffed the air, scowling at the steaming bathwater as he stood and removed the last of his clothing.

"Lavender," she answered, busying herself with preparing the bed for God knew what. He swallowed hard, tearing his gaze from her. When she bent over, that damned delicious arse of hers outlined by her skirts, he was tempted beyond belief. And, as he was now fully naked, that was not the ideal state to be in. Clearing his throat, he clasped his hands in front of his groin.

"Lavender?" His scowl deepened. "I'm not some debutante that needs lavender water added to their bath. I need a good, strong soap and nothing else to get me clean."

"Which is probably why your scars bother you so,"

Heloise said patiently as, done with whatever the hell she'd been doing, she turned to face him—only to pause, eyes widening and traveling down his body. Which did not help his state of increasing arousal.

But she was made of stronger stuff than he was. Instead of closing the distance between them as he was damn close to doing, she smiled firmly and pointed to the tub. "Let's get you in that water, shall we?"

He paused, eyeing the fragrant bathwater with distrust. He had never in his life smelled of flowers, and he wasn't about to start now.

Heloise, however, was having none of it. She planted her hands on her hips, cocking her head in mock disappointment. "You are acting like a child."

"No, I'm not," he grumbled. Which, no doubt, only served to make him look even more like a petulant child.

Heloise sighed dramatically. "Just trust me in this, won't you?" she begged.

It was a playful comment, made for the express purpose of getting him in the tub. For some reason, however, it gave Ethan pause. He gazed at her, that damned softening in his chest spreading through his whole body as a realization came over him. Before he knew it, he spoke that realization, the words pouring from him as if they could not be contained any longer.

"I trust you in everything."

It shook him how much he meant the words. When they'd first met, he'd been so certain he could not trust her. He'd gone into this affair as a way to keep her close and watch over her, had ordered Keely to look into her background. He'd considered her an enemy from the start.

Now, however, after a mere week, he found his feelings for her were quite different.

Heloise's gaze turned warm at his words. So warm he felt the comforting heat of it across the distance between them.

In the next moment, however, she pressed her lips tight, straightening her shoulders into an unforgiving line.

"I will not allow you to distract me," she declared, pointing to the tub with a shaking finger. "In."

Shaken himself at their peculiar exchange, Ethan quite forgot to continue fighting her and stepped into the water. It enveloped him as he settled against the copper wall of the tub, and though he would rather die than admit as much after his spectacular balking, it felt like a warm hug. Without meaning to, he sighed and let his muscles relax.

"There," she said brightly from somewhere behind him, "doesn't that feel lovely?"

"It would feel lovelier if you were in here with me," he mumbled, only half teasing. "But is lavender water truly necessary?"

"Lavender has healing properties," she replied. There was the sound of her rustling and moving about. But with the sweet floral scent surrounding him and filling his lungs and the warmth of the bath seeping into his muscles, he found he didn't care what she might be doing. Suddenly she was beside him, a bar of soap and a washcloth in hand. "It will do much to soothe your skin, as will the Epsom salts I added. And," she continued, holding up the soap so he might see the bar of milky white sprinkled with pale purple blossoms, "this will help as well. No more rough, damaging soap for you."

He considered it before turning to study the other items she had laid out by the hearth. His suspicion had eased much, to be replaced with a deepening interest. "Your botanist friend provided all this?"

"She did," she replied, dipping the soap and washcloth in the water. He watched her strong hands work the soap into a creamy lather against the washcloth, transfixed. He was tempted to grab her wrist and urge her into the tub with him. From the way she had gazed at him, her eyes hot on his body as he'd stood before her in all his nakedness, he didn't think it would take much effort on his part.

But this wasn't about that. His chest warmed again as he thought of all she had done here for him. No, this went beyond the physical.

It occurred to him that this was veering dangerously into a deeply emotional connection. He had never in his life experienced something of that sort with a woman. Oh, he'd had the odd affair, with women who were content with a quick tumble, never wanting anything more from him. And he had never wanted anything more from them.

But with Heloise...

Before he could finish that thought—thank God, as he didn't think he was at all ready for where it was heading— she moved behind him, hands on his shoulders, gently pushing him forward, hands splaying over his scarred back. And then—

Nothing. Her hands remained motionless, the only movement the slightest curling of her fingers against the ridged flesh. He stilled, his head tilting slightly to one side in silent inquiry, even as tension began to thread his muscles. She had never had cause to see his scars quite so clearly before. Did they disgust her? God knew they had disgusted women before, though those women had done their best to hide that fact from him.

But the moment was gone in a blink, her hands soon moving against his back as she gently swept the soapy washcloth against his skin in large, slow circles, not a bit of hesitation in her touch. And it was, quite simply, glorious. The rest of the world melted away then, the tension in his shoulders easing, his head falling forward onto his bent knees. For some minutes she continued her ministrations, the healing suds bathing his abused skin. They were both silent, the playfulness of a moment before gone, a subdued intimacy taking its place. An intimacy he had not expected, and that was further deepened as her husky voice washed over him.

"I hope the men who did this to you were given their just deserts in some way. It would be too unfair if the universe left them unscathed."

He let loose a rough chuckle, muffled as it was against his knees. "Oh, I did not wait for the universe to act. I took care of them myself when I had the means to."

Her hands stilled in their washing. "What do you mean?"

It should be an easy question for him to answer. He did not feel any guilt over what he had done, after all. The men had deserved every bit of retribution he had piled on their heads.

But he found himself pausing. Would Heloise think him a monster for it? And why did that idea bother him so much?

He frowned into his knees as she resumed the slow circling of the washcloth on his skin.

"You will think me cruel if I tell you."

"I sincerely doubt that," she said, the words light yet with a peculiar tightness to them. "Considering what they did to you, I rather think they deserved whatever they got."

"I know they deserved it," he replied gruffly. "I took away everything they treasured and had them sent to debtors' prison. They are mere shells of the men they were. And I'm glad of it. They will never be able to do to another what they did to me." He turned his head to the side again, this time almost in defiance. "I'm glad I did what I did, and I would do it again a thousand times."

Would she denounce his actions now, declare her disgust at his cruelty? He half expected she would. Even he, who had been the one to suffer at the hands of those men, at times cringed back from the memory of how far he had gone in his revenge all those years ago.

But she did not condemn what he had done. Instead she said, voice quiet, "I'm sorry I brought up memories that bring you such pain."

He shrugged, even as he was achingly aware of a deep relief that he had not turned her away from him. "Most of my memories bring me pain. But, strangely enough, it feels freeing telling you about them." And then, after a heavy pause, "No one has ever done anything like this for me before. Thank you."

"You're welcome," she replied quietly.

* * *

While Ethan would have been content with the bath, his entire body feeling decidedly pampered, Heloise, it seemed, was not through with her ministrations. Before he knew what she was about, she had maneuvered him onto the bed and on his stomach. The sheets were pleasantly cool beneath him after the warmth of the bath, and this, combined with the darkness of the room and the soft sounds of her moving about, nearly lulled him to sleep.

Until she joined him on the bed. But it was not to seduce him as he'd dearly hoped. No, she positioned herself on her knees beside him, clothed only in her chemise, and placed a tray on the bed near his head.

"Now," she said as the tinkling of glass echoed through the room, "just relax."

Alarm shot through him, banishing the last remnants of tiredness. The only time anyone ever told a person to relax was when something unpleasant was coming. *You trust her*, he hastily reminded himself. But it didn't seem to do a bit of good. After all, when one was bare-arsed naked one could not be too suspicious, especially when it came to surprises. He braced his hands on the bed, ready to rear up and bolt out of her reach.

Until her hands, those wonderfully strong yet graceful hands, splayed over his back. Warm and slick, they pressed into his scars, moving in slow, firm circles.

But this was not unpleasant at all. In fact, it felt good. Quite good. "W-what...?"

"It's oils," she murmured softly. "Lavender, like before. But mixed with primrose and rose hip. All conducive to easing the discomfort of your scars. That, along with the massage, will do much to bring you relief."

He was silent as she continued working. No, he was speechless; there was a decided difference. Full as his heart was, words would not form. The bath had been one thing. This, however, was something more. Her fingers pressed into his skin, down into his muscles, easing tension he had not even known was there. The slickness allowed her hands to move unfettered, the warmth of the oils sinking into his scars and to his very bones. He groaned as her fingers, those wonderful fingers, found a particularly tight spot in his skin.

She pulled back immediately. "Did I hurt you?"

"God, no," he moaned. "Please, don't stop."

She huffed a surprised chuckle. And then her hands were back just where he wanted them. Her fingers were clever as they worked, pressing into his skin, down into his muscles, bringing him a relief he had never thought possible. He had believed all this time that discomfort would be his bedfellow for the remainder of his life, that the trauma of his past would forever mar him, both inside and out.

Now, however, Heloise was soothing his scars, bringing him such comfort as he'd never experienced. And he began to wonder deep down inside if she couldn't begin to heal his heart as well.

The thought so shocked him, he could not breathe. Where the devil had that come from? His heart didn't need healing. But even as he told himself that he had not experienced any damage to that useless organ, that there was nothing to damage, he knew it wasn't true at all. He thought then of all the pain and devastation that had touched him over the years, causing his life to veer off course in heartbreaking ways. From his father leaving, to the false theft accusation, to the punishment after, to his mother's ensuing death. And then after, the worst one of all, Gavin's betrayal and death. Each of those things had molded him, shaped him, as surely as a sculptor shaped a ball of clay. But it was not a beautiful vase that had been the outcome of it all, but something misshapen, with cracks and dents and gaping holes. Something that no one in their right mind would ever want to claim.

Yet here was Heloise, with her healing touch and kind heart, who either intentionally or unintentionally was smoothing out those defects, making him whole in a way he had never thought possible.

His breath hitched in his chest, surprising him. And Heloise as well, if the way her hands stilled was any indication.

"Ethan?" she asked, voice soft. Which only succeeded in making his breath hitch again. What the ever-loving hell was wrong with him?

"I'm fine," he said. But the words came out as a croak.

And he recognized the lie in them. He was not fine, and he hadn't been in a very, very long time.

Heloise somehow understood immediately. Placing the tray on the side table, wiping the oil from his back with a soft towel, she gently urged him up the bed and under the sheets. Then, climbing in beside him, she pulled him into her arms.

It was a simple, sweet act, not sexual in the slightest, offering comfort. And it broke something in him, that seemingly impenetrable dam he had built up over the years. It crumbled to dust as she cradled his head to her chest, dragging her fingers through his hair in soft strokes. He did not cry, of course. He never cried. Yet he could not deny the moisture that tracked down his cheeks as he lay there in the quiet, held in her embrace. And as the exhaustion of the morning finally claimed him, and he felt himself falling headfirst into a dreamless sleep, he knew he had somehow, someway, fallen in love with her.

20

It occurred to Heloise some hours later that she should have taken advantage of Ethan falling asleep so totally and completely. She still had not located the jewels, after all, and the date of the Ayersleys' anniversary ball was quickly looming closer. And what was this affair with Ethan for, if not gaining access to the private places in Dionysus so she might find said jewels?

But Julia and her dilemma had been far from Heloise's mind when she'd held Ethan as he had drifted off into slumber. No, the only thing on her mind had been Ethan, and the emotions he'd dredged up in her as he'd held back, much to her shock, tears.

Had she expected her actions to touch him as much as they had? No. But she had been even more unprepared for how his response had affected *her*. All she had wanted to do when she'd heard that telltale hitch in his breathing was to hold him and never let go. Even now, as she banked the fire in her forge and put her tools away and washed herself at the basin after several hours at her anvil, she wanted nothing more than to return to his side. She had a job to do, she attempted to remind herself as she left her workshop and made her way through the back garden of the Wimpole Street house, and she'd best focus on that and that alone.

Yet no matter how many times she repeated it, it was a faint thing in her head, drowned out by the louder voice telling her that Ethan could not possibly be guilty of the crimes she had thought him responsible for.

Reaching her room, she changed into a simple muslin gown before falling into a tired heap in the wingback chair nearest the window. She was exhausted in body, yes. This past week she had felt like one of the tightrope walkers she had seen once during a visit to Vauxhall Gardens, balancing on the thinnest rope, trying to keep everyone and everything balanced along with her. One wrong move one way or the other and she would fall, bringing it all down with her.

But there was also an exhaustion of spirit. She had believed this whole endeavor to be straightforward and simple: Those at Dionysus had taken so much from Julia, and she and the Widows would take it back, even if it meant ruining the club.

Now she didn't know what to believe. Or what to do about it. Though she knew she needed to see this thing through, with Julia's very life on the line if she did not, the realization that she was deceiving Ethan, who had known so much pain and heartbreak, had her feeling sick to her stomach.

She turned to gaze out the window, hardly seeing the overcast sky, her heart heavy as iron in her chest. She fully believed someone at Dionysus was involved in cheating Julia. She also fully believed that things of this sort were not one-time occurrences, that they were typically a long-standing rot from within, a cankerous sore.

No matter that she told herself that, however, she could not help the ache in her chest when she thought of Ethan's quiet crying, the way he had gripped her to him as if she were his lifeline. Which, while it had initially touched her deeply, now only brought about a horrible, lowering shame.

It was not only someone within Dionysus who was deceiving him; she was as well.

She closed her eyes as pain ripped through her. She could not do this, could not hurt him. No matter that someone at Dionysus was doing heinous things, Ethan did not deserve to pay for it.

You could confide in him. The thought whispered through her mind, stunning her breathless. Could she? It would make things so much easier, after all, if she had his help in locating the jewels. She could be done with this whole debacle in no time.

But in the next moment she violently recoiled from the thought. Her suspicion that he was innocent was just that: a suspicion. She could not endanger the Widows and everything they had worked toward for something so uncertain. Nor could she entrust Julia's safety and well-being to someone who was so deeply entrenched in Dionysus, the living, breathing beast at the center of it all. No matter how deep her feeling of guilt because she was deceiving him, or how dearly she wished to trust him.

As if Heloise had summoned her simply by thinking of her, there was a knock on her door, and it was being thrown wide, and Julia was there.

Heloise bolted to her feet. "Julia?"

The other woman stood in the doorway, looking paler and more drawn than ever. She clenched her hands in her skirts, giving Heloise a smile that died out before it could even take hold.

"I'm sorry if I'm intruding, but Strachan told me I should show myself up."

Heloise hurried forward, taking Julia's hand in hers. As before, it was ice cold. But now it trembled, proof of her worsening mental state. She silently cursed herself, even as she tugged the bellpull for tea. "You're not intruding at all," she said, guiding the other woman to the sofa before the hearth.

"I'm sorry to have come unannounced," Julia fretted. "It's just that the date for the anniversary ball is approaching, and Lady Ayersley has been making comments about the jewels, and I just don't know what to do—"

Her voice cracked on a sob, and she pressed her fingers to her lips. Heloise, feeling powerless in a way she hadn't since Gregory's death, could only watch helplessly as Julia struggled to bring her emotions in check.

"I'm sorry," Julia repeated, her voice a mere whisper.

"You have nothing to be sorry about," Heloise said, guilt wrapping about her neck, a noose that tightened with every breath. "I'm the one who is sorry. While I thought sending you letters via messenger with updates would be enough, I should have realized you needed something more. But can't you quit that house and that horrid woman? You can live here. We would love to have you."

But even before the words were out of her mouth, Julia was shaking her head. As Heloise had expected. The suggestion had been made numerous times in the past weeks. But Julia, despite her kind heart, had an equally strong will. The very fact that she was able to support herself, no matter how heinous her employer might be, was worth everything to her. Gregory had instilled that strong sense of self-preservation and pride in her, Heloise knew. And there would be no talking her out of it.

Gregory. Guilt flooded her, as it always did when she thought of her late husband. Though while she usually pushed away the memory of his final moments, she forced herself to relive them now, a kind of penance for her weakening resolve. If only she had not asked him to run that errand for her; if only it had not begun to rain after he had left; if only she had insisted he take his umbrella...There were so many *if only*s, but only one truth: He had died because in a moment of weakness she had let down her guard and asked for help. And she would never forgive herself for it.

"I do appreciate it," Julia said now, sitting a bit straighter, that damnable Marlow pride like an iron rod down her spine. "But I cannot. As soon as the jewels are found I'll search for a new position."

She said it with confidence, no doubt in an attempt to let Heloise know that she believed Heloise could accomplish what needed to be done. But there was no hiding the faint taste of fear in it. A fear mirrored in Heloise's breast as well. And for the first time she truly began to worry that she might, in fact, fail. The thought came to her then, what Julia might face if the jewels were not recovered. It was something that had always been in the back of Heloise's mind, an evil presence she kept firmly at bay. Now, however, with its breath hot on her neck and its claws digging into her spine, and she could ignore it no longer.

There was a knock at the door, and the maid entered with the tea tray. Thank God. The distraction allowed Heloise to calm herself, the familiar, mindless preparing of the tea and plates of food a balm as she gathered her thoughts. Now was not the time for despair. No, now was the time for focus, and determination, and to make certain that she saw this through to the end.

A vision of Ethan attempted to manifest, as if mocking her, proof of her weakness. She brutally pushed it down to the very depths of her soul and turned her full attention to Julia. She would no longer allow herself to become distracted. She only hoped she could locate the jewels quickly and end this thing with Ethan, before her heart was irrevocably lost to him. And before he found out how deeply she had deceived him.

21

*T*wenty-four hours. It had been a full twenty-four hours since he had seen Heloise.

Actually, it had been over twenty-four hours. Not that he was keeping track. Ethan shifted in his seat, even as he cast a covert glance at the clock on the mantel and quickly calculated exactly how many hours it had been. Something that caused him to huff a small laugh. Very well, mayhap he *was* keeping track. But was it any wonder, considering what had occurred between them?

"Ho, what's this?" Teagan sat forward, peering at Ethan closely, as if he were a naturalist studying a new and strange species of insect. All the partners, as well as Copper the floor manager, were gathered in the owners' suite to discuss the upcoming masquerade and the progress on the boxing venue. A meeting that Ethan wished fervently would finish soon, and not only because he should have retired to his bedchamber hours before for some much-needed sleep. Since he had received Heloise's message last night that she had things to see to and would not be able to return to Dionysus until this evening, he had thrown himself into his work in an attempt to exhaust himself and make the time go by more quickly.

Though he had failed horribly in that, hadn't he? Not only was he completely awake, but the time was passing with aching slowness. Even that, however, could not dampen his mood.

"Is Sinclaire here smiling?" Teagan continued, narrowing his eyes. "What peculiar phenomenon are we witness to?"

The smile—one he hadn't realized he was doing—should have dropped the moment Teagan had begun to tease him.

Yet it didn't. Strange, that, he mused as he glanced around the circle of men, all of whom gazed back at him with various degrees of confusion and surprise. Any other time he would have glowered and snapped at them. Now, however, he merely shrugged.

"I hardly think it's anything to comment on," he murmured, to which Parsons snorted.

"The smile could perhaps be overlooked," he said, raising a pale brow. "But not your reaction to Teagan. Even I want to punch that smug grin off his face. Yet you're sitting there unfazed."

"Oh, I didn't say I didn't want to punch him," Ethan countered. "At least, I want to punch him as much as I typically do."

"There!" Isaac exclaimed, sitting forward and pointing an accusatory finger at Ethan. "That right there is suspicious in and of itself. You should want to punch Teagan *more* after a comment like that."

Ethan stared at him. "So there is something wrong with me because I don't wish to do *more* violence to him?" Which was so ridiculous a bark of laughter escaped him.

Every man in the room started and stared at him, mouths agape.

"Was that a laugh?" Copper asked in a loud aside to Isaac.

"I think it was," Isaac replied. "Should we check him for fever?"

Ethan rolled his eyes. "You're all a bunch of arses."

"Well," Teagan conceded, "we can't deny that's true. But there is something different about you." He tapped one long finger against his lips.

"No, there isn't," Ethan said, his light mood of a moment before beginning to dissipate. Truly, they were all maddening to a one.

"No," Isaac said, "Teagan is right. There is definitely something different." His expression turned sly. "That couldn't be the doing of our lovely Mrs. Marlow, could it?"

To which Ethan didn't have a reply. Except, that was, for the heat that flooded his cheeks. Something that was as loud as a shout, if the reaction of every man in that blasted room was anything to go by.

"Aha!" Teagan crowed, sitting straighter, eyes wide as he glanced around the room. "Did you see that? He blushed."

"I did not," Ethan grumbled.

"You did, too," Isaac countered, grinning.

"Oh, yes, it's definitely due to Mrs. Marlow," Parsons said.

Ethan stared at him. "You as well?"

Parsons shrugged. "I'm not an idiot. I see the way you make cow eyes at her and disappear for hours at a time when she's around."

"I'll bet even Copper here has noticed," Teagan said.

"Well," Copper replied with no small amount of pride, "it is my job to notice the unusual. And Sinclaire here showing attention to any single female is highly unusual."

"So you've all just been watching me like I'm some damned animal in the Tower menagerie?" He glared at each one in turn. "I'm glad to see I've given you all such a fertile source of amusement."

"And there's the glower back in place," Isaac grumbled, deflating against the back of the couch. The very same couch Heloise had straddled him on just days before. Which, naturally, brought his blush back. Not just on his cheeks, though; his whole body burst into flames.

Desperate that the other men not renew their damned teasing, he cleared his throat and said, his voice ringing through the room, "But we came here to discuss the masquerade. Let us put our focus on that, shall we?"

Blessedly, they conceded, though reluctantly, the draw of teasing Ethan too great for them to pass up with any willingness. Soon, however, they fully immersed themselves in the subject at hand. At the end of an hour, finally done, they rose and, deep voices rumbling together like stones in a metal drum, began to take their leave.

But though Ethan had been eager to find his bed, he found he was reluctant to do so just yet. Walking over to the damask couch that Isaac had vacated, he looked down at it for some time, remembering Heloise straddling him, legs strong as she'd moved over him, her sighs and cries of pleasure as she'd taken him inside her...

"Penny for your thoughts, Sinclaire."

Ethan started, glancing over his shoulder. Teagan was there still, though alone now, arms crossed and head tilted to the side as he considered him.

"They're hardly worth a penny," he replied. He would never tell the man that recollections of Heloise were worth more, much more. Hell, they were damn near priceless.

Ethan made to move around him. Teagan, however, was apparently not quite through. His hand snaked out, snagging on Ethan's sleeve.

"You have to admit," he said softly, "that our teasing is warranted, this time more than ever. You've never been one to mix business and pleasure, and have certainly never brought a mistress to your rooms."

Mistress. Why did the word sit like acid in his stomach? He had never thought less of women for taking lovers, after all. Even so, it felt wrong here somehow. Mayhap because the term could never encompass all that Heloise had become to him. And hearing her referred to that way made his blood boil.

Pulling his sleeve from Teagan's grasp, he turned to face him. "I'll thank you not to speak of the lady in that manner again."

Teagan's eyes widened infinitesimally at Ethan's quiet warning. The next moment, however, and his face was wiped as clean as a schoolboy's slate, his dark features rearranged into his typical easy-going charm.

"My apologies. I won't do so again. But damn me if this isn't a surprise. I've never seen you in such a state over a woman in the more than thirty years I've known you."

Thirty years. At the reminder of how long they had known one another, Ethan found his anger abating, his shoulders easing. They had been through much together, he and Teagan, Parsons, and Isaac. Even Copper and Mary and the myriad workers at Dionysus had been part of his life since their days on the streets, people who had all felt want and hunger and the utter unfairness of the hand life had dealt them. All their lives were connected, like links in a chain, their decades together having created attachments that could not be broken.

The thought had no sooner washed over him than Gavin's face flashed in his mind, an apparition come to taunt him. Hadn't he believed the same of his brother as well? That link in the chain had shattered. And there would be no putting it back together again.

Teagan's grin faltered as the man seemed to sense something shift in him.

"What I'm trying to say in my clumsy way," he said, voice more subdued than Ethan could remember hearing it, "is that I'm glad for it. I know things have been difficult since Gavin—" He closed his mouth with a snap of teeth at the same moment that an unintentional hiss of breath escaped Ethan's lips. They had not spoken of Gavin since his death. Or, at least, no one brought him up in front of Ethan. Given the ease with which Teagan had spoken his name, it seemed Teagan, and quite possibly the others, were not so reticent.

It was something he suddenly wished he could do, shrug off the permanent, debilitating pain that came from remembering his brother and how he had betrayed them, think of him without feeling he would go mad from the anger and grief.

The realization took him aback. He had willingly locked every weak emotion he possessed in a strongbox and thrown it into the gray, turbulent ocean of his heart, letting it sink into the depths where it could never be found again, all in an effort to forget his brother and the pain his memory brought.

Yet somehow, someway, that strongbox had risen to the surface, had opened the smallest crack. And those emotions he had thought forever dead to him were seeping out. Why? What had changed?

He knew the answer to that question even before it had fully formed in his head: It had been Heloise, with her strong yet gentle hands, with her passion, with her too-curious eyes that seemed to see to the very depths of his soul. She had revived something in him he had thought forever dead.

Shaken, he took an involuntary step back from Teagan. Though he had realized he'd fallen in love with her, he had never thought it could change him in such a way. And he did not know how to feel about it.

"I'll take my leave now," he mumbled. Then, without another glance at the other man, he bolted from the suite.

* * *

Heloise carefully replaced each paper, making certain they all appeared undisturbed before sliding the desk drawer closed, letting loose a silent sigh as she did so. "Damn and blast," she swore softly, looking about the dark room, eyes scanning the dim interior for anything else she might have missed. But no, every possible place of concealment had been gone over.

And now there was no other room in this hall to search. Over the past hour, since her stealthy arrival at Dionysus at noon, she had worked her way through all the offices in this section of the club save for Ethan's, offices she assumed were used by the other partners, richly appointed rooms that showcased the personalities of their owners. Like this one, done up in rich greens and burgundies and gold accents, a luxurious place that could belong only to Mr. Teagan. Going through each in turn, she had searched every drawer, every cupboard, every possible hiding place. To her utter frustration, however, the jewels were nowhere to be found.

But at least now she knew where they were *not* and could focus her attentions on other areas of the club, she told herself bracingly. Filled with a new determination, she moved for the door and opened it a crack, peering out and glancing down the long hallway. As all the times before, it was empty, quiet. Letting loose a slow breath, she slipped out, closing the door carefully behind her. Then, reaching into her bodice, she pulled the slender picks from her corset. Euphemia had crafted the cunning columns of fabric in the undergarments specifically for the Widows' more advanced lock-picking tools. Working quickly and nimbly as Iris had taught her, she inserted the picks in the lock, maneuvering them until she heard the faint click of the mechanism that secured the door again. But it brought her no relief. She told herself her unease was simply due to being unable to locate the gems. The clock was ticking ever closer to Julia's deadline, after all. And with her sister-in-law's wan face still fresh in her mind, the fear that Heloise would fail her was acute, a freshly whetted blade slicing her bit by bit.

Yet she knew that was not her only source of unease. Against her will, she glanced back along the hallway, pressing her lips tight in frustration as her gaze snagged on Ethan's door. Just as she had each time she had left one of the offices and stepped into the hallway, she felt the pull of something deep within her, like a cord behind her navel, urging her to go to him, to climb into bed beside him and forget her troubles in his arms.

There was a heavy thump in her chest, rattling her ribs and leaving her breathless. She pressed a hand over it, as if she could force the unruly organ beneath into submission by pure will alone. She had decided after Julia's visit that she must distance herself from Ethan as much as possible, and her body's unruly reaction was proof of why she should. She had begun to see him as something more than the means to an end, the tool that she would use to save Julia. Without her realizing it, he had opened something deep inside her that she feared she would never be able to close again.

And it frightened her. She rubbed her chest, blinking back a sudden moisture in her eyes. Yes, she was prideful. But she was not so prideful that she could not admit—to herself, at least—that she was frightened of the emotions he dredged up in her. She had gone through life knowing she was not wanted, knowing she was replaceable. And she had acted accordingly, keeping herself distant from everyone, hardening her heart into a shapeless lump, like the scrap metal in her forge.

But then Ethan had come into her life, had taken hold of that petrified, cold mass of iron, and like Hephaestus had plunged it into a fire until it was malleable, molding it and shaping it until she could no longer identify it as the ugly thing it used to be.

As if to attest to that, her heart gave another lurch in her chest. Blinking back tears, she scowled down at her chest, as if she could shame her heart for betraying her. Then, concealing the tools in her bodice again and pointedly turning away from Ethan's door, she started off down the hall. She had managed to complete the day's task without being discovered, but she was tempting fate by standing here, mooning over something that could never be. She would return to the Wimpole Street house and convene with the Widows to plan what was next...all while leaving her emotions firmly out of it.

She had not taken two steps, however, before the unmistakable sound of a door latch caught her ear. Before she could take a breath, much less look for a place to conceal herself, the door at the end of the hall swung wide to reveal Mr. Isaac Sinclaire, with an expression on his face that did not bode well for her.

22

"Mrs. Marlow, I did not expect to see you here at this hour."

That makes two of us. Heloise smiled, though it felt stiff on her face. She had wanted to quickly get in and out without meeting anyone. No matter that she had an excuse for being here, both as Laney's manager and as Ethan's lover; the fewer eyes on her, the less worry about being suspected should things go awry.

Even so, she should not feel this level of unease. She had always found the younger Mr. Sinclaire a pleasing, good-natured man. Now, however, he looked almost dangerous as he considered her from the hallway door—a position in which he essentially trapped her.

"Laney wished me to check in on the boxing venue," she explained with a calm she didn't feel. "While here, I thought I would visit Ethan."

His eyes narrowed ever so slightly. If she had not been watching him so closely, she might have missed it. The hairs at the nape of her neck stood on end.

"And did you manage to see him?" he asked.

The question was lightly asked. But there was the

slightest tension in his voice that snagged on Heloise's attention, like a burr on clothing.

"No," she replied evenly, even as her mind whirled at a dizzying speed to formulate a reply that would assist her in slipping out of the snare Mr. Sinclaire seemed to have laid for her. Though the question burned in her mind: *Why* was he setting a trap?

"I had hoped to," she continued, "but I have not."

There. Simple and truthful, something Ethan could corroborate if need be. As long as Mr. Sinclaire did not continue to question her, of course. Which he looked about to do. She steeled herself for whatever was to come; by the looks of it, she would need to not only keep her balance like those long-ago tightrope walkers but have the dexterity of the acrobats as well. Before he could open his mouth again, however, a hulking figure came up behind him, a shadow in the stairwell. By instinct she reached up, fingers finding with practiced ease the thin blade in her collar, gripping tight the grooves in the hilt, ready to pull it free...

Until the second figure stepped into the hallway, and the light pouring in through the windows revealed a very familiar, very dear face.

"Ethan," she breathed quite without meaning to, hand dropping to her side.

"Heloise?" He frowned in confusion before the expression melted away, to be replaced with something warm that had her insides melting as well. "I didn't expect you until this evening."

"I wished to see you," she replied, shocked to realize how very true it was. And not only because the threat of Mr. Isaac Sinclaire was well and truly neutralized. No, she wanted to see him just because it was *him*.

His eyes, those dark, hard eyes, softened considerably.

Without taking his gaze from her, he reached out and clapped a hand on his brother's shoulder. "Don't you have somewhere you need to be?"

In an instant the Isaac Sinclaire she had come to know was back. He grinned, a lopsided thing that set his eyes to sparkling. "Say no more," he quipped. "I know when I'm not wanted."

"That you are not," Ethan murmured.

Mr. Sinclaire laughed. Then, sketching a bow, he took his leave. Equal parts relieved that she had escaped his too-knowing gaze and shaken that the encounter had happened at all, Heloise looked to Ethan, prepared to school her features into a look of pleasant unconcern. That plan, however, quickly flew out the window as, with the click of the hallway door signaling they were quite alone, he wasted no time in striding toward her, pulling her against him, taking her lips with his. And she did not recall what she was supposed to be doing for a very, very long time.

* * *

"Heloise. Heloise!"

Heloise started so violently that the papers in her lap slid off and fell to the ground. Flushing furiously—after the interlude with Ethan that afternoon, the last thing on her mind was this latest meeting with the Widows—she dropped to the floor and gathered the pages into a messy pile. "I'm sorry, what was that?"

Sylvia gave her a long look. The woman had to know something was amiss with her. She had, with increasing frequency lately, been giving Heloise that very same look, one that asked far too many questions for Heloise to be at all comfortable with. She half expected Sylvia to interrogate her about what was distracting her. Instead, she pasted a patient smile on her face as Heloise resumed her seat. "I asked how your search of the office spaces went this morning."

"Ah." Heloise cleared her throat, praying the heat that suddenly flooded her face did not translate to a blush. "I managed to search just about every room in that wing of the club. There was not a jewel to be found."

"I see." There was another long look from Sylvia, so long that Heloise squirmed under the woman's seemingly all-seeing gaze.

Finally she broke the contact, peering into her teacup as if attempting to read the future there. "It's as I suspected, of course. They are not stupid men, and would not leave something so valuable easily accessible."

Euphemia's eyes narrowed in concern. "I know you've already stated the jewels have not been sold off. But are you still certain that isn't the case?"

"I am," Sylvia replied firmly. "I have had my informants scouring London for the slightest whisper about those jewels, and not a peep has been heard. And with such well-known gems, they could not have been sold off without some trail of breadcrumbs being left behind. No," she continued, nodding with certainty, "those jewels are still in the possession of Dionysus. I have no doubt."

She sat up straighter. "With Heloise searching Dionysus, we can narrow down where the more valuable of the club's assets are kept."

"But wouldn't that be the main vault?" Iris asked. "The one behind the floor manager's seat? Surely Heloise needn't go through all this trouble to verify something so obvious." She cast a quick glance Heloise's way, though she could not mask the emotions in her eyes, her concern almost a palpable thing in the air. Something that made Heloise squirm.

But Sylvia shook her head. "That is exactly why we cannot focus on it. It's much too obvious."

"I agree," Laney chimed in. "The ground-floor vault will be the place for the money needed for the nightly play. The long-term earnings, the surplus, the property and deeds and miscellaneous winnings they take in that cannot be used on the casino floor will be kept elsewhere, far from the general populace."

"Which is why we must secure everyone's position for the night of the masquerade." Sylvia leaned forward, peering at the rough map laid out on the low table before them. "For anyplace secured to such a degree will need a distraction to access. And not just any distraction, but an unprecedented one, something they could not begin to guess they need to protect themselves from. Heloise will soon find the location of whatever safe we need to access. Until then, we will continue our plans for the upcoming event, so we might know our places when the time comes."

She sat back, a small smile curving her formerly tightly pinched lips. "But I have received an interesting bit of news." She looked about at them all, a spark in her eyes. "It seems someone is quietly searching for anyone who might have been cheated by Dionysus."

The change in the atmosphere was immediate, the air fairly snapping with electricity. The papers slid from Heloise's lap again, but she didn't notice them for how focused she was on Sylvia. The news was validating. Julia had been right all along about Dionysus. And yet...

And yet it caused a lump to form in her chest that she could not dislodge. She realized in that moment just how desperately she had begun to hope she was mistaken about Dionysus. Or, rather, Ethan. For something so heinous could not be going on under his roof without his knowledge.

Bitterness filled her mouth until she thought she would choke on it. Resolutely swallowing it down as best she could, she said, "So there truly are others as we suspected."

"There are indeed. I've let it be known—discreetly, of course—that I am willing to meet whoever might be inquiring and have already received a reply. I am waiting for confirmation of the time and place of the meeting."

"But that could be dangerous." Iris began scratching at the skin of her wrist, a sure sign of her distress.

Laney laughed, taking Sylvia's hand in hers. "Do you forget I'm a renowned boxer? I'll protect Sylvia with my life, have no fear."

"I wish to go as well," Heloise said before she knew what she was about. Why? Why did she have to go? But she knew the answer almost immediately: She needed to hear the information, the damning news that would finally harden her heart again, with her own ears.

But Sylvia seemed to have been expecting her request. She shook her head, an emphatic no. "You have enough to do," she stated.

Heloise, however, was not about to be dissuaded. She could not hear this secondhand. "I will go," she said, gently but firmly, so Sylvia would know there was no talking her out of it.

Once more Sylvia considered her silently. Though wasn't there the faintest hint of sadness in her look? Finally she nodded, letting loose a sigh.

"Very well. I'll inform you once the time of the meeting is agreed upon."

As Heloise watched everyone rise and take her leave, she knew she should feel some sort of satisfaction that everything was falling into place, that her decision to start them off on this scheme had been validated.

Yet as she silently filed out after them, she felt only a deep sorrow that she had been right.

* * *

Ethan didn't take any particular notice of Keely when he arrived unannounced in his office the following morning. Business between them had reverted to the usual routine, after all, the search for information regarding Heloise coming up empty and the rumors simmering about the club having all but disappeared. Even Keely with his extensive web of connections and informants seemed to be coming up empty now, no rumbles shaking the foundation any longer. A relief, surely. It could very well mean that the rumors had been just that, mere rumors. Wasn't there always false information to wade through, someone with a grudge against the club who sought to damage it?

The lack of new information was also further proof that Heloise had never been plotting against him. That what they shared could be something true. What that something might be, he didn't have a clue; while he knew he had fallen in love with her, he was unsure where her heart lay, if her heart was involved at all. But just the fact that their connection wasn't polluted with intrigue and secrets was enough for him. For now, at least.

It seemed, however, that the quiet days devoid of new information had been just a sweet interlude.

"You might want to sit down for this one, Mr. Sinclaire."

Ethan, who had been searching through the bookcase behind his desk, stilled, heart dropping like an anchor into the depths of his stomach. "You have learned something new."

It wasn't a question, but Keely answered it nonetheless. "Aye."

Nodding grimly, he went to his chair, sinking down into

it. "Well then," he prompted as the man sat across from him. "Out with it. What did you learn?" *And what subject—the cheating rumors or Heloise—is this news about?*

The answer to that came quickly enough, thank God. Keely knew not to delay bad news any longer than he had to.

"I've found someone who claims to have been a victim of cheating at Dionysus."

The breath left him in a rush, though he did not know if it was due to shock and despair that they had actually located someone and the rumors surrounding the club had not been a fever dream, or relief that the news was not about Heloise.

Whatever it was, he didn't have time to coddle it. Pushing it aside, he sat forward, hands planted flat on the desktop. "Have you met with them?"

"I'm set to. Tomorrow, just after sunrise in Hyde Park, beneath the bridge that spans the Serpentine."

"I'll go with you."

Keely started, staring at Ethan with wide eyes. "You want to go yourself?"

"Yes."

A sharp, surprised bark escaped Keely's mouth. "Do you think that's wise?"

Crossing his arms over his chest, Ethan scowled at the other man. "I see nothing wrong with it. It's my club; therefore it's my responsibility to see this taken care of."

"Which you can do through me."

Ethan's scowl deepened. "And what is wrong with me going?"

Keely shrugged, motioning down at himself. "You have to admit, I'm not the most formidable-looking fellow. If anyone can make this person feel safe enough to tell what happened to them, it would be me. Whereas you…"

His voice trailed off as his gaze tripped over Ethan, the sideways glance and the curl of his lip saying louder than words that what he saw didn't please him a bit.

Ethan knew all too well that people did not look on him favorably, that he would never be invited into a Mayfair drawing room except as an oddity, something to be gawked at. And he had long ago made his peace with that.

Even so, it stung. "There's nothing wrong with me," he grumbled.

The look Keely gave him spoke volumes. "Whatever you say, Mr. Sinclaire," he said, touching a finger to his forelock.

The damned cheeky bugger. "Regardless," Ethan gritted, "I shall be there, if only to keep out of sight and step in if necessary." He glowered when Keely looked about to protest. "And that is final."

Keely deflated in his seat before, his typical optimism springing back, he straightened, rising from his seat, tugging his jacket down with a determined yank. "As you like, Mr. Sinclaire. Meet me on the footpath beneath the Serpentine bridge closest to the guardhouse, tomorrow at quarter to five."

Ethan watched him hurry off, a strange mixture of anticipation and trepidation simmering in his breast. Tomorrow, he vowed, his hands balling to fists on the arms of his chair. Tomorrow he would have the answers he had been searching for.

23

The air was crisp, a cool fog having settled over the landscape as Heloise, following closely behind Sylvia and Laney, hurried through Hyde Park to the designated meeting place. A fine mist peppered her face beneath the edge of her hood, though it did little to cool the heat on her skin from her galloping heart. The path was empty this early in the morning, the dim gray of the coming dawn barely lighting their surroundings, giving the whole scene a macabre feel, like something out of a gothic novel. She half expected a tragic masked figure enveloped in black to stumble out of the shrubbery to set a curse down upon their heads.

Blessedly, none did. That did not mean, however, that Heloise was any more at ease. Truthfully, she only grew more anxious with each step, perceiving each rustle of leaves, every call of a bird, as if it were a harbinger of doom. As they made their swift way along the wide path running parallel to the Serpentine and the bridge loomed into view, elegant stone arches spanning the dark waters, a sudden movement in the corner of her eye had her reaching for the knife tucked in her sleeve. There was no small blade in her pelisse collar today. No, each weapon she had secreted on her person was long, wickedly sharp, and intended to inflict maximum damage. The steel flashed in the fitful predawn light as she turned, hand outstretched, eyes straining as she scanned her surroundings...

Only to see a swan on the bank of the river stretch its wings and give them a good flap before settling back down and tucking its head along its back in obvious unconcern.

She let loose a shaky breath. "Damn swan," she muttered, glaring at the creature.

"What was that, Heloise?" Sylvia whispered, looking back, face barely visible under the edge of her hood.

"What? Oh, nothing. Nothing at all." Sliding the knife back within the leather sheath she had strapped along her forearm, Heloise stretched her head from side to side in an effort to relieve the strain in her neck and hurried on after the other women. Soon they were at the bridge, stopping just short of the tunnel that spanned the path. It yawned before them, a great maw, hiding God knew what—or whom—within. Heloise shivered in trepidation.

For a long moment they barely dared to breathe, ears straining for any hint of sound. But there was nothing to indicate anyone had arrived.

"Are we too early, then?" Laney asked, the words quiet on the still, heavy air.

Before Heloise could think to reply, a voice floated out of the shadows. "Not a bit," a man said. "I'd say you're right on time." With that, a figure stepped out of the mouth of the tunnel. The fog swirled about him in agitation as he moved toward them with a practiced, unconcerned ease.

At once, Heloise's hand was back on the blade strapped to her forearm, fingers curling around the hilt. Not that the man appeared threatening. In fact, with his slight frame and nondescript clothing, he looked like an average man you might encounter on the street, a fellow who could easily blend into any crowd without suspicion.

Though Heloise knew that the ones who appeared nonthreatening were often the most dangerous of all. Subtly shifting, she moved just in front of Sylvia, muscles tensed and ready.

Proving that he wasn't as harmless as he seemed, the man's eyes glittered beneath the brim of his cap, his lips curving up ever so slightly as he caught the movement. "I understand your caution," he said in a soothing voice that only heightened Heloise's apprehension. "But I swear I'm not here to cause you harm. I really am looking for people who may have been cheated at Dionysus."

"And what do you hope to do with that information?" Sylvia asked. As was typical when she wished to hide her identity, her voice took on a rougher cadence, a callback to her less-than-elegant upbringing before she married a viscount and entered into the aristocracy. And a subtle threat that she was not to be trifled with. It never failed to take Heloise by surprise, the change in tone making Sylvia seem like an entirely different person.

"I have an interested party who's looking to make things right," the man replied. "But to do that, he needs to interview the wronged parties."

"Is he not a 'wronged party' himself?" Laney asked. "That was the impression we received when we learned there was a search for victims."

His lips curved at the corners ever so slightly. "Yes, he's definitely a wronged party. But he's of a position to correct things as well."

A statement that caused the hair at the nape of Heloise's neck to stand on end. Something was definitely off here. This was no mere cheated person looking for others. A thought reared up in her mind, a beast with bared teeth: What if this person worked for someone within Dionysus itself? It could very well be a trap.

Inching closer to Sylvia, she eyed the man with even more caution than before. "I think it would be best if we leave," she said, voice low and tense.

Sylvia glanced at her sharply, eyes glittering in the shadows of her hood. The air turned heavy and electric as the other woman considered her. Heloise thought she would refuse. She had gone through much to find someone who might have been affected as Julia had, after all.

In the end, however, Sylvia nodded once, then turned to face the man. "We'll be taking our leave now." Then, taking hold of Laney's arm, she turned and started back down the path.

Heloise, relief making her nearly sag, nevertheless could not let her guard down just yet. Keeping the stranger in her peripheral vision, she moved off after Sylvia. Which allowed her to see just when the man realized his plans had gone awry. He took a step toward them, hand outstretched. "Wait—"

Before the word was fully out of his mouth, Heloise pulled the blade from her sleeve once more, swinging to face him, arm raised. Fortunately, the man was not stupid; he stumbled to a stop, eyes fixing wide with alarm on the knife as it caught the early-morning light. Unfortunately, her swift, fluid movement caused her hood to fall back.

The world seemed to freeze on their tense tableau, the very breath stalling in her lungs as she grappled not only with the possibility of violence and what she could do to protect Sylvia and Laney, but also with the knowledge that her identity was now fully revealed. Which could be a problem if this man worked for Dionysus. Blessedly there was not a hint of recognition in the man, not even the slightest start to indicate he knew who she was, and she believed herself to be safe.

Until a strangled gasp echoed through the crisp air. But it was not from the lips of anyone she could see. No, it came from off to the side of the path, within the shadows of the shrubbery. Before Heloise could right her hood and conceal her face again, there was the rustling of leaves. And then a hulking figure stepped from the bushes and onto the path—and began striding right for her.

Laney's and Sylvia's cries rang out in the air, setting up a cacophony of sound in the quiet stillness of the early morning, sending the fowl on the water's edge into a flutter of agitated feathers. But Heloise hardly heard it for the clatter of her blade falling from her numb fingers to the ground and the ringing in her ears. This man was certainly no stranger to her. Those dark eyes were the same ones she had gazed into while in the throes of passion, those full lips the same ones she had kissed. Though weren't those eyes on fire now, those lips an unforgiving line? And then he reached her and spoke, proving what her eyes could hardly believe.

"Heloise," Ethan rasped. "What the hell are you doing here?"

* * *

It couldn't be she. He refused to believe it.

Yet as he stared down at that same face he had come to care so deeply about in the past weeks, there could be no doubt that it was. Here was that stubborn jaw, there those pale blue eyes. Though wasn't her jaw slack now, her eyes wide with a mixture of shock and something close to fear?

His heart squeezed, and he ached to rub his hand hard over it to relieve the pain there, to reach for her and pull her against him and beg her to tell him this was all a dream and they were in fact back in his bed at Dionysus. Instead, he kept those traitorous appendages at his sides, balling his hands into tight fists.

"Ethan," she whispered through suddenly colorless lips, looking close to keeling over on the spot. As if to give proof of it, she swayed ever so slightly. He instinctively stepped forward, reaching for her, but froze when she took a step back, hands raised as if to ward him off.

Which only served to spark his anger from a small, flickering flame into a burning blaze. "I repeat, madam," he said, taking another step toward her. "What are you doing here?"

The two women she was with made small sounds of alarm in their throats. Not Heloise, however. Instead of retreating, she held her ground, drawing herself taller, eyes turning hard and cold as chips of ice.

"I could ask the same of you," she countered, raising her chin. Of course she would not be cowed, not his Heloise.

No, a voice roared inside him, *she was not* his *anything*.

Instead of answering her, he looked to the two women just off the path. They clung to each other, their shock evident though their faces were still obscured. The moment his gaze found them, the taller of the two stepped in front of the other, feet planted wide, shoulders rounded, and arms raised in a traditional pugilist stance.

Which was exactly when the pieces of the puzzle fell into place.

"Mrs. Laney Finch," he said, eyes narrowing on her. "You are part of this as well, are you?" He glanced at the woman standing just behind her. "And I assume your partner is Lady Vastkern, judging from our previous interactions."

Mrs. Finch, to her credit, did not so much as flinch. Nor did she relax her posture, her fists coming up even higher in front of her. "Mr. Sinclaire," she said, voice flat and hard. "If you don't mind, we'll take our leave now. It's so very early, you know."

Lady Vastkern, however, was not about to be ushered away, it seemed. Stepping in front of Mrs. Finch, she drew back her hood, revealing the mass of steel-gray curls atop her head and her ageless, striking face. "Actually, Laney, my love," she said, giving Ethan a considering glance from the top of his head to the tips of his boots, "I find I would like to speak to Mr. Sinclaire. I believe there is ever so much we can learn from one another. If you're not opposed, that is, Mr. Sinclaire."

She raised one perfectly manicured eyebrow, and he had the impression he was being weighed and measured. He very nearly laughed, though it would have been full of all the bitterness of having been made a fool of all this time.

Against his will, his gaze sought out Heloise. She stood as straight as if a post had been driven into her spine, her face expressionless. It was like looking at a stranger, a sad echo of the warm woman he had come to know. Which served only to drive the blade of betrayal deeper into his chest.

Setting his jaw, he returned his gaze to Lady Vastkern. "I think, madam, that would be a wise course of action considering these very…questionable circumstances."

She nodded regally, then turned and strolled down the path as if it were the middle of the afternoon during the height of the Season. Ethan was impressed despite himself at her complete confidence—until a movement out of the corner of his eye caught his attention and he turned to see Heloise bending to pick up her blade from the ground and concealing it in some hidden place within her sleeve. He watched her soberly, waiting for her to look his way, to show even a small bit of emotion beside the cold indifference she had shown since her initial shock.

But she did not, instead looking straight ahead as she followed Lady Vastkern and Mrs. Finch. It should not have hurt as much as it did. After all, hadn't he just received confirmation that his initial suspicions regarding Heloise's intentions had been valid? And yet...

He took a deep breath with effort, dragging the cool morning mist into his lungs by sheer will. But his chest remained tight, as if some cruel god had taken hold of him in his fist and was relentlessly squeezing. He felt as if something inside him had shattered and could never be put back together again. Giving Keely a quick, hooded glance, he strode after the retreating women. He would get answers soon, no matter what it took. The only question was: How much would those answers destroy him?

24

Ethan had heard from Keely of the house on Wimpole Street that Heloise shared with these ladies, a place of refuge for widows. But he'd never thought he would set foot within its walls. It had been just some vague structure, this place where Heloise lived. Mayhap if his life had not taken the path it had, if he had lived a life of respectability that had made him at all worthy of courting someone like Heloise, he might have visited here on occasion, calling on her, bringing flowers.

His lips twisted. But no, his true origins would never have allowed that. In truth, if not for this whole mess with Dionysus, he would never have met her in the first place. He would have been like manure beneath her shoe, not worthy to approach the black lacquered door with its fan-shaped window above, much less to set foot within. As he was doing now, following the three women into the front hall, boots clicking on the polished inlaid wooden floor.

He cast a look her way, recalling the hard expression on her face when she had pulled the knife on Keely, the shock and dismay, quickly wiped away to be replaced with cold indifference, when she had caught sight of him stepping from his hiding place in the bushes. But then, he told himself grimly, she was not the same woman he had believed her to be, the same woman he had come to love. In fact, the woman he had come to love didn't exist at all. That Heloise was a mirage.

A squat, hard-faced woman stormed toward them from the bowels of the house before he could so much as get his bearings, her face like granite as she scowled at them.

"A visitor?" she barked in a rough Scottish accent. "At this hour of the morning? Are ye daft?"

"Hello, Strachan," Lady Vastkern replied with impressive poise, considering she was being scolded by a servant, handing over their voluminous capes to her. "This is Mr. Ethan Sinclaire of Dionysus. Would you be so kind as to bring a fresh pot of coffee to the drawing room? Although," she continued, raising one steely gray brow as she considered him, "mayhap you would like something a bit stronger? I know it is fully morning now. But you do not keep the same hours as most."

Said by anyone else, it would have been a scold. But, for some reason, it did not come across as such said by Lady Vastkern. If they had met in a different time or place, he might have liked the woman.

Now, however, he just felt numb, thoroughly overwhelmed as he was by Heloise's dark presence not five feet from him. "Coffee is fine," he replied stiffly.

The viscountess nodded before returning her gaze to the woman. "Coffee then. And a plate of biscuits. I find myself famished."

The servant snorted. "That's because ye rose before the skreigh o' dawn. Would serve ye right if I were to let ye starve."

With that she spun about with all the finesse of a general in battle and strode off, stout boots clomping like horse hooves across the floor.

Lady Vastkern gave him a cool smile. "Please, pay no mind to Strachan. She is abrasive at the best of times, but she is indispensable to us all. We would be lost without her."

Mrs. Finch, who had kept close to the viscountess's elbow the entire morning, scowled at him before sending a hooded glance Heloise's way. "Do you truly think it wise to bring him here?"

"Actually," the woman murmured thoughtfully, "I do. Mr. Sinclaire, if you would be so good as to follow us to the drawing room?"

Without waiting for his acquiescence, she made for the stairs, skirts snapping about her ankles as she ascended to the first floor. Mrs. Finch, shooting him one last dark look, hurried after her. Leaving him and Heloise alone in the front hall.

He balled his hands into fists, refusing to look her way yet painfully aware of her presence, the air so thick with the tension between them he could have fairly cut it with that bloody knife of hers. *Say something*, his heart begged against his will. *Tell me this is all a misunderstanding, that you haven't been playing me for a fool all this time.*

But his silent plea went unanswered. Without a word she started after Lady Vastkern, and he was left to follow, his steps as heavy as if millstones were attached to his ankles.

* * *

The drawing room was as eclectic as the women themselves, all manner of luxurious yet mismatched furniture crowding the space. The women were already seated as he entered, their eyes intent on him. All except for Heloise, who was determinedly looking out the window to the bright morning sky.

"Please, have a seat," Lady Vastkern said, as pleasantly as if he were an acquaintance arriving for a friendly visit. Yet he could hear the faint thread of steel in the command. This woman would be a worthy opponent, that he could sense readily enough. Though how truthful she would be in the next minutes was anyone's guess.

But he was adept at playing such games, wasn't he? He had made a living off of reading bluffs and anticipating moves. Setting his jaw, he made for the sturdy leather armchair in the small circle of seats, the one the furthest from and directly across from Heloise. He could not stand to be near her just then for how desperately he wanted to reach for her and beg her for answers. Yet he needed to see her face, to gauge her reaction, to see if there was something, *anything* of the woman he had believed himself in love with still there.

He spoke first, wanting to claim the upper hand in this macabre dance of hidden motives and camouflaged intent. "My man told me you claim to be a victim of the house cheating at Dionysus."

Was that a look of grudging admiration in her steely eyes? If it was, it was gone as quickly as it had come. "Oh, we are not the victim. However," Lady Vastkern continued, settling back in her seat in an easy manner, "we do represent someone who is."

He narrowed his eyes. So it had not been a complete lie. "You know of someone. Who?"

Her lips curled ever so slightly. "That, I fear, is information we cannot divulge. At least, not just yet. Not until you tell us why you are searching for victims in the first place."

A valid request. He dipped his head in acknowledgement. "You have heard of my reputation, I assume? That I expect honesty and fair play at my club?"

"We have," Lady Vastkern replied.

"Those are not mere words, my lady. I expect everything to be aboveboard when it comes to Dionysus. And, indeed, everything in my life." His gaze darted to Heloise, anger simmering in his blood as the realization began to sink in of just how deeply she had fooled him. He expected her to keep her eyes firmly on that blasted window she seemed to be enamored of at that moment.

But for a split second her mask broke, and she looked his way. And the pain in her eyes nearly stole his breath. Pain? She was the one who had fooled him; she had no right to feel pain…or to dredge up this strange, misplaced guilt in his gut because she did. Just as she had no right to feel pain, he had no reason to feel guilty. No, that lay squarely on her shoulders.

Which only served to make his anger swell until it was a barely banked fury. Pulling himself together by sheer will, he returned his attention to Lady Vastkern, who was watching him much too closely for his comfort.

"I have heard whispers that something…unsavory is going on at my club," he continued. "I wished to locate someone who could help me flush out the infection."

Lady Vastkern pursed her lips. "That is prettily said, Mr. Sinclaire."

His vision began to go red at the edges at her obvious mockery. "They are not mere pretty words, my lady," he growled, shifting forward.

Mrs. Finch, who was positioned between him and the viscountess, moved at once, placing her body more directly in front of the other woman's. He scowled at her, very nearly snapping that he would not do anything to hurt Lady Vastkern, that he was not so despicable as that.

At the last moment, however, he reined in his tongue,

holding up his hands as a sign that he was not a threat. He was an overlarge brute, yes. But he had a feeling their caution had less to do with his appearance and more to do with the fact that he was simply a man. And for that he could not blame them, not at all.

"My livelihood and the livelihood of everyone within Dionysus depends on my reputation for honesty," he continued in a more even voice. "I am determined to oust the cause of the rumors, be it someone spreading malicious gossip or a person within Dionysus causing harm to others. And to do that, I wish to locate those who have been harmed, not only to find the answers I need but to right the wrongs that have been done to them."

All three women looked at him then with wide eyes. Even Heloise, from her seat across the circle, had turned her gaze on him. But he couldn't look at her if he was to keep his head.

"Do you mean to say," Lady Vastkern said slowly, "that you would punish one of your own people if you learn they are cheating your patrons?"

"Yes." Gavin's face flashed in his mind, bringing with it the stab of pain that always accompanied it. Though wasn't it worse now than it had been in the past weeks? He'd had the cushion of Heloise's kindness dulling it. It had begun to feel manageable, with the muted ache of a healing scar, like the ones that crisscrossed his back.

But now, her betrayal like a freshly whetted blade, she had sliced that old wound open again, even deeper this time, nearly to the bone. And it hurt so much worse than before. Heloise had known how cruel lies had shaped his life, that he abhorred deception of any kind. And still she had done this to him.

But this was not doing him any good, and there were

still answers he needed. "Now it is your turn, madam," he said. "Who is this victim, and what are the claims against my club? I vow to take any accusations seriously and to investigate fully to make things right."

Once more the women stared at him, though now their surprise was palpable. "You are serious," Lady Vastkern said.

"I am."

She considered him for another long moment, as if weighing his words. Something in his face must have revealed his sincerity; her mouth closed with a snap and she nodded. "Very well. Though as this case is closest to Heloise, why doesn't she provide the information you require."

Closest to Heloise? His gaze snapped to her, but her features didn't betray an ounce of emotion, her gaze staying quite firmly upon his chin.

"The person in question is very close to me," she began, voice a carefully modulated monotone. But she couldn't control it as well as her expression, agitation making it quake ever so slightly. For some reason, that fact gave him some relief. She was not as unaffected as she would have him believe.

"She was present during your last masquerade," she continued. "Her employer brought her and funded her play. But in the process, massive losses were incurred. Including the very valuable ruby jewelry set her employer was wearing that night. When my friend returned the following day with the funds to reclaim the jewelry, she was told there was no record of such a thing being lost to the house."

That took him aback. They were meticulous in their records, each win and loss recorded, no matter the size. And as a rule, if someone wished to reclaim property lost to Dionysus, they were allowed to purchase it back. At twice the cost of the loss, of course, but even so, he was not so cruel that he would not allow that much. After all, they were not in the business of collecting jewels and houses and horses, but of making a profit.

"The jewelry is quite precious," Heloise continued, voice tightening. "Her employer informed her that, as it was lost while my friend was playing, if it is not recovered in its entirety, she will be reported for theft."

Which meant this friend would be either hanged or transported. The stark realization of the danger this person was in settled on his shoulders, made all the heavier with his history giving it weight.

Even so, someone losing much more than they could afford was not uncommon. It was the gamble one took, quite literally, when playing with stakes as high as those under Dionysus's roof. "It is unfortunate, I will give you that," he said, sitting forward, resting his elbows on his knees and steepling his fingers under his chin. "But why does this person believe she was cheated by Dionysus?"

Finally emotion showed on Heloise's face as her cheeks flushed with heat. "My…friend has a certain talent." She paused. "She is able to predict with impressive accuracy the cards that will be played."

"You mean she counts cards," he replied dryly.

Heloise paused ever so slightly before giving a stiff nod.

Ethan let loose a heavy sigh, leaning back in his seat and running a hand over his face. Counting cards was a talent, yes, but a rare one, and with the harm it could do his club, one they understandably discouraged, to the point that if a person was discovered doing such a thing, they were barred from Dionysus for life.

In this case, however, he could not fail to see how such a person would be invaluable in identifying not only cheating but also the perpetrator involved. "I can see you are very protective of this…friend of yours," he said. "But would it be possible for me to meet with her?"

Heloise paused, her eyes darting up to meet his. And the distrust there had his fury boiling once more. What right did she have to distrust him, given how cruelly she had been playing him for a fool all this time?

In the next moment, however, a voice of reason whispered through his head: In truth, she had no reason *to* trust him. She had been driven by the fact that this friend of hers—whoever she might be—was in danger because of his club. No doubt she had gained access to Dionysus—and himself as well, though he could not think of that deception without wanting to tear his heart from his chest—with the sole purpose of recovering the lost jewels. She was fighting for her friend's life.

And so he was not at all surprised when her gaze dropped once more to her lap and she mumbled, "I will discuss it with her and let you know."

Which, he knew, was all he would get from her today. Just then the woman named Strachan entered, holding a heavily laden tray aloft with one hand. But the thought of taking coffee with these women made him physically ill.

As the housekeeper deposited the tray on the low table, he rose. All the women started, looking up at him with surprise.

"You are leaving, Mr. Sinclaire?" Lady Vastkern queried, motioning to the tray. "Before refreshments?"

The nutty scent of fresh coffee reached his nose. Any other time he would have gladly accepted a drink. He was a man who could appreciate a good coffee, after all, and with the hours he kept, he imbibed it generously.

Not now, however. No, now just the idea of it turned his stomach.

"I'm afraid I have somewhere to be," he said smoothly. "I shall await word from you on your friend, Mrs. Marlow."

At his use of her name, so formal, so cold, she visibly flinched. But she raised her chin, nodding stiffly before turning back to look out that damnable window.

Giving her one last long look, he sketched shallow bows to the other women before striding from the room, achingly aware of Heloise behind him—as well as the hopes and dreams he had left with her, like a spilled deck of cards at her feet.

25

*H*eloise had not allowed herself to think or feel since Ethan's departure the day before. To do so, she knew, would be to invite heartache and self-recrimination and a bone-deep guilt she would not be able to shake, which would affect what little time was left before the jewels needed to be recovered. No, she could not afford to let emotions rule; she had to focus. And to do that, she had to keep herself from thinking of Ethan beyond the very limited scope of their plans.

It helped, of course, that she didn't see him. There were no trips to Dionysus to check on the boxing ring, and certainly no visits at night...

But the time of shutting herself off from him, she knew, was at an end.

"That Mr. Sinclaire is back," Strachan grumbled from the doorway of the drawing room.

Heloise, who was perched on the edge of her chair, nodded with as much poise as she could manage. "Thank you, Strachan. Please show him up."

The housekeeper gave her a scathing glare before she harrumphed and turned about to make her way down the stairs.

Beside her, Julia fretted, her slender hands tearing at her handkerchief. "What was I thinking?" she babbled, voice reed thin. "I cannot meet Mr. Ethan Sinclaire. I thought it would help. But what if this is a trap? What if he's lying—?"

"Mr. Sinclaire is not lying, Julia," Heloise said firmly, laying a comforting hand over the girl's. No, Ethan was not lying to them. He truly was trying to flush out the villain in his club. He'd had no part in the cheating, was as much a victim as Julia was.

Which made the way she'd used and tricked him all the more abhorrent. Truly a feat, considering how horrible she'd already felt deceiving him before receiving confirmation of his innocence. Her control slipped as the rogue thought came through. Which was when Ethan entered, his bulk filling the doorway, snapping the tight leash she had on her emotions.

"I'm glad you acknowledge that, Mrs. Marlow," he said, his voice even. As before, she felt the chilly use of her married name down to the very depths of her soul.

But while she could not hope to control the heat in her cheeks from his overhearing her, she could retain her composure. Ignoring his comment, she dipped her head in his direction. "Mr. Sinclaire, thank you for coming."

He nodded in response, but his eyes slid past her and anchored firmly on Julia, who, in her anxiety, gave a small squeak at Heloise's side.

"This is the woman you were referring to?" he asked. "The one who is a victim of Dionysus?"

It was not the first time Heloise had noticed him indicating that Dionysus as a whole was at fault. Though he didn't know the identity of the one creating havoc in his club, he could easily put the blame on that person.

Yet by indicating the club itself was at fault, as owner,

he was essentially taking the blame on himself. Something softened inside her chest at the very thought.

But no, she reprimanded herself, it was the least he could do in such a situation. As the head of the beast that was Dionysus, it was his duty to assume responsibility for such things. Sylvia would do the same should something occur in the course of one of the Widows' investigations.

The realization, however, did little to refreeze her quietly thawing heart.

But she was heading down a slippery slope. Once she truly allowed such thoughts to take hold, she was done for.

"Mr. Sinclaire," she said as he took a seat across from them, "this is Miss Julia Marlow."

"Marlow." His gaze darted to her, his surprise evident.

She dipped her head in acknowledgement. "She is my late husband's sister."

What was that sudden change in his eyes? A sad realization perhaps?

A moment later, however, it was gone as he turned his full attention to Julia.

"I am very sorry," he said, voice gentle and expression somber, "that you have suffered at the hands of Dionysus."

Julia, clearly startled, darted a quick, anxious glance Heloise's way. Heloise smiled in reassurance, though her insides were quickening their thawing, sending her emotions in a spin. She had not expected much from Ethan beyond a cold gathering of facts.

But she saw now she had been a fool. Yes, he could be brusque and hard. Yet she had seen that softer side of him, the vulnerability beneath the surface that he disguised so well. It felt like a gift, that he had revealed that part of himself to her. Her heart constricted in grief that she would never be given that gift again.

"Th-thank you," Julia said, fingers strangling one another in her lap.

"I certainly don't deserve your thanks," he said. "I should be the one thanking you for coming forward. I know you must have already disclosed the details of your ordeal several times over. But would you mind doing so once more for me?" At her pause, he continued in an even quieter tone, as if he feared she was a skittish rabbit that would bolt at the first wrong move, "It would help me immensely in making things right."

The effect of Ethan's words and tone on Julia was by no means immediate. Yet Heloise, seated as she was beside her sister-in-law, could feel Julia's body slowly relax, her rigid pose easing.

"Yes," she said, voice shaking only slightly. "Yes, I can do that."

Over the next hour the two talked quietly, with Heloise silently watching. Every detail was gone over meticulously, and yet with such care on Ethan's part that at times it brought tears to Heloise's eyes. Why did he have to be so wonderful to Julia? Why did he have to take such care in making her feel at ease? And why, when she should be relieved that Julia was being treated with respect, was she getting so damned angry?

It didn't take Heloise long to figure the answer to that last question, however. It quickly became apparent that her anger was not directed at Ethan at all, but rather solely and firmly at herself. And every single self-recrimination she had tried so hard to smother since the previous morning came crashing over her head, a powerful wave that stole the very breath from her lungs. Had she done all she had to save Julia? Yes. But in the process, she had used and manipulated Ethan. Worse, she had played to his emotions and hurt him dreadfully. After all he had endured over the years, it was an unforgivable sin on her part.

But his emotions had not been the only ones involved, had they? It was one thing to feel guilt over what she had done. It was quite another thing, however, to experience this bone-deep grief. The very idea that she had hurt him when he had already been through so much was like a knife to her heart. And it was then she knew, without a shadow of a doubt, that she had fallen in love with him.

She sucked in a sharp breath as that realization slid into place like a key in a lock. Ethan and Julia glanced at her sharply.

"Heloise," Julia said, placing a hand over hers, brows drawn together in concern, "is something wrong?"

"What? Oh! No, I'm fine." She tried for a smile, but it trembled on her lips. "Please, don't mind me. You were saying?"

Julia's concerned frown turned to one of puzzlement. "We were just finishing. Mr. Sinclaire," she continued, rising and holding her hand out to him, "thank you for everything."

"It's the least I can do," he murmured, standing and taking her hand in his.

Julia smiled and dipped into a shallow curtsy. "I'll be off, then. Heloise, I shall see you later?" Then she was gone. Leaving Heloise and Ethan quite alone.

Which was when Heloise realized this was the first moment they had been alone together since learning the truth about one another—and since she'd realized she was in love with him. Any hope that she could face him without bursting into tears was thrown right out the window when she glanced at him and felt that new and painful twisting in the region of her heart. Did it hurt her pride that she couldn't even remain in the same room with him without making an utter cake of herself? Yes. But such was her need to escape that she didn't care.

"Well, then," she said, perhaps a touch too loudly. "I do hope that helped. I've much to do; I'm certain you won't mind if I don't show you out." With that she made a beeline for the door.

Ethan's voice, however, stopped her cold.

"I think," he said softly, quietly, "that you owe me some kind of explanation, Heloise."

She might have been able to ignore him and continue on her way—if he hadn't used her name. His speaking something she had not thought to hear from his lips again had her feet faltering on the plush carpet. The draw of him too great, she took a deep breath and, steeling herself for the conversation to come, turned to face him.

* * *

By God, his chest ached just looking at her.

She appeared almost defiant as she faced him, hands bunched into white-knuckled fists at her sides, chin lifted ever so slightly. A day ago it would have infuriated him, that seeming unconcern for what she had done to him.

But his fury had not lasted long. In fact, it had already begun to transform by the time he'd left this house the morning before. How could it not, after he'd learned why she had done what she'd done? How could he blame her for trying to save her sister-in-law, the relationship making her sacrifice all the more desperate?

Sacrifice. The word left a bitter taste in his mouth. But why else would someone like her wish to bed someone like him? He had been pursued for the thrill of sleeping with someone of crude origins before, and he had not minded then. Or, at least, not minded much. It had been purely physical, without emotion, a mutual fulfilling of a need, however base.

But with Heloise, it had been more than that. So much more. It had not begun as such, of course. Then, he'd been certain she was up to something, that she was somehow connected to the swirling rumors about his club—and it tore at his heart now, seeing just how right he had been, that his instincts had been correct, as much as he wished now he had been wrong.

Their intimate moments, however, had quickly developed into a deep, emotional connection. For him at least, he thought bitterly as he gazed at her. Had she truly not been affected? Had it really been just the means to an end?

And did he really want to know if it had?

"I would think," she said, blessedly oblivious to the torturous thoughts decimating his insides, "you could have guessed my motives by now."

Either she was saving herself the effort of explaining the obvious, or she was saving him the pain of hearing the full, raw truth. It would be an easy thing to decamp, to take the out she was giving him. God knew it would prevent the mountain of grief that would come with the answering of his question.

But apparently he was more of a glutton for punishment than he'd ever suspected.

"I think I deserve to hear from your lips the whole truth."

She looked at him a long, tense moment, lips pressed tight, as if debating if she should acquiesce to his request. Finally she nodded, a sharp thing. "Very well," she bit out. "I could see no other way around it. I need to save Julia, and to do that, I need to locate those jewels. The only option I saw was to gain access to your club. But acting as Laney's manager only got me so far. And so I..." Her voice faltered before she lifted her chin and continued, the words spilling from her lips as though she needed to expel them from her body with force. "I seduced you to gain access to portions of the club I could not otherwise."

It should not have hurt as much as it did to hear that. He'd known it was the truth, after all, that she had used him to access the club and find those blasted jewels.

Even so, the depth of the pain had him nearly gasping for breath. It was by sheer will alone that he kept himself still, kept his face impassive, kept his chest from caving in.

"I...see." He swallowed hard at the lump in his throat, but it didn't budge, only lodging more firmly in place. "Thank you for being so blunt."

Finally a reaction as she flinched. Her hands were not just balled into fists now. They had taken hold of her skirts and were doing their best to strangle the cloth. "It was not a decision made lightly," she said.

He nearly laughed at that. As if the fact that she had agonized over seducing him would ease the pain. If anything, it only hurt more, knowing his suspicions that she had sacrificed herself in his bed were true.

But he supposed it was a kind of apology. Granted, a sad excuse for one, but her attempt nonetheless. And he suspected it was the only one he was going to get.

He dipped his head in acknowledgement. "You do not have to explain further. To save someone I care for, I suppose I would have done the same."

The cold mask finally fell at that. But she was looking at him much too intently, as if trying to figure him out and confused by what she saw. To divert that damned all-seeing gaze of hers, he blurted, "You must have searched a fair amount of the club over the past week."

She physically recoiled as if he had slapped her, her cheeks heating. "Yes."

As he'd suspected. He had a vision of her then, sneaking about when no one was around, opening drawers and digging through cupboards. It was such a ridiculous image that if he'd been in any mood to laugh he would have. But he was the furthest thing from laughing in that moment. In fact, he rather thought he was much closer to crying.

But he was beginning to lose sight of the main purpose of all this, in that this whole, quite literal, affair had begun in an effort to save Miss Julia Marlow. Something he was determined to finish to make things right again. And perhaps, when it was completed and Heloise's sister-in-law was saved—God willing, they could locate those damn jewels—he could leave Heloise and everything to do with her behind him.

He nodded. "Very well. Then I shall finish what you started."

Eyes wide, she took a step forward. "I can help—"

He took two steps back to her one, holding up a hand. No. God, no, he could not spend any more time with her than absolutely necessary. This right here was hard enough as it was. All he wanted to do was take her in his arms and beg her to see him as a man and not as the means to an end.

There was a flash of pain in her eyes that she quickly covered up. Was she hurt at his refusal? And why did that small tell make him yearn for her even more than before?

"I can handle that myself," he said. "But you must know that there is a very good chance the jewels are not within the club. Everyone else affiliated with Dionysus has their own homes separate from it, you know. The logical place to conceal them would be off-site."

Composed once more, she retreated a step and nodded,

hands now clasped in front of her as if holding herself back from advancing again. "I had considered that. But not knowing who might be responsible, I had to limit my search to Dionysus alone. Did your conversation with Julia give you any insight into who the perpetrator might be?"

He ran a hand through his hair in agitation. "No. I had hoped it might, but as yet I don't have a clue who it is."

"I had feared as much." She chewed at her lip before, giving him a cautious glance, she took a deep breath, as if bracing herself for something unpleasant. "But now that we have your assistance, we may be able to flush out the perpetrator."

He stilled. "Flush them out?"

"Yes." She cleared her throat, looking toward the open door as if seeking assistance. When none came, she faced him once more, expression resigned. "We believe that if we cause a diversion the night of the masquerade, it's quite possible the villain at the center of all this will show himself."

A diversion. He saw it then, how Lady Vastkern and Mrs. Finch and Heloise all had their places in Dionysus. And, no doubt, the other widows they resided with were in on it, too. A realization hit him then, like a punch to the gut. "You have been planning a diversion for the night of the masquerade from the beginning, haven't you?"

She nodded, but did not meet his eyes. "It was always our plan if the jewels could not be located in time. Though it will be significantly easier having you assist us."

She tensed, as if bracing herself for an outburst. No doubt she expected him to lash out in fury that they had been planning to use the masquerade and boxing match to infiltrate his club and do God knew what manner of damage.

But though he knew he would have reacted thus just a

week past, now he felt only a sad resignation that it had to come to this.

"Very well," he said. "Please let me know what I may do to assist in any way I can."

She sucked in a sharp breath, her shock palpable as she met his gaze. "Why are you being so kind?"

The question took him aback, and not only because this was the first truly vulnerable moment she had shown him since the heartbreak of the day before. Shaken, he was tempted to shrug her off. But there was something almost like pain in the question, as if it grieved her that he could be kind to her. It made him pause, that pain, and give her question much more thought than he normally would have allotted it. And he found he was as surprised by his response to her as she was. Normally deception, especially to such a degree, would be an unforgivable sin to him, and he would have been glad to rain down fire and brimstone on anyone responsible.

Yet looking in her eyes, seeing the emotion she was trying so damn hard to conceal, all he wanted to do was hold her.

He swallowed hard, trying his best to find a reason that was not tears for the burning behind his eyes. "After these past weeks, did you think me a monster?" he finally asked quietly.

"No," she replied, voice hoarse, arms snaking about her middle. "No, I never thought you a monster."

He gave a humorless chuckle. "I suppose I should be content with that." Then, because he could not stand there a moment longer without betraying his heart in the process, he dipped his head and strode from the room.

26

The echo of the front door closing had not faded before Heloise crumpled to the ground. Ah God, what had she done?

She had expected Ethan's coldness, his anger. She had been so certain their first confrontation alone would be filled with yelling and recriminations and bitter words wielded like swords to wound in the most brutal way possible. It was what she deserved, after all.

Instead he had been kind, and generous, and understanding to a fault. And she had felt the devastating pain of it more than she would any freshly honed blade.

Wrapping her arms about her middle, she bent her head, fighting to control her breathing, trying to keep the sobs at bay. But they came anyway, inevitable like the tide, tearing from her throat, dragging high keening noises from her chest. She would never, for the rest of her life, forget the grief in his eyes. That had been the greatest source of pain to her. There should have been hate, distrust, fury present in their dark depths, turning them cold, as frigid as the ground in winter. Instead he had seemed to be quietly begging her to tell him that her seduction of him had not been starkly relegated to her plans for his club. What could she have said to that? That she had begun to develop feelings for him? That she had nearly abandoned her promise to keep Julia safe and her duties to the other Widows in her growing affection for him?

And why not? The question swirled in her grief-stricken mind, taunting her, stealing the breath from her lungs. Why not? Because there was no future for them. Because you could not build a relationship on lies. Because...

Her tears fell in earnest now, dripping down her nose, darkening her gray skirts. Because she loved him, so very much. And she did not deserve his affection, whatever that might be, after hurting him like this. That heartbreaking realization only drew more sobs from her, so violent she felt her bones shudder, seemingly unending.

Until a pair of soft arms came about her, and she was drawn into a gentle embrace.

"My God, Heloise," Euphemia cried. "What has happened?"

"She was to meet Miss Marlow and Mr. Sinclaire," Sylvia said somewhere above her. "Something must have occurred."

"Did he harm her?" This from Laney, whose voice was tight with anger. "If he did, I swear by all that's holy I shall put an end to him myself."

"I'm certain he did not harm her," Iris fretted. "At least not physically."

Heloise attempted to gain control of herself, to speak. She never allowed herself to lose control of her emotions around anyone lest they think her weak, lest they believe she could not do her job and be of use to them. Yet her sobs only grew harder as she heard how they worried for her. She had thought her relationship with these women was purely business, had spent the past two years making certain the line was not crossed into something more personal. Hadn't she been told since she was small that her only worth lay in what she could do for others, that without that she was not needed?

Yet here were these women, worrying for her, giving her comfort. And demolishing every barrier she had put up against them. Ethan's words came back to her then, from the day she had confided in him about her treatment by her uncle and aunt and their family: "No one should have to earn their place in anyone's life." She saw now the truth in those words, how these women had welcomed her in, loving her unconditionally, from the very first day.

She collapsed against Euphemia then, melting into her embrace, letting emotions that she had not known she possessed wash over her like a cleansing balm. Euphemia pulled her in closer, one hand caressing her back as she murmured quiet words of comfort that were unintelligible to Heloise's ears but nonetheless soothed her. Soon her sobs quieted, her tears stopped flowing, and she lay in an exhausted heap in her friend's arms.

Yes, her friend. No mere business partner would do what Euphemia, and indeed all of the Widows, was doing for her.

Sylvia dropped to her knees before her, pressing a handkerchief into her hands with a gentle smile. "Better?"

Heloise nodded, dabbing at her swollen eyes, blowing her running nose. "I'm sorry about that," she said, voice hoarse.

"There is no need for an apology," Sylvia proclaimed, patting her arm, before giving a small chuckle. "But let us move this party to the sofa. My knees are not what they used to be."

Heloise nodded, and at once hands came beneath her arms, helping her to stand, guiding her to the circle of seats she had just vacated with Julia and Ethan. At the sight of his untouched teacup, the tears threatened anew. But the collective strength of the women around her bolstered her spirits, helping her to feel she was not so alone in all this.

"Did he harm you?" Laney asked from beside Sylvia, the tight control she was exercising over her voice evident.

"No," Heloise croaked before trying again. "No, he did not harm me. I swear it."

Euphemia, still close to her side, leaned into her, her warmth a comfort Heloise had not known she would need so very much. "Do you wish to talk about what happened?"

A week before, a day before, hell, even an hour before, and Heloise would have stated emphatically that no, she did not wish to talk about it. She did not do that sort of thing; after all, did not share her troubles with anyone. To do so, she had been led to believe, was to make herself a burden.

Now, however, looking about the circle of faces that showed unwavering affection and care and worry, she wished, for the first time in her life, to lean on another. And the words spilled forth then, like a dam being torn down and a river finding its proper path through a rugged and unforgiving terrain.

"I've hurt Ethan horribly," she began, closing her eyes as she recalled his stark face. "He was innocent in everything, and I betrayed him. It's stupid, I know, to regret my actions. It was my decision, after all, to seduce him in order to gain access to the club. And no matter how often I think about it, I have never been able to come up with a different way to accomplish that." She drew in a shaky breath. "But I do regret it, so very much."

Sylvia leaned forward, placing a hand over Heloise's. "Because you care for him," she said quietly.

Heloise looked up in shock to find Sylvia's steady gaze on her. The other woman smiled faintly.

"I daresay you did not know yourself until today. Else why would you have reacted so violently to giving him pain?"

Heloise shook her head in confusion. "You knew I was falling for him?"

"Not until yesterday, when I saw you together in Hyde Park, and then after, when we brought Mr. Sinclaire here."

"Ah, God." Groaning, Heloise dropped her head in her hands. "I'm such a fool. I put everything at risk."

"You are most certainly not a fool," Euphemia declared. "You were willing to do so much, to give up so much, for love of your sister-in-law, as well as to protect us and make certain we succeed. Those are not the actions of a fool. Rather, those are the actions of someone exceptionally brave." She rubbed Heloise's back in soothing circles. "And besides," she continued gently, "I do not think you would have fallen for the man if you had not sensed he was good."

"It seems your heart knew who he truly was before your head did," Iris piped up.

"Well said, Iris dear," Sylvia murmured. "And it worked out for the better, now that we have his assistance in recovering the jewels." She gave Heloise a long look. "What happens between you and Mr. Sinclaire when this is over is anyone's guess."

Why did her heart leap at that? It was obvious things were over between them, that he would never be able to forgive her for what she had done. And that she would never be able to forgive herself.

"There will be nothing between us then," she said. "I assure you."

Sylvia's lips kicked up at one corner, as if to say, "We shall see." Before Heloise could respond, Sylvia leaned forward.

"But we have a mere three days until the masquerade. If Mr. Sinclaire cannot recover the jewels by that time, we shall have to put our plan into motion to flush out the villain who has taken them. That will be our last chance to save Julia. And so, though Mr. Sinclaire may come through for us before then, there is still a very high chance we shall have to trigger our plans for that night."

Julia. Of course. Once more Heloise had lost sight of what this whole endeavor was about. Though this time it had been due to the faintest hope of a future for her and Ethan. A hope that, now that it had broken through the hard outer shell of self-disgust that had contained it, seemed to be growing strong roots that attached to her heart and would not let go.

"Yes, our plans," she said in an attempt to control her quickly spiraling thoughts. But as she and the other Widows went over in meticulous detail everything that must happen the night of the masquerade, there was a part of Heloise that was thinking of the days after, and that hoped-for, yet hopeless, future with Ethan.

* * *

Ethan's footsteps were heavy as he ascended the stairs to Gavin's apartment, a place he'd certainly had no intention of visiting. After his devastating visit with Heloise, however, his feet had brought him here through no clear will of his own. His heart pounded in his chest as he climbed the familiar treads. The rooms, in a fashionable neighborhood in Mayfair, the place his extravagant brother had been infinitely proud of, should have been given up upon his death. There was no reason, really, to pay the exorbitant rent when no one lived in the place.

Yet Ethan had not been able to let it go. No matter what

Gavin might have done, he had still been Ethan's brother, and Ethan had never lost his love for him even through the years of hurt.

He stopped at the door and closed his eyes, taking a steadying breath before, turning the key in the lock, he opened it wide. He had not been back here since his brother's death three years before, unable to set foot within these walls that Gavin had called home. Yet he had made certain to pay not only the rent but also for the meticulous upkeep of the place. Every week someone came and dusted and swept and made certain the rooms were aired. At first it had seemed a better solution than covering the furniture in shrouds. It would have felt like burying his brother all over again.

He saw now, however, what a mistake that had been. Everything was just as Gavin had left it, from the chair pulled out from the table to the book lying haphazardly on the sofa cushion to the quill on the desk, dried ink still coating the nib. He went there now, picked up that quill, gripped it tight in his hand, as if he could still feel the warmth of his brother's touch through it. Leaving this room as a kind of shrine might have lessened Ethan's grief at the time—or, at least, not added to it. But it had also prevented him from truly laying his brother to rest in his heart. Standing here like this, surrounded by things that still held Gavin's energy within them, he felt that at any moment his brother would step into the room with his crooked smile and hearty laugh.

Just thinking of that now made his heart seize. He dropped the pen to the desk and rubbed at his chest, willing the ache to go away. But it did not, instead spreading until it filled every inch of him. Gavin would not be coming back, he told himself brutally. It was something he should have come to terms with by now. Ignoring everything that had to do with his brother, however, rejecting his pain, had only made things harder in the present.

His head swam, his vision clouding and his throat closing. He swayed, reaching out to steady himself, leaning heavily on the desk as he did so. Emotions bombarded him, those damned feelings he had buried since learning of Gavin's betrayal and death soon after, when his world, that world he had so carefully built, had come crashing down about his head. It had been a mistake to come here, a mistake to face this most agonizing part of his life. And all because Heloise had opened his heart up, that traitorous organ that should have remained closed but was now left exposed. He had to get out of here, had to find a way to close himself off again before he was completely destroyed by it.

But as he turned to go, ready to stumble his way from this place and never, ever return, the front door swung wide, and Gavin himself stood in the entrance.

He stared in disbelief, his mind unable to wrap itself around what he was seeing as he was transported three years into the past. Until Gavin moved, stepping over the threshold, and Ethan's fevered mind finally recognized the difference in movement, the slight dissimilarity in features, the bulkier build. And then the figure spoke, the deeper tone shocking Ethan back to the present.

"Ethan, what the hell are you doing here?"

"Isaac," he breathed. His body gave out and he lurched sideways, his hip crashing into the desk.

Isaac was at his side in an instant, arm about him as he steadied him. "Are you well? What happened?"

Ethan was tempted to lean into his brother, to garner some strength from his last remaining family, this man who had been the scared, wide-eyed boy he'd raised after their father's abandonment and their mother's death.

His senses, however, were coming back to him, that familiar armor that had protected him for so long. So what if there were dents and kinks in it, if one well-placed arrow could find its way past his defenses? Right now, in this moment, it gave him the protection he needed.

"I'm well," he replied gruffly, pulling away from Isaac, taking a step to put some distance between them. His brother stood frozen, arms extended in the air like a marionette's before he let them drop heavily to his sides.

"I did not expect to see you here," he said, voice quiet. "You have not been back since...well, since."

"No, I have not." Ethan narrowed his eyes, a sudden realization dawning. "But what are *you* doing here?"

Isaac shrugged. "I come from time to time, to figure things out." His lips twisted. "Though maybe it hasn't been as healthy for me as I believed it to be."

"None of this is healthy," Ethan muttered, looking about the place, heart heavy. He let loose a harsh breath. "It's time to let it go."

Isaac gave him a sharp glance. "You will get rid of the apartment?"

"It's the best solution, don't you think?"

"I do," Isaac replied slowly, carefully, his eyes wary as he considered Ethan. As if he feared one wrong word would act like a grenade thrown into the tentative calm that was between them. "But why after all this time?"

Why indeed. Heloise's face swam up in his mind, the gentle compassion in her eyes that told of understanding and commiseration. *No*, he told himself fiercely, *she has been playing me all along. Everything about her has been false, including those feigned emotions.* No matter how harshly he berated himself, however, he could not force himself to believe that those moments of their affair had been faked.

But Isaac was waiting for an answer. An answer Ethan was not ready to admit to his brother, much less himself. Clearing his throat, he tugged at his jacket sleeves. "I'd best be going," he muttered. "I'll leave you to close up, then."

Before he reached the door, however, Isaac's voice stopped him. "Aren't you going to ask me what things I try to figure out when I come here?"

Ethan turned his head and regarded his brother cautiously. "I daresay it's none of my business. You're a grown man; you can do as you like."

"But it is every bit your business," Isaac replied softly.

Was it? And even if it was, did he have any right to hear it after the way he'd pushed Isaac aside these past years? He very nearly shrugged him off and left, the comfort of solitude like a beacon.

Until a small voice in his head, Heloise's voice, urged him to wait, just a moment. And that small moment was all it took to shift his mind entirely. As he continued to look upon his brother's familiar features, the echo of Gavin in them, he saw it: the tightness about his eyes; the faint trembling of his lips before he pressed them tight together; the clenching of his hands into fists that told of great stress, a stress that Isaac was attempting to hide with a mild expression and easy tone. Ethan saw how he'd left his brother to deal with his grief alone while he'd shut himself off from the world, and how his brother had attempted to mask that grief to protect Ethan. As he was still doing. That door Heloise had opened in his heart opened even further and he knew, no matter how loud that creature of self-preservation was within him, he could no longer turn his back on Isaac.

"Tell me," he said, voice gruff as he turned to fully face him. "Tell me why you come here."

Isaac's eyes flared wide, his lips parting. Then, as if he feared Ethan would take advantage of the lull in conversation to turn and bolt from the room—he was tempted to, God knew he was—he quickly gathered himself and began.

"I keep thinking over that last day with Gavin, when we learned he was the one responsible for the cheating at the club."

A memory washed over Ethan at those words, a vivid recollection of the moment they had discovered that Gavin was the viper in their midst, the way his stomach had dropped when they had discovered the missing funds in his brother's desk, his world falling apart in an instant. Isaac, in his youthful fury, had rushed to Gavin, to confront him. And it had been as Gavin had hurried back to Dionysus that he had made a fatal misstep, had careened into the path of a speeding carriage and been thrown from his horse and died before Ethan could beg him for a reason why he had done what he had.

"Yes," Ethan said through numb lips. "I recall it well."

Silence filled the room, heavy and bleak, nearly suffocating him as the horror of that day seemed to manifest between them. And then Isaac spoke, his voice reed thin.

"If I had not come here in the heat of the moment, if I had been able to control my anger, Gavin would not now be dead."

Ethan's head snapped back in shock. "You cannot have been blaming yourself for his death all this time?" But he saw with painful clarity that Isaac had been. Dear God, his brother had been dealing with guilt on top of his grief? He had not even considered the extra burden Isaac must have carried.

He took a step forward, laid a hand on his brother's

shoulder. "You are not to blame," he said hoarsely. "It was an accident and nothing more."

"Perhaps," was all Isaac said. But that one word was enough to reveal that Isaac didn't believe it one bit.

"Be that as it may," he continued, in an obvious effort to steer the conversation to safer waters, or at least the tumultuous waters he was familiar with, "I keep mulling over that last conversation I had with him. I was angry, and distraught, and so was he. Yet there has been something bothering me about it these three years, something that keeps me awake at night and sits like a vulture on my shoulder during my waking hours." He paused. "And lately I believe I've come to understand what that thing might be."

Why, Ethan thought as he gazed upon his brother's suddenly haggard face, did it seem as if everything in his life would shift in the next moment? And then it did, in a flash.

"I'm not certain Gavin was guilty of the cheating."

Ethan froze, shock paralyzing his lungs until spots began to swim in his vision. But his brother was looking at him with something like fear and worry, and he could not allow his disquiet to show lest he add to his brother's burdens. "Tell me why you think so," he said gently.

Isaac released a shaky breath, wiping his hands on his pants. "He said one word, and one word only: 'How?' That was all he said to me before leaving, before he rushed out of here in an effort to get to you." He closed his eyes and shook his head, as if trying to dislodge something infinitely painful. "That last word is still ringing in my ears, as clear as if Gavin just spoke it. I can still hear the disbelief and pain and fear in it. But after three long years, I'm beginning to wonder if that single question was not asking how we could have found out about his betrayal, but rather how he could have been blamed when he was, in fact, innocent."

Those quiet words, said with a sad resignation and a thick guilt, nevertheless hit Ethan like a wave smashing against a cliff face. And he saw then those questions deep in his heart that he had been ignoring since the latest information regarding the corruption at Dionysus had cropped up: What if this betrayal was not new at all, but a continuation of the one from three years ago? What if the perpetrator had been lying low all this time after the tragedy of Gavin's death, letting everyone believe in his brother's guilt, an act of cowardly self-preservation—letting a dead man, someone who could not defend himself, take the blame?

His breath left him in a rush. Truly, it made perfect sense. Which meant that all this time, as he had been thinking his brother a villain and closing himself off from everyone, the one responsible for the betrayal in the first place had been safe and secure at Dionysus. The cuckoo in the nest.

"Fuck," he growled, slamming his fist down on the desktop.

Isaac, however, misconstrued the source of Ethan's anger. His face paled, the trust of a moment ago gone. "If you would just listen—"

But Ethan was not about to allow miscommunication to come between them again. Nor was he going to keep information from his brother that he had every right to know. "I believe you," he cut in gruffly.

Isaac's face went slack. "You…do?"

"Yes."

"Oh." And then, quietly, "Thank you."

A humorless laugh tumbled from Ethan's lips. "Thanking me is the last thing you should be doing. In fact, you should be cursing me. If not for me pulling away from you, we might have had this conversation sooner, might have come upon the truth long ago." He swallowed hard. "Especially as it seems whoever was responsible for the cheating the first time may have resurfaced."

Isaac stared at him. "What?" he breathed.

Ethan nodded and ran a hand over his face, a new fury boiling up in him. Had the perpetrator purposely framed Gavin back then? Had they been the one to cause the tragic chain of events that had led to their brother's death?

But losing control of his emotions right now would not help anyone. No, he had to maintain a cool head. "These past weeks I have been tracking new information on corruption at the club."

Isaac frowned, confusion clouding his vision. Then, suddenly, the clouds lifted, a dawning light entered his eyes, and Ethan could fairly see the moment his brother realized that he had been under suspicion, that Ethan had believed he could be the guilty party. He braced himself, expecting fury and grief that Ethan could think him capable of something so horrendous.

Instead, Isaac breathed deeply and placed a comforting hand on Ethan's shoulder. "Thank you for telling me." His lips tilted up at one corner. "Though I hope you know you cannot keep me out of working with you to unearth the culprit."

Ethan gaped at him. "You aren't angry with me?"

Isaac snorted. "Oh, I'm plenty angry. But I understand why you did what you did."

Ethan shook his head, unable to speak. Finally he managed, voice hoarse with guilt, "I'm sorry for turning my back on you when you needed me most. I essentially abandoned you."

Isaac gave him a small, sad smile. "Will you take on the guilt for this as well? You really do take pleasure in pain, don't you?" He chuckled lightly. "You never abandoned me. You simply did what you had to in order to survive."

Ethan shook his head. "No matter the reason, as your elder brother it was wrong of me."

"Bullshit."

While Ethan was stunned at the vehemence in that one unexpected word, he was even more so seeing a small, affectionate smile lifting his brother's lips.

"You're an idiot, did you know that?" Isaac murmured. "Despite what you wish people to believe, you're human. And you were hurting, worse than I've ever seen you hurt. I knew you were dealing with that hellish situation in the only way that you could while keeping your sanity. And not once did I ever resent you for it. Nor do I resent you for this."

Why, Ethan wondered blearily, was everything going hazy in his vision? He blinked furiously to clear his eyesight—only to feel the warm track of tears trailing down his cheeks.

But at the moment he didn't give a damn that he was crying. All that mattered was the feeling of the great gaping hole in his chest that had been punched clear through him at Gavin's death beginning to close. No, that wasn't right. It had begun to close this past week or better. And it was all because of Heloise. She had touched something deep inside him with her caring and had begun to heal him, no matter that her efforts had been born from desperation for her sister-in-law. Without her, he would never have found his way out of the fog he'd been wandering aimlessly in for three years, leading him here to this moment with his brother. As he wordlessly pulled Isaac into a hug, he vowed it would not be wasted.

27

The night of the masquerade came much faster than Ethan expected. Especially as every moment he was not scouring Dionysus from top to bottom—alongside Isaac, of course, who refused to be left out of even the most trivial details in the search for the jewels and, more importantly, the person responsible—he spent thinking of Heloise. And each moment with her on his mind and not at his side was the worst torture. Was she well? Was she eating? Was she losing sleep as he was, thinking about what had been between them? And, worse than all those questions combined: Would she ever forgive him for the part he'd played, however unknowingly, in her sister-in-law's misfortune?

Forgiveness. He sighed, looking down on St James's from his rooms, watching the quiet crawl of traffic, traffic that would soon be as constrained as the sand in the neck of an hourglass as the time of the masquerade arrived. Mere days before, he would have scoffed at the idea of wanting Heloise's forgiveness for anything. His hurt had been too great, the sense of betrayal too acute for him to even consider such a thing.

Yet after the sleepless nights he'd spent going over all that had happened, one thought in the whole debacle stood out first and foremost: what she must have gone through, the fear and anxiety and worry, all because of his club. And he knew she had done only what she'd felt she'd had to do. Was he still incredibly hurt from finding out the truth? God, yes. The pain in his chest was so sharp, at times he thought he would never draw breath again.

But he understood her. Or, at least, he understood why she had done what she had. Which only added to the guilt that pressed down on him like stone slabs on his chest.

"Penny for your thoughts," Isaac's voice said in his ear.

Ethan jumped, glancing sharply at his brother, who had somehow materialized at his side. "When the hell did you get here?"

"I did knock. Several times." Isaac pursed his lips as he considered him. "Though I daresay you have much on your mind."

"That's an understatement," Ethan mumbled, turning back to the scene out the window, glancing up and down the street once more. "Shall I take it the jewels were not found during your final search of the lower offices?" he asked quietly.

"No. Though we both knew they wouldn't be."

"Yes," Ethan murmured. He and Isaac had scoured every inch of Dionysus from top to bottom these past three days, and not a single penny had been found out of place, much less a full set of priceless rubies. He had desperately hoped they could locate them, that tonight and all the dangers that would accompany it would not need to happen—and that he could finally be free of the guilt and yearning that Heloise dredged up in him. Now, however, there was no alternative but for their plans to commence.

A carriage slowed in front of the club then, and he tensed, peering down at it, waiting for it to stop and a familiar sable head to emerge from within. But it kept on rolling down the street. He let out a harsh breath, not certain if he was frustrated or relieved that Heloise was not yet here.

"Looking for Mrs. Marlow?" Isaac drawled.

Once more Ethan's gaze snapped to his brother, only to find him grinning with unabashed glee. "You *are* looking for her," Isaac said.

"Whelp," Ethan grumbled, even as his gaze returned to the street.

Isaac was silent beside him for a time, his posture easy, and Ethan relaxed just because of his presence. Tonight's plans to flush out the villain, all while they hosted their largest event of the year, were fraught with tension and anxiety. Though he knew it needed to happen, that they needed to oust whoever was responsible for threatening Dionysus's hard-earned reputation, ruining lives such as Miss Marlow's, and indirectly causing Gavin's death three years earlier, that did not mean he did not worry about the repercussions. All they had worked toward could very well be at risk.

But having his brother beside him, knowing they were in this together no matter what might occur, was the greatest comfort to him.

Until said brother opened his mouth and spoke again on that subject Ethan had no wish to discuss.

"What will happen between the two of you after this night is through?"

Ethan clenched his back teeth so tightly he felt the ache of it radiate to his ears. "Nothing will happen."

"Why?"

A sharp bark of laughter escaped Ethan's lips. "Why? That should be obvious."

"What, because it started out under false pretenses?"

"I would think," Ethan managed through his teeth, "that is a good enough reason."

He expected his brother to concede. Which was truly stupid of him. His brother had never conceded in his life. If anything, opposition only made him more tenacious.

"You're an arse."

"What the hell…?" Ethan muttered before he glowered at his brother. "How am I an arse for believing there is no future for us?"

"Because, dear brother," Isaac proclaimed with a disgusting amount of self-assurance, "while it began with a lie, it's obvious that the feelings you both developed during said affair are not."

Why, Ethan wondered, did his heart leap in his chest at that? But he would not be swayed by that traitorous organ. "Bollocks."

Isaac shrugged. "Why else would you be brooding? Not that you don't brood most of the time," he corrected himself. "But this brooding is different. And it only intensifies whenever Mrs. Marlow is mentioned."

"It doesn't matter how I might feel," he gritted, his cheeks heating because Isaac had been able to see to the heart of him so easily. "What matters is that everything Heloise proclaimed to feel was false."

There was a heavy pause. Then Isaac said, tone thoughtful, "I believe her feelings are much more real than even you can imagine."

Before Ethan could think how to react to that, Isaac adjusted his cravat and said, "I'd best be off now. There's still much to do before the evening commences. Though," he continued, sobering considerably, "are you quite certain we cannot confide our plans to Teagan and Parsons?"

Ethan sighed, though not from frustration at his brother once more bringing up such a contentious subject. No, this sigh was born out of pain, plain and simple. There was nothing more in this world he wanted—besides Heloise, of course, but that was a fruitless wanting—than to confide in his two closest friends.

"I truly wish we could," he said. "But though I'm fairly certain of their innocence—"

"They *are* innocent."

He dipped his head in acknowledgement. Or, rather, his deep need to believe in their innocence. With his certainty that Isaac was not to blame, his desire to think only the best of Teagan and Parsons had become so powerful, he was having a hell of a time ignoring it. God knew that even considering one of them as the source of the betrayal at Dionysus devastated him. But it was made so much worse when he thought of Gavin's death three years earlier—and that the one responsible had allowed Gavin to take the blame. How could either of them have done something so heinous? It had been one thing for someone to cheat their patrons and betray the trust of everyone who worked at the club; it was quite another to play the coward, inadvertently leading to Gavin's death.

But he could not shy away from learning the truth. No matter how much it might gut him.

"You know as well as I," he said, voice soft, "that the fewer people who know about this the better."

"I know," Isaac replied, shoulders slumping. In the next moment, however, his chin came up, a determined gleam entering his dark eyes. "The fewer people who know about it, the safer we'll all be, Teagan and Parsons included." He grinned. "As well as Mrs. Marlow, whom I have every hope of calling my sister-in-law someday."

Before Ethan could think how to react—God knew the war that was going on within him, part of him rejoicing at the very idea and another part wanting to reach out and punch Isaac in the face—his brother winked and was out the door.

"That little shit," he growled to the empty room before going back to staring out the window, trying and failing not to think about his brother's words becoming reality. It was a relief when Mary arrived. That relief, however, was short-lived.

"Mr. Sinclaire, sir," she piped from the doorway. "Mrs. Finch and Mrs. Marlow have arrived, along with several other fine-looking ladies."

Why did his heart leap at that? So violently, in fact, that if he weren't certain it was being held in by his ribs, he'd expect it to burst from his chest and bounce across the room. Frowning, he glanced behind him to the empty street below.

Mary, bless her, was one step ahead as usual. "They've arrived by the back door. Shall I show them up?"

"No," was his quick reply. Too quick, if Mary's widened eyes were anything to go by. But having Heloise here, in this place where they had lain together, in the place where he had loved her, would be more than he could bear.

He cleared his throat. "I need to show them about the boxing hall," he explained.

Mary, thank God, nodded as if that made perfect sense. "I'll inform them you'll be down momentarily."

"No." Once more that one word burst from his lips. Once more Mary looked at him as if he'd taken leave of his senses. "There's no time to waste, after all," he said by way of excuse. "I'll accompany you."

Which must have been the right thing to say—again— for the maid smiled and spun about, leading the way from the room. But though her pace was quick, it was not quick enough for Ethan. It took every ounce of control he possessed not to push past her and sprint down to the ground floor and Heloise. In the end, however, he managed to control himself, and even walked with a semblance of poise into the main room of the casino. That poise, however, was short-lived. The moment he spotted Heloise, all coherent thought fled from his mind. And as he approached the cluster of women—women he did not even see, as focused as he was on *her*—and gazed down into her beloved face, into those clear blue eyes that had always seen so much, he thought back on Isaac's words and found himself feeling that most dangerous emotion of all: *hope*.

* * *

Heloise had spent the past several days telling herself that she was strong enough to do this, that seeing Ethan would not affect her in the least, that she could separate herself from her heart for one evening to make good on that promise to her dying husband and protect his sister.

The moment she saw Ethan enter the casino, however, looking so tall and commanding and utterly wonderful, she realized that her silent assurances to herself had been made of mere smoke and mirrors. How, she wondered desperately as something cracked in her chest, could she get through tonight?

His eyes alighted on their group immediately. Was it just her, or did he seem to exhale as if in relief? But no, she told herself severely, that exhalation was merely an indication of his aggravation. Regardless of his kindness the other day, he could not be happy about this entire situation. He would be glad to see the end of it. Just as she was.

Why, then, she thought as he reached them and she gazed up into those dark eyes that were incredibly dear to her, did she have the overwhelming urge to cry, knowing tonight would be the last time she would ever have cause to see him?

"Good evening, ladies," he murmured as, finally breaking his gaze from hers, he glanced at each of them in turn. His features were grim, thinner than before. Was he not eating?

"Mr. Sinclaire," Sylvia said, dipping her head in that regal manner she had. "I trust we are not late."

"Not at all. You're just in time."

"Splendid. I'm glad to hear it. But you have not yet met our companions." She turned to Iris and Julia and made the necessary introductions, as if Ethan had indeed never met them.

It was all a predetermined interaction for the public spaces of the club. Yet Heloise grasped each cool, emotionless word that spilled from his lips as if it were the sweetest nectar. Dear God, she had missed his voice, had missed *him*. No matter how things had ended between them, she was determined to cherish each and every second she had with him before they were separated forever, to take with her into the lonely years that loomed ahead.

Ethan guided them to the back of the casino and the long hall that led to the boxing venue. About them, Dionysus had been transformed into an unfamiliar landscape. She had noticed it in a very vague kind of manner upon her entrance to the club, of course. But now that the initial meeting with Ethan was behind her, she could finally take in her surroundings. And what she saw had her in awe. The walls were no longer covered in heavy red velvet as before, but in rich ivory decorated with twining vines, gilded grapes dripping from their tendrils. Faux stone columns stood at intervals, statues of mythical gods scattered around, everything elegant and shining as if they had stepped into an ancient palace. The employees had exchanged their typical stark black garb for deep amethyst jackets embellished with shining gold thread, similar to the one Ethan currently wore. They all scurried about, putting the finishing touches to the decor, preparing platters of champagne, wiping down already sparkling surfaces. They would all don their masks soon, she knew, Ethan and the partners included, completing the transformation, giving the final magical touch.

Over the past weeks Heloise had become aware of many of the intricacies involved in planning such an event. Yet this was the first time she had fully understood the effort, time, and money it must take. Guilt surged. She'd been so concerned with finding those damn jewels, she had not fully comprehended the scope of this event and what it meant for this place Ethan had poured his heart and soul into. And it could all be ruined in one fell swoop this evening if things went wrong.

She did not fail to notice the irony that she was now concerned with Dionysus's fate after being more than happy to destroy the gaming hell in order to recover the jewels. But after having been brought into Ethan's confidence, after learning what he had gone through to build this place from nothing—after falling in love with him—she could think of little else in this moment but the devastation their plans could wreak on him.

They reached the back venue just then. As with the rest of the casino, Heloise found herself shocked at the change. She had witnessed firsthand the work to turn this once-empty space into a place suitable for a grand boxing match. Nothing had prepared her, however, for how it would look once the workers and craftspeople and equipment and debris were removed. The ring stood in a place of honor in the center, the platform a thing of beauty with its raised dais and sturdy ropes and thickly padded posts. Surrounding it, the newly constructed seats gleamed in their fresh varnish. Pendants and ribbons hung from the balcony above, where even more seating had been constructed.

"It's perfect, Mr. Sinclaire," Laney said with satisfaction as she stepped forward, spinning in a circle to take the grandeur of it all in. "As I expected. I could not have dreamed of a better venue to host my return to the ring."

"I'm pleased to hear it," he replied. Suddenly he turned Heloise's way. "I hope the venue is up to your expectations as well, Mrs. Marlow."

Mouth suddenly dry, Heloise swallowed hard and forced her reluctant voice to work. "It is, Mr. Sinclaire. Thank you for your efforts; it will be a splendid affair indeed."

"That we can guarantee," came a jolly voice from the shadows. The group turned to see Mr. Teagan, along with Mr. Parsons and Mr. Isaac Sinclaire, emerge from the doorway leading to the upper level. Mr. Teagan grinned as they approached. "And not only because of our preparations. Rather, your match itself will be the highlight of the evening. Though I daresay it would be even if we held it in a barren field."

Laney laughed merrily. "I knew I liked you, Mr. Teagan. But please allow me to introduce you to my friends here." So saying, she turned to their group, face animated and hands busy.

Which was Heloise's cue to get Ethan alone. Not that she particularly wished to get him alone. God knew what it would do to her composure, not to mention her heart. But a private discussion regarding the evening's upcoming events was imperative, the danger of something going wrong too great.

She sidled up to him on shaking legs. "Mr. Sinclaire, would you be so kind as to show me the changing room, so I may prepare things for Mrs. Finch?"

His eyes when they met hers were not the cold, distant ones she'd expected. No, they fairly burned. But whatever he might be feeling toward her, the rest of him did not betray it even one bit. He dipped his head. "Of course," he said in a neutral tone. "Please follow me."

They exited the venue in silence, the sounds of voices and laughter growing fainter as they stepped from the space and turned into a small room off to the side of the hall. Without a word, Ethan closed the door behind them, shutting them in. And it took Heloise everything in her not to throw herself into his arms.

"We can speak freely here," he said quietly.

Taking a deep breath, Heloise schooled her features and turned to face him. But what little composure she had managed to retain slipped dangerously as she caught sight of his face. That burning in his eyes was still there. But his features were no longer calm, no longer emotionless. Instead of the anger she had expected, however, there was pain and longing.

She froze, forgetting to breathe. Longing? That made no sense at all, unless his longing was for her to get out of his life once and for all.

"I trust Euphemia's position has been secured," she said, clasping her hands in front of her to conceal their shaking—and to prevent her from reaching for him.

His expression cleared. "Yes. She'll be working as a footman this evening." His lips quirked humorlessly. "She is quite the master of disguise. As was proven by her infiltration of the craftsmen, of course. But meeting with her tonight truly showed me what she is capable of."

"Yes," Heloise replied almost by rote, finding a strange comfort in the innocuous conversation, "her talent is unmatched. She is the person responsible for all our specialized garments, split skirts and trousers and corsets…"

"And places to conceal blades, no doubt," he finished for her when her voice faltered.

She recalled that early-morning meeting at Hyde Park, when she had pulled a knife on his man Keely, and her cheeks warmed. "Yes, that, too." But this conversation was veering into the personal, which made her feel as if she were in a listing ship on a ravaged sea.

"But we are here to discuss our plans for this evening," she said firmly, determined to get them back on track—and her heart under control.

"Of course," he murmured.

She nodded, the tilting ship finally righting some as they returned to the business at hand. "As discussed, at the conclusion of the boxing match, Euphemia will make her way to the gas valve and cut off the supply, dousing every lamp within Dionysus. If we have judged the villain right, the ensuing chaos will force him to reveal himself."

He frowned. "And you are certain that will flush him out?"

"Certain?" she gave a small, sad laugh. "Nothing in this is certain, I'm afraid. We are counting on human nature. If it's as we suspect, the villain is using the anonymity of the masquerades to cheat people. By flushing him out late in the evening, we have every belief he'll have already made his move and stashed his ill-gotten winnings somewhere in the premises, and his anxiety over being found out in the ensuing chaos will force him to reveal his hand. That, or he will use the diversion to secure more."

"But human nature is a capricious thing," he murmured softly. "Is it not?"

Her heart twisted painfully. No doubt he thought her the most capricious of all.

But she was allowing her emotions to rule, which would only lead to disaster this evening. She had to keep herself under tight control until the bitter end.

"It will be a gamble, yes," she replied evenly enough. "But we don't have the luxury—or time—to do it any other way. As much as we may both wish it otherwise."

He gave no response to that, but his gaze changed, that longing back in place. Once more she had the insane urge to take him in her arms and beg him that they begin again. Her feet inched forward against her will. It was only with incredible willpower that she managed to stop herself.

"You indicated in your correspondence with us that you have apprised your brother of what is to happen here this evening?" she said almost desperately, needing the change in subject.

He continued to look at her for a long moment. Finally, blessedly, he nodded once, breaking the spell. "Yes, Isaac is aware of everything."

"And you trust him."

"With my life."

She knew it wasn't a reprimand. Yet it only added to her guilt, knowing how he must have struggled with all of this. She dipped her head, her cheeks burning hot. "I'm sorry for questioning your judgment. It's not what I intended."

He was quiet, gaze unreadable. And then, voice tight, "My judgment is not infallible. You have every right to question it."

Which must be a reference to the trust he had mistakenly placed in her. Tears blurred her vision, and she ducked her head lest he see. But there was no hiding her emotions when she said, "Ethan, I'm so sorry I deceived you. It was never my intent to hurt you in any way."

"I know."

Her gaze snapped back to his at the tenderness in his voice. "What?" she breathed.

The smile he gave her was painful to behold for the

sadness that saturated it. "I know you felt you didn't have a choice. I understand."

Those simple, earnest words, spoken with such gentleness, were more painful than obscenities screamed at her. At least she would have felt she deserved that. But she did not deserve this kindness and understanding from him, not even a bit. And she knew, in that moment, she could not do this to him.

"I'm sorry, Ethan," she managed through a throat tight with unshed tears. "I'm so sorry it's come to this. I'll put a stop to it. Let me go tell the others."

She took a step toward the door, needing to escape this, to escape him, to find any other way but this.

His soft voice, however, stopped her more surely than if he had physically blocked her path.

"No, you won't," he said. "This is happening."

She shook her head, so violently it threatened to bring down the intricate braids she'd carefully pinned up. "It's not too late. We can end it before it begins."

He sighed. "You would give all this up now, after the effort you have put in?" There was frustration in his voice that only intensified as he asked—nay, fairly begged, "Why?"

Why? Because I love you. But she could never say those words to him. She didn't have the right to say those words.

"It could ruin everything you have built," was her logical but completely lacking answer.

She could fairly feel him shrug. "If that happens, so be it. In truth I'll have deserved it for what the club has done."

She hugged herself about the middle, closing her eyes against the pain in his voice. "It's not your fault."

"Perhaps not. But that does not mean I should not take responsibility for it. I have to make things right."

She shook her head again. "No. I won't allow it."

He huffed a soft laugh. "You cannot stop it."

"Try me."

Again that laugh, though with some humor to it this time. "If you insist on this, I'll have no choice but to tie you up to make certain tonight happens."

Which brought about an altogether different picture in her head. But she could not go down that path, now or ever again. "But—" she tried.

"No *but*s," he declared firmly. "We shall see this through. Now, let's finish what we've started and save your sister-in-law and I expect many others as well." There was a heavy pause. And then, "Including me."

She looked at him, only to see her own pain mirrored in his dark eyes.

He gave her a sad smile. "Go now, and prepare the others for tonight."

What else could she do? Giving him one last mournful look, she turned toward the door. His sudden hand on her arm, however, stopped her feet in their tracks and her breath in her lungs. Her gaze flew to his, shock making her heart pound in her temples.

His eyes were back to burning again. No, they didn't just burn. They blazed with fire. Without realizing it, she swayed toward him.

"But first, promise me you will be careful tonight," he said, voice hoarse. "That you will not do anything unduly dangerous, that you will fetch me the moment something occurs."

Tears threatened and she blinked them furiously back, for it sounded almost as if he cared what might happen to her. But he was waiting for her to reply. She swallowed hard. "Very well, Ethan. I promise I shall be safe."

"Thank you," he whispered. And then, giving her one last scorching look, he released her and left the room.

28

Heloise tucked her arm about Julia, keeping her close to her side as they hugged the wall of the boxing venue. Around them patrons crowded the space, vying for the choicest seats, the best vantage. Spirits were high, the excitement over the coming match reaching a fever pitch.

"Should we attempt to secure seats?" Julia fretted, hand shaking as she checked—for quite possibly the hundredth time that long night—that her mask was still secure on her face.

"We won't be staying in this portion of the club for long," Heloise reminded her in a low voice, lips close to her ear. "Once the match begins we shall all take our places on the casino floor. We need to be ready before the culmination of the fight, for once the lights sputter, everything will happen very quickly."

"Oh dear," Julia moaned under her breath. She swayed, and Heloise feared she would faint.

Iris and Sylvia approached then, slipping among the thickening crowd like fish swimming upstream. Though Iris fairly twitched in her anxiety, her fingernails relentlessly scratching at her wrist as proof of her nervousness, she nevertheless forced a falsely bright smile beneath the edge of her floral mask. The Widows as a whole had considered whether it might be best to leave her home for this evening's plans. Crowded social events, after all, were a source of great stress for her.

Iris, however, had been adamant that she attend, refusing to sit out any longer.

"It is all quite exciting, isn't it?" she proclaimed now in carrying tones. At any other time Heloise would have winced at her horrible acting—Iris, while a genius with all manner of flora and fauna, was decidedly lacking in anything remotely approaching stagecraft. But her gratitude to Iris for braving something she feared so much, not to mention her relief in having someone to assist her with Julia in that moment, was too great.

"Immensely so," Sylvia proclaimed, sidling up to Julia's other side, tucking her arm through hers. To anyone observing them, it would have seemed the affection of a dear friend. Heloise, however, could see it for what it truly was: extra support for Julia should she fail to gain control of herself.

Blessedly, it was enough to snap her sister-in-law back to the present. Shaking her head, she straightened, quickly following their lead with a shaky smile.

"I'm quite looking forward to Mrs. Finch's match," she said. "Do you think she shall be the victor?"

"Good girl," Heloise whispered in her ear before raising her voice. "I do hope so. I've got a hefty sum on her, after all."

Everyone in their small group laughed, giving a fairly good impression of genuine high spirits, and Heloise breathed a small sigh of relief. The entire evening had been trying for her sister-in-law. Like Iris, she had insisted on coming, certain she could help, perhaps by identifying the villain by some small sign only she would be able to see. Yet the atmosphere, as well as the anticipation, had taken a toll. *Just hold on a bit longer*, Heloise thought, casting a concerned glance at Julia's pale features.

* * *

The sound of flesh hitting flesh carried over the sounds of cheering and yelling from the crowd. Heloise glanced toward the fight, gnawing anxiously at her lip with her teeth, only to see Laney take a solid hit to the jaw. She winced, tightening her hand on Sylvia's arm. They should have left some time earlier, the moment the women stepped into the ring.

Yet nothing, it seemed, could tear Sylvia away.

"We really must go," she whispered desperately in her friend's ear.

"Just one more moment," Sylvia replied, eyes never leaving the ring. "You know this match will last for quite a while. If there is anything my dear Laney has, it's stamina." She tried for a mischievous smile, but it came across as more of a grimace, her face pale beneath the edge of her gilt mask, her lips thin and bloodless. At another sickening fleshy sound she winced, her entire body seeming to shrink in on itself.

Heloise could understand her reluctance to leave. Truly she could. If it had been someone who was her whole world in that ring—God, if it had been Ethan getting pummeled to within an inch of his life…A horrible vision of just that happening filled her head then, one so abhorrent she felt sick to her stomach. Her gaze shifted to Ethan near the ring, as if to assure herself he was in truth safe. His face was completely concealed by the gilded mask, but even so she saw clear as day his eyes on her. It bolstered her, that steady gaze, though she had no right to be given strength by him at all.

But if they did not adhere to their plans, God knew what could go awry. There was no room for error. And that meant they had to stick to their scheme, no matter how difficult it might be.

That did not mean, however, that she could not buy Sylvia a sliver of time.

"Julia, Iris," she said, turning to those women, who were fairly plastered to the wall in their need to stay as far from the wild crowd as possible, "you know what is to come, what places we are to take on the casino floor, correct?" At their wide-eyed nods, she smiled reassuringly, though it was the very last thing she felt like doing. "Why don't you go on ahead? Sylvia and I will meet you there in just a moment."

The words were barely out of her mouth before the two women, arms clasped tight, fairly bolted from the room. Heaving a sigh of relief that one portion of the plan was at least underway, she turned back to Sylvia—

—Only to find her look of brave determination being replaced with one of horror. Gaze snapping to the ring, Heloise was just in time to witness Laney, obviously hurt, spit out blood before planting her foot and landing a solid punch to her opponent's jaw. The other woman stumbled back from the impact, causing a frenzy of cheers to go up that subsided to raucous grumbling as she quickly regained her balance.

The moment of reprieve did not last long, however. For just as Sylvia, finally in control of herself once more, reached for Heloise's hand in preparation to leave the event hall, Mrs. Holburn took advantage of a drop in Laney's guard to land another punch to her jaw. This one, however, did far more damage than those before it, snapping Laney's head back, causing her to stumble and crash into a corner post of the ring.

"Laney!" Sylvia cried. Eyes wild, she turned to Heloise. "What do I do?" she wailed. "I cannot leave her."

Before Heloise could reply—what could she even say?—Mr. Isaac Sinclaire was at their side.

"Let her stay," he said low under the wild cheers from the crowd. "She can take my place here. I'll go with you to the casino floor."

Heloise nearly sagged with relief. But now was not the time for weakness. Nodding her thanks, she turned back to Sylvia. "Be safe. We shall see you soon."

As she turned to leave with Ethan's brother, however, Sylvia grabbed her hand.

"Thank you," she said to the both of them, voice thick with emotion. Then, giving Heloise's hand a brief squeeze, she pushed through the crowd toward the ring.

But though Heloise should feel some relief now that the snag in their plans had been dealt with, the tension in her muscles would not leave her be. Some dark premonition had taken hold of her and would not easily let her go.

The cavernous casino was considerably quiet when they reached it, only a few patrons having chosen to forgo the much-anticipated match to continue their luck at the tables. Across the room, Julia and Iris had taken up their respective positions, the better to keep an eye out for any signs of suspicious behavior. But something was wrong here, the atmosphere not right.

Before she could gauge the reason, however, Mr. Sinclaire hissed a low curse.

"Damn it, why aren't the lanterns lit?"

Heloise's stomach sank in an instant, her gaze flying wildly about the room. He was right. The extra oil lanterns they had set up about the space, a necessary safety precaution to make certain they were not plunged into complete darkness when the gas line was turned off, were all dark. Without those lights, this huge, windowless space would turn into a veritable tomb, the stampede that would surely follow causing the injuries and possibly the deaths of many of the patrons.

"Dear God," she whispered in horror.

Mr. Sinclaire grabbed the nearest footman. "What happened in here?" he demanded, voice rough. "Why have the lanterns been gutted?"

The man's eyes widened in alarm behind his gilded mask. "We was told it was too bright, sir, that the extra light ruined the mood, and was instructed to extinguish them."

"Fuck," Mr. Sinclaire hissed. "Did you douse them elsewhere? The boxing venue as well?"

"Y-yes, sir."

A roar of fear and fury escaped Mr. Sinclaire's lips. Terror, however, did the opposite for Heloise, petrifying her chest until she could hardly draw breath. They had been so intent on the fight and making certain everyone took their places that they had not noticed those vital lanterns had gone dark.

"All of you light them again," he barked. "Now!"

As the man scurried away to do his bidding, several other workers who had been listening in bolting after him, a raucous cheer went up from the venue behind them. Heloise tensed, looking to the gas lamps, expecting them to sputter out at any moment. The undulating sounds of the crowd continued, however, like waves against the shore. Heloise nearly sagged in her relief.

"Can you get to Euphemia?" she asked Ethan's brother

now. "Should the fight end in the next several minutes, she will need to delay turning off the gas. We need time to get the lanterns relit."

"Of course," Isaac said. And then he was off, sprinting back down the hallway.

Heloise grasped her skirts in her hands and turned then, intending to race to where Julia and Iris stood and have them help in the relighting—only to find both women hurrying her way, no doubt having sensed that something was very wrong.

"What has happened, Heloise?" Iris asked breathlessly, thin body fairly trembling in her agitation.

"We need to assist the footmen in relighting the lanterns, now," she said.

Neither woman needed further urging, both no doubt hearing the desperation and fear in Heloise's tone. They immediately located tinderboxes and turned for the closest lanterns, going to work without a word. Heloise had not gotten far, however, when one of the employees, in the same deep purple jacket and full face mask as everyone else who worked at the club, passed by, heading back to the boxing venue. "What's that you're doing there, Mrs. Marlow?" he called out.

That rough voice could only belong to Mr. Copper. "Mr. Sinclaire has ordered the relighting of these lanterns," she explained. "Can you please make certain the ones in the boxing venue are relit?"

"Of course," he said with a dip of his head. "And if I'm lucky, I'll be able to catch the end of the match as well."

He exited the casino. But she hardly saw his departure because Julia, suddenly back at her side, dug her nails into her arm. Heloise glanced down in shock—only to see her sister-in-law staring after Mr. Copper, fear having dredged every last bit of color from her face.

"Heloise," she croaked. "I recognize that voice. It's him, the man at the table that night, the one who took the jewels."

Heloise's heart dropped into her stomach. "Mr. Copper? You are certain?"

"Yes."

Ah God. Her gaze flew to Iris, who had come rushing back over, and saw some of her own shock mirrored back at her. She should feel relief, of course, that they had discovered the culprit so quickly. With luck Mr. Sinclaire had reached Euphemia in time to stop her from dousing the gas lighting, and they could cancel that portion of their plans altogether. This could hopefully be wrapped up quickly, with little damage to the club.

But relief was the farthest thing from her mind just then. For besides his brother and Mr. Teagan and Mr. Parsons, Mr. Copper was the person at the club Ethan trusted most, so much so he had conferred the important position of floor manager to him. He had known Mr. Copper since he was a boy, had grown up in the same rough streets, had a shared history with him. More than that, though, she knew Ethan considered the man a friend.

"I have to go tell Ethan," she whispered, even as her heart broke for him.

Just as she was about to step away, however, a roar went up from the boxing venue, louder than ever, a sound that didn't stop. That was it, she realized dazedly, the indication that the match was over, the proof that Euphemia had been waiting for. But had Mr. Sinclaire reached her in time? She looked to the massive chandelier that soared above the casino floor, dread and a hopeless kind of hope nearly suffocating her— just in time to watch the flames on it flicker and go out.

The roars of triumph and despair changed then, yells and shouts taking their place. And then the rumbling came as hundreds of pairs of feet sought a way out. And that rumble was headed her way.

Instinctively she pushed Julia and Iris against the wall, fear snaking under her skin as her eyes strained to adjust. A good number of the lanterns had been relit after Mr. Sinclaire's orders. But would they be enough? The crowd from the boxing venue began streaming into the main casino then, a mass of dark, undulating bodies. The faint, fitful light glinted off gold and jewels and illuminated the faces of the patrons, highlighting the panic that etched their features. It was a panic she and the Widows had counted on. But was the low lighting—lower than they had planned on—making that panic more than they had bargained for?

Blessedly, the footmen had truly taken Mr. Sinclaire's orders to heart and were even now doing their best to illuminate the space, all while trying to calm the terrified horde of patrons. Equally a blessing, the slowly increasing light also allowed Heloise to find just what she needed in the crowd: Mr. Copper, mask off now, hand clutching a bundle to his chest, ducking into the stairwell that led to the upper floor.

She should wait to tell Ethan. She knew she should. Hadn't she promised him, after all, that she would not take any unnecessary chances, that she would remain safe?

But the very idea that, in the time it took to inform Ethan, Mr. Copper could conceal proof of his thefts had Heloise panicking. For she knew that if he was not caught in the act, he would never reveal the location of Lady Ayersley's jewels. She had to follow him herself, *now*. But how could she leave Julia alone in this chaos?

Just then a slim male figure, one of the many footmen who littered the place, materialized at her side. "Heloise, have you seen anything yet?" he asked in a familiar feminine voice.

Heloise's knees nearly buckled in her relief. "Euphemia, thank God. I think I've found the culprit. Stay with Julia for me?"

As Euphemia hooked a protective arm about Julia, Heloise turned to Iris—only to have the breath sucked from her body. Iris had her hands pressed to her ears, eyes squeezed tight, and was hunched against the wall as if in physical pain. Damn it, how had she forgotten Iris's panic in crowds? She had to get her out of this mess.

"Iris," she shouted over the din, hugging an arm tight about her shoulders in that way that seemed to ground her when she lost control, "I can bring you someplace quiet. Can you trust me?"

There was a pause, barely a heartbeat, but it was enough to make Heloise want to scream. Finally Iris nodded, tucking her head into Heloise's shoulder.

It was all the encouragement she needed. Holding Iris tight against her, she fought their way through the crowd, pushing through the mass of people. Finally she made it to the door to the upper level. About her, more and more lamps were being lit, the employees' voices begging for calm, guiding people out. The cacophonous sound of coins crashed over the scene, the harsh voices of men yelling as someone took advantage of the chaos and attempted to steal from the abandoned tables. But she ignored it as, a rising fury filling her at the pain and grief that Mr. Copper had caused in his greed—and that was still to come when proof of his betrayal came to light—she and Iris followed Mr. Copper into Dionysus's dark abyss.

* * *

Ethan had fully intended to put his entire focus on sticking to the impressively detailed plans that Heloise and the other Widows had set out. Success was paramount, after all, and it could be achieved only if everyone did their part, each of them a cog in a very intricate machine.

But when the lights had flickered out, and the screams had begun—so much more panicked than any of them had expected—he had known deep in his gut that something had gone wrong. And as his eyes struggled much more than they should have to adjust, that something wrong was made frighteningly obvious: It was too blasted dark. A few meager flames flickered at the perimeters of the room, but the majority of the extra lamps were not lit. Why? But even as he cast wild eyes about, trying to understand what had happened, there was one thing and one thing only that filled his mind: Heloise.

Vivid images crashed through his brain as the crowd surged like an angry, storm-churned sea—of Heloise lifeless, trampled beneath hundreds of feet. Bile rose in his throat and he forced it down. No, he told himself fiercely, as, mask off, he pushed his way through the mass of people desperate to escape the cloying shadows of the boxing venue, she was safe. She was strong, and capable, and would have things in hand. He trusted her.

Trusted her. Those words should shock him, considering how she'd deceived him. Yet they felt right. But he could not think of that now. A woman stumbled in front of him, her towering powdered wig falling to the floor and immediately trampled. He reached out, steadying her, nodding distractedly as she thanked him profusely, even as his eyes strained to make out anything useful in the feeble lamplight swinging in pendulous arcs as his workers guided the horde of people out to safety. They were owed extra pay after this, he thought grimly, squinting through the gloom.

He came to the ring then, taking up one of the lamps hanging on the outside edge, quickly lighting it and peering within. There, in the middle, was Lady Vastkern, propping up a bloodied Mrs. Finch. Mrs. Holburn was there, too, with her manager, and he let out a sigh of relief to see that they were all safe.

"You are well?" he shouted over the noise.

"Yes," the viscountess called back, her face set in fierce lines of determination. "But something has gone wrong. Heloise—"

But he could not think of her now or he would go mad. "I shall help guide everyone out, and then I shall find her," he replied. "I promise."

She nodded, her thanks fairly screaming from her eyes as she returned her attention to Mrs. Finch. And then there was no time for Ethan to think as, turning back to the crowd, he went to work. Lantern held high, he helped guide the fearful people toward the exit, assisting one gentleman who had lost his footing, calming a wailing young woman, directing his employees. All the while he fought the panic that had burrowed like a vole beneath his breastbone, trying to dig in deeper with sharp claws.

Finally, he guided the last of the patrons through the long hallway and into the casino itself. But there was no reprieve from the panic surrounding him. Though the room was better lit than the boxing venue had been, the shouts and cries were more enraged here. Through the gloom he spotted several close masses of people on the floor, men fighting each other for the abandoned bounty at the tables, his employees doing their best to protect Dionysus's coffers.

But lost earnings were the least of his concerns. He stopped in his tracks, scanning the cavernous room wildly even as patrons flowed around him, like a raging river around a boulder. In one corner, Teagan was assisting a crying woman, guiding her toward the exit. In another,

Parsons was using his fists to push back a group of violent young men as they attempted to crawl over a table. And there, not ten feet from him, was Isaac, using his body to protect a feminine form against the wall. *Heloise.*

He pushed toward his brother like a madman, desperate to get to him, to *her*. But even before he reached them he knew by the height of the woman that it was not Heloise at all. That was proven a moment later as he came abreast of them and Miss Julia Marlow's pale, fearful face turned his way.

Disappointment crashed over his head, quickly transforming to a strangling panic as he realized Heloise would not have left her sister-in-law's side. Unless...

"Where is Heloise?" He attempted to keep the fear from his voice, but it was there, coating the words like molasses, thick and clinging.

Isaac's eyes tightened at the corners, his perpetually smiling mouth a pinched line. Dread snaked under Ethan's skin.

"Heloise has followed someone to the upper floors." A footman nearby spoke up in a cultured feminine voice that momentarily shocked him until he recognized Mrs. Euphemia Blount in her disguise.

"Who?" he demanded. "Who did she follow?"

"Copper," his brother replied, fury threading the word.

"Copper," Ethan breathed.

Isaac nodded sharply. "Yes, the bastard. I would have gone after them myself, but Miss Marlow was in danger of being trampled."

Ethan looked to Miss Marlow then, who stared back at him, her expression at once fearful and furious.

"I recognized Mr. Copper's voice," she explained tremulously. "Heloise and Mrs. Rumford followed him when the lights went out."

His heart pounded in his chest, in his ears, in his temples, and his vision went dark at the edges. She had promised him not to do anything unduly dangerous. And yet she had willingly walked into a known danger. But he could not be angry that she had broken that promise. No, right now he just needed to see her safe.

"How long ago?" he demanded.

"Fifteen minutes at least."

Fifteen minutes. Much could happen in fifteen minutes, especially with someone as skilled as Copper, who had been raised on the same streets as Ethan, who had been schooled in violence.

He recalled Copper's face then that fateful night three years before, how he had stood with them as they'd looked down at the missing funds in Gavin's desk, how he had voiced his outrage along with the rest of them, how he had stood grim and silent at Gavin's graveside. And all the while, he had been the one to put him there.

Bitter gall filled his mouth. How could he have done it? He had grown up alongside the rest of them, after all, had been a trusted friend. And he had betrayed them. Worse, he had committed the crimes that had led to Gavin's death.

And Heloise had followed him.

Fury and fear battled within him as, without giving his brother or the two women another glance, he stormed through the crowd and toward a reckoning that was long overdue.

29

Heloise's trembling fingers skimmed over the wood-paneled walls of the stairwell as they reached the landing, eyes uselessly wide in the pitch black, breath overloud and ragged in her ears. Iris, in control of herself now that the chaos and noise were behind them, gripped tight to her gown, following close behind her. Thank God. Heloise's focus had to be solely on locating Copper before it was too late.

How had they missed proof of his complicity? Every inch of Dionysus, Copper's office included, had been gone over. And yet nothing had been found? A frustrated curse knocked at her lips, but she swallowed it back. It didn't much matter how they had missed it. The important thing now was learning what he had done with those damn jewels and stopping him from doing to anyone else what he had done to Julia.

Finally she found the now-familiar handle on the door to that secret hallway where she knew Copper's office to be. Letting out a shaky breath, she carefully pushed the panel inward. As before, it did not betray so much as a whisper of a creak as it gave way. And there, at the far end, was the faintest sliver of light.

Copper.

Iris made a small noise in the back of her throat at the sight. Heloise reached back, squeezing her hand in silent warning before tugging her forward down the hall. Copper's office door stood ajar several inches, and they crept to it on silent feet, easing up to the crack to peer within.

A small lamp burned, illuminating the room in a faint glow, and the scene that was revealed had Heloise's jaw dropping nearly to her chest: Mr. Copper, face stark in the dancing shadows, peering down into a hidden space beneath the raised top of his desk.

She shook her head, rubbed at her eyes. The fitful light must be playing with her vision. Yet when she looked again, the scene was the same. The entire top of the desk was raised as if it were a lid on a box, and Mr. Copper was rifling through the contents of the cavity beneath. To deposit his most recent ill-gotten goods, no doubt. Heloise pressed her lips tight as fury simmered in her veins. He had cheated Julia, stolen from her, not only Lady Ayersley's jewels but her life as well. God knew how many other people he had done the same to.

Iris moved forward, bending low beneath Heloise, peering through the crack. She sucked in a breath of surprise, quickly clamping a hand over her mouth to stifle it. But it was too late. Mr. Copper's head shot up at the whisper of sound, dark eyes—made darker still in the harsh shadows—narrowing as he looked toward the door. Heloise wasted no time, grabbing Iris's arm, hauling her down the hall and around the corner. There they stood, backs pressed to the wall, waiting, listening. The faintest sound of footsteps and the door being pushed open reached them. Was he listening for them as well, fearful he had been found out? That could make him very dangerous indeed. They waited, hardly breathing, for what felt an eternity. Finally there was the sound of shuffling, of wood meeting wood, and the glow of his lantern illuminated the wall opposite them. Would he come this way? Heloise bit her lip hard even as she felt along her collar, finding and gripping tight to the small blade hidden there. The echo of the door closing reached them then, the scrape of metal and a lock clicking into place, loud in the tense silence. Soon footsteps sounded, not approaching but receding, muffled by the plush runner that ran the length of the hall. Finally they quieted altogether, the meager light from the lamp going with them. Had he gone back to the casino floor? She closed her eyes and breathed deep, counting the seconds, needing to be certain. When a full minute had passed and there was no indication of him returning, she peered around the corner. Not even a hint of light showed, the darkness pressing on her eyes. He was gone, then. Thank the heavens. Turning back to Iris, she whispered, "Have you got the lamp?"

Iris didn't hesitate, the rustling of fabric telling Heloise the other woman was searching her pockets for the necessary items. In the next moment a small tin box was pressed into Heloise's hands. She went to work immediately, each movement practiced so many times at Sylvia's insistence that she did not need her vision to do it. Releasing the latch, she pried the two halves of the box open, folding out the third, glass-fronted panel before taking the small candle within and securing it in place. Just as she finished, a spark lit the close space, the char cloth in the tinderbox Iris held catching fire. Wasting no time, Iris set the sulfur-tipped match to the char cloth, waiting for the flare of it catching before, fingers shaking, she set the small flame to the candle.

A soft glow lit the hallway, and Heloise held the pocket

lantern aloft, a breath of relief escaping her lips. As one they moved around the corner and to Copper's now-closed office door.

Iris wasted no time, reaching into her bodice, pulling the long lock-picking tools from the boning channels of her corset, inserting them into the lock. Before Heloise could blink, the faint click of the pins falling into place sounded. Iris opened the door and they slipped within, Heloise daring to breathe only when the door closed silently behind them.

"It is ingenious, that's for certain," Iris murmured, moving into the room and around the desk. "Now, if I can only locate the lock."

Heloise followed, watching her carefully for any further nervousness. But no, this was where Iris was in her element. Her eyes fairly glowed with excitement now as she took the lantern from Heloise and bent low, moving quickly and methodically, running the sensitive pads of her fingers over the gleaming mahogany. The seconds ticked by, each one excruciating. The sounds from below were barely discernible, the faint echo of raised voices a chilling accompaniment to the pounding of her heart in her ears.

Then triumph as a small, satisfied squeal came from Iris.

"I found it," she whispered, leaning in closer to study the mechanism. She gave the small lamp to Heloise, her hand back at her bodice, more tools appearing as if by magic. With a frown of concentration, she bent and worked at the lock, head tilted to the side, listening intently. Soon there was that soft click again, accompanied by a hiss of pleasure from Iris. And then she was lifting the top of the desk, revealing the hidden compartment beneath.

"Oh," Heloise breathed as the small light of the lamp illuminated the contents within. Banknotes and coins and papers of every kind filled the space, as well as the small bundle Copper had brought here to conceal. And there, half peeking from beneath a narrow box, was the glint of rubies.

The jewels.

"We've found them," she managed around a throat suddenly tight with tears. "Thank God, we've found them."

But as she reached for them, desperate to get her hands on the pieces and finally—finally!—claim the means to save Julia, the door swung wide to reveal Mr. Copper—and the telltale glint of a gun in his hand. A gun that was pointed right at her.

* * *

Ethan heard them before he reached them, tense, unintelligible voices echoing through the dark hallway, Copper's rough cadence and Heloise's strong tones bouncing off one another. He broke into a run, heading for the golden glow at the end of the hall, fury like fire in his veins. What he saw as he turned into the room, however, was enough to transform that fire into ice: Copper, looking wild in his fear and anger, the gun in his hand pointed at Heloise.

"Heloise," he choked.

Copper's eyes fairly rolled in his head as he swung them to Ethan. "Damn it, Sinclaire, you should be below."

Though a voice screamed in his head to tackle the other man and tear the weapon from his grip, he fought for composure. One wrong move and a bullet could lodge in Heloise's chest. A brief flash of her, lying motionless at his feet, crimson blossoming on her bodice, had him nearly casting up his accounts. "Why don't you give me the gun?" he said as calmly as he could manage. Moving slowly, he reached out.

"No," Copper hissed, backing away, stumbling against

the wall. His hand shook violently, the gun wobbling dangerously—and still aimed at Heloise.

Given Copper's volatile state, this could all turn tragic in an instant. Fear pounded through his veins, that damn vision of Heloise lying lifeless coming back to torture him. If he lost her…

Panic flared and his gaze flashed to her, as if to prove to himself that she was well. She stood straight and tall in the light of a small lamp, one hand resting near the collar of her gown. Mrs. Rumford's pale, frightened face peeked out from behind her. Before them was Copper's desk, the entire top propped open in an odd manner. But he hardly noticed all of that, his entire focus on the trust in Heloise's eyes. It bolstered him, giving him strength he hadn't known he needed.

"You are well?" he asked, desperation making the words harsh.

A small, tremulous smile ever so briefly crossed her lips. "Yes, we're well."

"Good," he breathed before turning his gaze back to Copper. "Why don't we let the ladies go? They've nothing to do with any of this."

"Like hell they haven't," Copper snapped. His eyes darted back and forth between Ethan and Heloise, confusion and anger and fear twisting his features. "What I can't figure out, though, is why they're here in the first place. How did they know—?" He gritted his teeth, shaking his head violently. "It doesn't matter how or why, I suppose," he mumbled, seemingly to himself, the words almost manic. His expression, when he turned it on Ethan, was tortured, that of a man burning from the inside out. "Damn it, why couldn't you have stayed below?" he cried.

"It's over," Ethan said in a soothing tone that nevertheless shook from fear. "Just give me the gun."

"Like hell it's over," Copper snapped. He looked to the desk with its strangely open top in fury and longing. Ethan followed his gaze, catching what he hadn't before: the glint of coin, the piles of papers. So this was where he had been hiding it all, some secret compartment, right in plain sight. He pressed his lips tight in frustration. No wonder they had been unable to locate the jewels.

He breathed deep, trying to control his rising fury, but it betrayed itself with one tortured question. "How long has this been going on, Copper?"

The man's eyes blazed fire before, in the blink of an eye, he seemed to deflate. "Does it matter?"

"It matters to me," Ethan replied harshly. "Why did you do it? Did you need the money? Are you in trouble?"

The words came out almost as a plea. And no wonder. Here was a man he had known nearly all his life, someone he had trusted implicitly. But even a response in the affirmative wouldn't alleviate the sense of betrayal that suffocated him.

Again that fury was in Copper's eyes, though it was threaded through with pain. "You don't know the things I know," he hissed.

"Try me."

Copper clenched his jaw tight, as if fighting against the words. But they would not be held back, pouring out of him like water from a pitcher. "The patrons, they treat you and the other partners with deference. They see you as men of power, who can make or break their miserable lives."

His nostrils flared, his vision going dark. "But I straddle our world and theirs. I'm the invisible brute lumbering in their midst, a cockroach that they tolerate. I hear how they truly see us, that they think we're vermin. That, if given the chance, they would crush us beneath their polished boots. We're a joke to them."

His lips twisted cruelly, a defiant look hardening his features. "And so I took from them. So what? The amounts were so small they could never miss it. Mere pocket change to them."

Despite his knowing he needed to keep a clear head, red began to bleed at the edges of Ethan's vision. His hands curled into fists at his sides. "Notwithstanding the fact that in cheating our members you are dishonoring every person at Dionysus," he gritted, "not everyone you stole from could afford it. For some it was the difference between life and death."

Something in Ethan's tone must have gotten through the outraged haze in Copper's head. He frowned, glancing to Heloise and Mrs. Rumford.

"Yes," Ethan said quietly, "they are here to save a life that you have put in jeopardy."

Copper faltered, uncertainty taking hold of him. The gun began to lower, ever so slightly.

But the vulnerable moment was quickly gone, his features hardening once more. "It doesn't matter. One person doesn't matter in the grand scheme of things."

Heloise made a strangled noise in her throat, her body shifting as if she would attack Copper. Ethan held up a staying hand, praying she heeded his silent plea, even as his furious gaze remained on his former friend.

"More than one, I'm thinking," he growled low. "What of Gavin? How does he fit into your *grand schemes*?"

At the mention of Gavin's name, Copper flinched. "I never meant for that to happen," he rasped.

"Didn't you?" Ethan's body fairly vibrated with the need to beat the life from Copper. "Didn't you mean to distract us by putting the blame on Gavin, to throw us off your scent?"

"It was an accident—"

"An accident? Gavin died because of you."

"I know!" Copper cried. "Don't you think I know? It has tormented me every hour of every day. But it truly was an accident. I swear it."

Why, Ethan thought with the one portion of his mind still capable of reason, did the man sound sincere? "Explain," he demanded through numb lips.

Copper let out a harsh breath, looking to the ceiling as if for support from the heavens. "You were all searching for the reason behind the rumors swirling about the club," he began, the words tremulous, a long-buried secret finally breaking free. "I'd meant to move the goods to someplace you could never locate them, but I was nearly discovered. I ducked into the closest room I could access, Gavin's office, hid it all there. I'd meant to go back for it later, when things cooled down. But it was found before I could."

He ran a hand over his face, suddenly looking a hundred years older. "It all happened so fast after that. And then Gavin was dead, and it was too late."

"You should have said something," Ethan hissed. "You should have come clean before—" His voice broke, and he clamped his lips tight, breathing hard through his nose.

"I should have," Copper said, the words fragmented with emotion. "Yes, I should have."

But in the next moment that hard look was back in place. "Even so, if I were to go back I would make the same decision. Those rich bastards deserve to be stolen from, to be dishonored in such a way. And the rest of you are too cowardly to see it."

That red haze was back, clouding Ethan's vision until he could hardly think straight. The need to end this overriding his common sense, he lunged forward, determined to take the weapon from him.

Before he could reach him, Copper jerked the gun up, arm straight, not a hint of shaking in his limb now as he leveled it once more on Heloise.

Ethan froze. "Let her go!" he roared.

Copper let loose a chilling, manic laugh. "I don't think so, Sinclaire. If it was your own life on the line, I'm certain you would do something stupid." His lips twisted. "Mrs. Marlow, on the other hand…"

Ethan's blood congealed in his veins as Copper turned his head slowly to her. "Yes," he said, almost to himself, "with Mrs. Marlow's life on the line, you're more likely to behave. We all know you're in love with her."

A small sound escaped Heloise. It took every ounce of Ethan's control not to look at her. He should refute it, tell Copper he didn't give a damn about Heloise, that she was a good fuck and nothing more. It could quite possibly save her life.

Yet he couldn't give voice to the lie, no matter how hard he tried; the thought of Heloise believing he didn't care for her, and one of them dying before he could tell her the truth, seized his tongue.

But no, neither of them would die. He would make certain of that. To do so, however, he had to draw Copper's attention from Heloise and her friend as quickly as possible.

It was as his mind worked feverishly, trying to think of some way, any way, that he could get Copper to redirect the gun to him, that a light suddenly appeared in the hallway behind him. On the heels of that came angry male shouts bouncing off the walls, Teagan's and Parsons's and Isaac's voices mingling in a cacophony of fury. He saw it the moment Copper realized it was over. He hissed a curse, spinning to face the new threat, gun turning with him. Before Ethan could so much as tense to spring forward, however, there was the flash of silver in the lamplight. In the next instant a blade buried itself in Copper's hand. The sound of the gun clattering to the floor mingled with Copper's screams. And then all hell broke loose, a mass of huge bodies pouring into the room, tackling Copper, who was clutching his bleeding hand to his chest.

But Ethan didn't care if the world burned down around his ears; all he could think of was Heloise. He looked at her, barely noticing her wild eyes, her arm extended toward Copper from throwing the blade. The only thing he could register was that she was safe. In the next instant he was around the desk and dragging Heloise into his arms, feeling as if his world was finally whole.

30

"Miss Marlow here to see you. Again."

Heloise pursed her lips to keep from smiling at the disgust in Strachan's voice. Putting aside the blade she'd been polishing, she took up a rag and wiped her hands. "Thank you, Strachan. I'll be in momentarily."

The other woman scoffed. "As if I'm your messenger, Mrs. High-and-Mighty," she grumbled as she turned to leave the smithy.

"I can hear you," Heloise called after her, not bothering to subdue her smile.

"You were meant to," Strachan snapped back, storming off.

Heloise chuckled as she removed her leather apron and tidied up. But her humor was short lived. As it had been these past two days, ever since she'd said goodbye for the last time to Ethan.

She had a flash of memory then, quick and sharp, but it was enough to grab tight to her lungs and prevent her from drawing breath: Ethan's face when her blade had struck Mr. Copper, the stark relief in his eyes as he'd rushed to her. And then his arms about her, so tight she'd thought he would never let her go. No matter how busy she kept herself, how much she poured into her work, how focused she was on her duties, that memory would insist on surfacing, tormenting her, making her want to run back to him and beg for a chance to remain by his side.

Shaking her head to dispel the idea that their story had a happily-ever-after—especially as, following the events at Dionysus, she had not seen or heard from him once—she finished cleaning up and headed out of the forge and to the main house.

She found Julia in the drawing room, but she was not alone. No, it seemed the whole of the Wimpole Street house had come out to see her.

"I do hope you don't mind," Sylvia said with a smile, passing Julia a cup of tea, "but we have all decided to join you this afternoon. We're anxious to learn what the outcome was of the return of the jewels."

Not long ago Heloise would have minded, very much. She felt the echo of sadness for her former self when she thought of how clearly she had drawn the line between personal and business with the Widows. Now she saw these women for who they truly were: a group of dear friends who genuinely cared about her. She would not close them out again.

"Of course not," she replied, taking a seat beside Julia. "In fact, if you had not come, I would have called you here. It is all our triumph, after all."

"Indeed," Sylvia murmured, eyes shining with emotion. She turned to Laney at her side then, taking up her hand and pulling it onto her lap, wrapping her fingers about it as if she would never let her go. "And it gives my darling Laney a chance to be about people instead of locked up in our room with only me for company."

"I will never complain about being locked up with you,"

Laney said, smiling at Sylvia before wincing, hand coming up to gingerly touch her lip. A split lip, however, was the least of her injuries, the fight from the other night having been a brutal affair. There was not a place on her face that did not have some sort of cut or bruise. And her injuries did not end with her face, as was proven as she shifted in her seat and tensed, the hand that had been at her lip dropping to cradle her ribs. The smile she gave Sylvia, however, belied her physical discomfort.

Julia leaned forward, eyes wide in her face. "But Mrs. Finch, you were incredible. I have never seen two women fighting before."

"You didn't see Laney's fight, either," Heloise drawled with a grin. "What little time we spent in the boxing venue, I rather think you watched the floor much more than you watched Laney."

"Yes, well," Julia said, giving her a sheepish look. Her eyes, Heloise noticed, were clear, and dancing with wry mirth. "That, however, does not negate my admiration."

"Nor mine," Iris piped up, leaning forward, eyes wide with excitement. "It was quite fascinating. I wonder," she mused, largely to herself, as she fiddled with a small triangle of sandwich on her plate, dismantling it in her inattentiveness, "what prompts the human species to pummel each other in such a manner for mere enjoyment."

"I do wish I had been able to witness it myself," Euphemia grumbled. "I missed everything."

Sylvia held the platter of biscuits out to her, as if offering her a consolation prize. "I am sorry, my dear. But know you had the most important job of the evening, and we could not have caught Mr. Copper and recovered the jewels without you."

"Well," Euphemia said with a pout and yet a pleased

blush, taking a biscuit from the platter, "I suppose that does help some."

"But we are getting off track," Sylvia said, turning to Julia. "I'm dying to hear how things went with your employer. Or," she continued with a hopeful cock of her head, "judging by your relaxed expression, shall we call her your former employer?"

"You may," Julia replied. She gave a happy sigh as she placed her teacup down. "Lady Ayersley received her jewelry back with little grace. But then, I did not expect anything more from her. She showed more emotion when I told her immediately after that I would be leaving her service."

"I'm proud of you, Julia," Heloise said around the sudden tightness in her throat. Here was this girl she had helped to raise, now a woman, coming out the other side of a horrendous situation with a smile on her face. "Gregory would be proud of you."

Julia turned bright eyes on her. "Do you think so?"

"I know so." Reaching out, she took her hand. "And now we shall help you get back on your feet. Don't worry a bit; we shall find something new for you."

"Oh, but you needn't do that," Julia said. "I have already secured a position."

Heloise blinked. "You have? But how?"

"I have told you of Miss Newberg, Lady Ayersley's cousin who has been staying with us for some months?" At Heloise's nod she continued. "She overheard my last… conversation with Lady Ayersley and approached me as I was about to depart. It appears she is in need of a companion for her travels. She has asked me to accompany her." She grinned, squeezing Heloise's hand. "I shall travel the world, Heloise."

Something lifted from Heloise's shoulders at that, a

burden she had been carrying for too long. She felt it then, the release from that promise she had made Gregory, for Julia, it seemed, was well and truly grown now.

"I am happy for you, dearest," she managed through a throat tight with unshed tears.

The rest of Julia's visit passed swiftly, the time cheerfully spent talking of her bright future. Too soon, however, it was time for her to go.

"Miss Newberg has secured rooms for us to stay in until we depart," Julia said as they all stood. She grinned. "It seems she liked her cousin even less than I did, which truly is saying something, and could not wait to escape her house. But I shall be certain to visit before I leave. I promise."

"I shall make certain you keep that promise," Heloise replied.

Most of the Widows said their goodbyes then and returned to their rooms. Sylvia, however, gracious hostess that she was, accompanied Heloise down to the ground floor with Julia.

"I shall see you soon," Heloise managed, pulling Julia in for a hug.

Julia hugged her back, slender arms tight about her. And then tearful words sounded in her ear: "Thank you so much, Heloise. For everything."

In the next moment she descended the front steps, was handed up into Sylvia's carriage—which Sylvia had insisted she use—and waved cheerfully from the window. And then she was off, the carriage clattering down the street. Heloise watched until it was out of sight, painfully aware of the mix of sadness and happiness swirling in her breast. She had loved Julia like a sister, yet at the same time had been painfully aware of the burden of having to watch over her.

She saw now, however, what a blessing that "burden" had been. And she would miss it, would miss *her*.

Suddenly Sylvia was at her side, arm going about her waist. "Well, it looks like Julia has finally found her place in the world," she said. She turned to Heloise. "Now that the chick has left the nest, perhaps it is time for the mother bird to find her own wings."

Why, she wondered, did that make her yearn so desperately for Ethan? She forcefully ignored the ache in her chest and smiled. "I have found my own wings, here with all of you. There is no other place I would rather be."

Sylvia, however, must have heard the lie in the words. "Isn't there, though?" she murmured. Then, giving Heloise a wink, she disappeared inside the house, leaving her alone on the front steps with only her futile dreams for comfort.

* * *

Dreams that did not disappear as the day wore on. No, they only grew, swelling like the tide until, finally, in the lonely quiet of her bed, they could not be ignored any longer.

"Ethan," she whispered into the darkness, as if giving voice to her longing could ease it. But it only made it more acute, the soft echo of his name making her realize how desperately she missed him. She bit her lip, squeezing her eyes tight against the wave of grief that crashed over her. But her efforts were no help. The warmth of tears tracked down her temples and into her hair, a sob escaping her lips. In the next moment she was on her side, her body curled in on itself, her face pressed into her pillow in an attempt to quiet the cries that were being expelled from her heaving chest with a force that stunned her. God, she missed him so much, loved him so much. How could she live the rest of her life without him?

As if determined to torment her even further, her mind conjured again that last embrace with him. She had fought against the memory of it with every inch of her being, knowing it would destroy her. Now, however, she was too weak to fight it any longer, too weak to push it away. She could still feel his arms wrapped about her, his hands cradling her as if she were something infinitely precious. But other details of that embrace came back to her now, simultaneously filling her up and beating her down: his chest heaving, the way he'd pulled back as if to verify she was well before pulling her back in again, how it had felt as if they were in their own world as chaos erupted about them…

His words, low and desperate in her ear, "Oh, thank God, love. I would have died if anything had happened to you."

The sobs that had been falling from her lips suddenly stopped, the breath hitching painfully in her chest. Did she remember that right? But no, it was just said in the heat of the moment, when emotions had been running high. He hadn't meant it.

But then a question whispered in her mind: *What if he did?*

Hope, that damned hope she had been fighting against, was resurrected in her heart, growing stronger with each steady beat. Copper's words came back to her then, a comment that had struck her like a fist to the stomach at the time but that she had forgotten until now: "With Mrs. Marlow's life on the line, you're more likely to behave. We all know you're in love with her."

In the moment, she had fully expected Ethan to refute it. She knew he didn't love her, and so declaring that fact, the right thing to do in that volatile situation, should have been easy and quick. Copper had been holding her hostage to control Ethan, after all.

Yet Ethan had not denied it. Oh, she had watched him, bracing herself for the pain when he did. But the words had never come. Instead he'd looked as if he were fighting some great battle within himself, a battle he lost. Had he been unable to refute the claim that he loved her, then, because it would have been a lie?

She was out of bed and on her feet before she knew what she was about. Was there every chance that she was reading into things? Yes. But that small chance he did love her, that sliver of light at the end of the dark tunnel she'd believed her future to be, could not, would not be ignored.

She lit a lamp and went to the wardrobe, pulling out the first thing she could get her hands on. She would go to Dionysus and find out, once and for all, if they had a chance together, even if she was destroyed in the process. Which, she thought as she pulled her gown over her head with shaking hands, she very well could be.

31

Ethan was exhausted, quite possibly the most exhausted he'd ever been in his life. Yet he knew that no matter how hard he might try, there would be no sleep for him.

Of course, the noise coming from the casino floor alone would have prevented him from sleeping. With no little amount of bemusement, he looked down at the milling crowd, a crowd that was significantly larger than what Dionysus drew in a normal evening. It seemed that the chaos and panic of the night of the masquerade had, instead of ruining them as Heloise had feared, only served to whet the public's appetite for the club.

Heloise. At the thought of her, so unexpected after he had managed to keep his mind off her for, oh, the past ten minutes at least, he sighed wearily. After her blade had struck Copper, after he had ascertained she was safe while Isaac and Teagan and Parsons had finished subduing the floor manager, there had been too much to focus on to give her proper attention. From relighting the gaslights, to making certain all their patrons were safe, to filling his partners in on what had occurred, he'd not had a moment to spare for Heloise. By the time dawn broke and he was able to draw breath again, she had been gone, without even a note of goodbye.

Not that he had expected one. *Give her time*, he'd told himself. The night had been traumatic, after all, as well as exhausting. Not to mention there were the jewels to return and her sister-in-law to look after.

But though he'd waited, there had been not even a whisper from her. Which was akin to torture; he missed her so much he could hardly breathe.

"You know," Teagan drawled from behind him, "if you're going to sit around brooding all day and night, you may as well go visit her."

Ethan started, glancing back into the dimly lit owners' suite. Teagan, Isaac, and Parsons stared back at him, their expressions betraying varying degrees of amusement. Even Parsons, whose smiles of the past decade Ethan could count on one hand, had a vaguely amused tilt to his lips.

He scowled at them. "I'm giving her time."

"Wasting time, is more like it," Isaac rejoined. He leaned back in his chair, crossing one foot over the opposite knee. "I'm getting damn tired of waiting for you to make Mrs. Marlow my sister."

The longing that brought Ethan was physically painful. "As if that's a possibility," he mumbled.

Isaac rolled his eyes as if asking for celestial guidance. "Well, it's not if you don't get your head out of your arse and ask her."

"It's not that easy."

"Isn't it, though?" Teagan asked. He held his glass up, studying the amber liquid within as if divining the future. "I thought recent events would reduce your stubbornness, but it seems you're just as stubborn and thickheaded as ever."

"What the hell does Copper's betrayal have to do with my stubbornness?" he demanded.

There was a moment of heavy silence, that betrayal still infinitely painful to each of them. As it would be for some time, no doubt. Their shock and fury at learning the truth of that tragic event three years ago, as well as finding out that the corruption had not stopped in all that time, had been extreme. Especially as it had all been committed by someone they had grown up with, been friends with, trusted.

But while each grieved it in his own way, Ethan had noticed the change that had occurred among them all. There was a closeness there now that had been missing for the past three years, a return of the camaraderie that had been shattered with Gavin's death. It had started as a fragile thing, as new and green as a spring shoot. But it grew stronger every minute of every day. A fact that Ethan was infinitely thankful for.

"This has nothing to do with Copper," Isaac said now, the pain of a moment ago having blessedly passed with few residual effects. "Rather, it has to do with your affair with Mrs. Marlow and everything that came from that. Namely an opening up of that rusty piece of tin you call your heart."

"Shut up," Ethan grumbled.

"We will shut up when you finally come to your senses and go after her," Teagan declared.

Ethan glared at them. "Do the two of you enjoy joining forces against me? At least Parsons here has the sense to leave me be."

The man in question, however, shifted in his seat, looking as uncomfortable as he ever had, and cleared his throat. "Actually…"

Ethan gaped at him. "Not you as well."

He shrugged. "I may be slow, but I'm not blind. Anyone could see you were happy with her."

Isaac gave Ethan *a look* and motioned to Parsons with both hands as if to say, "There, you see?"

But this was all too much, and was making Ethan want things that he could not allow himself to want until Heloise was good and ready—if she ever would be. Thankfully, Keely knocked and opened the door just then.

"Keely," Ethan exclaimed, perhaps a touch too loudly, if the stunned looks the other men gave him was any indication. But in that moment he didn't care that he was acting out of character, as long as the conversation turned from that one subject that gave him the most painful hope. He motioned expansively for the younger man to enter. "Come in."

"Mr. Sinclaire, Mr. Sinclaire, Mr. Teagan, Parsons," Keely said, nodding at each of them in turn.

"I trust you have news for us," Parsons said, back to looking as imposing as ever.

"Aye. I saw the boat Mr. Copper was on set sail myself this afternoon."

Ethan nodded, looking back to the casino floor, though he hardly saw it as the rest of the men talked behind him. He had expected relief at knowing Copper was well and truly out of the country. But he felt only a heavy sadness that it had all come to this. The four partners had discussed at length Copper's fate—after giving the man the beating of a lifetime, of course—and had decided to a one that, to honor their long-standing history, a history that Copper himself had besmirched, they would not turn him over to the authorities. No matter what he might have done, they had no wish to see the man dangling at the end of a rope. And, as Isaac had so poignantly put it, Gavin would not have wanted such a violent end for him, either.

And so they had bought him passage to America, warning him never to return, and witnessed him boarding the ship that very afternoon. They'd left Keely to keep watch, to make certain the ship set sail, to verify that Copper was well and truly on his way across the Atlantic. Yes, he should feel relief that it was over. But he didn't. And as Keely departed and Ethan turned back to look at his partners, he knew they felt the same.

Teagan downed the remainder of his drink, pulling his lips back from his teeth in appreciation. "It was the best decision we could have made given the circumstances."

"Yes," Ethan replied softly before rallying and giving Parsons a wry glance. "Besides, if he had stayed in England, I do believe Parsons here would have finished the job he'd started and beat the very life from him."

Once more Parsons's lips quirked up at the corner ever so slightly—truly, this was a banner day for wringing emotion out of the veritable stone that Parsons was. "I was only finishing the job that Mrs. Marlow started."

"If I had known the woman was as talented with a blade as all that," Teagan murmured with a raised brow, "I would have snatched her up myself."

Isaac chuckled. "It will be handy, having a sister-in-law with such skills."

And so they were back to this, were they? Ethan bowed his head and sighed, even as his heart pounded out that damned hopeful beat again in his chest. "You won't stop harping on this subject, will you?"

Isaac grinned. "No."

Ethan pursed his lips, considering them all severely. "You truly plan to drive me to the brink of madness until I go after her?"

"Oh, absolutely," Teagan drawled.

"And nothing I say will dissuade you?"

Parsons snorted. "As if we ever listened to you in the first place."

That bit of unexpected sarcasm finally earned a bark of laughter from Ethan. But his humor was short lived. He expelled a heavy breath, rubbing at the back of his neck. "And what if she won't have me?" he asked, the words low and harsh.

Isaac frowned, his confusion palpable. "What do you mean, what if she won't have you?"

He gritted his teeth, pressing the heels of his palms into his eyes. "It was because of the club that her sister-in-law was in danger, that she had to resort to an affair with me in the first place. I cannot imagine the fear she must have felt to do such a thing. How can affection grow from that? And even if, by some miracle, she could come to love me, would she be able to withstand the memories of what happened? I'll be nothing but a source of heartache to her. No matter how deep my affections for her, no matter the future I may hope to share with her, I have to respect her choice. Even if that choice is to be without me. Though I do believe it will kill me if that is what comes to pass." He sighed heavily. "I cannot ask her to live with those memories, no matter how much I may wish to."

There was a beat of silence, the loudest silence he had ever heard. And then a voice so sweet filled the room, one he'd never thought to hear again.

"I can assure you," Heloise said softly, "that the pain of those memories is insignificant compared to my love for you."

He sucked in a breath, head jerking up, eyes scanning the dim suite, hardly noticing that Isaac and Teagan and Parsons had somehow quietly departed while he'd been pouring his heart out. No, the only thing he could see in that moment was a face incredibly dear to him.

"Heloise," he breathed. He must be imagining things. She could not be here. But then she approached him, a nervous smile on her lips, and reached up to cup his cheek in her palm, and he knew his hopeless dream had somehow, someway become a beautiful reality.

* * *

It had taken every bit of bravery Heloise possessed to come to Dionysus and seek Ethan out. That hope that had taken root in her, after all, had taken a beating during the drive here, every possible reaction to her confession filling her mind, battering her with growing uncertainty. But she had done it, had entered the club and climbed the steps to that dark hallway and found her way to the suite. And there he had been, looking so magnificent she'd wanted to cry.

The last thing she'd expected to hear when she'd finally found him, however, was him pouring out his heart.

The partners had seen her immediately. With wide smiles—well, except for Mr. Parsons, though that little curve of his lips could certainly be deemed a grin considering how dour he typically was—they had crept from the room, leaving her alone with Ethan. Leaving her to soak in each and every tortured word pouring from his lips, filling her up until she thought she'd burst. And then she did burst, her confession spilling from her, her love for him unable to be contained any longer.

His eyes were wide and disbelieving when he looked at her, her name on his lips full of such longing it brought tears to her eyes. It was an easy thing then to walk across the room, to reach up, to cradle his face in her hand.

The breath left him in a rush, his eyes caressing her face

as if he could not believe she was in front of him. "Heloise," he said again.

"I'm sorry it took me so long," she whispered. And then, the words stronger, filled with every emotion of their parting, "And I'm sorry I tricked you, that I betrayed you. I'm sorry I believed the worst of you. I'm sorry that I ever made you believe I didn't care for you—"

But he was shaking his head. "I should be the one apologizing for what you were forced to do because of my club. And I will, profusely, for the rest of my life. But that's for later. For now, just tell me again what you said when you arrived."

It didn't take her long to realize what he was asking for. She smiled, her heart full. "I love you, Ethan—"

She was in his arms before the words were out, his mouth on hers, as if he would swallow her confession down to the very depths of his soul.

"Again," he demanded when he broke the kiss, eyes blazing down into hers.

Her smile widened. "I love you."

He kissed her eyes, her cheeks, her nose. "Again," he breathed.

She laughed—her joy was so great—even as tears prickled her eyes. "I love you," she managed through a throat tight with emotion.

He pulled back, gazed down at her. "Thank God," he whispered. He cradled her to him, his eyes scouring her face as if he could not get enough of looking at her. One hand came up and cupped her cheek with such tenderness that those blasted tears threatened to spill over. And then, his voice shaking with emotion, "I love you, Heloise."

Her tears broke free then, trailing down her cheeks. He kissed them away, one by one, each touch of his lips reverential. Which only made the tears come faster.

"I must be dreaming," she whispered. Yes, that was it, she was still back at home, in her lonely bed, just dreaming of this beautiful moment.

He looked down into her eyes, his own brimming with tears. "If you are dreaming," he managed hoarsely, "then I am, too. And that I will not condone."

She gave a watery laugh. "And how do you propose we ascertain it is not a dream?"

He smiled tenderly. "There really is only one way." When she raised a brow in question, his smile widened. "I shall just have to take you to my bed, and make love to you until dawn."

Which, Heloise thought happily as he lifted her in his arms and strode through the club to said bed, was a very good idea indeed.

Epilogue

One month later

"Heloise, dear, some letters have come for you."

Heloise, in the process of inspecting a sword in the makeshift fencing salon at the Wimpole Street house, glanced up excitedly. She never received letters, after all, having no one to write to. Except…

"Julia?"

Sylvia smiled. "It appears so."

Heloise needed no further urging. Placing the sword aside, she sprinted for Sylvia, tearing into the first letter the moment it was in her hands. Her eyes fairly raced over the page, devouring every elegantly penned word before, with a happy sigh, she read it a second time, slower now, relishing every happy sentence.

"She is well?"

Heloise grinned at her. "More than well. Oh, Sylvia, I never believed she could find such joy in life. She and Miss Newberg have had the most wonderful adventures already, and only a month into their trip. It is as if she was made for traveling the world."

"How splendid. It appears Lady Ayersley did her quite the favor forcing her to quit with that whole jewelry fiasco."

She gave Heloise a sly look. "And she is not the only one who has bloomed from the rubble of that mess."

Heloise's face heated, even as she smiled. That was too true. If not for Lady Ayersley and her propensity for gambling well beyond her means, she would never have lost her jewelry at Dionysus, and Heloise would never have met Ethan, and they would not have fallen in love.

Her heart thumped happily in her chest as she recalled their promise to meet that evening at the club. Not that they did not meet nightly as it was. But that did not stop the giddy anticipation from filling her. Yes, it had been serendipitous, indeed. If only…

She stopped the rogue thought in its tracks. No *if only*. Did she wish to spend every possible moment with him? Yes. Did she wish they had a place of their own that was away from Dionysus, a haven that was just for them? Also yes.

But she would not complain, would take him wherever and whenever she could have him, and gladly.

"As I said," Sylvia murmured, "she is not the only one who has bloomed. But what is that second letter you have there?" She indicated the missive Heloise had tucked beneath her arm while she'd read over Julia's letter.

Still smiling, certain this was yet another letter from her sister-in-law that had gotten delayed in the post, she opened it as well—only to be met with an unfamiliar scrawl. Frowning, she quickly read the short note.

"This is not as happy a message as the first, I take it?" Sylvia queried.

"No, it's not," Heloise replied. "It seems someone is in need of our help."

"Have we got another job to do, then?" She sidled closer to peer over Heloise's shoulder. "They appear quite desperate. You should visit them straightaway."

Heloise glanced at her in surprise. "What, now?"

"There really is no better time than the present, my dear," Sylvia replied. Then, placing a firm hand at the small of her back, she steered her toward the door. "I shall inform Strachan to prepare the carriage for you."

"I cannot go this minute," Heloise balked, trying to dig in her heels. But Sylvia, to her surprise, was much stronger than she'd believed.

"Oh, but you must," the other woman said, her tone firm and brooking no argument.

"But Isaac, Teagan, and Parsons are due to arrive shortly to continue our fencing lessons."

By then they had reached the landing. Sylvia, hands firm on her arms, continued to propel her down to the ground floor. "Strachan," she called out. "The carriage please."

That woman glanced up with a scowl before, huffing a beleaguered "Aye," she stormed off.

Sylvia gave Heloise a bracing smile. "I am quite certain the men will not mind the delay," she proclaimed with certainty. "And in any case, I should dearly love to visit with them. It is not every day a person has three gaming hell owners at her disposal." She laughed delightedly.

Just then they reached the front hall. Before Heloise could continue her resistance, Sylvia grabbed her outerwear and helped her put it on. Or, rather, she forcibly tugged it on before spinning Heloise about and pushing her out the front door. And then the carriage was pulling up in front of the house, and she was ushered inside and was on her way.

Later, much later, when her senses had returned to her, Heloise would laugh at herself for not realizing that there was no way in heaven or on earth that the carriage could have been readied and in front of the house in such a short time, much less know where to go without her telling the driver. The only thing she could wonder in that baffling moment was why Sylvia was so eager for her to leave, and what exactly was waiting for her at the address in the mysterious letter—an address that they reached much more quickly than she could comprehend.

The driver opened the carriage door, offering a hand, and helped her down to the pavement. Still quite dazed, Heloise looked about, blinking in surprise when she saw the long row of elegant town houses, all shining in the early morning sunlight. Brook Street. The name had not fully sunk in when she'd initially read it. Now, however, as she stood on the pavement gazing up at their destination, with its quietly beautiful bright white stone and sparkling windows, she recognized what this place was: a fashionable street in Mayfair, most certainly not where their typical clientele came from.

Suddenly inexplicably nervous, Heloise cleared her throat and smoothed her skirts before climbing the steps to the front door.

Her knock was answered immediately, a stoic butler pulling the door wide before the sound echoed away, as if he had been waiting on the other side of the door for her.

"Madam," he said, bowing deferentially, stepping aside so she could enter.

Blinking, Heloise paused for the briefest moment before, taking a deep breath, she crossed the threshold. The butler closed the door behind her, indicating she should follow him.

The nervousness that had begun to fill her upon her arrival multiplied tenfold as he led the way up the curving staircase to the first floor and no doubt the drawing room. The house was light and airy, decorated in gentle blues and ivories that reminded her, strangely enough, of Ethan's private apartment at Dionysus, with the addition of the pale greens of her own rooms at the Wimpole Street house. It gave her a feeling of familiarity that should have been jarring, yet it felt oddly comfortable. Which only served to increase her nervousness even further. Why, she wondered a bit wildly, did she feel as if something momentous was about to occur, as if her life would be forever changed in the next minutes? That feeling only intensified as, much to her bafflement, they bypassed the doors on the first floor and headed for the next staircase and what no doubt were the private apartments.

"Excuse me," she called after the butler, "but are you certain I should be shown to the family floor?"

"Yes, madam," the man said, not so much as glancing back, keeping on his determined path.

Still utterly confused, Heloise nevertheless continued after him. Finally they stopped at a white paneled door, and the butler threw it wide.

"Please wait in here a moment," he murmured with a bow. A bow he did not rise from until Heloise, on shaking legs, stepped into the room. One glance about the space, however, and she quite forgot the man altogether.

While the rest of the house had seemed vaguely familiar, this room felt as if someone had reached into her mind and filled it with everything she loved. There were several swords displayed on the wall, ones eerily similar to those she'd made herself, as well as books she loved, paintings of some of the places she dreamed of visiting, even an embroidered pillow that looked like one Sylvia had been working on these past weeks. And then there was a faint sound at the door, and she turned to see that person she loved more than any other enter the room.

She shook her head in confusion. She was supposed to

be meeting a client; what was Ethan doing here? She must be seeing things. But he remained solid and wonderful as he strode toward her. And then he smiled, a nervous, lopsided thing, and took her hands in his, and she knew that her future, that future she'd been so certain was soon to change, was about to become more beautiful than she could ever have imagined.

* * *

Ethan had never been more nervous. Even so, as his insides quaked and his legs trembled beneath him, he knew he had never been happier. Heloise had given that to him, had brought light and joy to a life that had been nothing but darkness and anger, had worked her way into his heart and cleared away the cobwebs of his unhappy and brutal past, replacing it with a bright and shining future.

He had never given his future much thought before now. It had been something to bear, to get through, a burden he'd been forced to shoulder. Now, however, as he held Heloise's hands in his, that future beckoned him, like the warmth of the sun rising, ending the pitch-black night his life had been and lighting his world with beautiful, brilliant color.

"Ethan?" she asked faintly.

He soaked in the sound of his name on her lips, a beautiful sound he would never tire of hearing.

"You're finally here," he breathed.

"Here?" She cast a glance about the room. "Just where is *here*? I thought I was meeting someone who required my help. And yet here you are." She frowned slightly, her confusion palpable. "In a house that is far more familiar than it should be."

"I'm the one who requires your help," he managed.

Her gaze returned to him, wide-eyed now. "You?"

He nodded. "And you're the only one who can save me." He drew her closer, wrapping his arms about her, his eyes scouring her face. "I have a proposition for you, you see, a particular case that will be a lifelong commitment should you be willing to take it on."

Understanding began to soften her eyes then, along with the tears that began to well in their pale blue depths. A small, tremulous smile lifted her lips at the corners. "Let me hear this proposition, then, so I may determine if I should accept."

His heart pounded in his chest, carrying him ever closer to that happiness he had never thought to reach. There was just one final step to take, one last leap of faith...

Pulling back from her, he reached into his jacket pocket for the small item within, still warm from his body. And then he dropped to one knee and held that physical manifestation of his promise out to her.

Her mouth opened in a soft gasp, her hands going to her chest, the soft tears that had been pooling in her eyes spilling over.

He smiled, even as he felt the answering tears in his own eyes tracking down his cheeks.

"You have given me a happiness I never thought to claim, never thought I deserved," he rasped. "And if you let me, I will spend the rest of my life dedicating myself to you. Here, in this house I've purchased for our future together. To love each other, grow old together..."

His throat closed at that, and it took some seconds before he was able to speak again. When he did, the words poured from him, that question he had been aching to ask her since the moment he'd realized he loved her.

"Will you marry me, Heloise?"

The smile that lit her face was as bright as the sun. In the next moment she dropped to her knees in front of him, her strong arms going about him, her tear-streaked face pressing into his neck. Her voice sounded in his ear then, more beautiful than any music.

"Yes, Ethan," she choked out. "Yes, I'll marry you."

He crushed her to him, achingly aware of their hearts pounding as one against each other. "I love you, Heloise."

"And I love you, Ethan."

He pulled back then, taking her hand in his, his heart fuller than he'd ever imagined it could be as she gave him a watery smile. And as he slid the ring on her finger and pulled her close to claim her lips with his, he felt he'd finally come home.

About the Author

CHRISTINA BRITTON developed a passion for writing romance novels shortly after buying her first at the impressionable age of thirteen. Though for several years she put brush instead of pen to paper, she has returned to her first love and is now writing full-time. She spends her days dreaming of corsets and cravats and noblemen with tortured souls.

She lives with her husband and two children in the San Francisco Bay Area.

You can learn more at:
  Website: ChristinaBritton.com
  Facebook.com/ChristinaBrittonAuthor
  Instagram @ChristinaBrittonAuthor

Get swept away by Forever's historical romances!

Rebellious Heroines x Forbidden Love

HOT EARL SUMMER
by Erica Ridley

Nothing will stop Elizabeth Wynchester from seeing justice done. But when her next mission drops her at the Earl of Densmore's castle, she isn't prepared to be locked inside! And her trusty sword cannot protect her heart from the handsome rogue guarding the keep.

When Stephen Lenox agreed to impersonate the earl, he didn't expect him to vanish. Nor could he predict the arrival of his new blade-wielding bodyguard. She'll share his bed until their adventure concludes. Unless he can convince her to surrender her heart...

DUCHESS MATERIAL
by Emily Sullivan

Phoebe Atkinson is what society might call unconventional. Instead of marrying well and taking her place in society, she chose to be a schoolteacher. But when her pupil goes missing, she has only one option: to beg the Duke of Ellis for help.

William Margrave never expected to inherit a dukedom, but he's determined to act the part. Phoebe might not be duchess material, but as they fall further into the mystery, William discovers that he never got over his childhood crush on her.

Witty Banter x Murder Mystery

LADY CHARLOTTE ALWAYS GETS HER MAN
by Violet Marsh

Lady Charlotte Lovett has been promised to a man who, rumor has it, killed his previous two wives. To get out of this engagement, Charlotte will need to prove that Viscount Hawley is as sinister as she thinks. And the person who would know best is his very own brother.

Dr. Matthew Talbot is the exact opposite of his sibling—scholarly, shy, and shunned by society. But as he and Lady Charlotte grow closer to each other, they are also getting closer to a dangerous confrontation with Hawley.

A GOVERNESS'S GUIDE TO PASSION AND PERIL
by Manda Collins

When governess Jane Halliwell's employer is murdered, the former heiress is forced back into the world of the ton—and made to work with the lord who broke her heart.

Lord Adrian Fielding never noticed Jane when they were younger, so her icy demeanor confounds him—as does his desire to melt the tensions between them. But first he must find his mentor's murderer and ensure Jane's safety when she insists on joining the investigation. With a vicious killer circling, will it be too late for their chance at forever?

Find more book recommendations from Forever on social media
@ReadForeverPub and at Read-Forever.com

RAISING READERS
Books Build Bright Futures

Thank you for reading this book and for being a reader of books in general. As an author, I am so grateful to share being part of a community of readers with you, and I hope you will join me in passing our love of books on to the next generation of readers.

Did you know that reading for enjoyment is the single biggest predictor of a child's future happiness and success?

More than family circumstances, parents' educational background, or income, reading impacts a child's future academic performance, emotional well-being, communication skills, economic security, ambition, and happiness.

Studies show that kids reading for enjoyment in the US is in rapid decline:

- In 2012, 53% of 9-year-olds read almost every day. Just 10 years later, in 2022, the number had fallen to 39%.
- In 2012, 27% of 13-year-olds read for fun daily. By 2023, that number was just 14%.

Together, we can commit to **Raising Readers** and change this trend. How?

- Read to children in your life daily.
- Model reading as a fun activity.
- Reduce screen time.
- Start a family, school, or community book club.
- Visit bookstores and libraries regularly.
- Listen to audiobooks.
- Read the book before you see the movie.
- Encourage your child to read aloud to a pet or stuffed animal.
- Give books as gifts.
- Donate books to families and communities in need.

Books build bright futures, and **Raising Readers** is our shared responsibility.

For more information, visit **JoinRaisingReaders.com**

Sources: National Endowment for the Arts, National Assessment of Educational Progress, WorldBookDay.org, Nielsen BookData's 2023 "Understanding the Children's Book Consumer"